Speed Trap Murder

Margo's Manic Dream

Speed Trap Murder

Margo's Manic Dream

By P. G. Knudson

ISBN: 979-8-9994362-0-7

Dedication:

This subtle peek into the scourge of mental illness is intended as a source of encouragement for those who suffer yet are searching for hope, and is dedicated to anyone who has had to deal with a loved one who suffers from any form of it; and to the health practitioners and scientists who tirelessly strive to improve the lives of its victims, always with one goal in mind—perseverance, then victory.

.

Prologue:

A Wayward Child
October 9, 1992
Burntwood Prairie, Minnesota

It seems that no one understands Margo Toralf—never did. Gone for years, but here she is; back again, seeking a tranquil life.

She turns at her parent's mailbox, then brakes at the entrance to the two-track driveway, her last chance to change her mind and turn around. The old farmhouse looks quiet and the lights are all on, just like always.

"What am I doing here—another mistake that I'll regret for the rest of my life?"

With a forlorn love for her parents, yet with mounting apprehension, she slowly drives up to the house, imagining a round of shouting that is bound to come.

"Dad will kick me out," she mutters, remembering her last threatening words, that she'd never come back. She forgets; has it been ten years? Eight? And what was Dad's prediction, something about seeding wild oats? Or was it reaping? He'll probably say, "I told you so!"

Well, now she's here, by herself and parked under the oak tree that she remembers well, alongside her father's rusty, old station wagon. Expecting a stormy reception, she's glad that she left young Toby behind with her boyfriend, Stanley Nelson. Seeds of her plan had already been planted, years beforehand. So, is it time to plant again, or is it time to harvest? Maybe neither one, but—whichever—it's exactly the way she wants it. For now, that is.

To Margo's surprise, her mother and father are happy to see her, in the way parents seem to welcome *a wayward child*, especially years after most hard feelings have dissipated. They aren't surprised when Margo tells them that she's unmarried yet has a baby.

During the so-so homecoming, she discovers that she has missed the country lifestyle.

By morning, Saturday, October 10, 1992, she finds herself in the hayloft of the barn, swinging on the old hayfork-rope, reminiscing, imagining herself as a horse-rancher. Gazing out the hayloft door, high above the ground, she sees visions of herself riding across the south forty on a powerful stallion. From her vantage point, she stares across the fallow fields, reliving an old desire to turn that idle dairy farm into a first-class horse ranch.

She instantaneously makes up her mind: "The farm is destined to be mine!"

She calls her best friend, Maria Richardson, who almost immediately shows up with two horses, saddled and ready to ride. Renewal of their past friendship is automatic, as they revive old horse-ranching plans, all to take place on this farm still owned by Margo's parents.

Speed Trap Murder

That night, the two old friends *go out*; crash a music jam, then shark pool games at The Corner Bar. The two of them skunk a young man named Martin Martl, to a crowd of cheering onlookers. The young women relish the look of panic in Martl's eyes when he realizes that his female opponents will run the table.

Martl complains that the money he lost isn't his; that it belongs to some other guy who will kill him for losing it. When the Martl kid leaves the bar, in fear for his life, the two girls laugh, scoffing at his fears and pocketing their cash, feeling satisfied that they haven't lost their touch. Neither knows that Martl will disappear before morning.

The next day, a sunny Sunday, the two friends ride horseback on the cross-country trails. Near the end of the day, after skinny-dipping at a remote swimming hole, it's time for Maria to go. On her way home, she drops Margo off at the far-corner of the Toralf farm. Margo walks across her father's fields, dreaming of what her future holds but not imagining how her friend, Maria, will never make it home; only as far as an obscure forest road on the county line.

SPEED TRAP MURDER

MARGO'S MANIC DREAM

Chapter 1
The Ominous Phone Call
October 11, 1992

It was a quiet Sunday night at the Justus County Sheriff Office, except for loud snoring coming from the office with a view. The telephone rang, startling the elderly Sheriff, a peaceful man named Homer Anders. He bounded to his feet, chair-wheels screeching, rolling away from the desk. Loose papers drifted to the floor.

A bit disoriented, he felt like his head was still resting on a pillow of unopened mail. He glanced to the switchboard, noticing that line-one was flashing. Frustrated that the dispatcher had taken the night off, he made his way to pick up the phone.

"Doggone it!" he lamented. "It was peaceful, around here, until someone had to disturb a perfectly good, work-related dream!"

Before he could say *hello*, a blood-curdling scream blasted from the earpiece, then static obscuring an incomprehensible voice. He guessed that the scratchy-sounding call was originating from a remote location on the fringe of wireless reception.

"Try to find a better cell," he said, offering advice to the anonymous caller. Straining to hear the broken-up words, he distinguished a few: *Emergency . . . bloody . . .* and something about a *big swamp*. Then, a dead line—not even a click.

The ensuing dial tone droned while Homer Anders pondered the only audible words, hoping he could figure it out.

"*Swamp*—there's only one *big* one", he said, thinking out loud of the vast, forested bog, part of the great Boreal forest-type that extends into the United States from Canada.

He knew that area well—the terrain, timber, and sphagnum bogs —since his youth when his grandfather introduced him to hunting and fishing. Access was limited, except for a few skid trails; *ice roads*, as the old-timers spoke of them.

He panned his finger across the mosaic of black-and-white aerial photographs that hung on the wall, looking for familiar details, stopping at the edge of *Wilderness Swamp*.

"County Line Road—the only way in," he quickly surmised. "Emergency? This is gonna tick-me-off, if it's an early Halloween prank," he muttered.

He radioed the only officer on duty that night, Deputy Clarence Smith. With an all-business *10-4*, they arranged to meet on a logging spur just off the County Line Road.

Tires rolled immediately. Sheriff Anders wore his western-style hat, as he felt naked without it. The full moon was already high in the sky, the vibes unsettling. "A fine night for the crazies to come out of the woodwork," he said, turning left at the only traffic light in Burntwood Prairie.

An autumn chill bit at the late-night air, prompting him to roll up the windows on his cruiser. Heading north, into the wilds of northern Minnesota, the sleepy sheriff spun the dial on the dashboard, hoping for AM-skip that would bring in some lively music from far away—maybe, Nashville—entertainment that would keep his eyes open. Curiously, he stopped the knob at a signal from Chicago, attracted by political talk, an encore broadcast of that evening's three-way presidential debate between the entrepreneur, Ross Perot, the relatively unknown Arkansas Governor, William J. Clinton, and sitting President George H. W. Bush. He listened as he sped through the inspissate fog that hovered above the asphalt.

The timely political broadcast was of special interest to Homer Anders. The presidential debate kept him alert, as he deadheaded to the scene of the alleged crime. He seemed more interested in the upcoming presidential election than in his own re-election bid.

"Who's this amazing politician—this . . . Clinton?" Homer mused out loud, as he rubbed his sleep-starved eyes, listening to the debating candidates. He searched, through wisps of fog, for glimpses of the white-dashed line on the blacktop, fast-disappearing, then appearing again just below the fog line.

"He's kickin' that . . . Bush! Poor ol' George; kinda like the guy, but he'll probably get squeezed out of the whole deal, between this new guy, Clinton, and Ross Perot—the third-party spoiler." Homer cracked a smile, then chuckled with a certain admiration for the new guy, William Clinton. He liked the way that Candidate Clinton preferred to break from tradition by only using his nickname, "Bill".

Chapter 2
The Yellow-Haired Girl

It was almost midnight when Sheriff Anders arrived at the remote meeting place on the south edge of Wilderness Swamp. Deputy Smith was already parked on the loose gravel, seated in his patrol car, headlights on high beam with the heater running. His spotlight was aimed across the ditch, into the dense timber, casting a beam of bright light far into the popples.

Sheriff Anders parked alongside Smith's patrol car, stopping just behind an occupied horse trailer, still attached to a farm pickup truck.

The sheriff stepped out of his car, glancing at puffs of his own breath that had instantly condensed into a billowing fog, quickly rising in the frigid air. The sky was in motion, crisscrossed with eerie beams of vertical lights, green and red, undulating above the treetops and high into the black but starlit sky. They were wavering back and forth, like a collection of search lights, searching for a lost soul somewhere in the Great Beyond.

"Invigorating!" Homer said boldly, shaking off the heebie-jeebies as the moonlight was downright spooky that night, especially combined with the undulating ribbons of colored lights, directly above. He was stretching stiffness from his arms, when Deputy Smith approached.

"Weird ionosphere—electrical forces going nuts," Smith remarked.

"I've always liked the Northern Lights," Anders said. "Intellectually stimulating, although a bit extreme tonight."

"My wife, the purist, would kill me if I didn't use the scientific term—Aurora borealis," the deputy said. Small talk, instead of a greeting.

"Is the caller here?" Anders asked, glancing all about but not seeing anyone.

"Who?"

"The *caller*, of course, the person who called in the emergency. Poor reception: had to be on one of those new-fangled, cellular telephones, where you can't understand anything."

"Ha!" Deputy Smith almost laughed. "Don'tcha love those portable antenna-jobs!"

"I'd expect that the caller, after going through the trouble to make the call, would've at least shown up. Who'd make such a call, if it was a legitimate emergency, then go into hiding?" He angled his thumb at the truck and trailer. "Whose rig is this?"

There was a reverberant murmur, from a horse inside the trailer. Deputy Smith shrugged his shoulders.

"So—what's up, Clarence?" the sheriff doubtfully asked, thinking that the deputy, himself—the office jokester—may have been the one who spoofed that call.

"It's a shocker. Come and see for yourself!"

Sheriff Anders followed his deputy into the edge of the woods, the patrol car's spotlight at his back. Suspicious that co-pranksters from the office had led him to this obscure place, in the middle of the night to participate as the sucker in some hilarious Halloween prank, Homer stayed alert. He expected to hear a spurt of laughter, or Halloween hoots emitting from the dark shadows. He was accustomed to going along with a limited amount of nonsense, hoping his staff would get their kicks over with, and that everyone could get back to work.

After following Smith for a short distance, Homer slowed his steps to a stop. Not seeing anything unusual and seeming confused, as to the purpose of this late-night trek into the forest, he asked, "Deputy Smith, what's going on—a snipe hunt?"

Clarence laughed at that, then pointed with his flashlight. A lifeless form, almost hidden among the ferns—pale skin and a splash of blood—shone in the center of the light beam. "I told you, Boss, it's a shocker. This girl has been murdered!"

"No—not in *my* county!" cried Homer Anders, seeing *the yellow-haired girl* lying on fresh-fallen leaves. Breathless, he stared at the dead blonde's face, hoping she was not someone that he knew. She was not.

"Beautiful hair, like new corn silks—"

Chapter 3

A Picture for the Files

"Keep this outta the newspaper . . . and no TV!" the sheriff demanded, his voice shaking. With wobbly knees, he crouched over the lifeless body of the young woman, taking a closer look at the gaping wound in the center of her back.

"Holy Mackerel! Must be an axe-cut—my God!" the sheriff gasped. He staggered away on weak legs, stooped, and vomited. Holding his trembling hands on his knees, it took Homer a moment to stabilize.

"Clarence, get *a picture for the files*—just one—that's all. Makes me sick! We'll need clarity, to satisfy the crime lab, so use the new camera," he said quietly, feeling compassion for the dead girl.

When his deputy went to get the camera, Sheriff Anders stood in the center of the bright spotlight beam. With his handkerchief, he wiped his mouth, then splotches of barf from his shoes. He stood next to the cold body, staring into the darkness until Officer Smith returned.

Smith focused the single-lens-reflex camera on the spot where the sheriff aimed his flashlight. The electronic flash was brilliant in the blackness of the forest, overpowering both the flashlight and the spotlight.

"Looks like she was running. Somebody caught up to her," Homer supposed, pointing out apparent facts. "She only made it about fifty feet. No wonder she didn't get away—tight blue jeans . . . and cowboy boots! How can anyone actually run in cowboy boots?"

"I hope your campaign-ad will show up in tomorrow's paper," were Smith's only words.

The two officers silently walked back to the vehicles. Officer Smith searched the cab of the dead girl's pickup truck.

"How in the world did this young woman end up here, parked on a dead-end logging spur, facing the wrong direction? And horses in a trailer?" asked Sheriff Anders, totally befuddled.

Officer Smith showed Sheriff Anders the dead woman's driver's license, found in the glove compartment.

The sheriff held his flashlight against the thin cardboard document, read the name and address, then fumbled with a small, blue-lined notebook. "We can't change the plight of *the yellow-haired girl*," he acknowledged. "Put all the evidence in a bag."

Deputy Smith went about his work, and the sheriff walked to the front of the horse trailer where two curious horses held their heads out the side windows. He gently rubbed the nose of the closest mare. The friendly horse nickered and sniffed Homer's hand.

"What did you see, Girl?" whispered Homer, as if he expected the horse to reveal details of the killing, after witnessing the whole thing. "My God, if you could only talk!"

Deputy Smith suddenly stepped to Homer's side and handed him the evidence bag.

Speed Trap Murder

"What in God's name happened here? What was this young woman—this Maria Richardson—doing way out here, more than forty miles from home?" the sheriff asked. Not expecting a response, he continued with his train of thought, "Ya never know; could be anything, I suppose, like the work of a psycho, or maybe a love-affair gone amok. Hurry up and get the measurements, before the ambulance gets here. Call and tell 'em there's no hurry. Nobody can save this poor girl now."

* * *

At that very moment, in the middle of the night, Margo Toralf lied quietly in her old bedroom, amazed that after years of being away, it felt great to be back on her parent's farm where she had grown up. Just visiting for the weekend, and having joyous thoughts about the wonderful day she had just spent renewing her friendship with her all-time best friend, Maria Richardson, she was too excited to sleep. Reliving that day's trail ride gave her a sense of tranquility. She finally zoned out, just as the first beams of morning sunlight permeated the thin curtain which hung over the east window.

Chapter 4
A Crime Against Humanity

Irked by beams of sunlight that glared across his desk, Sheriff Anders was still functioning on his pre-midnight power nap. The beginning of a gut-wrenching homicide investigation, coupled with the tedious, long night was catching up to him.

He was tired of waiting for someone on the other end of the line to provide answers to his many questions. He toyed with the coiled phone cord, the agonizing moments seeming like an eternity. Accustomed to bureaucratic slowness, he tried to be patient, adjusting the horizontal blinds to eliminate the glare of the rising sun.

"No, I can't wait for normal office hours! This is a murder investigation, and that's all ya got—we found a dead Sunday School teacher? I hafta have more information than that!" He let go of the cord and watched it recoil, like a spring. "I haven't been up all night, for nothin'! This was a young woman, cut down way-too-early in life —*a crime against humanity*! I've already got her name and address; there must be more."

Perplexed, Sheriff Anders quietly hung up. He took a short sip from his cup and sifted through the limited facts he had assembled about the deceased girl, all jotted down on the tiny pages of his shirt-pocket notebook.

"Maria Richardson—single; lives with her parents," he muttered to himself. "An innocent farm girl."

He pinpointed the location of the Richardson farm and grabbed his copy of the weekly paper. Only glancing at his own likeness, he rolled it up and tucked it under one arm, while snugging the sweatband of his hat into place.

On his official visit to the parents of the deceased girl, delivering the tragic news, he admitted that he was puzzled by the brazen murder and how easily the unknown perpetrator had vanished. He was troubled that he was not able to answer grievous questions, posed by the girl's parents. And he was disappointed that this visit produced no evidence, but he got his first clue: the Richardson family knew where Maria had spent the weekend. They gave the name, Margo Toralf, a longtime friend of their daughter.

At the end of the sheriff's visit, Maria Richardson's grief-stricken parents began to show their anger. "That unstable Toralf girl! The prettiest ones are always the craziest," said Maria's father.

"Why didn't she stay away, as she had all these years? Insane person—nothing but trouble—that entire Toralf family!" fitfully remarked the dead girl's mother.

Sheriff Anders offered his condolences, then returned to his cruiser, remembering a kid he had once arrested—Billy Toralf—a two-bit con-artist. "He must have a sister."

He remembered where the Toralf farm was, and he deadheaded in that direction. His only lead, just a young woman's name, was not much to go on.

"Trouble runs in families," he muttered, turning off the highway, soon stopping near the back porch at the run-down Toralf farm.

It was a routine visit. The Sheriff told the Toralfs of the tragic news, asked a couple questions, and scrutinized their reactions.

Margo was as shocked as everyone else, that her old-best-friend had been brutally murdered by an unknown assailant. It was hard for her to grasp, that she had just accompanied Maria the previous day; and before that day was through, her friend had been killed. Unbelievable.

After the sheriff left, her initial shock grew into severe grief. Hair-pulling anguish.

After Maria's funeral, Margo returned to her rented trailer house near Minneapolis, still devastated by the violent death of her friend and by the second curtailing of her dream, to have a horse ranch. She fell into a profound sadness which lasted for months. Stanley Nelson, her boyfriend and father of her baby, was the only one who could console her.

The murder of Maria Richardson became a political issue, barely a week before Election Day. Having an unsolved crime, and all the questions it brought, was an embarrassment for Sheriff Anders. His re-election campaign slipped into a stall. And it didn't help that a Fargo newspaper picked up the story, that the farmer's daughter was mysteriously killed by someone dubbed, "The Hatchet Murderer".

The Sheriff had to publicly admit that he had not assembled any meaningful evidence, even though he had assigned his most experienced officer, Deputy Clarence Smith, to investigate the crime.

Speed Trap Murder

"This is the first time that I've hit a dead end, in an investigation," he was quoted in the Otter Tattler. "I will not retire, nor will I rest from my duties as your faithful sheriff, until this murder is solved!"

With that promise, Sheriff Homer Anders successfully squeaked through re-election, even though his opponent, Aino Pekka, played upon the fizzled murder investigation.

After the election, the case went cold.

Chapter 5
Secret Swimming Hole

The winter was typically cold, until February when an unexpected thaw began. All this time, Henry and Bette Toralf never heard from Margo; but with the promise of an early spring, the changing future began to roll out quickly.

Out-of-the-blue, their daughter landed a nursing job in Burntwood Prairie. This miracle, finding employment within easy commuting distance of her homeplace, gave rise to the resurfacing of her childhood aspirations of having her own horse ranch.

Ecstatic, she abruptly returned to the farm, announcing that she was moving in. She introduced Toby to her parents, then took over her old bedroom. The place was full of her childhood memories. It still held the same magic; it provided the place of solace that she had craved. She was *done* with the big-city life.

By mid-March, the wintery blanket of accumulated snow had succumbed to the daily onslaught of 50-degree warmth. The fields became bare, runoff trickled, and the ditches overflowed. The weekend finally came when Stanley Nelson drove up to the farm. First time.

Margo was excited to show him around. Her *secret swimming hole* was the first stop, but the water was high. No matter, Willow Creek commonly overflowed its banks.

She looked up at the knot at the end of the rope, far out on the oak-limb where it was tied. She tried not to think about Maria Richardson who had been killed only hours after the two of them had last swung on that rope. More than 5 months had gone by, yet the memory was fresh in her mind.

"Maria did this so well," Margo whispered, wanting to remember the good times but none of the sadness. She braced her foot against an exposed root and glanced, over the rushing clay-colored waters, unconcerned that the creek had risen to a dangerous flood-stage level.

The rope felt thick in her hand. She remembered how it took both hands to grip it fully, years before when she was a little girl. She snuck a glance at Stanley Nelson who stood off to the side.

Stanley wore a spring jacket and blue jeans, with no intention of jumping in. He watched from the riverbank, absorbing her ever-present magical aura that always lured him in. He adored her, her form perfect. Beautiful. Even from a distance, she looked like a calendar girl. His eyes couldn't stray, as she was poised to plunge into the eddy-pond that swirled below.

Knowing that Stanley was watching gave her a special feeling of excitement. She wanted him to be impressed with her daring stunt, something she had done many times, in the past.

"Take one last look," she called out flirtatiously. Margo knew that she looked sexy in her cut-off jeans and white T-shirt, and that she had just shown enough charisma to make any man look twice. She tightened her grip, glanced at Stanley once more, and cried out a hoot.

P. G. Knudson

Stanley flinched, then pulled at the collar of his jacket when he saw Margo sailing through the air, swinging out, over the floodwater.

"She's something else," he whispered to himself, hearing her screeching with delight as she let go of the rope at the point where height and distance coincided.

Stanley's heart pounded. He shouted a hoot of his own when Margo's body disappeared in the swollen current with barely a splash.

"She's totally nuts," he mused, after seeing her go under. He shuttered, knowing how cold that plunge must have felt. He was glad that he had decided not to go in, even though Margo had begged him to. Feeling a chill, he zipped his jacket a few more notches and anxiously watched for her head to reappear below the swirling pool of icy-cold water. He stepped to the water's edge but saw no sign of her.

What happened? He thought the worst. *Did she drown?*

He felt a fluttering in his chest, running along the creek bank, looking for some indication of life; possibly a break in the surface tension of the water.

"Margo—Margo!" he called out, stricken with fear.

Suddenly Margo's face burst through the surface of the water, farther downstream. She spit out a mouthful of water and called out, "What do you think of that?"

Relieved, Stanley caught his breath. "Pretty scary stuff, Margo," he said, trying to sound calm but pleased that she finally sounded happy, after months of gloom.

"You should've jumped in with me. The water's nice!"

Strong current! "Yeah—so you say. I might have tried it, if I was ten years younger."

28

"You're not old!" she said, knowing that she was stretching the truth but satisfied that he'd do anything for her love. For some reason, she preferred older men; and Stanley fit the bill.

Dogpaddling up to shore, she teased, "You're just chicken!" She nimbly stepped onto the sandy shoreline, hardly flinching from the bite of sharp sticks that poked the bottoms of her bare feet. Margo, her hair hanging wet, shivered and cradled her elbows in her hands. Her clothes clung to her shapely form, the excess water running down to her toes. "Not too shabby, huh?"

"Not bad," Stanley said, his heartbeat still winding down. He heard Margo's teeth chatter. *She needs a towel, but we don't have one.* "I've never done anything like that," he admitted. "I'd accidently kill myself, if I tried it."

"I did it!" she bragged, locking on to Stanley's glance and leering with ogled eyes. She liked to dim her eyes that way, to look like a sensual girl on the cover of a magazine.

The fact that Stanley seemed different than most men appealed to her. She considered him to be a new challenge, even though their baby was already a year old. She loved the excitement of a romantic chase, feeling that she had him, right where she wanted him—baby boy and a promise of eventual marriage.

Stanley either didn't mind the power play or wasn't aware of it. Either way, he didn't complain of being manipulated by a younger woman. He just knew that he felt energized when she acted that way.

"I think you're . . . looney!" he said, trying to pat her on the butt when she swayed past.

Margo dodged his hand, giggling. "Loons swim well. Thanks for the compliment!"

"I meant, 'you're nutty', jumping in like that. If it wasn't for the snowmelt, this little wide-spot-on-the-creek would've been too shallow. You would've broken your neck!"

Chapter 6
Tough As Nails

Without warning, Margo jumped onto Stanley's back, her arms around his neck. At first, Stanley thought he was going to get a big hug and a kiss. Instead, Margo gripped him with some sort of wrestling neck-lock. She held on, her feet swinging wildly above the ground, both legs finally wrapping around his hips.

"What—what are you doing? You're choking me!" He staggered, almost falling on the riverbank but grunted and stood his ground. Mislead by her mischievous giggle and not noticing her athletic maneuver of hooking one leg around one of his, he succumbed to her final move—the flip.

Stanley fell flat onto his back; and much to his surprise, Margo was still holding on.

"I learned that in the Army!" she said with a *tough-as-nails* overtone, a persona she rarely showed, except when feeling amorous. She tightened the scissor-grip of her legs, her wanting eyes melting with passion, then forcefully kissing him. It made her feel powerful.

She rapidly worked herself into a frenzy. She stripped off Stanley's jacket, tossed it into the bushes, and started pulling at his shirt.

Worried, Stanley finally said, "Hold it, Margo; not here!"

There was a belligerent groan before she let go. She stood up and made two angry slaps on her thighs, to brush off the sand, but the stubborn dirt was stuck to her wet jeans. She stepped into the shallow edge and glared into the continuous swirl of the swollen pond, not saying a word, seeming as cross as a bear.

Stanley sat down on the riverbank and calmly waited, as if he knew how to handle Margo's version of the old-fashioned *silent treatment*. Soon, they sat side-by-side, both quietly looking into the turbulent flow.

"Getting cold?" Stanley asked, trying to break the divisive silence.

"Oh, you're such a spoilsport, Stanley!" Margo whined and looked away.

"Just thought, you might want to dry off. What are you so grumpy for?"

"I'm happy!" she barked angrily. "And I don't have any other clothes with me. I'll air-dry, just fine. And it's not very cold; the warmest day we've had all spring."

"So, this is your secret swimming hole?"

"Yeah. Mom used to take us kids here, on a hot day—skinny-dipping—unless the boys came too, then we wore cutoffs. You should've seen Mom swing from that rope!" she said and laughed maliciously, obviously recalling an incident from the past. "No; on second thought, you wouldn't want to see Mom naked—believe me— you really wouldn't!" she continued her wild-hearted laugh.

"It doesn't look like a secret place."

"Well, it always seemed that way, to us kids. I just wanted you to see it, Stanley. It's part of my life, part of me; part of who I am.

Memories here, at this secluded place." Her eyes suddenly welled up with tears. "Memories? Oh, Maria!" she sobbed, suddenly getting a flashback in her mind. "She'd probably still be alive, if I hadn't brought her here!"

Stanley knew that Maria's death was still traumatizing Margo. He searched for a consoling word, as he usually provided, but couldn't think of a new one.

Chapter 7
Muddy Horse Tracks

S tanley and Margo sat on a fallen log, staring down the steep bank at the churning current.

"I'm glad you came. Mom and Dad will see you here, overnight, and know that you're serious about getting married."

"You told them, already?"

"I couldn't wait! It's exciting to be getting married—for a girl, anyway! But Dad said, he wishes that you would've asked him first. It's a custom, from the old days."

"Well, it sounds like you didn't give me a chance."

Margo laughed, "You should still ask Daddy; he'd like that. We're not getting married right away, anyway, so you have time." She hugged Stanley's arm.

"I've missed both you and Toby. He's really growing."

"I'm so happy," Margo whispered, softly stroking Stanley's thinning hair. She lightly kissed him on the side of his neck. "Mom tells me that my goals are not realistic—a man, kids, horses, and happiness. A family is full of pain, and I deserve all the grief that I gave my own parents—payback!" She laughed. "I think Mom gets these ideas from watching soap operas. I'll show her how wrong she is, though, now that we're getting married, buying the farm, and having our own family! I'm so-o-o happy! Thank you for coming into my life, Stanley!"

Stanley seemed puzzled. "What was that part—the part about *buying the farm*?"

"You don't have to say anything; just live it and enjoy it!" she said, ignoring his question.

"I love you, strange woman; but what's this talk—the farm—what farm?"

Margo suddenly grabbed onto his leg, trying to pull him back downhill, cackling mischievously all the while.

Realizing that he was suddenly within inches of being dragged into the frigid water, Stanley grappled for something to hold on to. He luckily hooked his fingers around an exposed tree root and hung on.

"I'm not letting go!" he boasted, laughing faintly, realizing that Margo was surprisingly strong. "You'll have to pry my fingers from this root, if you want to throw me in!"

Margo giggled, struggling in vain. "You win, Deputy Nelson!" she finally said, then tossed a feathery kiss and left him lying flat on his stomach. She scampered up the riverbank and sat alone at the base of the huge oak tree. She stared at the dangling rope that seemed to dance invitingly, over the creek. Stanley walked up and sat next to her, reclining against the bulged butt of the buttressed tree. The two calmly embraced, hardly realizing they were both covered with sand and river-muck from head to toe.

Margo giggled, giving an amorous glance. "Take your clothes off, Stanley. Nobody'll see us." She winked and pulled at his shirt.

"You like taking chances? Here's the deal—plain and simple: I can't risk it," he said, glancing through the dormant bushes that grew close to the creek. "It only *seems* hidden. It's a public place—not a secret place. If anyone sees us, the word would get out—somehow—and I'd end up losing my job. I'm finally in-line to get a promotion—Sergeant—and I don't want to mess-it-up."

"I understand," Margo said softly, locking her arms around his neck.

After a chilly rinse, they hiked a woodsy trail, waiting for their soaked clothes to stop sticking to their bodies.

"Horse tracks," Stanley said, observing gouged marks in the sand.

"Of course, they are," Margo said sarcastically, "we're walking on the horse trail. Gol-ley—let's get technical! You're always looking at the ground!"

"That's where the clues are."

"What clues are you talking about?"

"I see ruts from a car and *muddy horse tracks*."

"So, what?"

"Mud on top of leaves means, the autumn leaves were already lying there when the horse flipped the compacted soil on top of them, proving it occurred in the fall. And it proves that this is not a very secret spot. It's a busy swimming hole; lots of people come here, in cars and on horseback, to swing on that rope."

"Okay, okay; it was me! I rode Maria's horse through here, so they're probably *my* tracks. Mud on top of leaves—my God, you're a fanatic cop! Can't you take a weekend off?"

"I'm glad I kept my pants on! I'll still have a job, when I go back to work on Monday."

36

"Oh-h-h!" Margo fumed. "You sure know how to spoil a good time!"

"What did I do, now?" Stanley asked, not necessarily wanting a confrontation.

Angry, she marched ahead of him, down the brushy trail in double-time. She didn't say anything until they got almost all the way back to the swimming hole. "Get your nose up, off the ground, and let's go home!"

Stanley stopped along a wet depression, intrigued by more horse tracks, riddled deep in the mud. "Just one question . . . about Maria," he started to ask, scrutinizing the mucky maze of tracks.

"I told you about her—my best friend—dead."

"I remember; you told me she was murdered," he said, recalling the endless hours he had spent consoling her.

"After our last ride, she had to get going; farm chores—you know. She loaded up the horses and dropped me off by the south forty, so I could hike across Dad's land. I saw her pull onto the highway, Maria and her horses; the last time I ever saw her," she said, wiping a tear away. "And I told you about the dreams; they're horrid!"

"Which day did you girls ride your horses through here?"

"The same day that she was murdered. Somebody must have followed her home and . . . nobody knows; it's an unsolved crime."

"How was it, that she came down here?"

Margo hated being interrogated, upset that her own boyfriend was springing tough questions on her. "You know why; she came to see me! There's no law against that! When I told her I'd be home for a few days, she drove all the way down here; two horses in her trailer, so I could ride, too. She went home on Sunday, and I—I waited, until .

. . after her funeral to go back downstate . . . to our trailer. You remember that." Her reddening eyes were awash.

"Yeah, I remember; she never made it home, and you didn't get back until way-past midnight . . . a week later."

Chapter 8
Stiff Body

Stanley spotted something that would arouse the interest of any detective, a discarded canvas shoe, just off the side of the trail. He pointed a finger, so Margo would see it.

"Was that shoe lying there when you rode *this* trail, *that* day?" Stanley probed, wanting to ascertain the facts.

"I don't know! I just showed Maria the secret swimming hole. We skinny-dipped, but it was shallow! I want to go back to the farm now. Thinking about Maria's death is too upsetting."

Stanley mulled over the coincidence, that two young women would have been here, at this specific location, their horses spooked to make erratic tracks in the mud, and that one of the women was murdered just after leaving. *The killer must have been here, saw the activity, and followed the women when they left; but, if so, why did one of them—Margo—escape death?*

"Something's not right, here," he said, still gazing at the shoe. He walked over to it.

"What?" she sneered. "A lost tennie shoe is suspicious? On this trail, most people take their shoes off . . . to swim. Let's go!"

"Wait," he said, crouching near the abandoned shoe. He stared silently, then pointed to a second shoe, barely visible, and a patch of denim hidden under an inconspicuous pile of leaves.

"Blue jeans!" Margo gave an eerie gasp. She watched, as Stanley slowly pulled at the tips of a cluster of twigs, all stuck together and protruding from the pile of compacted leaves. The whole pile of small sticks and leaves slid easily, with his steady pull. He stopped pulling when he realized that he had exposed a dead body, clothed in blue jeans and a red-plaid, flannel shirt.

"Good God!" Margo cried out. She turned away, her hand covering her mouth.

"Look at that—*a stiff body*!" Stanley said fairly calmly. "Be careful not to disturb anything. This is a crime scene!"

"I can't bear to look," she whimpered, then stared at the leaf-littered body, the face half-buried in a bed of loose leaves. "It's a boy."

"Just a kid—maybe eighteen or twenty," Stanley said with cool concentration, like one would expect from a trained officer. "There's blood, down under, but I'm not going to roll him over. Not my jurisdiction—a job for the locals. Poor kid; he's been here a long time. There must be some worried parents, somewhere, wondering where he is."

Margo's face grayed, exhibiting a shock-like blankness. "Uh—the shirt!"

"What—you know something about the death of this boy?"

"Oh, cut it out, Stanley! I don't know anything, or whom he might be. I just thought of something, that's all; but . . . it must have been someplace else." She turned away from the body and away from

Stanley, so she could hide the look of surprise on her face, trying to recall where she had seen that red shirt.

After walking back to her car, Margo seemed only half-interested in watching Stanley use his trendy, bulky-looking cellular telephone to call the authorities.

Just one officer showed up—the Sheriff, himself—a wrinkled old man who seemed too old to be a competent officer of the law. He nearly tripped, getting out of his cruiser. He stumbled, again, on his first step past the ditch. Stanley slowly led the way down the woodsy trail, to the site of the body, hoping that the old sheriff would not fall and hurt himself.

Margo walked far-behind the others, numbed by the way that both Stanley and the sheriff approached the scene of the crime in a cold, matter-of-fact sort of way. She stopped by the oak tree, not wanting to see the body again.

"We just happened to see a sneaker—right there," Stanley explained to the sheriff, pointing at the innocuous yet gruesome pile of leaves. "I pulled on those sticks and—wham—a dead body! He must have been here all winter. The snow melted, over the last week or so—"

"Let me draw the conclusions, Son. We do our own investigating in *my* county," the sheriff said slowly, first glancing at the sneaker that lied in the leaves, some distance away, then at the corpse under the pile of leaves, by his feet, where the matching shoe was still tied onto one foot. He knelt and poked at the stiffened denim of a pant-leg with the blunt tip of a stick.

"Hm-m—still frozen," the old sheriff muttered, observing the flannel shirt that was half-covered with ice-crystals and fragments of dead leaves. "Who pulled that brush off the body—you?"

"Yes, Sir, Sheriff; that's what I said, just a minute ago."

"Oh yeah; I remember. You told me that—"

Stanley told the sheriff what Margo had said, about riding a horse past that spot, and that the horse tracks might be from her horse. He also mentioned that there were two horses, both belonging to Maria Richardson, the young woman that was murdered, just hours after the trail ride.

The sheriff's eyes snapped to alertness, recognizing the young woman's name. He also remembered the horses. "What? She was here, too—the platinum blonde, killed off the County Line Road?"

"Yes, Sir, Sheriff; last fall, both Maria and Margo passed through here."

The sheriff scratched his head. "Huh—preposterous—such an unlikely occurrence, don'tcha think?"

"I don't know;" Stanley said, seeming surprised at the off-the-cuff rhetorical question, posed by the old sheriff. "It's not a coincidence; the girls were friends."

The sheriff began scribbling notes into a pocket-sized notebook with blue-lined pages. He asked for names and numbers, which Stanley provided. "You two can go."

"Aren't there some forms to fill out?"

"Nah; when it comes to these kinda things, it's six-a-one-n'-half-a-dozen of the other. I've got what I need—for now. You didn't move the body, itself, didja?"

"No; that's what I . . . said—twice, already—"

42

"Good; those crime lab scientists go nuts, if the body's moved. I'll letcha know, if I need anything else from ya," he said. "In the meantime, I'll call-it-in."

"There are tire tracks, too. There must be something . . .," Stanley tried to volunteer.

"I see the tracks. Don't you worry about the details, Son. I'll get my number one deputy goin' on this, right away." The sheriff bowed his head, showing reverence for the deceased boy.

After a moment of silence, he said, "Take my card. Call me if ya think of somethin' else. And remember me on election day—November—when—ah-h, you know the date—"

Stanley glanced at the business card: *Homer Anders—Sheriff—Justus County, Minnesota.* "Sure-thing, Sheriff Anders, but . . ."

"Oh—didja think of somethin'?" *the senile sheriff* asked.

"Ah, Sir—about the four-year election cycle—wasn't the election held, just last fall?"

Chapter 9
The Beeline Drive

There was silence in Margo's old sedan, after she told Stanley to "shut up" about the dead body. Realizing that there was no point in getting under her skin, Stanley held his tongue almost the entire way, on *the beeline drive* back to the farm. This wasn't the first time he had to deal with the downside of her changing moods. Of course, this time there was an actual reason for her to be upset.

He stared out the window, making sure that his lips didn't move, listening to the hum of the wheels speeding on the gravel roadway, and hearing the rapping sounds of acorn-sized pebbles ricocheting off the insides of the wheel-wells.

After a mile, Margo unclenched her jaw, slowed down a bit, then complained about someone stalking her ever since she'd moved back to the farm.

"A stalker?"

"A deputy. He showed up at Maria's funeral. Strange—Maria's mother asked me who he was and what he was doing there. I told her, 'I don't know', but I figured out why: he was investigating *me*. It was snowing at the cemetery. I'll never forget, he stared at me through the flurries, from across the casket. His eyes were glued on me, even while the preacher prayed. Then he followed me to the farm. I saw him again, last month, when I was up here for the job interview. He came by the farm, when I was raking leaves by the mailbox."

"You saw him—the same guy?"

"Yeah; he stopped. He was a deputy, like I said, in the Justus County car."

"Did he say anything?"

"Yeah; we talked. He asked who I was, but he seemed to already know me. After all, he'd seen me before. He was ugly. Scary. He got very personal, so I walked back to the house."

"Did you get his name?"

"No. To tell you the truth, I didn't want to encourage him, so I didn't ask."

"All deputies wear a name tag; you should've read it."

"We can find out, if we want to, can't we? How many deputies can there be, in this county—especially ugly ones?"

"It wouldn't do any good to ask, now. Too much time has gone by, and it sounds like normal police work, anyway. It's common for cops to attend funerals of murder victims, because the culprit is sometimes there too. He might've thought you were the killer, since you knew Maria and you were present. What makes you think he's a stalker? You're not getting paranoid, are you?"

"Don't talk to me that way!" Margo cried, something short of screaming. "It's not paranoia when it's really happening! He's been back, looking up the driveway. And he stopped me, one day, by the speed trap; stared down my blouse and gave me a warning ticket."

"I give out warning tickets all the time. It's a common practice, but it's possible he might think you had something to do with Maria's death. After all, you told *me* that you were probably the last person to see her alive."

"But I wasn't doing anything wrong . . . and got stopped. I was scared—the creep! I don't want to talk to him again!"

"Maybe we should ask . . . um—" He reached into his pocket. "Sheriff, Homer Anders," he said, reading from the business card.

"That Homer Anders—what a stupid, old man! He didn't even remember me today. He's the one who questioned me about Maria's death! He took notes in that same little notebook—some investigator, he is! He did nothing! This poor, dead boy in the leaf pile; his case will never be solved either."

Margo came out of a sharp left turn, sliding through *Dead Man's Corner*, then let the pebbles fly.

She must know, high speed and corduroy road do not go together. Bouncing on his seat, Stanley grabbed onto the dashboard and frightfully asked, "Are we on the right road?"

"I know where I am," Margo said, sounding offended. She slowed down, her tail-end fishtailing over the bumps. "I still remember all these back roads. Maria and I came this way, last fall. And, back in the old days when I rode my trusty horse, he always knew the way home, and to the other swimming holes. There are other good spots!" she said and laughed mischievously, giving Stanley a flirtatious wink.

"Your mood changed—right there—just now, and for the better."

"No, it didn't!"

"Yes, it did. I saw it—a twinkle in your eye! You were grumpy, almost bounced us off the road, then . . . suddenly happy. You're fun when you smile, but not as much when your smile is up-side-down. You drive me nuts when you're moody."

"Complaints? What do you expect, after finding that dead kid in the woods? And now, what's next, police interrogations?"

"Don't worry about it. That old sheriff won't call us. I told him, I was a deputy in another county. I did all I can do; it's up to him, now —him and his number one deputy."

"Well, don't call me *moody*! I can't get Maria off my mind, that's all. She was going to help me start a horse ranch," Margo said, a quaver in her voice, the first time she had ever mentioned her old horse-ranch plan to Stanley.

"I just like it better when you're happy; that's all."

"You make me happy, Stanley. I'm so lucky to have you in my life."

"Do you realize that we'll hardly-ever see each other now, with you up here . . . and me down there; we're a long day's drive apart!"

"Then, quit your job. Move up here. You'll love it—all the seasons —especially winter!"

"Wintertime is cold up here!"

"Winter is good in the North; cold—true—but it's also a quiet place to live, away from that big-city nightmare. Lots of people actually go somewhere else, like Mom wants to do. She wants to go South, for the winters—way-down-South—warm air and bare ground. But me, I like it here. Good riddance to those who go away . . . and stay away!"

"You don't mean that, do you, about your own mother?"

"Do I wish she'd move away? Yeah, I do. She's crazy—you know —*certifiable*!"

Stanley laughed. "You're too much, Margo! That *is* funny! Nobody really means it . . . when they say . . . stuff like that. You're joking, right?"

"Don't get me started . . . about Mom! She's certifiable; of course, I mean it! I haven't told you about what happened to my dog, have I?"

Chapter 10
A Close Call

Who could hurt a dog? Believing the old saying, *a dog is man's best friend*, Stanley clammed up. He turned to the side window and stared outside, curious about what had happened to Margo's dog but afraid to ask.

After skidding through a sharp right turn, Margo said, "I'll tell you what she did to my dog, if you want to know."

Stanley saw a black limo-like car outside his window, parked in front of a paint-bare farmhouse, and a half-dozen all-black cattle huddled near an old barn. Faded, hand-painted letters on the mailbox read, *Jensen.*

"There it is—Dad's farm! Can you see it?" Margo said, pointing ahead.

No, he couldn't. He was still looking to the side, deciding not to pursue the dog-question. Outside his window, there was a new house under construction. "Where are we?"

"It's Elmer Jensen's farm. At least it *was,* until somebody—maybe some city-slicker—started building a new house. Damn, I hate it when that happens! Betcha they'll end up tearing down the old house—a place that actually has some style." Margo stopped and glared at the new ranch-style frame. "Tsk-k!"

"Where's your dad's farm?" Stanley asked, looking away from the construction zone and the sleek-looking car that had first grabbed his attention.

"It's the next place; see the barn—way over, across the hay field?"

Stanley looked beyond the clustered cattle. "U-huh—way over yonder; now I see it. I recognize the barn. It's your dad's place, alright."

Margo grimaced. "Never thought I'd see the day when there'd be a new house on our road! Another outsider, crowding out the farmers. Too many city-people moving out here! They should stay in the city!"

"Why do you say that? It looks like . . . progress, to me."

Gravelly rocks hammered at the undersides of the fenders, as she punished the accelerator-petal, holding it to the floor. Her old clunker lunged ahead and sped toward home. Road-dust billowed up, from unseen holes in the floorboards of her rusted-out car-body, filling the inside-air with dust.

With the cloud of dust inside the car, it was getting harder to breathe.

"Don't you think you ought to slow down? No need to floor-it, all the way home!" Wanting fresh air, Stanley began to roll his window down, only to hear a loud rumble, then the loud blast of a train-whistle. He turned his head to the right, then saw the yellow engine of a train, bearing down upon them. The whistle blared again, and the ground shook.

"A Train—Margo—a train!" he shouted.

Margo was too scared to scream. She slammed on the brakes, spinning the steering wheel to the left. Her locked-up tires slid on the loose gravel. The car spun around and stalled, crosswise in the middle of the road and just short of colliding with the passing freight train.

Shaking with fright, Stanley stared at the blur of empty cattle-cars whizzing past, almost close enough to touch.

Within seconds, the short train had rumbled past, narrowly missing Margo's car. Stanley rolled his window, all the way down, and groped for clean air. Glad to still be alive, he glanced through the dissipating dust and saw Margo's half-smirk.

"That was *a close call,*" he said.

After realizing that the danger had passed, Margo slowly began to laugh. "Sorry—I forgot about the train."

Stanley looked back and forth, up and down the county road, which was blocked by Margo's car. "This is an unmarked railroad crossing! Isn't that illegal?"

"I don't know; you're the cop, not me!"

Chapter 11
Nostalgic Memories

Margo restarted her engine, then slowly drove the remaining half-mile to her parent's farm. She splashed her tires through a small pothole and stopped partway up the driveway where patches of willow brush stood, dormant in the watery ditches.

"This is where I want a sign, one of those *big* ranch signs like you see in Texas. It should say, *Margo's Ranch*, or something like that."

"Are you sure your father wants a ranch sign?"

"It'll be for me—for us."

"Is that what you meant, about *buying a farm*? Did you mean, this place? We haven't discussed jointly buying this farm, or any other farm."

"I want to buy Daddy's farm, Stanley. Me and you, of course. Please, Stanley," she whined. "We can afford it. I'm starting my new job next week!"

Stanley looked perplexed. "Have you taken a look? Decades of decay. One glance tells me the whole place has gone downhill. The barn looks like it's about ready to fall down. It should be demolished. Even the house is in tough condition. Financially, it would be a disaster to take on this . . . boondoggle. You can't be serious!"

"I am . . . and we're not going to tear down the barn. I want to keep it. It's full of old memories."

"You once told me you want to forget about your entire childhood!"

"When I said that, I was in a bad frame of mind. Sure, my childhood was . . . not-so-perfect, but there are still memories. I dreamed about changing my life . . . in that barn, many times, over and over. It's the *dreams* that've kept me going."

Stanley didn't know what to think about her seemingly new passion—buying her father's farm. "*Dreams*—both good dreams and bad dreams?"

"Forget about . . . what I said about my old dreams; half of them were . . . crazy! There'll only be good dreams, from now on—*our* dreams—dreams to come true."

"*Nostalgic memories* and buying dreams? When do we get it, if it happens at all?"

"Soon, but don't say anything to Mom and Dad about it. If it's going to go *our* way, we have to be patient. Dad will surprise us someday and . . . just do it. He's so impulsive!"

Stanley seemed troubled that Margo would seemingly be willing to take advantage of her father's good will. "Fixing an old house, we'd go broke. It'd be better to build a new one."

Margo didn't agree, but made no rebuttal, saving that argument for another day; but she pressed the issue, concerning her ranch sign. "We'll get some tall poles and mount the sign over the driveway, high enough for everyone to see."

"If it's important to be high in the sky, why don't put it up there?" Stanley tried to joke, pointing to the tallest structure on the farm—the silo. "It would show up well."

Margo glared at him, as if he was an idiot. "Farm rule: nobody's allowed to climb up there. It's too dangerous!" A childhood memory of being thrashed with a willow switch flashed through her mind. She and one of her brothers had to endure severe punishment for climbing up the side of the silo. And they had to promise, to never do it again—never-ever. Margo thought about it but decided not to tell Stanley why the silo was out-of-bounds, or what it feels like to endure the sting of a willow switch.

With nothing more said about it, she lunged ahead and parked under the oak tree, next to the station wagon. Getting out of her car, she said, "Don't mention the dead body to Mom; she'll freak out."

"Your Mom and Dad will want to know."

"No, they won't! They'll hear about it on the ten o'clock news . . . and ignore it. They don't have to know that it was *you* who found it. Don't say a word!" she insisted, troubled by her mind already replaying the image of Stanley finding the dead body.

"What about the near miss at the railroad crossing?" asked Stanley, still shaken by the incident.

"What about it? Everybody knows, the train comes through here every day."

Chapter 12
Suppertime

"*Suppertime!*" Bette Toralf announced, the second that Margo and Stanley stepped into the house. The awaiting family meal was steaming in the center of the kitchen table. "You're both wet and your hair's matted down," she said critically, brushing her own bangs from the top of her butterfly-like glasses. "You look terrible! Where have you been?"

"Oh," Margo laughed lightly, "I showed Stanley the secret swimming hole, except he was too-chicken to jump in. I had to drag him!"

Bette smirked in a knowing way.

Stanley felt embarrassed. He walked out of the room and looked throughout the house for his little boy. He returned, in only seconds, asking, "Where's Toby, Missus Toralf?"

"Oh," Bette said, "he's sleeping. And you might as well call me 'Mom', now that you've almost tied-the-knot."

"Where is he, Mom? I can't find him anywhere."

"He's in the house trailer, next door—Grandma's trailer," Bette said.

"I thought that old trailer house was vacant."

"Grandma's gone to the rest home," Bette said, "but we . . ."

"So, who's watching Toby?" he wanted to know.

"He's okay; don't worry about him," Bette insisted. "We're right next door."

"He shouldn't be left alone," Stanley objected, got up from the table, and went outside.

"He's going to be a good dad," Bette said. "Toby needs a father—you know."

"Stanley *is* the father."

"He's no dreamboat. You could have done better than him," her mother said tauntingly, not able to resist sparring for a fight.

"Shush, Mom!" Margo whispered sharply. "Don't you know that Stanley might hear you?" She glared at her mother but stopped when she noticed that the wrinkling skin on her mother's neck was beginning to look like the expansion bellows of an accordion.

Hank Toralf, Margo's father, sat silently at the table absorbing all the interactions, his presence almost going unnoticed. He rubbed his pepper-streaked white whiskers, looking out from under his boyishly thick hair that spilled over the tops of his large ears. He mashed his boiled potato with a table fork, then chuckled when Stanley came back into the room carrying Toby.

Bette grabbed onto one toe of Toby's full-footed pajamas.

"How's Grandma's itsy-bitsy boy," she said in high-pitched baby talk. She nosed in and tickled his cheek. "Koochie-coo!"

"Leave him alone, Mom; he's tired!" Margo grumbled, then scolded Stanley, "Why didn'tcha let 'em sleep? We could've eaten, in peace and quiet!"

"It was dark in that spooky trailer house. No one could hear him crying, way over there. He wants to be where the action is!"

"Babies don't know the difference," Bette said.

Stanley ignored Bette's insensitive remark but raised one eyebrow, giving Margo a questioning glance. "What's this sticky stuff around Toby's mouth, glue from duct tape?" he asked, with a dead-serious expression.

Bette's eyes twitched, caught off-guard. "Ah-h, it might be," she said, seeming to be conniving a convincing response, on the fly. "That little mischief-maker; got hold of that big roll of gray tape today. I had to take it away!"

Stanley glanced around the table, looking for table-napkins, but there were none. He moistened a corner of his shirttail and wiped the stickiness from Toby's cheek. He had a suspicion but kept it to himself. *Something's not right—*

Margo's father wanted to ease the tense atmosphere. "So, Stanley," he said, "how was your drive today?"

"It was good," Stanley replied, seated across from him at the table. After fielding a couple questions about his past life in Arkansas, he glanced at the thick table-legs and the hefty, square top. "Great craftsmanship!" he remarked.

"Handiwork of my father," Hank said, impressed that Stanley had an appreciation for farm-made furniture. "Margo just got back from the floods—ya know."

"Floods?" Stanley repeated, surprised, knowing that the farmyard was nearly dry, except for a few puddles from the melted snow.

"Thoughtcha mighta heard about it on the radio, on your drive up here," Hank said. "The Red River valley; flooded—again this spring!"

He gravely shook his head. "Most rivers, around here, flow south into the Mississippi. Tell me if there's another river, besides this one, that flows north into frozen ground, instead of away from it. The snow melts, the ice jams, the water backs up; and those poor farmers, up there, hafta fight that floodwater ev'ry spring!"

"I mostly listen to recorded music—cassette tapes—on a long drive. It helps make all those miles . . . seem just a little shorter."

"Didn't Margo tell ya . . . 'bout the high water?"

"Daddy! I—I haven't had a chance," Margo said warily, not wanting her boyfriend to know where she had spent the previous week. "Stanley just got here this morning, after driving all night long; then to the ol' swimming hole, and—"

Margo suddenly realized who it was that had worn the red-plaid, flannel shirt. It was her nameless mark at the pool hall; the guy who'd lost his money, then feared for his life. With her hand covering her mouth, she suddenly rushed out of the room, almost certain that Stanley could read her mind.

"Now, what was that about?" Hank asked, watching Margo disappear down the hallway.

"That girl has a heart of gold, Stanley," Bette said, bragging a bit. "And she's not one to boast. When the call went out for volunteers, to hold the river back, she didn't hesitate. She tossed her sleeping bag in the back seat . . . and she was gone!"

"That's a lotta work, throwin' all those sacks fulla sand around," Hank added.

"Oh, Daddy!" Margo said, seeming embarrassed, quickly returning to the table. She nonchalantly wiped the remains of a tear from one eye.

"She learned howda work hard, like that, right here on this farm. And it don't surprise me that she went up there to help. Farmers help farmers; that's all there is to it!" said Hank boastfully, wanting Stanley to be impressed.

"Oh, Daddy! It wasn't glamorous—all that work. It was more like slave labor—almost like child-slave-labor!" she added with a boisterous laugh, repeating the first thought that crossed her mind. "You must remember those days, don't you Daddy—all your little kids—your little farm-worker-slaves, from dawn to dusk?"

Hank didn't seem surprised with Margo's cutting remarks, but didn't react either.

Stanley sensed a remnant of tension in the air, the return of past hard feelings. Resentment. He wished that Margo hadn't spoken so harshly to her father.

"All farm kids have to work hard, don't they?" Stanley asked, holding Toby on his knee. He fed his young son from his own plate.

"Farm kids work; that's just the way it was. Still is, on most farms," said Hank unapologetically.

"You never mentioned it," Stanley said quietly, to Margo, during a lull in the conversation, "Red River—sandbagging. What—sleeping in the car?"

Fearful that Stanley may have gotten the wrong idea, Margo couldn't look up. She stared at her plate. "Sorry. Maria's mother hates me, so she wouldn't let me stay at their place. I never left the worksite; spent half of the week scraping mud out of my car, all because some idiot told me where I had to park. When the sandbags gave-way, the whole parking area got flooded."

"Everyone was grateful for the volunteers," Bette commented. She stood up from the table and went to the window, nervously glancing outside. She paced the floor, repeatedly looking down the driveway, clearly expecting headlights. She disliked it when anyone was late for supper. And someone was guilty.

Chapter 13
Last-Second Mirror

It was peaceful at the table, in a dysfunctional sort of way, as the get-acquainted supper got underway. The men were eating, but the women were holding off. Bette was preoccupied, wondering what was keeping her son, Brian. And Margo was *done* with the sandbagging story, plus she couldn't get the dead kid in the red shirt off her mind.

She stared across the supper table at her mother's flabby neck-skin that seemed to droop much-too-far. To her, it was depressing to see crepey skin which showed no sign of elasticity. It was a sure sign of aging, revealing a predictability and an inevitability, as the ghastly affliction could likely affect her someday, too.

She was soon standing in front of a small wall-mirror that her grandmother had given her when she was a teenager—her *last-second mirror*, since it hung near the back door where it was handy for a quick vanity-check. She alternately pulled at the loose skin of her own neck, then let go of it, checking to see if it would snap back again.

The waiting was over. The rumbling sound of a rusted muffler on an old truck, vibrating the walls, meant that the evening milking was done at Miller's Milking Parlor. "Brian's here—my brother," Margo said to Stanley, then half-whispered, "freaking nuts, but you'll like him."

Betty dashed to the range to get another bowl of mashed potatoes.

Brian Toralf, a tough-looking but scruffy dude, dressed in a black leather jacket and tight blue jeans, suddenly burst through the kitchen door. He tossed his jacket at a hook on the wall but missed. He laughed when it fell to the floor. Almost tossing his hunting cap at the same hook, he changed his mind. He flopped it back on his head, covering up a cyclonic cowlick that had his hair contorted in a permanent, unruly swirl. He came straight to the table.

"You started without me, Mother," he grumbled, seeing that the others were eating already. Wearing a risqué T-shirt, he walked to where Toby was sitting and showed off his biceps.

Little Toby smiled, watching his Uncle Brian's antics with wide-eyed wonder.

Stanley, still holding Toby on his lap, bristled at the obscene graphic that was stretched across Brian's chest, depicting a naked woman on a motorcycle. Stanley was surprised that Margo's brother dressed like a motorcycle fanatic yet wore a camouflage hunting cap to the dinner table. Not only did he seem crude, but he didn't resemble anyone else in their family. In spite of Brian's quirky personal traits, Stanley waited to establish eye contact, wanting to be polite. And he expected an opportunity to introduce himself.

"Happy Birthday, Little Nephew! Yours is the same day as mine!" Brian announced, then tossed a gift-wrapped package onto the table in front of the one-year-old.

When taking his seat, Brian barely acknowledged Stanley's presence with a minute nod of his head. Stanley nodded back, realizing that a subtle introduction had just been made.

"Thank's, Momma—birthday supper—fried chicken and spicy gravy. To die for!" He grinned, his way of complimenting his mother. He immediately flopped a large spoonful of mashed potatoes onto his plate, then looked squarely at his sister's face.

"Watch out, Margo," he said angrily, nearly emptying the chicken platter. He raised a drumstick to his lips. "That pimple-faced cop—the coward who hides behind the Hazel brush—gave me a sixty-dollar ticket, just now, at the speed trap! Who can afford to pay these fines? Someday, I just might shoot that sneaky bastard; that'll show him!"

"Rowdy!" his mother scolded, then scanned the hushed faces of everyone sitting around the table. She seemed satisfied with the level of her motherly dominance.

"I'll make it look like an accident, Mom!" Brian sneered, spewing a devilish laugh.

"Don't talk that way, Rowdy! We have company," Bette retorted but finished calmly, in a sort of nicety that was reserved for the ears of their guest.

Bette, the proud grandmother, surprised everyone by suddenly placing a miniature birthday cake in front of Toby. The flame on the single candle flickered on top of the cupcake.

Margo joyously led with the song, "Happy Birthday".

Brian exchanged anxious glances with his mother.

"There's only one cake, Rowdy," she said.

Brian blew out the candle, since it was his birthday too. And it was also a protest.

P. G. Knudson

Everyone laughed when Little Toby smeared chocolate frosting all over his face. With only one cupcake, there was barely enough icing for a youngster to make a mess.

Chapter 14
The Stalker

When the double-birthday supper was over, Hank went outside and over to the trailer house. He sat down on a lawn chair, on the small deck that his father had built years earlier. He wanted to be as far away as possible from the unnerving sounds coming from the kitchen, sounds of dishes rattling and pots and pans colliding.

Since Brian was still eating, and not especially sociable, Stanley carried Toby outside. He joined Hank on the deck, feeling safer at that distance, too, while the women argued, gossiped, and cleaned the kitchen together.

Stanley sat on a plastic chair across from Hank, bouncing Toby on his knee. Even from that distance, Margo and Bette could be heard spreading stories about somebody. Stanley seemed to know that they were talking about him. He chuckled to himself when he overheard Margo ask her mother, "Does it seem realistic yet, Mom?"

"It's peaceful on the porch, this time of year; too early, in the season, for mosquitoes," Hank said, breaking-the-ice for conversation.

"We're lucky, I guess. When do the mosquitoes start bothering, Mister Toralf?"

"Usually not 'til the leaves come out on the popple trees; not yet anyway."

"Nice, warm weather—" Stanley said, trying to keep the dull conversation going.

"Yeah—not bad, for a winter day, but I'll tell ya what: these early springs always make me nervous. We missed all of that rain that fell, west of here. Damn lucky, or it would've flooded here, too."

Hank suddenly gave the hush sound. Leaning forward in his chair and looking through the blackness, toward the mailbox, he said, "Stanley, take a gander at that car, sittin' out there, lights off and prob'ly up to no good. My eyesight's not what it usta be."

Stanley peered in that direction and spotted the stationary glow of parking lights. He was suspicious of the mysterious car, too, since he remembered what Margo had said about a stalker.

"I wonder if it's the same one that's been by here a dozen times today. We don't see that much traffic, out here; not in a week," Hank said, an air of suspicion in his voice.

Stanley handed Toby to him. Without speaking, he quickly stepped off the porch, crouched down, and moved stealthily along the back side of the house. He disappeared around the corner.

Moments later, Hank saw the car suddenly speed away. When Stanley returned to the porch, Hank asked, "Didja see who it was?"

Stanley didn't want to say, but he had seen enough to conclude that it was a deputy. Not wanting anyone to worry, he shook his head *no*. "Whoever it was, saw me and took off!"

"Hm-m! I think it's a cop!" Hank said, stroking his chin. "It can't be about Rowdy's speedin' ticket. I wonder what's goin' on."

Stanley silently worried for Margo's safety. Without revealing her fear of a certain stalker, he took Toby from Hank's lap and held him close. He stood on the deck, looking past the barn at the passing lights on the highway. The constant hum of the traffic seemed normal.

"Game time, Henry!" came Bette's voice, from the house, wanting to liven up the party.

A simple game of checkers, between Margo and her brother, ended abruptly in a spat. Brian won and immediately demanded his twenty-five-cent payoff. After a family game of cards, around the kitchen table where Brian won again, everyone went to the living room. They sat in-line on a sagging, old sofa to watch a 1946 Ava Gardner mystery on the UHF band. The twelve-inch screen on the compact black-and-white television set seemed a bit small.

Margo complained about the snowy picture, so Stanley tried to adjust the UHF antenna. Hank solved the reception problem by wrapping a crumpled piece of aluminum foil around the loop. It didn't help, very much. Ten minutes into the movie, the screen went white and the sound became all-static.

Brian got bored and left early. Hank and Bette both dozed-off during the *ten o'clock news*, finally getting up and going to bed about ten-thirty. Margo and Stanley stretched out on the sofa, both noting that the local media had mentioned nothing about the discovery of a corpse.

"Just one more day, before I have to go back," Stanley whispered in Margo's ear.

"I'm going to miss you, really a lot," she said sleepily, hugging his neck. "Will you be back next weekend?"

"If I can get off."

"Get a job, around here," she said. "I miss sleeping with you."

"I already checked: no vacancies in this county. And I've mailed my résumé to every sheriff's office . . . all around."

"They could use your expertise, here, Honey; they haven't arrested anybody. I hate it, that it's an unsolved murder," she half-whispered. "I know that some insane freak is out there; probably going to do it again . . . to some unsuspecting girl. I need you, Stanley! Don't go back to your pitiful job, down there. Our future will be up here—"

Stanley noticed that she had dozed off. He lovingly covered her with a blanket, kissed her on the forehead, and went upstairs. He slept on the hardwood floor, next to Toby's crib.

Chapter 15
Vivid Dreams
March 28, 1993

Stanley saw morning frost when he looked out Toby's window. He re-tucked Toby's blanket and propped up a friendly-looking dinosaur so he'd see it when he woke up. Downstairs, the couch was empty, except for a pillow and a blanket swirled into a heap.

"Where's Margo?" he asked Hank who sat at the kitchen table, sipping coffee from his retired fart cup, looking as lonesome as a lost calf.

"Prob'ly in the barn; should be back soon, though, since I don't got no animals out there, anymore, for her to talk to," he said gloomily, clearly missing his farm animals.

The morning air was snappy-cold, Stanley seeing steam from his own breath escaping to the sky as he walked. *Swimming weather yesterday. What a difference a day makes!*

In the barn, he heard creaking footsteps above his head. *It's Margo, up in the hayloft.* He found the only way up, a crude plank-ladder nailed to studs and extending through the hay-chute. He quietly climbed the ladder, thinking he'd scare Margo with a *BOO*, at the top; but when he got there, he saw a teetering pile of hay-bales tumbling to the floor, with Margo holding on to the double-knot of a hay-fork rope that swung from high in the peak of the rafters.

By the time he ran to where the bales had fallen, the rope-swing was on the rebound with Margo still holding on. She sailed past him on the giant swing, her eyes closed and a satisfied smile on her face.

You are a nut, he thought affectionately, seeing the smile that he loved. He stood, thumbs in his pockets, proudly watching her swing until the momentum slowed to a stop.

She opened her eyes, as if gently wakening from a deep sleep, and said brightly, "Stanley, you're up! Isn't it a little early, for you?"

"Margo, what are you doing up here?"

"I'm concentrating, of course, exercising my brain."

"I thought you'd still be asleep. You need to catch up."

"No, I don't! And Mom's crummy davenport wasn't made for sleeping!" she blurted out with a laugh. "Too much sleep gives me *crazy* dreams, so horrid that they wake me up anyway! I can't take another *manic dream*!"

"What—*manic*? What kind of dream is that?"

"Good God, Stanley!" she vented, stopping the rope and eyeing him crossly. She could change moods at the drop-of-a-hat. "Maybe I shouldn't have used *that* word. I just hate those . . . *vivid dreams*; they're scary. I always get them. That's why I wake up so early."

"I just wondered where you were; you disappeared!"

"Well, Stanley, this is the way it is on a farm: you get up in the morning and go outside, before the chickens wake up," she said condescendingly. "No one disappears. It's a big place. If I was out on the back forty, half-a-mile from the house, I'd still be on the farm; get it?"

Frustrated, she snaked the rope, then began twisting it into a spiral, her stern jaw fortifying each successive twist. The tension on the rope was tightening, augmenting the statement she was making.

Stanley got the point: *she's angry about our farm-buying disagreement.*

Her body slowly twirled with the unwinding of the rope. "Before daylight, something inside me told me to get up and go outside. So, I did. Have you ever heard a voice like that?"

"You're hearing voices?"

A quick stomp of her foot stopped the rotation, telegraphing her exasperation. She hugged the rope and stared out the hayloft door, speaking in barely a whisper, "Just Maria's voice, calling for help. I couldn't help, of course, because she's dead. I saw her over and over again; the trail ride; the horse bucking; the dead boy; and some cowardly murderer chopping her in the back with a hatchet!"

It was hard to watch Margo cry. Stanley comforted her anguish, snuggling her in his arms, wondering how long she could endure her prolonged grieving. "It's not your fault. You've got to stop torturing yourself."

"What torture? I went outside and enjoyed the sunrise, then ended up right here, in the haymow. And I saw my dream—Maria's dream, too; it's still alive! It was all to happen *here*," she said ominously, a far-away look in her eye. "I still see it. The whole thing."

Stanley was confused. Margo's vacillating thoughts and her smile, mixed with tears, were hard to follow. "What is it that you see now, Margo? Are you still having a bad dream?"

"Do you mean . . . right now? No!" she laughed. "I'm talking about *my dream*, my future ranch, the dream I've had since I was a kid. It'll be right here, on Dad's dirt-poor farm. We'll have to fix it up, of course, change it around so it works for horses."

She's back to selling me her 'buy-the-farm' argument. "Margo, this old farm is dilapidated. We talked about this yesterday!"

"We're not done talking! Sure, the buildings are an eyesore, but the land—priceless!"

"I can understand that your folks might allow us stay here, but I don't think your dad wants us to change anything or give him extra work to do. He's retired, Margo. His farming days are over."

"I know that!" she huffed, almost like a horse snorting through its nostrils. "That's why it's time for me to take over; we'll buy the farm." She let go of the twisted rope. It spun alone, as she walked over to the open hayloft door. "You don't care about my dreams, do you, Stanley?"

"Don't get mad. I just don't think your parents want the changes. They like it the way it is. It's your father's farm, after all!"

"Being a city-kid, you've probably never run into this before: on a family farm, the old folks turn it over to the younger generation—the expected way of things." She stood on the threshold, her toes extending past the drop-off point, gazing across the farmyard and beyond. "I wish you could see it, Stanley—the potential! When I look out, across this old farm, I see beautiful white fences and horses running across the south pasture."

"There's nothing out there, Margo, just a hay field. That's all it was, even when you were little."

"We can change that—you, me, and Toby; make it into a ranch! When I'm up here, in the top of the barn, it's like being on top of the world. I can see it, as plain as day!"

Stanley understood Margo's lifetime dream, but very little of it passed his logic test. It was all really up to her father.

"Does he want to sell you the farm? Probably not, but if he did, how would that go over with your brother, Brian? He probably expects to get the farm, someday—not you."

Margo's eyes welled up, knowing that Stanley had read Brian correctly.

Stanley held her close while she sobbed. "When I get a deputy job up here, I promise you, I'll find the low-life animal that killed Maria!"

Chapter 16
Duck Pond

After breakfast, Margo and Stanley took a walk across the farm acreage, part of Margo's plan to sell the ranch-idea to him. It was not enough that he loved her; she wanted him to love the farm, too, as much as she did. Could she change a city-slicker into a rancher?

The crusty, white frost clung to the dead grasses and crunched under their feet but quickly melted with the warming rays of sunshine. She picked a Pussy Willow stem from the brushy edge of the field and stroked the soft blooms across her cheek. It was ironic that the same narrow willow stem that stung-so, when she was a disobedient child, now comforted her with its fuzzy catkins.

"I love it here in the spring," she said. "Do you hear that sound? Listen closely, Stanley."

"It sounds like frogs, croaking in the waterholes," he said, "just like down South."

"Hey, you understand the land, Stanley. You'll like it here. Just imagine—living on the land; a farm life for Toby," she said, deliberately working on Stanley's sensitivities. She pointed across the southernmost field. "I can see Toby riding his horse, in slow motion, inside my brain without closing my eyes, just like watching a movie. It's a beautiful thing. You can see it, too, can't you, Honey?"

Stanley didn't answer but kept strolling by her side. They circled around that field, cut across the dry corn-stubble on the east field, parted tall weeds on the fringes of a small wetland, and hiked the woods road through a back woodlot. Under the tall Ash trees, she suddenly took Stanley's arm and pulled him in close, a feverous look in her eyes and a quickening breath.

Something is different. Overcome with her beauty and her passion, Stanley kissed her lips, not able to resist, realizing that Margo was hot-to-trot and there would be no waiting.

Their roll-in-the-leaves was intense. Quick.

After that stroll in the woods, Stanley had more insight into what life would be like, if he were to live on the farm with Margo. It also gave Margo a chance to question him about money, something that was always prominent in her mind.

"Have you talked to your realtor, lately?"

"I haven't heard anything about the house. I think it's too remote."

"Darn! I knew your Arkansas house wouldn't sell! What about the refund of your Little Rock Retirement Fund?"

"My contributions? I checked on it, like you said to. If I pull it out, I'd essentially lose my retirement for the future. If I leave it in-place, I'd eventually get a reduced retirement."

"Yeah, when you're *old*. Honey, what good is a *reduced* retirement? We need that money now. You can start a new retirement fund when you get a new job—up here."

"I know; that's what you want. That's why I told them to pull it out. I signed the papers and mailed them, a month ago. When they wire it, lump-sum, you'll see it on your account balance before I even hear about it."

While in the woods, Stanley asked about an odd-looking tree. "It still has most of last year's leaves; they're all dead and dried but still hanging on!"

"That's a Bur Oak tree, known for its *persistent leaves*."

"It's the first one I've noticed. It's almost time for new leaves to emerge, but the dead, dried-up leaves are . . . persistent."

"You've got it! You understand this stuff," Margo giggled, walking hand-in-hand through the woodlot and out the other side. Before completing a large circle, encompassing most of the farm acreage, they stopped at the muddy edge of a secluded pond in the east pasture. A mating pair of Mallard Ducks suddenly rose from the surface of the water and flew away.

Stanley was startled with the sudden, buffeting sound of the pair's beating wings and the speed at which their flight began.

"You didn't tell me; there's a new pond back here; a nice water hole, but it's a mess—piles of dirt, never leveled off. The job site looks incomplete."

"You're right; it never got finished. The dumb guy got mad and pulled his equipment out, before it was done. I know it looks bad, but we can get a dozer in here and finish spreading it out. We can plant seeds and have a nice grassy patch back here," she said optimistically. "It will be a great swimming hole—our own private, skinny-dipping place, just for you and me!"

"Who dug this pond, and what could have made him mad enough to leave?"

Margo shifted her eyes, looking for a way out of this story. "Oh— a guy—*Ernie*. He has his own construction company; and he dug it for me—for Dad, I mean," she said, trying to ease the impact of the truth.

"Your last boyfriend," Stanley surmised. "I'll bet that you got mad at him and kicked him out, before he finished it."

Margo saw the slight grin on Stanley's face. "You jerk—you had that figured out! Yeah—that Ernie Niceski—he can be pretty stubborn, sometimes! You'll meet him someday," she said coolly and giggled. "You two would get along; he's a cornball, actually. By the way, did you ask Daddy yet?" Surely this diversion would stop the questions about Ernie.

"You just asked me this yesterday! No, I haven't. There's no hurry, apparently, until you say the word, Honey; it's up to you—ya know."

"We're not ready yet," she said bluntly.

"Toby's a year old already. When will you be ready, Margo?"

She turned her eyes away, seeming annoyed. "Soon."

"Whenever *soon* gets here, I'll ask your dad. Are those ducks nesting here?"

"It's too early to know. When spring-mating is over, the ducks will choose a place to nest. I hope it will be here."

"I'd like that—a pond for wild ducks. That's *if* we do the ranch-thing."

"The *duck pond* was a good idea, and it didn't cost me a dime!" she said with a laugh.

"Are you admitting that you took advantage of him—Ernie, or whatever his name is?"

"I didn't ask him to do it. He *wanted* to dig the pond, and I let him. I owe him nothing!"

"Why did you break up with that guy?"

"Old history, Stanley. He wasted two years of my time; two years of my life!"

"If that's the case, didn't you waste two years of his life too?"

Margo instantly got heated but bit her lip, determined to never mention Ernie Niceski again. Mentioning him to Stanley was an unintended error, one that went against her desire to bury all of her past life. He was one complication that she wished would go away. She knew that her past was only one memory away, though. A slip of the tongue could undo everything.

Chapter 17

The Rope Incident

Stanley and Margo strolled back to the barn without talking, walking through patches of tall, dead weeds that tore at Stanley's legs. He picked pokey seeds from his pant-legs, then followed Margo who didn't seem to have any problem avoiding the weeds and briars.

Stanley was troubled, having noticed the callous attitude she had shown, concerning her old boyfriend's contribution to her farm project. He realized that Margo had probably relayed her ranch-dream to Ernie Niceski, at one time or another, but it seemed unfair that the love of Ernie had been discarded under piles of dirt by the unfinished pond. He saw it as a warning signal that seemed to parallel his own romance with her.

"We need to make a corral, here," she said, pointing to the exact spot where she wanted the first post to be dug in. "All wood posts; no steel posts or barbed wire for horses. They hurt themselves easily. White fences are my favorite, and the barn should be Norwegian Red."

She entered the barn through the back door, the same door where generations of the Toralf's dairy cows had entered in the past.

"The gutters have to go; they're for cows. A horse could break a leg in those deep trenches. I've always hated them. You know how to fill them in with concrete, don't you?"

"Ah-h—yeah; it's possible, I guess," he said tentatively, not seeming to like the idea of accumulating a difficult to-do list.

"And the stanchions—they have to go. If you tie a horse in a cow-stanchion, it'll kill itself trying to escape. They need comfort, where they can move around, freely, without getting caught between-a-rock-and-a-hard-place."

"I didn't know you knew so much about horses . . . and cows," he said, listening as she unveiled more of her horse ranch plans.

"Well, I am a farm girl, but I'm not a carpenter. That's where you come in!" she said teasingly, then laughed. "It can't be hard to tear out all these mangers and make box stalls, is it? Can *you* do it?"

"Ah-h, I don't know—"

"You can surely swing a hammer; make 'em like that box stall in the corner, the one Grandpa made for me when I was a kid," she said, pointing at the cubical made from flat boards. "Yikes—that stall is broken to pieces! Dad must've had calves in there; they wrecked it! Oh, well, you can fix that too!"

Margo had an unexplained attraction to the upstairs of the barn—the hayloft. Soon, the two of them were up there, once again, standing by the suspended rope. Holding on to the knot, she let her eyes travel up, all the way to its anchor-point on the hayfork that was fastened to a steel track in the peak of the roof.

Stanley stood, mystified. *It looks exactly like the one at the swimming hole.*

"All us kids played up here, climbing, jumping—whatever. I could always swing it the farthest. I left my tennie shoe track by that rafter, once," she bragged, pointing to the peak of the roof, near the back end of the barn, "by that bee-nest."

Stanley followed her in that direction, then positioned himself directly under the gray paper-like hornet nest, looked straight up, and saw her historic footprint.

"You must've been a tomboy."

He looked for a response, but she had walked away, grabbed on to the dangling rope, and was standing in the middle of the empty loft, once more. He returned to her side, listening for more of her story, watching her fingers slide over the smooth fibers of the old memory-maker.

"I've never seen the haymow this empty," she said, melancholy heavy in her tone. "The hay was always halfway to the ceiling—all the time; food for the cows . . . and my horse. It gave this place life. Now, it's sad to see, the old hay is moldy, in no condition for fodder; no animals to eat it anyway. An idle farm is a sad sight—like death."

Stanley was having a hard time relating to Margo's childhood experiences on her father's farm, but he was trying to understand. He reached out and wrapped his fingers around the rope.

"Take a close look, Stanley—my favorite rope."

"What about it? It looks worn-out, to me. Aren't you afraid it'll break?"

"Ah-h," Margo started to giggle, "I remember when this rope was brand-new, absolutely the best thing on this farm! I played up here, for hours—by myself."

Suddenly, a change melted across her face, flattening her smile. Her voice quavered, then seemed to choke off. Her eyes froze, fixated on the woven fibers.

Something's wrong. She's fading away on me! He tried to push the dangling rope out of the way, as if to attempt a rescue, but Margo tightened her grip. He reached for her resisting arm, but his effort was met with a push. Then, all motion stopped. She stood stiffly, not responding to Stanley's touch. Not a sound. Strangely still.

"Margo-o-o!" Trembling, Stanley searched her eyes for a sparkle. It had disappeared in an instant. A deep fear gripped him; too scared to call out her name again.

He held her in a bear hug, tight around her rigid limbs. Motionless. Her face was warm but her hands, cold. He felt the stiffness gradually subside, back to flexible arms. Her eyes rolled, then stared at his face. A straight lip almost formed a smirk, like she relished the fearful chill that she sent through his body.

She almost laughed, her eyes growing large when Stanley flinched at her eerie whisper, done in a far-away-sounding voice, "It feels so good to swing from this rope—"

"What's happening, Margo?" he asked, letting go, retreating from her bizarre behavior.

She touched the rope to her lips, then caressed its smoothness against her throat. "Do you ever wonder what it would be like to tie this rope around your neck?" she whispered.

"What?" *What did she just ask me? What is this, a trance?* Shocked, Stanley had no idea of what was going on, and his legs began to shake. He took a half step backwards and shielded his face with one hand, as if avoiding danger.

"Do you ever think about swinging from a rope . . . around your neck?" she asked, staring into his eyes.

"No!" He took another step backwards. "Why aren't you talking in your normal voice?"

"Sure, you do," she argued eerily. "Everybody thinks about it— what it might be like to have the rope around your neck and . . . let it go-o-o." Her whisper was barely audible.

"Not me!" Stanley said, his voice shaking. "Come back, Margo. Come back to normal!"

"Everyone has these thoughts," she insisted, now being argumentative.

"No, they don't! I don't!" he said. "Snap out of it, Margo! You're scaring the hell out of me!" He grabbed her by the hand and swiftly escorted her down the hay chute, and all the way outside. He stopped to confront her, in the bright sunlight, just below the open door of the hayloft. He looked straight into her now-normal-looking eyes.

"What are you doing, Margo?"

"Whatever are you talking about, Stanley?" she asked in a burst of laughter, sounding perfectly normal and as boisterous as ever.

"I'm talking about *the rope incident*; the one we just went through. It sounded like you were talking about suicide. Tell me what's wrong!"

"I never said any such thing!"

"What was all that about, wanting a rope around your neck?"

"What?" Margo laughed scoffingly. "You have a big imagination!"

"But—"

"You're weird! I'm going in; you stay out here!" she said fitfully and bolted away.

Confused, Stanley watched Margo skip all the way across the yard, like an eight-year-old girl would do, until she slammed the screen door on the back porch.

Chapter 18
Advice Is Cheap

Hearing the slamming of the door, Stanley also heard a gunshot, the sound of a small round nearby. He instinctively crouched low, assuming a defensive position as he had been trained, although he hadn't determined where the percussion had come from.

Moments later, Hank Toralf emerged from behind an adjacent outbuilding, holding a short shovel in one hand and a .22 caliber rifle in the other. When he saw Stanley, he slowly approached, his understanding eyes prepared to reassure his puzzled-looking, future son-in-law.

Stanley looked to Hank apprehensively. "Did you hear that?"

"It was just one shot: this varmint gun, behind the chicken coop. Damn skunk. I shoot 'em and bury 'em, right where they fall."

"That's not what I was asking about," Stanley said, his thumb motioning toward the house.

"Oh—you and Margo? Ya got snookered into a game?" Hank chuckled. Stanley wasn't aware, but Hank had observed the odd confrontation just a few minutes beforehand.

A game—a mind game? Games are supposed to be fun; this was not fun!

"Well, stuff like that can happen sometimes," he said. "You'll just hafta get used to it. Learn to adjust. Shuck it off, like I do with her mother, and life will be a lot-more peaceful," he said, still chuckling lightly. "You must be going back soon, huh?"

That's it? The bizarre behavior is just . . . nothing? And I'm expected to adjust to it? It seemed awkward to confide in Margo's father, but Stanley was beginning to like him. He told Hank about his impending drive, the make-up shift, the graveyard shift—the whole 9 yards.

"Burning the candle at both ends, huh? Ah, you're young; you'll make it," Hank said.

"The drive back and forth is too much, though. I'm trying to find a job, up here."

"Margo mentioned it. Not much luck, though, huh?"

"I've sent out my résumé; no takers, so far."

"If ya wanna get *in* at the local Sheriff's Department, the best way is to get elected. The sheriff is gonna retire soon—ya know. That job'll be on the ballot, next time around, and there won't be *any* competition."

"Really?"

"Yup; time for Homer Anders—that ol' goat—to be put out to pasture!"

"I just saw Sheriff Anders, and he sounded like he's campaigning for another term."

"Well, keep your ears open. He's gettin' so old, no wonder he don't know what's goin' on! You could pro'bly get elected, if ya run for that office. They need somebody new, around here. That old

Homer—he'll pro'bly never live long enough to finish his existing term."

"Thanks for the tip, Hank. I'll remember that, in case nothing else comes up," Stanley said, not necessarily looking for a political position.

"Ya know, Stanley, *advice is cheap*. Ya either take it, or ya leave it!"

"Yeah?"

"The sheriff is the most powerful man in the county, didja know?"

"Well—"

"Being an elected official, he's got a lotta leeway. He can overlook any law or circumstance—push it, or ignore it. Ya know what I mean?"

Stanley doubtfully stared into Hank's aging eyes but saw a fatherly-like concern that seemed genuine. He listened with a certain ambivalence, but preferred discounting most of it.

"Some laws don't make sense—ya know—so he can make a judgment—"

"Are you saying that the sheriff can pick and choose which laws he wants to enforce?"

Hank laughed heartily. "Now, Young Man, I didn't use those words! To phrase it right, I'd need a silver tongue, like our new President, Bill Clinton. Now, there's a politician who can parse his words. No matter what he says, it's always convincing!" Hank detected the doubt in Stanley's eyes. "The sheriff position—not a bad job, if ya can get it! He decides who will go to jail . . . and who won't! If people don't like what he does, all they can do is vote him out! So, if ya win, Justus County is all yours! And if ya screw-up, your only penalty is losing the next election!"

Stanley absorbed the fatherly advice and listened for another well-intended word of wisdom, but Hank seemed to be done.

"Take it with a grain-a-salt, if ya want. But if yer interested, check it out. If ya miss yer chance, you'll hafta wait another four years."

"Seems like I've got a couple of years, before I have to decide anything."

"Oh, no! Politicking: that starts now! Press the flesh; don't underestimate the need for it. Folks hafta know who ya are, recognize your name, and all that kinda political boo-hoo." He stroked his chin, pondering the unlikely prospect that his future son-in-law would follow his advice, as Stanley began to walk away.

"Hey—I saw you and Margo walking across the fields. How didja like the farm?"

"Okay, I guess. I've never worked on a farm—ya know."

"That'll change, in a hurry, if you kids buy this place," Hank said doubtfully, trying not to show that he was staring at Stanley's smooth fingers that revealed no calluses—no sign of ever doing laborious work. "Did Margo mention it?"

"Yeah, she said something—*maybe* buying it. You don't want to sell it though, do you?"

Hank laughed. "Oh, I don't know—maybe—maybe not," he said, feeling that Stanley was not tough enough to be a farmer. "Bette and I —well, we'd hafta talk about it. I still wanna raise some pigs; maybe a few more chickens—"

"Hobby farming—that'll keep you busy."

Hank chuckled, sensing that Stanley was not actually interested in the farm. "Guess you could call it that."

Stanley caught his drift and breathed a sigh of relief. Then, feeling more at ease, he asked, "What were you doing behind the little shed, besides killing skunks?"

"That's not a shed; it's the pig barn! I was just fixin' a few broken boards and tacking-down the old fence-wires. The last pigs we had broke it up pretty good. They're hard on the facilities—ya know. They throw their whole weight against a fence. It hasta be strong! They'll dig right under it, if they find a soft spot in the dirt. I'll get it fixed up, pretty soon. If Bette agrees, we'll be gettin' some little piggies—starter-pigs, that is—just a few. I don't want very many. I'm retired; in case ya haven't noticed."

"Ah, that's what you say; but you can't give it up, can you?" Stanley asked, hoping the farm-ownership issue would settle itself.

"I think you've got that figured right," Hank said and laughed in his jovial way, a mannerism that Stanley liked about him. "It's the kinda thing that sorta grows on a man. I like this ol' place, now, more than I did when I was farmin' it! I don't want cows, though—too much work. I'd like to . . . just putter around."

Chapter 19
Farmer's Logic

The aroma of bitter coffee filled the kitchen at the trailer house. Margo briefly curtailed the arm-twisting that she had been subjecting her mother to, when her father came inside.

"I'll have a double!" Hank joked, then took his seat at the table.

Bette handed him a hot cupful, then glared at him, frustrated that the memory of his drunken days still haunted their entire family. And knowing that former alcoholics always seem to joke about drinking, only deepened old sores.

"What's up?" he asked, giving up a restful sigh.

"Same thing, again, about selling her the farm," Bette complained. "Stanley's taking a nap, so here she is: pestering me."

"It's already spring. I want to get horses, but I need the place in my own name, first," Margo asserted, using *farmer's logic*, something her parents would surely understand. "Like Grandpa used to say, 'Time's a-wasting'!"

"Do you know what your crazy nephew, Butch, wants his mother to do?" Bette suddenly blurted out, changing the subject. She traded glances with Hank's eyes, expecting a coordinated response, not wanting to be coerced into any sort of farm-give-away.

Hank picked up on the subliminal message, "Don't make me guess; nothing surprises me, with that kid!"

"Well, he's pretty upset about the Whitewater Scandal in Washington, D.C.," Bette said. "He expects his mother to buy him a bus ticket, so he can travel all the way across the country to protest in Washington—to the *actual* White House! Who can afford to waste money on such foolishness?"

"Mom!" Margo said angrily, recognizing her attempt to side-step the issue. "Enough about my stupid cousin, Butch! Who cares what Gerald-The-Idiot wants to do?"

"Oh—back to the farm-deal?" Hank remarked, realizing that Bette's ploy hadn't worked. He rolled his thumbs. "Ya know, Margo— I was gonna raise a piggy or two . . . and who knows what-else. There's no hurry to sell—"

"No, not for you; but what about me? I'm ready to start! Don't think, for a minute, Dad, that I'd stop you from having a few pigs, chickens, or whatever. When I'm the owner, you can dabble with anything you want. And rest assured, I'll keep the farm in the family. You know what Rowdy would do, if it was his; he'd sell it . . . and it'd be gone! You'd be forced into an apartment, in the city. He'd squander everything and end up living with you, in *your* apartment. Get the picture?"

"I just remembered, about Butch," Hank said, still searching for a way out of this discussion, "and his interest in politics. He was the first one, around here, who predicted that Bill Clinton would win the election. Now, ain't that amazing?"

"Margo, I think we need some time to think about this—me and Dad—alone," Bette said, irritated that she was being pressured to sell-out.

"Both of you are avoiding the inevitable. All I need is an answer, and you go off on a tangent!" Margo huffed. "Can I get a decision from you two? I've already been to the bank; they're ready to move on it, if you guys are. Just don't say anything to Stanley—not yet," she whispered. "He'll be gone, by morning; then we can go ahead on it."

"Why is it a secret, from Stanley?" her mother wanted to know.

"I can't tell you, right now, Mom. Stanley might hear us talking."

Bette diverted from the subject, again, "Do you know what your sister Francine did? She made Irvine sleep in the dump truck, all last week."

Margo laughed. "Good for her!"

"No; it's *not* good! Married people belong in the same bed. You know what happens to people who can't keep that straight! The last time this happened, Irvine almost left her. Francine promised that she'd never do that again. I've told her, she has to take her crazy-pills. I don't know why that's so hard for her to understand. What's a mother supposed to do?"

"Mom! She's thirty-three years old. She can do whatever she wants to. Did she say why she doesn't take her medicine?"

"She misses *the highs* too much."

"That's the same thing she told me. She's actually depressed all the time, if you ask me—pills or no pills. She's horrible to get along with. No wonder we fought all the time, when we were kids. Sh-h— he's coming in. Family only—remember?"

Chapter 20
Edge Of The Earth
March 29, 1993

S tanley awoke to the first daylight that permeated the lace curtains in Margo's room. "Monday, and I can't be late!" he said, thinking that he was talking to Margo and that she'd roll toward him with sleepy eyes. The other side of the bed was empty. He jumped to his feet and got dressed immediately, shivering in the cold room.

Frustrated that he wanted to say *good-bye*, but Margo was nowhere in sight, he skipped breakfast, quickly gathered his things, and carried them to the car.

"Margo, where are you?" he called out.

She suddenly came into view, standing in the always-open doorway of the hayloft.

"What do you want?" she yelled back.

"Time for me to go! What are you doing in the barn?" He saw Margo teetering on her toes, toying with danger, standing on the threshold of the drop-off. *Don't jump!* he thought.

Margo gave a frustrated huff, slid through the hay chute and came out the door. Wanting to rescue her, Stanley ran all the way across the yard.

"What's the panic about?" she asked. "I wasn't really going to jump. I just wondered what it would be like—"

93

Stanley was nearly out of breath. "Don't you have to go to work, too? Your new job starts today." He was feeling the pressure of his impending drive; plus now, the scare of Margo possibly injuring herself.

"I have lots of time, but you don't. You'd better get going, Cowboy," she said and kissed him lightly on the lips.

"What were you doing up there?"

"Well, I wasn't contemplating suicide," she said sarcastically. "I was imagining what the farm would look like, if all the buildings were painted red. I do my best thinking in the haymow. The time is right. Daddy's ready, I think . . ."

"Not the farm-deal; no time now. We can talk about this . . . on the phone. If I don't leave now, I'll be late."

"And if you get caught speeding, you'll get a ticket and then you'll get fired. Then you can move up here . . . to be with me on the farm," she laughed.

"Why don't you just come back with me? You liked it there."

"That trailer park . . . in the city? I think not! I have a job here, and I'm not moving—not again! Give me a good-bye kiss, Stanley," she begged mischievously.

Stanley didn't have to be asked twice; he loved that woman, in spite of her faults. He gave her a big smacker, right on the lips, and didn't care who might be watching.

"We were just getting our new life set up, and my new job, when you decided to come up here—up north, to the . . . *edge of the earth*."

"Oh—woe-is-me—cut it out, Stanley! Are you going to hit me over the head with that sorry song, every week, for the rest of my life?"

Stanley grinned, gave Margo a peck on the cheek, then got in his car and started the engine. "Get a portable telephone, this week," he said. "They're making them smaller now, so you don't have to lug a bulky one around; one like my trusty, ol' brick."

"It's more-like a cheese box with an antenna. It makes you look like a Martian!"

"Get a handy, small one that hooks onto your belt. I don't like having to leave messages on your mother's answering machine."

"No! I hate the idea of being saddled to a phone! You know about radiation, don't you—birth defects and deformities? What do you think the rest of our kids will look like, if I start carrying around all that toxic radiation on my belt, next to my ovaries?"

"They're safe; there's nothing wrong with a portable phone! Without one, I can never reach you; you're always unavailable—out in the barn . . . or somewhere."

"The purpose for being on the farm is to get away from distractions. I don't want to be joined at the hip, to a telephone. I stay away from them, on purpose! Why would I want to carry one around with me all day long—for the inconvenience and constant interruptions?"

Margo stood in one spot and watched Stanley's red coupe drive all the way to the end of the driveway and turn toward the highway. She loved that car—pure envy. She calmly touched her fingers to her lips, imagining how good it would look if there were a big western-style sign hanging over the end of her driveway.

"Margo's Ranch," she said aloud and liked the sound of it. "A perfect idea!"

Chapter 21
A Pushover

Margo stood at her last-second mirror, spraying curls with an aerosol can, while Hank kept his distance from the choking overspray.

"Daddy, I'm starting my job today; can you believe it?"

"Today? Guess that slipped my mind."

"Did you and Mom come to a decision? Idle land will go-to-pot—you know."

"We talked, but there's still Rowdy to consider; and Billy, of course."

"Billy's locked up in Stillwater, Daddy. He'll never want the farm. There's no one to steal from, around here."

Hank's incensed eyes riveted her, and his voice shook with anger. "I don't like it, when you refer to Billy that way!" It was unusual for Hank to lash out at anyone, concerning his delinquent son. He normally blamed himself, that Billy was in prison.

Margo knew her dad well enough to know that she had just stretched her luck. Fearful of his volatility, she spun around and rushed out the door. He angrily followed.

"I'm sorry, Daddy. I didn't mean it," she pleaded, wanting him to calm down, "but he has a problem—you know. He's a sociopath. When he sees a sucker, he can't help it; he rips 'em off. How long was he out of jail last time, two weeks? He found another victim—*wham*—back in the slammer!"

Hank was still a bit angry but understood the point she was making. "He might be in jail, but he never hurt anybody; there's no blood on his hands."

"Just not too smart, when it comes to making trouble. He'd lose the farm—for sure; all your hard work, down the drain, Daddy!"

Hank shook his head. "Yeah; you're right, I s'pose. That kid . . . and all the whiskey I drank, because of him!" He admitted the inevitable, "He wouldn't work out very well, as an owner. That's what your mother thinks, too."

"Exactly, Daddy! And Francine is married and gone; not interested. Bruce is in California, doing better than any of us. And, as for Rowdy—the jobless drifter and part-time farm hand—how could he afford it? He'd end up in the toilet—damned certain—as he's practically out of work right now! I'm the only one with a good job, Daddy, so you can get paid! And you want the farm to stay in the family, don't you—not lost to some stranger in a poker game?" She sensed that she had brought him to the point of persuasion.

"Your grandpa would be proud, if he only knew. That's who gave you the idea, years ago—pro'bly—keepin' it in the family, that is."

"Grandpa always talked about the old ways from the old days."

"Yup; that's the way they did it, way-back-when—the Scandinavian way—old folks settin' it up for the next generation. It was always the eldest son, though, that got the farm, or all the sons; own it together."

The *son-only* idea was an ancient tradition that angered Margo, but she tried not to let it show. Now was not the time to play the female-victim card. She watched her father's eyes, as he slowly deliberated, even glancing at the closed door of the trailer house, a clear sign that he wanted to talk to her mother. Margo almost pushed harder but instinctively held back.

"Your mother and me still want to be able to live on the farm; come and go, as we like. With her arthritis, and if that *global warming* doesn't come mighty-soon—warm things up so we can tolerate the winters—she wants to spend the cold months somewhere where it's warm. Maybe Texas or New Mexico where the livin's cheap. We'd come back, for the summer, stay until Christmas, and go South again —every year. We'd get the trailer; the house for you."

That sounded like a deal, but it came too easily. She had him pegged as *a pushover*, allowing her to stake her claim to the farm ahead of any other sibling, but it wasn't enough. She wasn't necessarily greedy, just wanted to sweeten the deal with a negotiated add-on.

"Can we dispense with the trailer, Daddy? It blocks my view of the woods. If I look out the window, what do I see? Certainly not a deer; just the damn-ugly trailer house!"

Hank's body language went into revolt. "You want it *gone*—a one-sided deal? Where would your mom and me live, if we got rid of it? It's all the security we'd have—the trailer; it hasta stay. We get to stay, free. You pay all the taxes . . . and everything! You've got a good job, after all. We'll sell it to ya cheap enough, but all of that detail hasta be part of the deal, or no deal!"

"What are you saying, Daddy, that I can buy the farm?"

"Well, I guess, I am. But what about Stanley? I'd like to hear what he has to say. If you two were married, I'd put both your names on the deed, thinkin' of his benefit. A married man ought to have equal ownership."

"No, Daddy, just my name," she insisted.

"Why?" Hank was confused.

"What if we get divorced . . . later—you know?"

"You're not planning to get divorced, are ya? You're not even married yet! Look at what your mother and I went through. We stayed married, through all the problems—through-thick-and-thin. Now, after some rough years, we're okay with each other."

"Just let my lawyer handle the details, okay? We have to move fast, though; complete the transaction before Stanley can stop me. Can you do it this week, Daddy? He'll be gone all week. The coast is clear!"

"What does he think of this, being dealt a hand from under the table?"

"Stanley has nothing to do with this, just you and me; he cannot know. There'll never be peace in our family, if he finds out."

"I see—we can tell your mother, though."

"Just a minute, Daddy. Not everything; not about screwing Stanley out of any piece of the farm. Mom's so unpredictable, she'd probably spill-the-beans," she whispered.

"Right—no spilling— ," Hank whispered back, not wanting Bette to overhear.

Margo gave her father a hug. "Call Natalee Zinger today; get on it —right away—okay? I left her number on top of Grandma's dresser; she's expecting your call."

Hank seemed surprised. "A woman-lawyer? What—you had all of this set up, already?"

"That's just the businesswoman in me, Daddy!" she said, turning to go, amazed that she had successfully manipulated her father. "I'll never let a man-lawyer take advantage of me!"

"Hey, Margo!" Hank called out as she was getting into her car. "Just one more thing: stop and see Grandma today, when you're at work—okay? She's so doggone lonely—"

"Sure, Dad. I'll try."

"Don't feel bad, if she don't remember ya; it's the dementia."

"I know, Dad. I'm a nurse—remember? She has Alzheimer's Disease."

"Yeah—Alz-z-z—whatever. It's sad to see her there, like that. She don't know what's goin' on. She didn't even know who I was, when I stopped to see her last week, and . . . I'm her son!" Tears came to his eyes.

"I know, Daddy; that's just the way it is—"

Margo squealed her tires at the end of the driveway but cautiously drove past the speed trap, a roadside park where the radar trap was usually set up, lying in wait of unsuspecting, out-of-state drivers. It wasn't always this way; she remembered that the Burntwood Prairie Roadside Rest Area was originally intended to be a picnic-stop for weary travelers, not a place for lazy-ass policemen to ambush commuters who were late for work.

Speed Trap Murder

When she saw that there were no police in sight, she floored it. She wasn't happy with the poor performance of her car, wishing it would go faster. Her engine sputtered and balked, all the way to town. At least, she made it on time for her first day on her new job.

Chapter 22
Horse-Crazy Girls
April 2, 1993

Margo was sitting in a quiet hallway at Shady Creek Rest Home, her first day going mighty slow. Bored to death, reading from a dictionary-sized volume of policies and procedures, her eyelids felt like someone had applied glue to the edges. The drudgery of fulfilling mandatory prerequisites was worse than the mundane weekly grind that she had left behind.

During the week, she forgot to visit her grandmother who was housed in the same building. She also missed all of Stanley's calls.

By Friday afternoon, just like clockwork, her parents had signed the papers; and Margo got the loan at Burntwood Settler's Bank. Along with this great news, she was ecstatic that Stanley's retirement fund had been deposited into her checking account, that same day.

By quitting time, she was flying on an emotional high, barely able to contain her joy. She asked her old friend, Eileen, to help celebrate her good fortune. They met at The Corner Bar.

"Eileen, I need your brain. What should *we* do first?" Margo asked, stirring her drink with a small straw. "Remember our horse-ranch plan?"

"Did you say *we*—you, me, and Maria, as when we were little?" Eileen asked.

Hearing the mention of Maria's name, Margo was stricken with gloom, then by a wave of guilt, feeling that it was her fault that Maria was dead. She picked at a stubborn hangnail, thinking back, remembering the mutual excitement of the three pals—the *horse-crazy girls*.

"Now, *we* finally get to do it; our good luck but a rotten deal for Maria."

Eileen sensed that Margo was dead-set on reviving the past, but she clearly was not. "I think . . . a lot of water has run under the bridge, since we were kids. Don't get me wrong, Margo; horses are wonderful, and I still love them, but the work and the commitment would be too much. We're not ten years old anymore!"

Margo fixed her stare on the row of bottles on a shelf behind the bar, feeling that her childhood dream had been sabotaged. "Maria is dead, so you—what—quit?"

"The hatchet murder was upsetting," Eileen said. "I almost puked when I heard. I got so scared that I couldn't go to her funeral; couldn't bear to see her cold, dead face." She quickly ordered a second round of drinks.

"Horse-ranching—I can't afford it," Eileen continued; true, but it sounded like another excuse. She chugged a second glassful. "Did you get any money from . . . what's-his-name—the millionaire?"

"Huh?" Margo blinked and snapped out of the initial effect of Eileen's tactless refusal. "Well, I'm not one to kiss and tell. A mistress doesn't rake-it-in, in this tiny town." She floundered her glass, spilling liquor on the bar, forming a puddle that resembled her duck pond.

"Are you still seeing him?"

"No! Life passed by—water under the bridge, like you say. I have a new boyfriend."

"And I don't know him? Does he have money?" Eileen reached over with a cigarette and said, "Here, take it—a cancer stick!"

"No, I can't. I told Stanley that I quit two years ago. He'd be mad if I started up again."

The bartender overheard, then nonchalantly left a folded napkin by Eileen's glass.

Eileen peeked under it, then smirked. "Sure . . . you can. How about a couple puffs on some *Mary Jane*—you old junkie!" She abruptly shoved the shaggy end into Margo's mouth.

"A joint!" Margo eagerly straightened the crinkled paper sleeve, twisting the tip to accept a flickering flame. It reminded her of the cherished but pointless comradery, high on weed in the bunkers, and how much she missed the infantry. She drew in, powerfully on her first inhalation, burning the tip backward a whole inch.

"Oh, God—we have a baby together, Eileen, and he wants to marry me!" she blurted out, blowing a gray cloud of smoke past Eileen's face.

"Congratulations, except you don't sound very happy about it," Eileen said coldly. "In fact, after your week of excitement and success, you don't sound happy at all. You don't even sound like you love this guy. What's the matter with him?"

"Nothing; he's damn-near perfect, and that's part of the problem: I'm not. He loves our baby. He'll be a good father," Margo admitted and started to cry, "but I'll be a lousy mother. I wish I knew how to do it right," she said, taking another long drag on the contraband, "but my mom's a bad example . . . and a worse teacher."

Eileen seemed unconcerned but was very calculating. "Sounds like a loser—get his money, then dump him! Plus, collect child support—free money—guaranteed by our leftist government. Ain't it great?" she jeered joyously. "I voted for that cutie, Bill Clinton, in three jurisdictions! And my grandmother—may she rest in peace—voted for him twice!"

"Wait a minute; isn't that illegal—a dead person voting?"

"Ha—what are they going to do about it, dig her up and throw her in jail?"

Chapter 23
Worthless Advice

Upset with Eileen, the quitter, Margo was ready to go. She slid off the stool but fell to the floor. Eileen laughed hysterically and pulled Margo up by the arm. "Take my advice," she said, "get the freebies, unless you strike it up, again, with Mister Moneybags. Even a commie, like me, could love a capitalist-millionaire! There's your ticket to happiness!"

"That's what Mom says."

"Hm-m—even your mother agrees with me!"

"The problem is, Stanley wants to change everything. He thinks the house is a dump!"

"So? Improvements are a bonus, the same as money in the bank. Get him to invest his own cash into your house. Remodel the whole place, if you can get away with it."

"I don't think he'd agree to investing," Margo started to say, but stopped, realizing that she had already gotten her hands on his retirement fund. "What if he gets suspicious?"

"If he's in love with you, he'll shell-it-out, like peanuts! Get him to pay for a lot of the little things; it all adds up. But if he starts asking questions, you've got trouble—time to bail out! Get all you can, as soon as you can, then dump the guy."

"I can do all that—legally? We're not married."

"Sure!" Eileen sneered and emitted an evil-sounding giggle. "It's almost like cutting his throat, except . . . not as bloody-messy, in case anything like that ever enters your mind. You'll need a good lawyer, though, to go for the gravy train. I know just whom you need— Natalee Zinger. Natalee's a genuine witch, if there ever was one. She can make 'em squeal, like a pig caught in a beaver trap! I'll give you her number."

"Ah-h, I'm going to have to think about this," Margo said, realizing that she had kept Stanley's name out of the purchase agreement, even though she actually respected him. And she had also retained Ms. Zinger to draft all the papers. She drew in, on what was left of the marijuana.

"Hey, after you dump him, find that millionaire-guy again, or introduce him to me!"

"I gotta go, Eileen. Stop out, at the farm, and see me sometime."

"Sure; and congratulations on . . . everything," Eileen said, and moved down the bar to hustle a man who was woefully staring at his brown bottle.

"Some friend you turned out to be, Eileen," Margo mumbled. In a drugged haze, she staggered to the door, angry with the betrayal and determined to reject Eileen's *worthless advice*. "You're out of the deal, now! And good riddance!" she cried out, telling-her-off. "Who needs you? I'll manage, by myself!"

P. G. Knudson

Margo felt a familiar calmness, as she sat at the steering wheel and passed out. The breather was short, however, as she suddenly snapped to awareness and fired up her motor.

With both alcohol and cannabis coursing through her veins, she was arguably stoned when she aimed her hood ornament toward the highway, knocking down a decorative fence and narrowly missing a head-on collision.

Without realizing that she had dived into a self-loathing mood, she suddenly turned off the road. She almost stopped in the sandy parking lot by Lake Lavender but got a suicidal impulse to plunge her car into the lake. She floored it, streaking for the empty beach. Gravel and sand sprayed on all sides when she quickly slammed on the brakes, just before her front bumper stopped against a *beach closed* sign that blocked the footpath to the water.

Some time passed. The spell of welcome silence calmed her thoughts. She turned the car around, as if to leave, but circled back; then stopped in the empty parking lot, facing the lake and staring through the orange hue, the beginning of a colorful sunset. Mesmerized by the shimmering reflection off the water, she began to imagine herself galloping across the length of sandy beach that stretched out, in front of her, riding bareback on a muscle-rippled steed.

Her mind leaped, imagining that she had her knees scissored against its powerful withers and that she felt the sure-footedness of its stride, the wind whipping at her face. Her exciting thoughts surged, in rhythmic time to her imagined steed's powerful hoofs that leaped through the air and thundered like timpani.

Her mind magically switched locations, to her south forty where the fleeting stallion never missed a stride, thundering out of sight at breakneck speed but leaving her behind.

"What—was I thrown? How did I get left here, all by myself?" She was saddened that a totally fictional horse could be that cruel.

Back to reality, or quasi-reality, Margo became aware that she was still seated at the steering wheel, surrounded by the rusted-out shell of her old clunker, and that the exciting bareback ride was just a small part of her giant imagination. Even though she understood that the magical horseback ride was no more than a mirage, she felt angry that the imaginary horse tricked her and left her alone. She loathed being alone, craving company.

"I want *that* horse—*that* mysterious black one!" she burst out, not wanting to give up on the black phantom in her mind. She looked to the vacant passenger seat, listening for Maria's advice. Silence.

"I know it's gone; just have to find another one—now," she said aloud, as if carrying on a conversation with Maria. "Do you know where I can get one? If anybody would know where I can find a fast horse, Charley Day would know!"

Chapter 24
The Transplanted Texan

Margo aggressively turned onto the highway, her car apparently doing its own navigating, because it went directly to Charley Day's ranch without missing a turn.

Her mood-change was instantaneous, excitedly telling the ghost of her deceased friend that she remembered where Charley Day lived, from her childhood days. Fond memories. It wasn't far, only about ten miles to his mailbox where she hung a right turn.

Proceeding up the sandy driveway, she drove under the wooden *Day Ranch* sign, from which hung an authentic, Ojibwe dreamcatcher —*a protector from bad dreams*—handmade from a hoop of willow, webbed with strings of rawhide and adorned with traditional feathers. The spiderweb-like symbol barely moved in the calm evening air.

She drove past a group of spotted yearlings that eagerly gathered by the plank fence, watching her pass by. There was a corral on each side of the driveway, all the way up to a modest-looking house.

Stopping at the turnaround, Margo stepped out of her car, momentarily staggered, then regained her balance. Clearly drunk. She blew a sample of her breath into her cupped hands, to self-determine if any alcohol remained on her breath. Not being able to verify her self-test for intoxication, she slammed the door, hoping Mr. Day would hear and that he'd remember her.

She spotted an elderly-looking man near the far-end of the farmyard, cobbling a horse-pen together with long Tamarack poles.

She flipped the latch on the farm gate and let herself in, then headed directly toward the old man, her memory flipping the calendar backwards, realizing that she was only about 12 years old when Mr. Day had delivered a horse to her father's farm.

"Eons of time—he won't remember." She took a deep breath, hoping the country air would stop her dizziness and give her courage to speak to a man she didn't really know at all.

Charley Day stopped working and looked up at the young woman who had suddenly appeared, walking toward him across the manure-peppered plane, the entirety of the corral. He grinned. It was evident, that his guest was not just a young woman dressed in white tennis shoes and hospital-like scrubs, but a real cowgirl who didn't seem to mind where she placed her feet.

Sizing him up as she approached the man, Margo saw a dark, weathered face and gray hair protruding, from under a crushed-looking cowboy hat that sported a single Barred Owl feather. She suddenly remembered that her father had once dubbed the horse trader as, *The Transplanted Texan*'; but there was something else about his appearance that itched at her mind.

She spurred her memory, "He's older, by more than twenty years." The slim cowboy seemed to become more and more scrawny looking, the closer she got. "I don't recognize him, at all, but he dresses like someone from Texas."

The thin, old cowboy flipped a pile of horse biscuits to the side, with a manure fork, and smiled when Margo got within speaking distance.

"Howdy, Ma'am," the cowboy spoke in a hoarse-sounding voice, and without facial expression, which instantly triggered Margo's memory.

"Mister Charley Day—do you remember me?" she asked respectfully, just as she recalled, that as a young girl, she had perceived him to be the spitting-image of the man on the obverse face of the Buffalo Nickle.

"*Cain't* say that I do, Ma'am," the old Indian said with a friendly smile and a somewhat refined but barely lingering Texas accent. He leaned the manure fork against a pole-railing, then pushed his hat higher on his forehead with the tip of his thumb. "How y'all doin'?"

Margo didn't know how to respond to that rhetorical southern greeting, so she stuck to business. "I'm Hank Toralf's daughter, Margo."

"Hank Toralf—that Norwegian cow milker? Y'all Hank's little girl?"

"Yup, that was me. You remember!"

"Yeah—the *little princess* who wanted a pony. Oo-oo-oo—back in time, many moons!"

"Remember the horse you sold to Dad—the black gelding? He became mine, and I named him *Black Lightning*!"

"Oh, yeah—good name—" Mr. Day pondered, thinking back to the very day that he delivered that particular horse. "That was no pony! How I remember that one—sixteen hands and nimble on his feet! He rode good; y'all couldn't tip 'em. And I recall your daddy, of

112

course, toilin' on that dairy farm, totin' that milk, one pail at a time. How's ol' Hank doin'?"

"Daddy retired; sold all the cows . . . and the farm. I bought it! I just want to raise horses, though. Do you have any for sale?"

"Ha!" The horse-trader laughed and gestured to both sides. "They're *all* for sale, Miss Margo!"

Being an experienced horse trader, he sensed that this young woman was a serious customer. And he knew that somewhere, amongst all of his animals, he had the object of her sudden shopping spree. He rotated his head toward the round-pens.

"Y'all can have your pick," he said. "But if ya wanna raise horses, it's a good idea to start with a mare that's already nestin'. Lookin' for a deal? Howzabout two for the price of one?"

"Really?" Margo shrieked with excitement. "I'd love to have a mother and a baby!" She held her hand over her heart, as if a little hand pressure would slow down the rapid beating. "I'm looking to the future, to build up a herd. And to get my ranch off and running, I need a good riding horse; one gentle with kids, since I have a little boy at home."

"Y'all better hurry—don'tcha know—Little Lady, if y'all want the two-for-one deal; *cain't* stop Mother Nature!" he said in his Texan drawl, crossed with a bit of acquired Minnesotan colloquialism.

"I don't want an ordinary brood mare. I want a fast rider; one with a few good years left in her."

"Hm-m—gentle, but . . . fast." Mr. Day thought of the paradox, for a second, then walked Margo past several pregnant mares. He moved quickly, for an old man.

Margo looked each horse in the eye and kept moving, trying to keep up.

"You have nice horses, Mister Day!"

"Yowza; got a couple well-trained riders, both fixin' to foal—them two, over yonder," he said, pointing to a round-pen closer to one of the rear barns. "Both ripe as a plum, ready to fall from the tree. I'm watchin' their signs, ev'ry day. They'll be in the birth-barn, by tomarrah—Saturday, I'm thinkin'."

Margo walked up to the pen and leaned on the railing. Both mares were beautiful animals; one, an Appaloosa; the other, a Chestnut Quarter-Horse. Either one suited her, just fine. "How much?"

Instantly judging Margo's ability to pay, based on her type of special-looking attire and her apparent urgency to buy something immediately, both indications that price was no object, the seasoned horse trader fielded a number: "Eight hundred 'n fifty—either one, ready to foal—two for one price—the mother and the foal, before birth. If y'all fixin' to buy, after the foalin', that's a whole nother deal." Voicing the wordy terms quickly was part of the horse-selling business, and he was good at it.

"It's getting dark," Margo said, ignoring the details. "I'll be back tomorrow. If I buy one, can you haul her to my place?"

"I'll carry y'all," he said. "Tell your daddy, Charley says *hi*."

"Okay!" Margo said happily and bounded across the carpet of horse manure. By the time she got to her car and pulled on the door handle, she had made an impulsive decision: "I want two!"

She beamed a smile and yelled back to the horse trader, "I'll see you tomorrow! You can depend on it, Mister Day!"

Day acknowledged with a wave of his hat.

Speed Trap Murder

Margo felt elated as she headed for home. She turned the radio on and sang along to a medley of Garth Brooks' songs, and she imagined her glorious life when her ranch would be full of horses. She envisioned buying both of the pregnant, good riders, when she would return the next day. Money was not a consideration; she had never felt richer.

Chapter 25
A Bad Mother

B ette was standing at the kitchen range, re-stirring simmering gravy, when she saw headlights turn in. "It's about time!"

When Margo finally got inside, she barely noticed that the evening meal was getting cold. With only horses on her mind, she was excited to tell what she had found at Charley Day's ranch.

"I'll buy two pregnant mares, so Stanley can go riding with me! That'll give me a jump-start at growing my herd. I get them tomorrow. Mister Day will do the hauling."

"I hope everyone enjoys the chicken supper," Bette said, without commenting about the excitement of getting horses, almost as if she hadn't listened to Margo's news. "It's our last meal, in this house, as a family. We've already moved most things out of here, today, Margo. I'll leave you this table, because there's already a perfectly good table at Grandma's trailer."

"Did you get to see Grandma at the rest home?" Hank asked.

"Ah; no, Daddy. It was just meetings—all week—plus all that time at the bank today. There wasn't an extra minute. Maybe next week—"

"Stanley called again," Bette said.

"Oh, I suppose I should call him back, but I don't know what to say."

"For starters, you can tell him that you bought the farm today," Bette suggested, sounding a bit perturbed. "Betcha he'd want to know that."

Margo thought for a second. She had almost forgotten about her boyfriend—almost, but not entirely. "No; think I'll wait until he gets back. He'd ask about Toby. What could I tell him? I haven't seen my baby, all week, Mom! I'm *a bad mother*!"

"No, you're *not* a bad mother. You're just a *busy* mother; starting a new job . . . and buying a house and horse shopping—all in one week. You're a busy girl! That's why I'm here; to help you, Darling," Bette said, embellishing beyond her normal expression of endearment.

Margo released a happy tear and hugged her mother.

At a calm point during the meal, Margo suddenly looked around the room, as in horror. "Where's Toby, Mom? Why isn't he here, at the table?"

"Oh, I've had his highchair at the trailer—five days already. I fed him there, an hour ago, and I put him to bed. You should call Stanley and tell him his little man is fine."

"I'm too tired, Mom. If he calls again, tell him I'm exhausted."

"Oh, Margo," her father said, "Rowdy was here today. He helped me move a lot of the furniture out of your way. He's coming back tomorrow, to do more."

Even though all the upstairs furniture was gone, Margo went up there; and with just a blanket and a pillow, lied on the hardwood floor in her old bedroom. She slept.

At the trailer house, Margo's parents prepared for bedtime.

"Horses, already—the first day?" Bette remarked. "Looks like she's spending money, like there's no tomorrow."

* * *

It seemed like a short night. Awakening in her own house for the first time, Margo experienced that new farm-owner feeling, something that's hard to put one's finger on, except her whole body ached from sleeping on the bare floor.

She stood up and stretched, letting her grandmother's hand-made quilt fall to the floor. The air in the bedroom was cold, making her naked body shiver as she stepped over and parted the lace curtains, trying to peer through the snow-like frost that had crusted on the inside surface of the windowpane. After scraping a peephole with her fingernails, she saw her barn. Despite its decrepit condition, it looked magnificent, its frosty roof gleaming in the morning rays of sunshine. She reminisced, how she used to be able to look out that same window and see her black gelding grazing in the east pasture, years before, when she was a teenager.

"I can't believe it, an equestrian showplace! And it's all-mine!" she cried out, holding her arms in the air, listening to the echo of her own voice reverberate through the empty rooms.

Her shivering worse, she reached down and picked up the blanket, then fell to her knees. With elbows on the windowsill, she stared at the farmyard, dreaming through the scratched hole in the frost.

"When the barn is red and when the white fences are done, it'll look like a million bucks," she whispered aloud. "No cows—just horses!" she shouted, as loud as she could, and listened to her own echo. "Who said I can't have my dream, Mom?" she called out, just to hear the echo again.

"What are you yelling about up there?" her mother's voice suddenly billowed up the staircase, from somewhere downstairs.

Margo spun around and jumped to her feet, clutching the blanket to her chin. "Mom, what are you doing in my house?" She saw a pile of her clothing, lying in a heap on the floor. She quickly dropped the blanket and slid her bare skin into a sweatshirt with matching sweatpants. She ran down the stairs, skipping the last four steps, then landing on the dining room floor with a thud that shook the room.

"Whoa—rein it in, Girl!" her mother said. "You're getting too old to jump like a kid, thinking you can arrive on the scene by flying without a plane!"

"I'm excited, Mom!"

Bette smiled. "Your dad told me it sounded like somebody was getting killed over here, so I hurried over to see what was wrong."

Margo's laugh turned into a giggle. "I'm so happy, Mom, I can't stand it! It makes me want to scream!" She screamed for her mother, and laughed louder, jumping up and down on the tips of her toes.

Bette grimaced, holding her hands over her ears. "Ouch! Good God, Girl! You make me wonder if we made a mistake, selling you the farm!" she laughed, shaking her head.

Margo gave her mother a big hug. "Thanks, Mom; you'll never regret it!"

"Don't you know how to turn on the heat?" Bette asked. "There's an oil furnace . . ."

"It's springtime. The house can warm up, when I open the doors and windows."

"You should mop this floor. It's filthy!"

"You left me a dirty house and my bed is gone! Where's my bed, Mom? You didn't even leave a mattress! I shouldn't have to sleep on the floor, like a barn-cat!"

"We thought you were buying new furniture, so we threw everything out."

Margo acknowledged her wish to go furniture-shopping. "I can't afford to buy *all* new furniture, Mom. I still need my bed. And I hope you left my real-feather pillows. Grandma hand-sewed the tick, including my initials."

Bette started out the door. "If you want any of it back, look for it in that pile outside." She turned around and added, "Come over for breakfast. It was on the stove when I had to come running over here. And *our* heat is on. Come over and feed your own kid!"

"In a minute, Mom," Margo said, blankly watching her mother skip across the car-path, up onto the wooden deck, and into the trailer house.

Margo stared contemptuously at the unsightly trailer house that came along with the deal. The peeling paint exposed the underlying rust on the steel panels. "It's ugly, and it's mine; but what can I do about it?"

She reclaimed her discarded, feather pillows from the trash pile in the front yard. When returning to the back porch, with the pillows balanced over both arms, she caught the breakfast smell of ham-n-eggs, coming from Grandma's old, wood-burning cook-stove, now her mother's favorite appliance in the trailer house.

Speed Trap Murder

"Last call for breakfast," Bette called through her screen door. "Just because it's Saturday doesn't mean that I'm running an all-day restaurant!"

Chapter 26
Margo's Rant

Toby was tapping his plastic cup on the tray when Margo walked, bare-footed, into her mother's kitchen. Toby tried to talk.

"Goo-goo-ga-ga," Bette mockingly said, holding a piece of toast in front of his face.

"Mom, let him talk!" Margo said, sounding frustrated. "You can't talk *for* him. And stop that baby-talk! How is he going to learn anything, if you don't speak normal English to him?"

"Oh—for Heaven's sake! Even *you* grew up on baby-talk. A little *coochy-coo* never hurt anyone. Sit down and enjoy your baby when he's still little. I've got your eggs in the pan. I'm making them, just the way you like them, sunny-side-up."

Hank came in, from outside, and sat down on the chair by the window. "A family breakfast; reminds me of the good ol' days when Dad was here and you kids were little," he said.

"Dad, that's where Grandpa always sat," Margo said. "It's odd, seeing you sitting there."

"Well, I'm the grandpa now, so I earned this chair!" he quipped and gave a jolly laugh.

Bette placed a large platter in the middle of the table. "Do you remember when Grandma, Grandpa, and our whole family sat around this table?" she asked Margo.

"Yeah, I do. It was crowded. I had to sit next to Billy, and he always stole my food."

"It was shoulder-to-shoulder, alright, but Grandma always made it work," Bette said. "Of course, you kids were a lot smaller then. There wouldn't be room for everyone, anymore."

"*Ah-h*, those were good ol' days on the farm," Hank said, smacking his lips as Bette flopped an omelet onto his plate.

"*What!*" Margo blurted out. "We never had *good days* on the farm!"

"Oh, it wasn't so bad," Hank maintained, with a carefree chuckle.

"You were drunk, most of the time! How do you know if it was good or bad?"

"Have some eggs, Margo!" Bette snapped, then slapped Margo's special plate down in front of her face.

"Well, it was no smorgasbord, but . . . it was a good life," he insisted.

"No, it wasn't. It was *Hell!*" Margo exploded, her face turning red. With a pouting lower lip, she watched the egg-yolks run, repeatedly jabbing them with a fork and stirring them into a slurry.

"Milk prices weren't very good, in those days," Hank recalled, rubbing his whiskers.

"Prices? All the farmers, around here, got the same price for milk!"

"I know, a pittance. We barely survived, but it was better than living in some big city—the only alternative. It was a good life, all-in-all," he concluded, looking for Bette to concur.

"It was difficult for all you kids; wish it could have been different, but we can't do it over again," Bette contended.

"Can't *do it over*? No kidding, Mom!"

"I meant to say, there's no second chance to do it over again—for anybody!"

"You had *lots* of chances to do it over, Mom! What about my first year of high school, your first chance to do it over? Or, what about my second year of high school, your second chance to do it over? Do you remember anything?" she asked sarcastically, knowing that her mother's treatments left her with nothing to remember. "And my junior year—where were you, Mom?" Margo started to cry, sobbing heavily as she ranted. "Do you know where I was, on prom night? I was sitting in the barn on a wooden stool, holding a pail between my knees and filling it to the foamy top, one squirt at a time, over and over again until a dozen cows got milked. Dad was at the tavern *relaxing his nerves*, and you were gone, Mom; and you never told us where . . . or why. I was here, doing *your* job and raising *your* damned kids!"

"Now, Margo—take it easy," her father cautioned. "You were young then, and you wouldn't have understood the *shock therapy*, or all the other stuff your mother went through!"

The upsetting voices made Toby cry. Bette moved his highchair closer to her seat.

"How can a mother just take off, like you did? You had kids who needed you! Where did you go, Mom?" Margo sobbed. "All I knew was, there were cows to milk twice-a-day, and all the ten-gallon cans had to be full and cooling in the water tank, by the time the milk truck came—every morning. That was our lifeline—the only money we got. I had to hide any cash I found in the house, so Daddy wouldn't drink it up. Dad and I ran the farm; or I should say, *he helped* when I hid the bottle."

Hank leisurely sat and listened, like he had heard it all before. Defenseless.

"After the milk shipped out, there was hay to pitch, cows to feed, calves to nurse, and manure to shovel. The work was never completely done. I don't ever want to see another dairy cow, for the rest of my life!" she bawled.

Hank fidgeted in his chair and Bette rose to her feet. She paced the floor, holding Toby in her arms while enduring *Margo's rant.*

"I had to bathe and dress my little brothers and sister, so they could go to school. I missed the school bus, myself—many days. There was the laundry, cooking meals, and shoveling snow! I don't know what I would have done, if it wasn't for Grandma. Oh—I miss you, Grandma-a-a!" Margo screamed to the ceiling, even knowing that her grandmother had been moved to the senior rest home. Her head fell onto the center of her plate. She dug her fingers into her scalp and cried profusely, her face floundering in the yellow egg-yolks that mixed into the strands of her auburn-colored bangs.

Bette handed the baby to Hank and rushed around the table, to Margo's side. She tried to give Margo a hug but was pushed away. That didn't stop her; she tried again, lifting her daughter to her feet and embracing her, runny eggs and all.

After her mother's consoling words, Margo's crying subsided. Bette handed her a towel. Margo rubbed briskly, and Bette pointed out the missed spots. Margo scrubbed until her mother was satisfied.

"Are you okay now, Margo?" Bette asked, showing a deep, belated concern.

"You were a horrible mother, gone for three years of my life!"

Bette said nothing, realizing that she couldn't remember much of the past, but knowing that it was all probably true.

Margo suddenly bolted for the door, kicking the screen door and falling to the deck, groaning with pain.

"You'd better go out there, Henry," Bette said in a near-whisper. "She probably cut her foot. Go see . . . and talk to her."

"She might bite my head off," Hank objected. "I don't know why she cut-into you that way, Mother. Sorry, I never expected her to do this, not the very-day-after we sold her the farm—ungrateful kid!"

"Oh, she's just venting. So much of the fallout came down on her shoulders, in the past," She motioned toward the door with her thumb. "Get out there, Dad! Besides, her memory is better than yours. If anyone deserves this farm, it's her!"

Hank started to get up from the table but hesitated. "She's awful-mad at me, for almost drinking-away the farm," he whispered. "She never forgot." He slowly approached the door, peeking through the screen to see if Margo was still there. He cautiously pushed the door open, seeing Margo sitting on the steps, facing the other way and massaging her foot with both hands.

"Boy! You really gave that door a kick—like a mule—didn't ya, Margo?" he said, chuckling cautiously.

Speed Trap Murder

Margo turned her head toward her father and showed a half-smile, holding her sore toes in one hand. "Next time, I'll have boots on. Then I'll kick anything I want to, around here!"

Hank laughed, in a sparsely measured amount, "It's your place, now, My little Princess. I expect you'll do whatever you desire. You can kick all the doors down, if you want to," he said. Then a serious expression came across his face. "Just don't kick me and your mother out. That's our deal! We sold you this farm, cheap, so you could afford it; but we get to stay—no matter what!"

"And . . . you don't get to interfere in my life. Don't forget that part of the deal!"

Chapter 27
Like Winning the Lottery

Margo was rushing against the clock. When she came out of the house, headed for her car, her father held a salvaged, old fencepost and was pulling handfuls of half-rotted grass from its attached, rusted wire.

"What about Charley Day . . . and the horse-deal?" Hank asked, dismayed that the fallen fence components were in such poor condition.

"I'm on top of it, Dad; later, in the afternoon."

"Most of the fence is broke down, like this worthless post. You'll be chasin' loose horses, from now till kingdom come!"

"Can you fix up something, today, Daddy? I'd do it, but I'm . . . stretched a little too thin. I promised Mister Day, I'd be there, and I want to get those mares home before they're too-far-along. If either of them foals, before they get here, the whole deal will be screwed up!"

"Fix . . . something? I can try, but it's a lotta work for an old geezer like me."

"Make-do . . . somehow, okay? Stanley can take over when he gets back. He'll normally do most of the work."

128

"That Stanley—he don't know how to work! Ya woulda been better off with Ernie! Now, there's a guy that can afford to raise horses!"

"Cut it out, Daddy! Ernie might be rich, but he's a slob! Besides, he pissed-me-off. It cannot be forgiven!"

"You know what you want, My Little . . ."

"I have to run, Daddy; we're burning daylight!"

Hank waved slightly as Margo began to drive away. "That girl will send me to an early grave."

"Margo!" Bette suddenly yelled and came running out the screen door.

Margo stopped the car and stuck her head out the window. "What?"

"I forgot to tell you," Bette continued, "Stanley called, early this morning. He wants you to call him back. It's important!"

Hank knew better than to listen to the cat fight that was about to start. He tuned out the argument and began searching the dead grass for more posts to salvage, almost wishing he hadn't promised anything.

"By the way, I called Ernie Niceski," Bette said. "He'll be coming over for supper tonight, since Stanley can't make it. It seems like the perfect time—"

"*What?* Why would you do that, Mom, to drive a wedge between me and Stanley?"

"We owe it to Ernie . . . to do *something*; it's the least we can do. He dug that pond for us . . . for nothing! We should have paid him something, long ago."

"He dug it for *me*, Mom—the cow and the free-milk-deal, like in the joke! Do I look like a *joke*, Mom? I'm not going to revisit that arrangement!"

"Try to be ready by six o'clock, Margo. I might even need a little help in the kitchen."

"Count me *out*! Do you remember . . . a guy named *Stanley*?"

"You must miss Ernie, don't you, someone who's made a name for himself, a nice guy and a millionaire—a prominent man in the community?"

"I can't believe you're doing this, just because Stanley's not here!"

"Ernie's got wherewithal. Don't you miss having cash, any time you want it? You lived with him—for what—a year or two?"

"Ancient history, Mom!"

"Comparing them, Stanley's a loser and Ernie's a winner—purely the truth!"

"You think of Ernie, *like winning the lottery*. Stanley's the father of my baby, and we're in love. There's a difference!"

"You're not happy, unless you're miserable. This might be your last chance; and it comes at a time when you'll be needing a lot of money. Come to grips with reality!"

"That's what this is really about, isn't it, Mother—*your* chance to get *your* hands on Ernie's money? You lost your right to criticize me, when you left us—all of us—remember? I don't have to listen to you!" she shouted, then peeled sand all the way down the driveway.

Black smoke spurted from her tailpipe, as her clunker sputtered past the frontage of the farm. She gunned the gas pedal, to keep the engine alive, while searching for a rocking song on the radio that fit the untamed side of her spirit. She found a Rock song that suited her mood and turned up the volume knob until the dashboard vibrated. She stripped off her sweatshirt, then replaced it, pulling on a cotton blouse that just happened to be lying on the front seat; all before coasting through the first stop sign.

She couldn't contain her proud feelings of personal accomplishment, combined with the anticipation of spending money. "Yaw-hoo!" she yelled out the window, like a G.I. on R&R.

Chapter 28
Demon Possessed Nonsense

Hank and Bette stood over the pile of salvaged posts, contemplating the urgent need to rebuild the fence and wondering how they'd gotten roped into doing it. Hank hopelessly kicked at the flaky end of a partially rotted post.

"I wish you would've used your head, Henry!" Bette said, their daughter out of sight.

"What did I do now? This fence-job is an emergency!"

"You let her have this place, and you knew I was against it!"

Hank became suddenly confused, as Bette seemed to have turned-a-180 on him. Scratching his chin, he asked, "You're having second thoughts about selling the farm? I thought we discussed this; and didn't you tell me, just this morning, that Margo deserves to be the new owner?" The two walked back to the trailer house together.

"The ink's not even dry yet, and look how she's treating us. You let that little devil twist you around her finger, Henry, and you should've known better! She'll kick us off this farm, the first time something happens that she doesn't like." Bette angrily slid the coffee pot across the wide cast-iron top of the old cook-stove.

"There's nothin' to worry about; she's our baby girl!" Hank said, ignoring the metal-to-metal scraping sound and dropping into his father's chair.

Bette hurriedly splashed some coffee into Hank's cup, then plunked it down in front of him. "There's plenty to be scared about—with her! I think she's *demon possessed*. Remember the time she tried to burn the woods, next to the trailer house? Go ahead; tell me that the Devil had nothing to do with that! She begged you for matches to play with; you told her *no*, so she stole them from your smoking drawer."

Hank chuckled. "Yeah; she sorta outsmarted me, that time." Grinning at the old memory, he took a sip.

Still angry, Bette insisted, "Conniving, like the Devil! There is such-a-thing as *exorcism*—you know. Maybe the priest . . ."

"*Demon possessed nonsense!*" came Hank's firm voice, just as his clenched hand bounced off the surface of the table. "Let's be sensible. She sometimes has a mind of her own, that's all!"

"Sometimes? All the time!"

Hank paused to think and to let his wife calm down. "Well, if she's gonna live here—all of us on the same farm—she'll just hafta be patient; give us old folks a chance to readjust. It's her place now, and you know it's gonna be different than when she was a little, snotty-nosed brat."

Bette's anger subsided, nearly to a state of depression. Her downhearted stare was directed at a faded picture of a chicken that Grandma Toralf had hung on the back wall, above the table, years before anyone could remember.

"If our daughter doesn't have demons," Bette continued in a calm but ominous voice, "then you explain to me, what else could have bestowed her to take a butcher knife from my kitchen and go on a rampage, slicing the heads off a dozen of my laying-hens. If your father had been alive, he would've killed her!"

Hank laughed boyishly, slowly spinning his cup on its saucer, remembering the decades-old incident. "A strange day, to be sure, but that was a long time ago, Mother! Margo's a grown-up woman now; has a kid, even—our grandchild! And now, she owns the farm. Things'll be different, under her control."

"The future is now, Henry; same person—full of old anger—no change. I'll tell you one thing—one thing for certain: I'll never trust Margo with a knife in her hand!"

Hank stood up and gave Bette a hug. "You must not remember, Dear, but all the chaos that led up to that incident was traumatic for Margo. Her taking of your best knife was symbolic, and so was her childish rebellion. We've had some tough times, Mother, but . . . all is not lost. Do you remember, our good neighbor, Red Wilson, gave us the replacement chicks that eventually grew up to be our new egg-layers? And . . . we got to eat most of the dead chickens, anyway, except for the one that Margo buried in the manure pile, out behind the barn next to her dead dog."

Chapter 29
Notorious Speed Trap

With shopping on her mind, Margo forgot to watch out for the *notorious speed trap*. She sped headlong through the invisible radar-beam. It wasn't that she hadn't seen the front end of the black police car, poking out from behind a thicket of bushes, but rather that she didn't seem to care.

She heard the siren, over the volume of the radio and over the open-window noise that buffeted her ears, then glanced in the rear-view mirror. Flashing lights were closing in.

She pounded her fist on the steering wheel. "I'm S-O-L, now!" She braked to a stop, just past the entrance sign for the Roadside Rest.

As the Minnesota State Trooper pulled up behind her, Margo reminded herself, "Think, Margo, think! Do the routine."

She nervously buttoned, then unbuttoned her blouse three times, trying to decide how much cleavage to show for this cop. She decided halfway was enough, knowing that she wasn't wearing a brassiere, just as the officer approached from the rear.

Her engine sputtered, so she revved-it-up, sending out a plume of black smoke just as the officer walked past the tail pipe. Knowing that she only had seconds to prepare, Margo closed her eyes and took a deep breath, trying to reverse her negative frame of mind.

By the time the Trooper stood at her open window, unscathed from breathing the black exhaust, Margo had a seductive smirk on her face, a bosom partially exposed, and her driver's license held between two fingers like she used to hold a cigarette.

The officer took the license and asked, "Ma'am, do you know how fast you were going?"

"No, Sir. My car was misfiring . . . or something. I was just trying to get it running better," she said, sounding accustomed to this sort of interrogation.

Just about that instant, the idling engine gave one last sputter and died.

Margo laughed. "See? I don't know what's wrong with it. Was I going too fast?"

The Trooper observed Margo toying with a button on her blouse. "That's not going to work with me, Mizz Toralf," the well-groomed officer said, reading every word on her driver's license. "I clocked you, speeding sixty-five miles per hour in a fifty-five zone."

"That's amazing! That's how fast we all could legally drive, before Richard Nixon. Remember him? It was President Nixon, according to my father—my highly-respected father—who lowered the speed limit to fifty-five during the Seventies-Energy-Crisis. Such a shame—fifty-five; never thought this old heap could go any faster than that! Do you know how to fix cars?" She flashed her fake, helpless-lady smile.

"No, Ma'am. You should take it to a reputable mechanic," he said, after politely enduring her practiced and sometimes-used monologue.

She then began her fake sincerity-act, telling the handsome officer all about buying a house yesterday, her mother watching her baby today so she could buy furniture, and that she was out of milk for her baby. Again, she playfully flipped her finger at a button and giggled.

The officer grinned slightly. "You're a long way from home, aren't you, Mizz Toralf?"

"Huh?"

The officer pointed to her driver's license, still in his hand. "It says *Minneapolis*—"

"Oh, that—my old, old address, before the trailer, even. I moved back home, just last week. And I just started a new job! I told you that I bought a house, here, didn't I? Actually, I'm just moving in, Sir," she said, fingertips still fidgeting with the button. "There's so much to do, when you're moving. I'm just on my way to buy furniture, like I said."

"Yes, I heard. You understand, of course, I'm going to have to write . . ."

"Oh-h-h, do you have to?" Margo cut him off, then wailed, not wanting a speeding ticket. She clutched the fabric of her shirt, closing the top of her collar with nervous fingers and massaging her throat, all in one motion.

"I have to write a—a *warning ticket*, this time," the officer continued, seeming to back off. "A second offense will be different!"

"Oh, I appreciate that, Sir. It'll help me save money—milk for my baby."

The policeman handed back her driver's license, along with her warning ticket.

"Thank you, Officer," she said, sparing no charm, "for being so thorough and so kind."

When the Trooper walked away, she restarted her car, ruminating this traffic-stop. The old car faltered, and black smoke rolled before the wheels turned. Back on the road.

"Stupid son of a bitch!" she jeered, checking her mirrors to be sure that the trooper was not following. She laughed and turned the radio volume, up high.

"Yaw-hoo!" she crowed. "Calm down, calm down," she restrained herself. "Remember what the doctor said. No—I can control it," she said argumentatively, talking to the empty seat.

Her euphoria transferred directly to the accelerator. She quickly overtook two semi-trucks but slowed down at the city limit sign. The Cowboy's Friend Western Clothing Store would be first.

Chapter 30
Exhilarative Buying-Spree

Buying an expensive pair of western-style boots was a must for Margo. She had never owned an actual pair of cowboy boots, so the experience of trying on the real thing was almost titillating. She impulsively added a new pair of blue jeans and a western shirt, to match, while she was at it. And she couldn't resist buying a thick belt with a super-sized, silver buckle. The total purchase price was extravagant, but her checkbook was overweight with Stanley's withdrawn retirement fund. She was thrilled, feeling especially rich on her *exhilarative buying-spree.*

On-a-roll, ready to buy more, she parked at the curb in front of the furniture store. The front doors were propped open wide. Seeing the alluring price-reduction signs taped to the windows, Margo tried to visualize her mental checklist of items she wanted to buy but realized that she hadn't actually made a list.

The leather soles on her new cowboy boots slipped, a little bit, on the blacktop surface of the street. She danced onto the sidewalk, and was just about to enter the furniture store when she heard someone call her name.

Squinting across traffic, Margo saw someone waving from the front of Runo's Music Store. She waved back and immediately crossed the street.

"You were at the music jam, last fall," the bearded man said with a friendly and high-pitched voice. "You're Maria Richardson's friend; said you were moving here—"

"You knew Maria?" she asked, instantly feeling at ease with him.

"You tried my guitar . . . and sang a Johnny Cash song."

Margo's eyes grew large, with surprise. "I remember that." She smiled, enjoying the notoriety. "You have a good memory, but—"

"You can call me *Bummer.*"

The odd moniker, an obvious label from a previous era, surprised Margo; but she was good at concealing her reactions. "You didn't tell me that—before—did you?"

"No. It's really *Jim Johnson,* but the new name stuck."

"Bummer—where did you ever come up with a nickname like that?" she asked with a whimsical smirk on her face, as if she could guess what the answer might be.

"I can't remember," he admitted and laughed lightly. "It was back in the Sixties, something you probably wouldn't understand—wrong generation, for you."

"Right on! I've never understood that old hippie-culture stuff," she giggled.

"Anyway, welcome home, Margo! Still playin' yer guitar?"

"Yeah! I mean—well, I don't actually *have* one!"

"I was tight with Maria," Bummer said, tearing-up and trying to make his voice sound lower. "Did she tell ya, she used to play *fiddle* with me, all around the Red River Valley area? She sang alto; her harmony, always on-the-money, a good match for my tenor voice."

Margo couldn't hide her feelings for Maria. She had a big empty spot in her heart and the void was painful. She stood in a state of blankness, as a flashback of the final trail ride popped into her mind. All the details. Stinging tears blurred her eyes.

"Maria was my all-time best friend," she said, gripped by a sensation of loneliness.

Bummer empathized with her, then offered a ragged piece of red cloth for her tears.

Margo dried her eyes into Bummer's worn out, paisley handkerchief, remembering the duet of Bummer and Maria at the jam, doing a nostalgic rendition of a Merle Haggard song.

"Your guitar-picking and Maria's fiddle-work—amazing," she said. "I want to be able to play, like that!"

"Old-Time music—nothing like it—songs about life, love, and all the human emotions that everyone experiences. Not a bad thing! It was Maria, who made it work. I miss her."

"Can you show me how to pick out a good guitar?" Margo asked impulsively. "I don't want a piece of crap. Maria would have wanted me to buy a decent-playing machine—one that sounds good with her fiddle!"

Before he could answer, Bummer noticed the remorseful expression on Margo's face, caused simply by his mentioning of Maria's name.

"I live here now—for good—so I can come to the jam again!"

"Good! I'd like to hear it again—that favorite song of yours—*Red River Valley*. That song, now that Maria's gone, means more to me than you can imagine."

A heavy weight sank in Margo's chest. She closed her eyes, visualizing Maria singing the ominous words which ultimately came true. She was truly gone—gone from the Red River Valley. A sensation of irretrievable loss engulfed her.

Moments of silence passed, bereft moments, Bummer wondering what had happened to Margo's state of consciousness. Not understanding, he deftly asked, "Are you okay, Margo? Margo—Margo—"

When she hadn't responded, fear seized Bummer's very being. Not actually knowing her, he didn't know what to think of it; however, Margo seemed to be coming around.

Mildly dizzy, she recognized the storefront of Runo's Music Store, then Bummer's voice, after she snapped out of it. She wasn't aware of her temporary state of incoherence that only lasted a few seconds, or that she had put a scare into her new friend.

To Bummer's surprise, she seemed to respond to a question which he hadn't asked: "Oh; it was such a simple song—too elementary for the rest of you good players, I'm sure! For me, it was fun playing along, even though I didn't know what I was doing."

"Ah-h—it was a classic," Bummer said, cautiously playing along with her game, not understanding what had just happened, miffed that he didn't know why Margo had spaced out on him.

Margo impulsively turned to leave.

"Hey—I'll show you how to pick out that guitar—the guitar you asked about."

Margo stopped and turned around, confused but remembering that she had indeed just asked Bummer that very question. "I'm losing it," she joked and walked back.

"Imagine that—we're both goin' to the music store, at the same time!" he said.

"Oh—well—don't read too much into that, Bummer," Margo joked, as she got her mind back-on-track and led him into the store. "But we did show up at the same time."

Chapter 31
A Beauty

As the door shut behind them, Margo gazed down the long row of stringed instruments that filled the wall, for the entire length of the store. "Wow, guitars everywhere!"

"Yeah; good ones and the . . . not-so-good ones. If ya wanna play bright-sounding Bluegrass, just skip over all these first guitars," Bummer advised. "The Bluegrass crowd only wants to hear acoustic —just the sound that vibrates off of *real wood*."

Margo was impressed with Bummer's knowledge of the instruments. "Just a wooden guitar—the basics. That's what I need!"

Bummer passed over the beginner-quality instruments. "You should probably choose a quality guitar," he said, lifting a flat-top guitar from the first row, rear wall. "This baby'll cost ya more than a grand, but you'll never regret it. Just listen to the sound—"

All six strings responded to Bummer's experienced fingers, vibrating with a loud but mellow sound that filled the music store.

"Gee—that's . . . not bad, but you're a maestro," she said, impressed.

"Not bad?" Bummer grinned, then strummed a full bar-chord. He continued by smoothly and rapidly plucking a series of ascending notes, culminating at the resolve of the G-run. "Far out!"

Impressed with his John Denver-like exclamation and now feeling the excitement, Margo reached for the guitar. She confidently gripped the neck in her left hand, ready to start.

The store clerk, Harvy Wead, suddenly appeared and towered over her. He adjusted his thick glasses and cleared his throat, making it plain that he intended to make a sale.

Looking up, Margo was startled to see the tall, balding man, bending over her. His blue, fluttering eyes seemed tiny, to her, the refraction viewed backwards through his pop-bottle-like lenses.

"You're holding six strings of pure bliss, Young Lady! What's your name?" the scary-looking clerk asked.

"I'm Margo Toralf; mostly a singer, but I need a guitar."

"Well, you found my finest acoustic guitar, Little Missy, right-off-the-bat! Natural Mahogany—*a beauty*! How do you like it?"

"I like it . . . very well," she said, even though she hadn't actually tried it out yet.

"What do you do, Miss Margo?" Mr. Wead probed.

"Oh, Bluegrass and Country. I can sing Rock, too."

"No!" Mr. Wead laughed, then hacked at a frog in his throat. "I mean, what do you *do* for a living? Can a young lady, like you, afford to buy my highest-priced instrument?"

"Oh!" Margo almost laughed but was irked by the patronizing question. "I thought you meant—"

"She's a Bluegrass friend of mine, Harv," said Bummer, cutting in protectively.

Margo instantly became angry, her feminine proclivity insulted, nothing lost as a proponent of women's personal rights, ever since the 1970s. "I'm a professional woman with a high-paying job," she said boldly, not letting anyone speak for her. "I'm a nurse, and a damned good one!"

All eyes were on Margo, followed by commanded silence.

She held the beautiful instrument up, almost touched it with her lips, and admired the fine details of its construction. She liked how the expensive-looking finish brought out the subtle colors of the exquisitely figured wood grain. It caught the light, shiny with luminous depth.

"Try it, Margo," said Bummer. "You can do it!"

Margo open-plucked the strings, each just one stroke. "Good tone."

"Good? That's impeccable," Harvy said. "They don't make 'em any better!"

"I'll take it!" Margo announced, wanting to impress the others. She giggled, "I love it!"

Bummer was flabbergasted. "Aren't you going to . . . try it . . . first? It's big bucks—"

Margo felt rich, writing a check for the full amount, not giving it a second thought. And she carried her new guitar to her car, enclosed in its handsome hard-shell case. She put it into the trunk of her car, before going into the furniture store.

The furniture store was an interesting place, to Margo. She was weaving through the turns and bends of the floor displays, browsing the amazing variety of living room sets when she was suddenly pursued by three members of the sales staff. The leader of the gang carried a brown clipboard, a credit application clipped under the clamp. He immediately began pumping her for personal information, seeking financial data, and generally making her feel anxious.

That was *enough* for Margo; she didn't feel like explaining that she had a job and that she could afford to buy furniture. An odd sensation flooded her head, compounded by the frustration of high-pressure sales tactics, causing her mind to spin. Overwhelmed, it didn't take long for her to walk away from the furniture debacle.

Deciding to go straight home, she drove down the main drag of Burntwood Prairie, daydreaming about expertly playing her guitar—someday. She was contently humming a Willie Nelson tune, before noticing a cherry-top tailing behind her.

"I'm not speeding," she said worrisomely. "I'd better not get stopped, twice, on the same day!" She made a panicky right turn. The officer followed.

"That was a test, and you failed it, Mister Policeman! Who are you, and what's going on?" She drove around the block, observing all traffic rules, then turned back onto the thoroughfare. The police car followed. This time, partway through the turn, she glanced backward and recognized the officer. It was her stalker, the ugly deputy.

Her heart pounded. A chill of fear shot up her spine. She slowed down, near a traffic signal that was about to change. When the light turned to amber, she promptly lunged across the intersection, leaving the patrol car at the red light. That didn't stop the officer; he ran-the-light to catch up.

"That was stupid! What's going on with this jerk?" She made a quick left turn, down a residential street, and stealthily turned into a driveway. When the patrol car shot past, in search of her faded automobile, she backed out and sped home. She lost him.

Chapter 32

Margo's Manic Dream

Margo saw Brian's truck parked by the apple tree when she drove up her driveway. She parked under the oak tree, as usual, but had a different awareness about her favorite parking spot. Since she was the new owner, the parking space actually belonged to her, a satisfying feeling.

Brian's slouchy body was lounging on the deck, lying in wait of her arrival when he heard Margo excitedly shout to the sky, "It's mine!"

Brian hated it, that she deliberately rubbed-it-in that way, triggering his pent-up hostilities, old feelings that he had never put to rest. Plus, he was already stewing in new anger, over Margo's surprise-purchase of the farm. He'd missed his chance and was ticked off.

Scornfully, he watched his sister carry a large shopping bag to the house, the very house where they both grew up. He jumped to his feet, got right behind her, and followed her up the steps into the kitchen. "So—you're the privileged one!" he verbally attacked.

Margo was expecting a rude display of sibling rivalry. Apparently, this was it.

"What are you talking about, Rowdy, some problem over the farm?"

"I would've bought it, and could've paid for it as soon as my ship comes in." Harbored feelings of envy were erupting. He unloaded on her, insults and accusations. "By the time I heard about the farm-deal, it was already sold!"

"Dad said I was the only kid who had the income to pay for it. He needed the money, not a promise to pay someday in the far-distant future."

"You didn't pay *real* money; you got a loan—a bad deal, at that!"

"My banker would've told you nothing about my personal finances."

"Dad told me what you're paying for a mortgage. You got screwed!"

"I did not! I'm proud that I'm a successful woman; got my own financing without the help of any man!" She was mad at Brian for complaining, and felt betrayed that her father hadn't kept any of it confidential. The argument went on, but she brushed it off; however, furious that her brother knew the details.

"I bought it . . . fair-and-square! What's your beef? You hate this house; why?"

"You can have this crappy, old house!" he said, glancing about the room with disdain. Peeling paint. Torn wallpaper. A worn-through linoleum floor and dingy cabinets with broken hinges. "I wanna build a new house on the south forty. Sell me some land, Margo! I only need a small piece of ground."

"In-a-pig's-eye! What kind of a farm would I have, if I sold part of it to you? Besides, I don't want neighbors—not that close!"

"What do ya need that south forty for? It'll just cost ya, in extra taxes."

"It's part of the farm. It would never be a *real* farm again, without the land."

"You don't need all this land. What for?"

"Horses. I need the grazing area . . . and the hay. Horses eat hay—you know."

"You'll never make this old place into a horse ranch. That's just a childhood fantasy. I'm tired of bending over backwards, like I've done for years, for *Margo's Manic Dream!*"

That remark triggered her anger. She pointed a shaky finger, "Don't you ever say that word again, Rowdy!" Her face turned beet-red with fury. "Remember our family meeting? All that . . . *manic talk* is to be dead and buried!"

Brian knew that any critical mention, true or false, of her state of mind would trigger a hair-on-fire response. It was the sort of rage he could have predicted and should have avoided, yet he often enjoyed stirring the pot. Once she lit into him, he held his tongue, having both fear of and respect for Margo but glared at her anyway.

After calming down, a few notches, Margo tried to sound reasonable. "You liked the horse-ranch dream, Rowdy. We rode together, when we were kids."

"Yeah; *me* on the plow-horse, and *you* on Black Lightning. Dad always gave you the best; and for me, nothin', except the short-end-of-the-stick. All I ever got to do was milk cows, shovel manure, and plow the fields!"

"That's how it works; we helped run the farm. Otherwise, none of us would've eaten."

"I hated all of that."

"Then, why would you want to build a house on the very-ground that you despise? Beat it, Rowdy! Come back for a visit when you get over this . . . farm-jealousy thing."

"Whatever you say, Manic Margo!" Gritting his teeth, he was gone in a second.

Chapter 33
New Cowgirl Outfit

Margo couldn't wait to wear her new western-style clothes. She carried her packages upstairs and changed into her *new cowgirl outfit*. She stood in front of a mirror and admired the fit, saying, "I like the way these jeans cling to my butt!" She pulled and poked the collar on her new shirt and brushed at the embroidered, butterfly designs with her fingertips. "I wish Maria could see this."

When fluffing her hair and gazing in the mirror, she began humming the tune, *Red River Valley*. A tear came to her eye, the lyrics hauntingly reminding her, again, that Maria was tragically gone; not only gone from the Red River Valley but gone from her life—gone forever.

There was a noise, a thud on the porch. The kitchen door opened with barely a sound. "Margo, are you in here?" came her father's voice.

"What is it, Daddy?" she called down the stairwell.

"I see that Rowdy left. What'd he want?"

"Oh, Daddy, what do you think he wanted?" she said, whisking down the steps, dressed in her new duds. "He wanted to argue over the farm."

P. G. Knudson

"That's what I figured," he said, not seeming to notice Margo's new clothes. "I heard fightin' words—your mom and me did; heard the whole thing from the trailer house. It was gettin' kinda loud, over here. I wanted to be sure he didn't—"

"Why did you tell Rowdy my private financial information, Daddy? He has no business knowing about my mortgage."

"Oh—I'm sorry, My Little Princess. He's a knucklehead, but he asked me, so I had to tell 'em; he's family. Are you okay with it, Sunshine?"

"No—no, it's *not* okay! He thinks I'm stupid and that I'll lose the farm, if I ever default on the loan! That can't happen, can it, Daddy?"

"Gee—I don't know. It's happened before—ya know—to others. You put the farm up, for collateral, after all—"

"That doesn't mean that I'd ever lose it, does it?"

"Not if ya keep your job . . . and pay all your bills on time, especially the monthly mortgage payments. That's all I know—"

"So, what does that mean, that I'm just the same as renting, until the bank takes it away? Why didn't you—?"

"You didn't bother asking for advice *before* you went off and made your own deal. Did you read those papers, before you signed 'em?"

Margo stood mute, chagrined, like she had been fooled by someone; tricked, because she was a girl, like her brothers had always done to her in the past—always tricks, someone playing upon her perceived female weaknesses.

"But you've got a good job; you can make it." He hugged her shoulder. "Just don't get lazy and stay in bed, for several days at a time. It's important to show up for work, every day—no matter what

154

—just like farming, taking care of livestock every day, even if ya don't feel like it. You can do that, can'tcha?"

Margo bit her lip and massaged a sudden pain in her forehead. "Doggone it! Whatcha do that for, Daddy? I don't want Francine to know, and any of the others; they don't have to know the details. It's confidential!"

* * *

Hoping for a cup of coffee, Hank sat down at his daughter's table. Nothing to drink. He couldn't relax, hearing the sound of restless boot-heels back and forth on the floor.

"The day's half-gone, and I still have to buy horses. How did you do on the fence this morning?" She saw the surprised reaction on her father's face.

Hank had started the mundane task, earlier, but took a break and forgot about it. He was in trouble, and knew it. After stalling for time, he finally said, "I had a senior moment."

"I thought you'd be done, by now! I don't want the horses to escape, as soon as they get here. The fence has to be fixed, and strong enough to hold them!"

That sounded like an order, something Hank had never had to deal with before; not since his father ran the farm, long ago, before he passed away. With his daughter now in charge, he was stuck in a subordinate position, a role-reversal, a technicality that he hadn't even thought of.

"I'll . . . get right to it! By the way, Aunt Pearl brought over some stuff for ya, today, when you were gone."

"What stuff?"

Hank led her through the house, pointing out the hand-me-down pieces of furniture that he and Brian carried in, earlier when she was in town.

Margo expected to see empty rooms, bare to the walls. Seeing a worn-out sofa and a mismatched chair, the only pieces of furniture in the living room, was a letdown.

"I refuse to sit in that ugly stuffed chair! Why didn't Aunt Pearl give me her big, color TV? Shoot—that would've been nice!"

"Ha!" Hank laughed. "She'll never give away her color-television-set. It's no secret: she never misses a chance to see Bill Clinton on the news. She claims she bought it, the day before the inauguration, so Butch could watch the Bill Clinton festivities. But if ya ask me, she bought it for herself, so she could admire President Clinton in full color. She loves him. If she had the chance, she'd hog-tie 'em and kiss 'em to death!"

Margo stared at her father, like she didn't believe what she was hearing and like there was no humor in knowing that Aunt Pearl was going *gaga* over the new president.

"What about the philandering accusations?" Margo asked argumentatively.

"Huh—you mean the political mumbo-jumbo, meant to discredit our fine president?"

"I think some people believe Paula Jones' story," she said.

"I hope ya didn't buy a bed. Aunt Pearl gave ya a good, solid bed, made of steel," he said, steering clear of any political innuendo.

"Did Aunt Pearl know that I had to sleep on the floor last night? She should've brought me this stuff yesterday!" Margo followed her father up the stairway, to see the rest of it.

"Nice bed, huh?" her father said, sounding nothing like a furniture salesman.

"Oh, it'll do," she said, a blue note hanging from every word. "I saw it, when I was just up here, but I was preoccupied with my new clothes." She jumped onto the bed and rolled over. The springs squeaked, and she sank far-into the sagging mattress. She began to laugh, "How old is this thing? Did Aunt Pearl bring it over on the Mayflower?"

Hank chuckled. "Kinda soft, ain't it?" He tested the mattress, both fists thrust down into the quilt. There was a twanging sound, coming from the stretched-out springs as he vigorously shook the bed with both hands. He smacked his lips. "We'll be able to hear this, way over at the trailer. It's good enough, though, ain't it?"

"It's junk, Daddy, but what are relatives for? To give you all their worn-out crap!" she laughed woefully. "It's no good, but I need it. What a pathetic life, huh? Even with a job, I don't have money for good furniture—not yet anyway." She struggled to climb out of the swayed mattress, sat motionless on the edge of the bed, and listened to the irritating sounds of its worn-out springs.

"So, what did you do in town—all that time?"

"Daddy! Can't you see?" she said, instantly changing her mood and jumping to her feet. She twirled around on the heel of one of her new boots. "I bought cowgirl clothes! See my saddle boots, embroidered shirt, and jeans?" She stepped back and showed off the tops of her boots, making sure he saw the finely stitched design that half-covered the calves of her legs.

"Wow—too nice to wear in the barn, but just whatcha need to stay in the saddle! Is that belt buckle . . . *real* silver?"

"Guess what else I bought, Daddy!"

"Me—guess? I don't know how a man can guess; never been able to figure out—"

"It's a special surprise, Daddy. It stays a secret, until you come to my car and see it!"

Chapter 34

Unveiling of the Guitar

Margo pulled at her father's hand, then ran ahead, wanting the *unveiling of the guitar* to be a special moment. Hank followed; but before he could catch up, Margo had sprinted to her car and opened the trunk. She lifted the fine instrument from its case.

"Look, Daddy!" She said excitedly, then strummed her thumb across the open strings.

Hank had to blink, to believe his eyes. The golden spruce top glowed in the sunshine. He leaned on the fender, expecting to hear a song. "Can you play it?"

"Just learning," she said, moving her hands into position. "Listen to this!" She tried to make a fretted note, but there was no connection between her fingers and her memory. She thought she knew the G-chord, but failed at each attempt to play it, not realizing how difficult it would be to perform in front of her father. "I need practice," she admitted. "I'll play you a song, one of these days, after I get good at it."

"Good! I'd like to hear your grandmother's favorite, *Red River Valley*," he said.

Margo's smile disappeared when Maria's image came before her eyes. A tear ran down her cheek. "No. I love that song, but don't ask again; not that song, Daddy. It makes me cry for Maria. I don't know when I can sing that song again." She put the guitar back into its case. "I'll stop by Grandma's room and play a different song for her, one of these days."

"Well, I'm sure she'd like to hear any song you can do."

"Ah-h, it'll be great. And I feel great now; now that all the depression stopped."

"I'm glad the pills are workin'."

Margo suddenly pressed her fingertips to her forehead and closed her eyes. A splitting headache had hit suddenly.

"Are you okay, My Little Princess?"

"Leave me alone! It's from sleeping on the floor, last night. At least I have a bed now. And I—I—I quit taking the pills, Dad; don't tell Mom!"

"You . . . what? You can't go *cold turkey*! You *need* those things!"

"No, I don't!" she shouted angrily. "Stop telling me that!" She glanced toward the trailer house, hoping that her mother hadn't heard.

"Are you sure?" he asked, knowing that she was only fooling herself.

"I hate that useless salt—lithium! Hate it—hate it—*hate it*! Besides, I don't need it."

Hank somberly looked straight into Margo's eyes and listened to her rambling excuses, then looked away with abandoned hope.

"Who needs meds? I'm doing better without them, anyway. I feel like a new person, now that I'm back on the farm."

"But . . . *the highs*, Margo. I'm afraid, I'm gonna hafta catch ya someday, tryin' to fly out of the haymow!"

"Daddy, you promised to never bring that up again!" she whispered, rubbing the rough spot where her broken collar bone had healed, decades earlier.

With his fence-fixing assignment in mind, Hank had just begun walking toward the tall grass when Bette suddenly appeared, standing next to the car.

Startled by her mother's presence, Margo jumped, as if she had been jolted by an electric fence. "Oo-oo—Mom, you almost made me jump out of my skin!"

"I thought I saw a guitar, when I looked out the window. I had to come and see it," Bette said, a bit taken back by Margo's excessive reaction.

"Oh—Yeah, Mom. Take a look; isn't it beautiful?" she said, her mood switching like it functioned by an on/off switch. She reopened the guitar case.

"Wow—shiny!" Bette exclaimed, very surprised.

"Listen to the tone, Mom," Margo said, then plucked a few open strings. "I need practice, but I'll play a song for you and Dad, as soon as I learn one."

"Yeah, I heard you tell Dad—"

"What—you *heard*?" She instantaneously went into a rage. "What else did you hear? Were you *eavesdropping* on me, Mother?"

"Margo, you're sounding paranoid. Are you taking your pills?"

"Ah-ha—just as I thought—you were listening! You heard me tell Dad that I quit the pills!" she said, wagging her finger.

"Margo!" Bette gasped in shock. "You can't—"

"Mom! Why were you listening to me and Dad?" She tried to compress the increasing pain, then contemptuously raked her fingers slowly downward, glaring at her mother through bare knuckles. "Keep quiet about this, Mother—remember—family agreement!"

Bette nervously clutched at the collar of her house dress, afraid of betraying her daughter.

"First of all, Mom, there's nothing wrong with me—zilch!" she contended, taking an aggressive step forward. "But if anyone hears that kind of talk from you, they'll spread it around until everyone knows. Do you know what would happen, at work, if they find out about . . . you know what? I'd lose my job—and hey, the farm. Guess who's footing the bill now? You don't want the money to dry up, do you, Mother?"

Bette's eyes thrashed left and right. This is what she had feared, all along. "Well, of course not."

"If I lose my job, we can all say *bye-bye* to this farm; get it?"

Bette could not answer. She understood the stigma of mental illness that could follow her daughter for the rest of her life, if anyone ever learned of it.

Margo was in total control; to her, a satisfying feeling. Just one more detail—horses awaiting—living proof that she was now in charge and could handle any challenge.

"Now that I can come home to my own ranch, every night after work—from the only place where there might be stress—I won't need pills. Please let me start my life over, Mom—my new job, new friends, and new boyfriend."

"I wouldn't call him your *boyfriend*; he's almost my son-in-law. You should call him your *fiancé*," Bette said, nearly always seeking an argument.

"Oo-oo—whatever! Just remember, Stanley cannot know either! Got it, Mom? And forget about those pills; those days are *over*!"

"Whatever—"

"Like the doctor told us, years ago," Hank said to Bette, "this distraction—it's gonna crop up once in a while, but we all understand how to deal with it. We keep it in the family; outsiders don't need to know."

Bette tried to smile, knowing how fragile her relationship was with her daughter. "I like your new cowgirl outfit, Margo—the slim-looking jeans and gorgeous boots; and my-oh-my, I love the embroidery on the yolk of that shirt!"

"Me too; but I have to go, Mom. Mister Day is waiting!" She got into her car. "And Daddy, the mares are going to foal soon. This fence has to be ready when they get here."

"Margo!" Bette called out, seeing the car lunging ahead. "Stanley called. He said—"

"She can't hear you, Mother," Hank said, the car already speeding down the driveway.

"Ernie's coming," Bette half-whispered, mostly to herself, as she and Hank watched Margo's car turn onto the distant highway, headed for Charley Day's place.

"Great having her home again, huh, Mother?" Hank asked, still watching.

Bette's eyes listed. "Great? We'll all get to see the train wreck," she said, dread showing on her face. "What'll we do if she kicks us off this place? We don't have anything, in writing, for us to stay in the trailer . . . forever."

"Ah, no worry, Mother. We have a father-daughter understanding: she needs us . . . to raise Toby. She's not stable enough to do it, herself. Don't tell her I said that; she'd kill me!"

"Oh—the money she must be wasting today—the clothes, that instrument that she'll never use, and who knows what else. She has no common sense, when it comes to value. What did she say when she saw the nice furniture that Aunt Pearl gave her?"

"She hates it—all of it. Normal for her, though. She'll get used to it."

"Hard to please; nothing's ever good enough for her—never good enough or soon enough! I hope she doesn't say anything critical to Aunt Pearl. It was an act of generosity, on Pearl's part—you know. Margo's criticism can be sharp, sometimes. It would hurt Pearl's feelings."

"I'm gonna need some help with this fence, Mother."

Chapter 35
The Maternity Ward

Cut Across Road was the fastest way to Charley Day's ranch. In a western mood, Margo drummed her fingers on the steering wheel and harmonized with George Strait on the radio. The equestrian ranch-life that she had always wanted, the fruition of her lifetime dream, was only hours away. She could feel it coming, and just the thought of it gave her goose bumps.

The herd of yearlings rushed to peer over the top of the fence when Margo turned in. Feathers of the dreamcatcher danced wildly in the stiff breeze, giving her the feeling of protection from bad dreams. She loved the idea of that, the Indian tradition.

Mr. Day was pitching hay into a round-pen, but he was not alone. He was talking with two black-haired young men, while working. One man was wearing a black business suit, not expected in a place where manure meets shovel.

"Hey, y'all made it!" Mr. Day called out when he saw Margo approaching. The two younger men left immediately, without saying anything to her.

"I told you I was coming," Margo said, noticing that Mr. Day bore a worrisome expression, in spite of his polite greeting. She glanced at the departing men and asked, "Is something wrong? Did I interrupt you—something important?"

"Ah—no—just tribal business. We're in federal court, right now—many tribes, actually—trying to get our treaty rights restored. They were systematically stolen from us, never truly recognized. Old history; but at the time, nothing seemed more important than Westward Expansion."

"I don't get it," she said, empathetic probity showing in her eyes. "If you win, does this mean that Native Americans will finally be able to hunt and fish without being arrested?"

"If the judge will listen and order the government to recognize the Treaty of Eighteen-Thirty-Seven and the Treaty of Eighteen-Fifty-Four as valid—even today, more than a century-and-a-half later—everyone will soon understand. But that doesn't have anything to do with our business today—gettin' your butt back in the saddle."

Margo suddenly got a huge grin on her face and deliberately kicked a pile of fresh horse droppings, then faked a cowboy swagger, stopping next to the old Indian cowboy with her hands on her hips and a subtle smirk on her lips, like she wanted to promenade.

"Nice boots!" Charley remarked, accustomed to ignoring horse manure stuck to footwear.

"Thanks; just got them today. I have to look the part—you know," she said with a grin. "When I say, *I'll be here*, you can depend on it!"

"It's off to the square dance, then!" he said. The horse trader grinned, turned on his heels and offered his elbow.

She was game for the fun, accepting his arm.

Mr. Day took the lead, dancing her toward the birthing barn, eager to satisfy a paying customer. "Y'all bring money?"

Margo giggled. "Your mares have been dropping babies!" she said, frolicking by his side and matching his rhythmic steps, observing three mares in the new round pen, each with a new foal.

"Yowza; been a busy place. All of those young'uns otta be inside, but I hadda make room for the newcomers. Still want that one y'all ogled last evenin'—the Quarter Horse, or maybe the Appaloosa?"

"Can I look again . . . at both of them? I want two."

"Yes Ma'am!" he said, his grin now stretching across the entirety of his face. He lengthened his stride, proceeding at a fast clip.

Margo had to speed up, to keep pace in the spring muck, her new boots sloshing along. "Have either of them foaled yet?" she asked.

"Well, only the Good Lord knows. I ain't looked at either of 'em for the last two hours."

Margo followed Day into the foaling barn. It was quiet in that building. The dirt floor was freshly raked, a new sprinkling of aromatic cedar shavings scattered on its surface. And there was the clean odor of well-groomed horses.

"Marvelous," she remarked enviously, her horse-loving heart melting.

There was a mare housed in each of the box stalls. They held their heads high, over the tops of the doors, silently watching the humans walk past.

"I call this *the maternity ward*," he joked, then peered over each wall, looking for possible new arrivals. "No news," he said, after checking the last two stalls at the end. "These last two ladies are the mares y'all liked, yesterday, Ma'am."

He stepped up to the gate where an uncomfortably pregnant Quarter Horse paced behind the wall. He leaned both arms over the rail. The Chestnut mare tossed her head and nestled her nose against his shoulder. He reciprocated with a hug.

"Nice," she marveled, noting Mr. Day's gentle way with horses.

While patting the Chestnut's neck, the horse trader stuck to business. "Y'all got a long-term plan, Little Lady?"

"I want to breed horses," she said.

"Business, huh? Then y'all want *color*. Drab-lookin' horses don't attract attention. Buyers will pay more for quality, and the Appaloosa mare has a lotta future color-potential."

"What about the baby she's carrying?" Margo asked, holding her eye on that animal.

"I betcha, y'all know how the genetics of horse-breedin' works; it's a crap-shoot—probability formulas be damned. Ya never know 'til the little guy's born."

"I've decided, I want both of them. I have my checkbook," she declared, confidently reaching to her back pocket.

"Whoa, Little Lady," said Mr. Day. "In a cash-deal, I like to get crisp-lookin' greenbacks. I can sometimes accept a check, if you're certain that it'll be good—same as cash at the bank. Now, how will I know this . . . today? It's Saturday."

Numbed, her eyes almost twitched, trying to match Mr. Day's scrupulous stare.

"Since the banks are closed, and horse tradin' is more than just a bunch of galloping fun," Day continued, "let's go over the figures— price times two equals seventeen hundred. Now, compare that against your balance—not too complicated or too much to expect. Just doin' y'all an accounting favor."

168

Forget about Margo's steady poker-face; she was taken back, not expecting scrutiny of her bank account. She knew that Stanley's retirement money had been deposited, but she had no idea what her balance was. In fact, she hadn't summarized the extravagant purchases she had already made that morning. Her typical knee-jerk reaction would have been retaliation, but she was operating on longstanding respect for Mr. Day, through her father's friendship with him. She wouldn't allow her deep-down, fighting nature to surface. Or would she?

"Give me a few minutes, Mister Day," she said agreeably, but was fighting back hostile feelings of persecution.

Mr. Day politely left Margo in the birthing barn, by herself, to reconcile her checkbook balance so he could accept a large personal check.

Chapter 36
Larceny-First Mentality

Rather than putting Margo at ease, the silence in the birthing barn heightened her anxiety. Her mind surged with vacillating thoughts, from feeling that Charley Day was suspicious of her motives, to an overwhelming desire to cheat him. "How dare he mistrust me!" she mumbled quietly, not wanting the horse trader to know her mind.

Angry that he had asked her to go over her figures, she sat on a wooden bench under the light of a window and pulled out her checkbook. Blank lines; no entries in the ledger for past checks written. She searched through the carbon copies and painstakingly did the math, a chore she hated.

"There's not enough money left, to buy both horses, even after Stanley's deposit!" She was baffled with the shortfall of cash, especially the surprisingly small amount of value he had recovered from his retirement plan. "I can't believe it! Am I *really* going to marry this penniless man?"

She began thinking of ways to get around Mr. Day's cash requirement, an old *larceny-first mentality* that she thought she had overcome.

"Buy two, anyway—who cares—bounce a check."

She nervously stood up and looked out the window, fearful that Mister Day had been spying; but no one was there. Suddenly, a confusing dizzy spell hit. She slowly re-seated herself on the bench, feeling like she might teeter and fall off. She rubbed her forehead. Convinced it was nothing, just a bit of drug-withdrawal from stopping her pills, she scanned her eyes across the ledger again.

"Pay attention to the numbers, Margo," she mumbled quietly, "or you'll be back on those pills again!"

"Howz it goin'?" Mr. Day suddenly asked, having returned unnoticed.

Caught in her thoughts, and with her mouth open, Margo's nerves jumped. She was still considering bouncing a check but was also fearful of the consequences. "Hm-m; the choices," she began slowly, disguising her pernicious thoughts and leveling off her heavy breathing.

"It's six-a-one, half-a-dozen of the other; just like every other decision in life, Ma'am!" he said, utilizing one of his acquired Minnesota colloquialisms.

"You are so-o right!" Margo laughed nervously, battling her guilty conscience. She sensed that Mr. Day already knew the exact balance of her checkbook, its plastic jacket already slippery with sweat and her hands feeling clammy. Beads of moisture popped out on her forehead. She was trying to work up the nerve to write out a check for insufficient funds, aware that she was battling an internal dilemma over right-versus-wrong and knowing that the profession she had chosen requires a great degree of integrity. And it was unnerving that Mr. Day looked her directly in the eye. It seemed that he could see inside of her mind; that he could sense her struggle with moral turpitude. She felt caught and tried to look away, but his honest eyes locked on to her psyche. The tension was building up, and she couldn't fathom it.

"Y'all need more time, Ma'am?"

Margo was glad that Mr. Day said something. It gave her pause to reconsider. She changed her mind. She could not cross him, a long-time friend of her father and a fellow horse-person.

"Can I use my credit? I have a good job."

"Now, Miss Margo, howz about like I done told ya—a friendly cash transaction?"

"Oh—I know that, but I want *two* horses. Doggone it; the truth is, I only have enough money to pay for one."

"You know the answer to that, Ma'am; y'all see any banker in this barn?"

"Oh! I was just asking," she said, feeling relief, again realizing that passing a bogus check was both a bad idea and a crime. "You'll get your money today, for only *one*. I just can't scrape enough cash together to buy two, but I plan to buy another one soon," she rambled on, feeling embarrassed that she had even considered cheating Mr. Day. And she knew that if she had done it, she would have relegated herself to be no better than her thieving brother, Billy.

With her options reduced, Margo's choice was obvious. "I want the Appaloosa. I love that her foal could be a winner!" she beamed with excitement. "I want to get her home, before she pops!"

"Sold! Her name is *Flower*. See how the spots on her back look like a field of spring flowers? *Git yer* checkbook. I'll *git* the horse trailer."

Margo leaned on the stall-gate and stared into the mare's deep eyes. She took one long, full breath of calming air, pleased that she had made an honest deal with Mr. Day, probably the fairest man she had ever dealt with; and now, a horse-friend—for life.

Charley Day loaded the horse while Margo dealt with the payment. She felt a new closeness to Stanley, as she pushed the end-button on the pen. She scrawled out the check, against a rough board on the wall. Adrenaline shot through her veins, making her feel like she had an endless stream of pure gold at her disposal. She grinned, savoring the moment, feeling rich.

Spending lots of money, all at one time, reminded her of the frenzied days with Ernie: exciting trips to Las Vegas, money blown at a whim since he could afford it. But she also remembered how terrible she felt in those days of being a driftless mistress—her life, worth barely the cost of a wild weekend.

Margo's daydream was interrupted when the horse trader asked, "Y'all ready?"

"Easy come—easy go, Mister Day," she said with a chuckle and handed him the check, not even concerned that she had just blown Stanley's entire retirement fund in one day.

"Thanks, Margo," he said. "But now that we know each other, just call me *Charley*!"

"That's a deal!"

Charley Day read the figures on the check. "Whew! Now I can pay the boys down at the feed mill." After securing the mare in the trailer, he said, "I'll follow y'all!"

Chapter 37
Old Indian Friend

"She's back!" Hank announced, recognizing Charley Day's homemade doodlebug-pickup truck pulling a small horse trailer and turning by the mailbox.

"But we're not done yet!" Bette said. "She should've done this herself. Who has extra time to spend on her hobby? I should be cooking supper; company coming tonight, too!"

"Margo can pitch-in; no reason she can't help in the kitchen. She owes Ernie—big time. And digging her pond ain't the half of it! Your spaghetti, done up right on Mom's old cook-stove, could be the magic formula needed. Old flames might reignite; maybe a spark left—"

"One problem: she's not coming, not with Ernie here," Bette said woefully.

"Hm-m—this stubborn streak of hers—"

"She hates him! At least, that's what she says."

"Well, she says she's getting married to Stanley, too, but . . ."

"Don't hold your breath, Henry. There's something wrong with that situation."

"You're tellin' me!"

Speed Trap Murder

Margo parked in her space and ran for the barn, motioning Charley to turn in that direction. She proceeded to direct his backing of the trailer, next to the spot where Hank was setting a wood post. Bette stepped out of the way.

"Wait 'til you see her; she's beautiful!" Margo said, watching the slowly backing trailer. She raised her hand in the air, shouting to Charley, "Hold 'er there!"

Charley stopped the truck and shut off the motor.

Hank walked up to renew his acquaintance with the horse trader. He watched his *old Indian friend* open the door and get out. "Charley Day—do you remember me?"

"You betcha, I remember y'all, Hank—you 'ol tit-squeezin' son of a dairy farmer!" Charley's smile beamed and he grabbed Hank's hand, shaking it eagerly.

"I'm surprised, ya haven't been deported, back to the southern range where *y'all* came from—you wild, Texas tumbleweed!" Hank joked.

Charley laughed. "Been a long time, ain't it? But don'tcha remember, Hank, Texas was never my *real* home? My *true home* is Minnesota. I told y'all about the *Last Indian Uprising,* how the shootin' got fierce and how my grandpa ran for his life. He left the Leech Lake Reservation in Eighteen-Ninety-Eight. Ended up in Texas, hidin' from investigators."

"Hm-m." Hank had heard Charley's story before, but couldn't remember the details.

"He didn't wanna disappear, like he did, but the federal agents were askin' questions. They wanted to know who killed Major Wilkinson at Sugar Point."

"Ah—now I remember—the gunfight. Who shot Wilkinson?"

"I don't know. It was *war*; people get shot in wars!"

"If nobody could be blamed, because it was *war*, why did your grandpappy run?"

"All the Indians ran. They won the battle, then scattered. They just wanted to be left alone. When the soldiers sailed their steamships back to Walker, everyone thought it was over."

"Well, it shoulda been over at that point, but . . . your grandpa—"

"Hell, that's when the cavalry rounded up every Indian in sight, lined 'em up to give 'em all Christian names, and told 'em to stay on the reservation."

"So, after the lineup, he took off?"

"The *Battle of Sugar Point* was . . . many moons ago. Grandpa escaped with his Ojibwe wife and his half-breed brother Thomas, long-before Daddy was born."

"And when you were a kid, you left Texas . . . for Minnesota," Hank pointed out, showing that he remembered parts of Charley's old story.

"I was fishin' with Daddy and his brother on the Red River, one day, on the Oklahoma line. The river was low; worst drought ya ever saw—Dust Bowl days. Life was tough, back in the Great Depression —ya know.

"Uncle Raven told us we wouldn't starve, if we went back to Minnesota to live off the land. He talked about our Indian roots in the Far-North, a place where my ancestors lived in peace; where they paddled birch-bark-canoes on clear waters and filled their bellies with venison, blueberries, wild rice, Brookies, and Walleyes. The food supply never ran out.

176

"I had only heard of Minnesota in family stories, but Uncle Raven knew the names—people and places. He missed this place.

"I was only six, but I got a feeling, a tugging at my heart to return to a place I'd never seen; a force I couldn't ignore. Daddy agreed. Before that week was out, he sold everything and bought a strong horse, a young Appaloosa stallion. Uncle Raven knew the way. I followed, riding bareback, my legs straddling the harness; baby sister and Momma in the cart, and Daddy running behind. We followed the dirt roads—over a thousand miles—to the land of my heritage," Charley recalled, wiping an emotional tear.

"That's quite a story, and prob'ly why I respect ya, Charley. Red River, huh? You moved from one Red River . . . to another Red River, the colder of the two," Hank said and laughed. They both laughed, in the way that old friends share memories.

Chapter 38
The Pregnant Appaloosa

Flower stood quietly in the trailer while the old men reminisced. "I still remember this place, y'all herdin' them Holsteins with a willow-switch and pitchin' hay with a three-prong fork," Charley said. "Seems like you did everything the old way, Hank—the hard way. Are the cows all gone?"

"Yup; decided to retire. It's my daughter's place now. There's the new owner, right there; you're lookin' at 'er!" Hank said proudly. "Been kinda lonesome around here, though, since I sold the livestock. Horses should make it feel like a farm again."

The anticipation was more than Margo could take, waiting to get her new horse on the ground while listening to old men talking like fence post philosophers. She giggled with excitement and boldly opened the back door of the trailer, herself. The rusty hinges croaked loudly when the heavy steel door swung open, almost by itself, from its own weight.

"Woah—y'all waitin' on me?" Charley quickly side-stepped his way into the trailer, showing he still had a lot of cowboy-dexterity left in him, slipping between the mare's wide belly and the steel-panel wall. "A cowboy hasta stay ahead of these horse maneuvers, to stay in control of the situation; don't want the four-legged critter to be the one who decides what to do. That's the definition of chaos!"

After working his way up to the horse's head, Charley untied the lead-rope. The Appaloosa backed out without any commands and stood alertly in front of everyone.

Charley looked up at Flower's head and admired the stance of *the pregnant Appaloosa*. "There's one helluva horse! Ain't she *perdy*?"

"Boy—she *is* beautiful!" Bette agreed. "Look at all those white spots—like a blizzard! She's fat, like a barrel, too!"

"She's full-term, Mom!" Margo giggled.

"When's that baby supposed to come?" Bette asked.

"Y'all otta know the answer to that, Miss Bette!" Charley laughed. "It'll be a surprise. The mare'll wait 'til nobody's around—my prediction."

"What are you going to do, Margo, when that foal starts to come, call a vet?" Bette asked.

"Mom! I'm a nurse—remember? It's the same as childbirth. Horses are just like people, except they're bigger . . . and they have four legs!"

Charley tossed four bales of hay on the ground, then threw a partial gunnysack of finely ground grain, on top of the last bale.

"This feed will gitcha started, Miss Margo. Give'er a coffee-can-full every day, especially after the foal comes. She won't produce enough milk, without the grain."

Margo carried the burlap bag into the barn. When she returned, Charley was ready to leave. He looked to the west at the darkening skyline, worried about the approaching storm.

"Gotta git home before the weather changes. See those black clouds over yonder? That means rain—tonight! Didja git yer fields planted yet, Young Lady Rancher?"

"No!" Margo laughed. "I might be a woman, but you can't fool me. It's too early for planting; corn seeds would rot before they have a chance to germinate!"

Charley smirked, then winked at Hank who was grinning with pride.

"It'd hafta be a cold snap in July to fool my little girl; she cut-her-chops on this place!" Hank said with a laugh. "Of course, her real smarts *wuz* all inherited!"

"Okay to brag," Charley said, just when a sudden gust of wind almost blew his hat off. He reached and caught the brim just in time. "Inherited her brain—from y'all, Hank? Maybe so, but it's plain to see that she got her good looks from her momma!"

Bette smiled, happy with the traditional, almost-obligatory compliment.

Charley put his hat back into place, facing into yet another strong gust of wind. "See? Big storm a-comin'," he warned, then pulled the brim down tighter and tilted it into the force of the wind, like any experienced rider would do. He gave Margo a wink. "Call me when that foal gets here, Miss Margo. I like to see 'em—ya know—after they're born."

"Yeah; sure, Charley," she agreed.

The empty horse trailer creaked as it tracked behind Charley's old truck, lumbering out the driveway.

"She should be in the barn," Margo said, "where it's safe."

"The stall's not ready yet. It won't hurt her, to be outside. She'll find a place to stand, out of the wind. I strung a wire around the lean-to, this afternoon. I'm thinkin', she'll prob'ly stand right there, under the roof. At least, we've got that much done. I'll take care of the repairs on the stall tomorrow."

"What about the fence, Dad?"

"It'll take me another hour; you'll have a small corral, when I'm done with it today. That's about it. You and Stanley can make it bigger, when you get around to it."

Margo looked critically at the cobbled-together, rusted wires, showing her dismay. "It's rusty, and this is *barbed wire*, Daddy—sharp and dangerous!"

"Well, the cattle never complained. You can replace it with barbless wire, if ya wanna."

"Hey, Daddy—no time to visit now. I have to clean up, to go *out*."

"*Out*—to celebrate?"

"No—to get out of here, before Ernie comes! How could you and Mom invite Ernie to dinner, then expect me to be here?" She ran to the house.

Later, Hank saw his daughter speeding out the driveway, just as he wound the last two strands of old wire around the corner post, then hammered-in staples.

Chapter 39
Petrified

Margo beeped *bye-bye*, seeing her father hammering on a fence post, then turned toward town, ignoring the last vestiges of the sunset being overrun by a black wall of clouds, the fast-approaching storm that Charley had warned of. The impending storm neither slowed her down nor impeded her racing thoughts.

Energized, since she had left just in time to avoid seeing Ernie Niceski, she forced her foot on the accelerator. Her mind was on expected good times at The Corner Bar.

Black clouds billowed above, as Margo searched the dial for some straight-up Bluegrass music. She couldn't hear the siren but saw the flashing lights closing in from behind.

"Police!" Her eyes refocused from mirror to speedometer. "Whew! At least I'm not going too fast, this time." She pulled onto the shoulder of the road and quickly slowed to a stop, turning down the volume at the same time. "I wonder what this jerk wants!"

With her foot on the brake, she reached for the buttons on her blouse, forgetting that she was wearing a western-style shirt. "Darn— pearl snaps!"

She yanked at her collar, popping two of the top snaps. She tried to flip the top open wider, but the starched collar retained its shape. Frustrated that her usual, diversionary routine was not going well, she glanced in the side-mirror. The officer was already out of his car and nearly to her door. She rotated the hand crank, lowering her window.

"You—again!" the officer lustfully snickered.

Margo's heart almost stopped. She recognized him, the ugly deputy, the same guy who had spooked her at the funeral, spoken to her by her mailbox, and chased her through town earlier that day. She was fearful, because the deputy seemed happy to see her again.

"Let's do this right. Good evening, Madam," the officer said, apparently starting over, sounding friendly but aiming a flashlight beam into her eyes, even though it wasn't dark yet.

"What's wrong, officer?" Margo asked, holding the top of her shirt closed, not wanting to suggest any ideas to this weirdo.

"You made a moving violation, Madam. Pull into the Roadside Rest Area. I'll be following, right behind you."

"I didn't do anything wrong, Sir. Why . . .?"

"Safety, Madam; it's almost dark. There's a streetlight, there, for your safety."

Margo glared suspiciously, since she had never heard of that sort of procedure.

"You can ask me anything you want to, after you pull in," he said, pointing to the entrance with his long, black flashlight that looked like a club.

Shaken, and not knowing the officer's actual motive, Margo slowly entered the vacant parking lot. Old visions of the same deputy flashed before her eyes, like still-photographs of his pimple-blemished face, plus total recall of their previous bizarre encounters. She steered into a parking space, directly under the one-and-only streetlight, and stopped.

The ugly deputy pulled alongside and immediately swung his door open.

Margo got a sudden impulse, to speed back onto the highway, but it was too late for evasive maneuvers. She was parked, facing the guardrail, and her motor was already off.

She quickly reached into the back seat, grabbed the sweatshirt that she remembered was there, pulled it over her head, then noticed that the deputy was standing by her door. He was thumping the heft of his long flashlight into the palm of his opposite hand.

"Step out of the car!" the officer said aggressively, seeming to position his feet for a wrestling confrontation.

Margo's heart palpitated. "Don't you want to see my driver's license?"

"Get out of the car!" his venomous anger surged, from zero to ninety-nine in one second.

Afraid, she clung to the steering wheel, wishing she had made a run for it.

Saliva dripped from the Deputy's lip when he repeated the demand. "I already know who you are; and don't give me any bullshit! I heard about your old Richard Nixon story!"

Margo obediently stepped outside. She finished pulling down on the body of her sweatshirt, fumbling with its lower edge, wanting it to fit correctly.

"Why the extra plumage?" he asked, seeming too concerned with her wardrobe.

"It's still wintertime," she said, reeling from his rudeness.

"Pretty-tricky maneuver you made, in town today; an illegal turn."

"Huh? I was following the law."

"I could arrest you—evading an officer."

"Was that you?" Margo asked, deliberately turning on the charm, one of her ticket-avoiding tactics. "If I had known you were so handsome, I would've stopped faster," she teased, hoping he'd back off.

She thought that her off-the-cuff acting would be convincing, confident that the officer would let her go; but that was not to be.

The deputy grinned, now seeming more relaxed, having something sinister in mind. "Do you really think I'm handsome?" he asked, followed by an obnoxious but accidental snort.

Margo refrained from answering that question, since it came across as being very weird. Fear flickered in her eyes, recognizing him to be dangerous, more so than just threatening.

"Can we talk, Mizz Margo Toralf?" the deputy asked, specifically using her full name.

"We're talking right now, aren't we?" Margo gripped one hand with the other, to stop the involuntary shaking, wondering why this officer had memorized her name.

"I mean, talk in a friendly way, like if we were playin' pool," he said, laughing coyly.

Margo realized that the deputy had probably seen her antics, out-on-the-town. "Not tonight; tomorrow would be better," she said, grappling for a way to get out of that situation. She tugged at the door-handle. "People are waiting—my husband—"

The officer angrily pushed the door shut, then grabbed her upper arm in the grip of his powerful fist. "Do not resist, Madam, or I'll place you under arrest!"

"This doesn't seem like . . . standard procedure. You're hurting my arm!"

"Go ahead and yell. Nobody can hear you out here. You just lied to me, Mizz Toralf. You don't have a husband! And you've been hiding from me, haven't you? You took off, after that funeral, too; gone a *lo-o-ong* time," he said ominously.

She recalled the deputy's penetrating stare from across Maria's casket, now realizing that he really had been stalking her.

"You didn't stay very long, to grieve for your friend—that blonde in the pine box."

That menacing reference to her deceased friend Maria made her heart gallop, spooked from thinking that this deputy could be Maria's killer.

"I want this discussion to take place at the Justus County Sheriff's Office, with the sheriff, himself, present!" she demanded, recognizing this situation was deteriorating rapidly.

The ugly deputy laughed cynically. "Request denied—you slut!"

"Do you think this is how a *normal* person picks up a girl!"

The insulted officer twisted his grip on Margo's arm. "What did you say, *normal*?"

Margo froze, fearing the twisted rage in his eyes, knowing that she was in trouble now. She had touched a malignant nerve in a dangerously insane person's head.

Suddenly his powerful grip spun her around. She flopped, like a rag doll when he dragged her, then kicked-open the trunk-lid. He grabbed an axe, closed the lid with one thrust of his head, and began marching her across the parking lot.

She saw how skillfully the ugly deputy flipped the axe, stealthily carrying it next to his leg. The polished axe-head was barely visible, hovering above the asphalt surface, then invisible in the weeds and brush. And she knew that Maria had been killed in a remote location, by someone with a hatchet.

Helpless, she became beyond-scared—*petrified*.

Chapter 40
Survival Dance

S ensing that her life would soon be over, Margo resisted, but pouting failed to alter the monster-like deputy's determination. And darkness was engulfing the periphery, the amount of light diminishing quickly as Margo was pulled further away from the parking lot, stepping over fallen branches, as together they plunged into the forest. He didn't stop until he got past the outhouses, almost out-of-reach of the beams of light which strayed from the single streetlamp. Once at his planned destination, he gave her a shove.

Margo almost fell but caught her balance. "What's the axe for?"

"What do you think?" the officer said, chuckling heinously. "It's all-yours, now; your name could just as well be carved into the handle." He suddenly swung the axe high into the air, pausing at the height of his swing to enjoy the frightened look on her face.

She felt like a caught chicken, an hour before suppertime with its head hovering above the chopping block. She closed her eyes, knowing that this was her chance to run, but imagined that Maria must have unsuccessfully run from a similar situation.

"You're free—skedaddle—one-two-three-go, Kiddo! Ain't ya gonna run-for-it?" the deviant deputy asked, fidgeting with the tapered grip of the handle.

Frozen in place, not wanting to be the running target that the dispassionate axe-man seemed to want, Margo stood silently.

The impatient axe-wielder quickly became frustrated, emitting a grunt of rage, then beginning a powerful downward plunge of the axe. The *thud* of the axe-head, burying itself in the sawn surface of a large Basswood stump, made Margo jump with fright.

"Don't kill me!" she pleaded.

"Eh-eh—ah-ha-a-a!" the deputy laughed hideously, then took off his gun belt and placed it on the top of the stump, perfectly aligned with the axe. He added his flashlight, meticulously keeping it straight, parallel with the other items on the stump. His evil chuckle was engulfed by the howl from a strong gust of wind, the storm testing its impending strength.

"What are you doing, Sir, undressing? Jammie time?" she asked boldly, although her voice shook with horror.

"Change of plans—just what you want—excitement at the speed trap!" the deputy joked. "You complimented me—my good looks—and lured me to this place. A date!"

"That's sick! What makes you think I'm interested?"

"You're game for it," he said, suddenly flashing a pair of shiny handcuffs in the sketchy light. He noticed that Margo seemed to be attracted to the glint of the polished nickel surfaces. "I'll save these for later," he said with a disgusting laugh, then loosely hooked them through a belt-loop on his uniform trousers.

Feeling trapped, Margo looked to her car, far away and situated under the streetlight, wishing she could run to it and speed away. But she already sensed that running would be a foolish idea, that she'd never make it. Still, she saw the axe gleaming in the partial light. Her quick mind gave her an idea, but she dismissed the impulse to grab it and defend herself. It might have been better if she'd already grabbed it and run.

Suddenly, the deputy stepped between her and the stump, putting an end to those ideas. He made a wanton glance, then started to brag about his primal abilities. Thinking quickly, Margo realized that her own abilities had to come into play; she had to do the only thing that came naturally to her, to somehow charm her way out of this ordeal.

She hated the thought of having to deal with the fetishes of an abusive man but realized that this wasn't the first time she had been thrust into a desperate situation with a pervert. Angry and fearful, she put that *boot camp* incident aside and tried to think.

"Escape plan needed, before it's too late," she whispered to herself, realizing that she was probably lucky to still be alive. She only half-listened to the boasting of the pitiful braggart who had abducted her, watching the handcuffs swing from his belt-loop like a hanging rope-swing.

"Like a rope," she almost whispered, a better idea forming—her ticket out of there.

Pretending to go along with the deputy's advances, she suddenly gave him a big hug, then made a swipe, trying to snag the handcuffs with hooked fingers. She missed.

"Hey! What are ya doin' down there—touchin' my leg?" the deputy said with a laugh. "You're more fun than . . . the crazy things, I've heard."

"Who told you about me?" Margo asked, trying to sound as flirtatious as a barfly, yet fearing that he might catch on to her plan.

"You're supposed to like it rough!" he said, forcing her body against his.

"Wait!" Margo objected, slipping free of his grasp, wanting another chance to seize the handcuffs. She glanced, one more time, and memorized where the cuffs were hanging—just to the left. "I'm going to teach you something."

The over-confident deputy grinned, hoping to learn a new, outrageous fetish.

"You've been going about it all wrong, officer," she said, smiling deceptively. Hoping another distraction would work, she threw her arms around his neck and planted a French kiss on his lips. "That's how it's done."

"Oooh-h!" The deputy relaxed, changing his disposition with the changing possibilities.

Seizing upon a flicker in his eyes, she took his hands, then backed him away from the stump, one short step at a time; almost like a waltz, except she was leading him away from the weapons that lied on top of the stump.

She recognized the rustling sound of persistent leaves, above her head, just as the shuffling of feet stopped. A two-inch-diameter sapling had caught the deputy on his backside. It was her last chance. She kept her *survival dance* in motion, pressing her body against his;

and his body shaking the small tree which stood erect at his back, the leaves quaking.

Surprised at his victim's unexpected aggressiveness, the delinquent officer hardly noticed the obstruction. The small tree flexed slightly, as he comfortably shifted his back to one side.

Margo knew she had to do something—fast; do it or forget it. Fear of dying drove her impulse to escape.

"You're not saying much," the officer said, pulling at her hand as Margo had taken a half step backwards. He tried to draw her nearer. "What's the matter—cat got your tongue?"

Margo grinned nervously, realizing that she had the loathsome brute standing right where she wanted him, leaning against a flexing but solid tree. She glanced to see the handcuffs again but had lost the beam of dim light. It was dark. She blindly reached, relying on her memory.

"What are you doing?" the aroused deputy asked, not realizing that Margo already had the shackles in her hand. "I'm ready for action!"

Margo's heart leaped. She found a stray beam of weak light, held up the handcuffs for him to see, and faked a flirtatious giggle.

The deputy snapped his head, in surprise, but was somewhat charmed. "What the Hell? You sneaky girl!" He laughed and shook his head, seeing the wide-open shackles dangling from her fingers, then shamelessly teasing him, one latch held between her lips.

"They're yours; you can have 'em. I bought 'em, special, just for you, Mizz Toralf. The soft leather won't bruise your wrists."

Margo was improvising her escape plan, one suggestive step at a time. She puckered her lips and gazed into her abductor's eyes, seductively playing into a dangerous game. It was too late to stop; she knew what she had to do, next, to stay alive.

The deputy gave a raunchy smile and began an evil chuckle.

Without saying another word, Margo suddenly took his wrist and hooked one of the cuffs onto it. She giggled devilishly when the officer flinched at the sound of the *click* of the locking mechanism. Wasting no time, she quickly spun around behind him, included the small tree in the hold of the chain and very deliberately clicked the second cuff onto his other wrist.

"So, you're into SM!" he said, and began waiting for sordid events to unfold.

Margo had successfully tricked the monster. He was tied to the tree but didn't know it. She stepped backwards, her knees shaking while marveling that she had gotten the upper hand.

Chapter 41
Run, Like a Scaredy-Cat

Margo watched the handcuffed monster test the strength of the chain, at first with gentle tugs, then with angry jerks, knowing that he had been tricked—outsmarted.

Miffed that he had stupidly let his guard down, the shackled deputy wrenched fiercely at the chain, testing the certainty of his newfound predicament: helplessness.

Frustrated that he had underestimated his victim, and that he had to immediately regain control, he crouched into a wrestler's stance, bracing his body to release a spurt of power. He took a double-deep breath, pumping up. Suddenly, with all of his strength, he surged his arms forward in one explosive jolt, expecting to break free. But, instead, the small chain held.

Margo was shaken, as she hadn't expected such a violent reaction. With bated breath, she bit at her knuckles, knowing that she'd be dead if the chain had broken. She heard his curses and saw the hatred in his eyes.

Now, it was her turn to fume, as she was angry, too. "Who do you think you are—you stupid bastard! Why are you harassing me?"

The astonished officer grunted, still yanking at the chain that pinned his arms behind his back. More persistent leaves fell, in front of his face, from his shaking of the sapling. One stray leaf landed on his shoulder. Margo stepped up, brushed the leaf away, and slapped his face.

"What are you going to do now," the deputy asked, acting tough, showing no apprehension, *"run, like a scaredy-cat?"*

Margo was close enough to spit on his face, but she didn't. After staring into his sunken–eyes that glared contemptuously, she strained to read his name tag. The glow from the distant light was barely enough. "Clarence Smith, Deputy Sheriff. Smith—that's your real name?"

The shackled deputy didn't answer.

"Why have you been stalking me, Mr. Smith?" she asked, in an unusually calm but domineering voice. "You were planning to assault me, weren't you, Officer Smith?"

"You're always game for a little action, ain'tcha?"

"Where'd you read that, on a bathroom wall?"

"Everybody remembers you. Your reputation stayed behind, when you ran off!"

"Everybody? Well, I've never heard of you—Smith—a real nobody!"

"I'm the best Deputy in Justice County. I got an award for *defending the public trust.*"

"You're a disgrace to your department and to the public—you pimple-faced pervert! And you don't look so tough, standing there with your arms around that baby tree—stronger than you—a Bur Oak!" she jeered.

The disgraceful deputy grinned, as if he had decided to enjoy this confrontation.

"Why don't you just leave me alone? I saw you stalking me by my house! Why don't you get a *real* girlfriend?"

"Huh; you're woman enough for me," he said. "I like your sassy tongue! Undo these handcuffs so we can get back to business. Still want to do the SM routine—here, or at your place?"

"Sadomasochism—with you? In your dreams!" she fumed. "You just stopped one girl too many!" she shouted and turned away, leaving him there, alone in the dark and tied to a tree with his own handcuffs. She started for the parking lot, feeling that the deviant cop had been humiliated enough.

The assailant looked through the growing darkness and saw Margo's silhouette against the light of the parking area, rapidly moving away.

"Hey! Where are ya goin'?"

Margo didn't answer but kept walking toward the cars. That would have been a good idea, to leave, then report the incident to Sheriff Anders. She had won the standoff and escaped, but had a pernicious thought: if he murdered Maria, she wasn't going to let him get away with it. Her suspicion grew. After all, Smith brandished an axe and threatened her, probably as he did with Maria. The not-so-coincidental similarities, comparing the murder of Maria to her own abduction, were becoming more apparent.

Seconds later, Margo had turned around and was walking away from the light, returning to the dark shadows, her mind full of questions.

"What's his axe really for? Why did he expect me to run? Did he tell Maria to run, too?" she asked, her voice muffled by the wailing wind. She had to know—now.

The invading arctic blast, not uncommon in Minnesota, made her shiver. Treetops swayed and pellets of sleet hammered the back of her head. She pulled up on her hoodie, as a downpour seemed imminent.

Once under the tall trees, her eyes readjusted to the darkness. She relocated the stump, then stared at the gleaming axe, wondering if it was the murder weapon. She visualized it flying through the air, the sharpened head striking Maria in the center of her back. She turned and glared at the ghostly-looking form of low-life that she had cuffed to the oak sapling. The restrained Deputy was staring back at her.

Wasting no time, she confronted Smith again. Sleet was snapping the persistent leaves, above the deputy's head, into a frenzy.

"You killed Maria, didn't you? I should leave you here for the coyotes, but you deserve to sit behind bars!"

"You're gonna end up in jail, when I get done arresting you, unless I kill ya first! Nobody's gonna believe your accusations!" the cuffed officer sneered. "The law's on *my* side! Just wait to see the charges, I'll levy against *you*!"

Alarmed by his violent potential, Margo backed away, fearing his threats as much as she feared his axe.

"You're in deep trouble now, Smartass—assaulting an officer! I'll see that you rot in jail! Or you can just swallow your white-trash pride and suck it up."

"You're crazy!" Margo screamed, then stomped her foot, tripping over something in the dark. She tumbled to the ground, momentarily lost in the darkness and entangled in the briars. She regained her bearings by looking toward the distant light, the only escape route.

Angry, she rolled over, rising to her hands and knees. There, right in front of her face, was the gleam of the axe handle. She had fallen next to the stump. She saw the Deputy's gun belt lying next to the axe.

Stunned, she had almost forgotten about the pistol, the weapon that was obviously strapped in its holster on the belt. Amazingly, all of it—the gun and the axe—lied directly in front of her within easy reach. If she'd picked up either one of them, she could have been in control, but she was scared and confused.

The precipitation temporarily stopped, leaving a strange stillness in the air; quiet, except for the sound of partially dry leaves crunching beneath the weight of her knees. Although she was free-to-run, she acted like she was trapped, not knowing what to do. She crouched lower, using the mass of the stump to block her assailant's view, fearful that the monster-like deputy would somehow free himself and attack.

"Hey! You out there . . . hiding! You won't escape me! I know where you live!" He laughed hysterically, panning the shadows and streaks of dim light that penetrated the brushy darkness, like a wolf trying to spot its prey. "I'll kill you, as sure as I can hear you breathing, right now!"

Chapter 42
The Absurd Proposition

A fraid to make a noise, or be seen, Margo stayed low. Slowly reaching above her head, she felt the smoothness of the leather strap and touched the cold steel of the gun barrel, wet with beads of precipitation. Her fingertips blindly recognized the feel of the pistol, a western-style revolver. She knew how to break a gun down and put it back together again, in the dark, if she had to.

Deputy Smith's angry voice radiated into the darkness. "When I get loose, I'll kill you—a promise! Nobody hog-ties me and gets away with it!"

That did it. Angry, she pulled the revolver from the stiff leather, turning it, trying to get a visible glance. A weak beam of light partially illuminated the metal surfaces.

"A Three-Fifty-Seven—and it's loaded!" Her fingers trembled, almost touching the tips of live cartridges protruding from the revolver's cylinder. With one hand over her mouth, she tried to muffle the sound of her hammering heart that echoed through her esophagus, throat, and out her mouth. A deep chill made her body shutter, dreading the confrontation in the offing.

Without a plan, and before she could level out her rapid breathing, she suddenly stood to her feet. Remarkably, she now saw the tied-up deputy clearly, as if she had found his flashlight. And with the revolver in her hand, she stepped forward, holding the grip of the pistol low, concealing the barrel behind her leg. Pulsating squirts of blood, inside her head, were painful.

"Oh, you're still here. I thought you were gone," Smith said.

"Did you kill Maria? Are you the *Hatchet Murderer*, Deputy Smith?"

"Hatchet?" The evil in Smith's laughter hissed from his lips. "It's an axe. Those stupid newspaper reporters can't get anything right!"

"It was you!"

"Damn sluts—I woulda killed both of ya, if you hadn't slipped away on me! Where didja go? I thought both of you whores were in the truck!"

"*You-u!*" Margo fumed, practically hearing an admission. "And *you* investigated the crime—surprise-surprise—no leads, no suspects —case closed?"

"It was disgusting—both of ya—swingin' from that tree, like naked simians!"

"What! You followed . . . from the swimming hole?" Margo's temper flared.

"I have rehabilitated myself!" Officer Smith laughed smugly, the sarcasm growing with his own amusement. His psychotic eyes glowed when they caught a spot of light, cast from the parking lot. "Let me loose. We can be friends."

Margo was *not* about to bargain with a murderer. She angrily lifted the revolver into view, deliberately holding it in such a way that Smith could see the glint of its shiny surface.

The cocky expression on Clarence Smith's face dropped. He was staring into the black hole at the business-end of his own pistol.

Although cowering, he acted calm, awaiting his chance to overpower his victim and regain control. He noticed the muzzle wavering; that the young Toralf woman was struggling with the weight of his hefty revolver yet had her finger on the trigger. He would wait her out, then make his move when she had a weak moment.

"Why-y?" Margo screamed, touching the coldness of the gun barrel against his face, shuttering at her own thoughts of vengeance that raced through her mind, realizing that she was angry enough to pull the trigger, if she wanted to.

"I was just minding my own business, then *you* and your siren! What—to rape me, or make me run so you could chop me in the back with your stupid axe!" She flashed the gun across the stray beam of light and zeroed it at the middle of Smith's forehead.

"So, you plan to shoot me . . . with my own gun? You'll never get away with it!"

Margo toyed with the pistol, again, liking how she could make the monster squirm.

"I can make it look like *you* killed your friend—that blonde! Don't doubt that, for a minute! You might not believe it, Missy, but I'm the only one who can get you out of this mess, now—now that you've gone too far!"

Margo was scared but ignored his defiant threats, knowing that she held the equalizer.

"If you shoot me, the department will track you down like a rabid skunk! But, if you know how to be smart, I can help you. I'm the only one who can—you know. Just *suck it up*," he said, simultaneously trying to kick Margo's feet out from under her.

Margo nimbly jumped out of the way. "How can I trust you, Clarence Smith—you poor murderer?" she jeered. "First, you suggest that I should run, so you can kill me with your axe. Then, you decide to rape me, instead; probably kill me later. Next, you threaten to frame me for Maria's murder. Now, you try to take me out by kicking me like a mule. I can't trust you as far as I can throw a dry cow-pie!"

"Just let me go. We can forget the whole thing. There's no evidence, and I won't tell."

"Yeah? But I will—I'll tell Sheriff Anders!"

"If you do, you'll be dead meat, just like the others—Maria and that double-crossing Martl faggot!"

"Oh—the boy, too? My, oh my—what a busy, low-life murderer you've been!"

"I saw the paperwork; it was *you* who found Martl's damn body! What are ya doin', checkin' up on me?"

"Oh—a paranoid murderer? And I'll bet, you're the one that Sheriff Anders calls his *number one deputy*. You cannot be trusted; you'd deny that you ever told me any of this. I can't let you go. How many other women have you done this to?" she asked furiously. The heavy gun weighed upon her hand. Her aim wavered. She reinforced her grip with her other hand, trying to rub away the pins-and-needles in her wrist.

"Ha—your hands are shaking! You can't hold a *hog leg*, not even with both hands!" he jeered. "You don't have the guts to pull the trigger! Think about it; we—that's you and me—we could be friends —partners, even!"

"In your dreams!"

"Unlike that stupid Martl kid, you've actually got some potential," he said, grinning, working on his own plan to escape. "With that rack of yours, betcha you could sell lotsa weed to those barroom drunks! We'll go twenty-eighty; that's twenty per cent for you, eighty for me."

"Oh—a drug dealer, too—maybe a little bit too convenient for a *protector of the public trust*? What makes you think that I'd go for a one-sided deal, like that?"

"Because I'm the only game in town; no dope-sales without my say-so!"

"Oh—an important man! But *the absurd proposition*—why so high—twenty-eighty?"

"Because I don't grow that stuff, and it costs money to get contraband to the point-of-sale. But your eight-ball scam—I'll letcha keep that measly profit, for yourself. How does that deal sound—fair enough? We'll be a helluva money-making team! Just unlock my hands and we'll shake-on-it." Smith's evil grin anticipated the unlocking of his handcuffs. "Reach in my pocket; get the key. We can both walk outta here, together."

Chapter 43
Hair Trigger

Clarence Smith leaned one hip toward Margo. "This pocket," he said eagerly, expecting that his intended victim had bought his spiel and was actually considering his nefarious offer.

Not trusting the murderer's long reach, Margo took another step backward. The shadow was deeper there, a better place to think. And out of the killer's clear vision; but her pause was not to consider his offer. She knew it was a ploy, buying time until he could strangle her, shoot her, or take advantage of another axe-throwing opportunity.

She had heard, on the street, that Smith was an oddball; but now she knew he was more than that, a homicidal madman. He admitted killing Maria Richardson and Martin Martl, facts that she wouldn't be allowed to take home with her. No way that he'd let her live; not to *tell* about it. She already *knew too much,* and she was aware of it. She had to be careful. He was desperate and would *not* be brought to justice.

"Hey, I'm waiting. What about our deal?" he called out.

Margo heard him. And she was done thinking about it—done with his lies and deceptions. Anger roared like a train—a torturous whistle inside her head. She wanted to leave before her head exploded.

Speed Trap Murder

The wind picked up. Swaying trees bent the sparse rays of light, causing alternating blackness and glimpses of discerning light.

Her fingers flexed, loose but comfortably closing on the grip of the pistol. Fury lit up her face. It looked red, even in the dark. With ice water in her veins, she took a step forward, giving the cylinder a spin, almost like she used to make the roulette wheel spin for Ernie Niceski, in Vegas. She coldly pulled the hammer back with her thumb; surprised, though, that it pulled effortlessly; fully cocked, ready to fire, before she had realized it.

Clarence Smith recognized the clicking sounds of the rotating cylinder. Even knowing that three chambers were empty, as he always carried it, he knew the odds; but now that she had randomly spun the cylinder, messing up his safety protocol, it was highly probable that a live cartridge had rotated into position, directly under the firing pin. He became terrified, not liking this version of Russian Roulette, the odds now impossible to calculate.

"Hey—wait a minute! There's a *hair trigger* on that thing!" he shouted in a panic.

"What was that you wanted me to do, Mister Smith? Open your mouth—you pervert. Suck on this!" She shoved the cold steel barrel into his mouth, in the space of a heartbeat, then mocked him. "Why don't you try to kick me now—you murderer?"

She heard him groan; however, there was no satisfaction in hearing it. "Get this straight, you axe-murdering freak: we are *not friends*! And I could *never* be any kind of *partner* with you. What are you going to do, if I let you go, turn on me, or leave me alone?"

Clarence's attempt to answer was futile, with the barrel of the gun obstructing his tongue. And, with panic in his eyes, it seemed that

Smith was looking far beyond her shoulder, maybe all the way to Eternity, mumbling something; but Margo couldn't distinguish his words.

Satisfied that the standoff was over, she decided that Officer Smith had had enough. She had won. As abruptly as she had shoved the gun into his mouth, she began to retract it, feeling vibrations of the steel barrel scraping across chattering teeth.

Without warning, the hammer suddenly fell.

BOOM!

The explosive sound of the fatal gunshot cracked sharply, instantly popping her ears, sending them into spasm. Persistent leaves flew, as the back of the man's head sprayed behind, into the black night. Margo fell backwards, the hefty pistol slipping from her numb fingers as if there had been no recoil.

Chapter 44
Pungent Gun Smoke

Snowflakes fell silently, landing cold on Margo's face, finding her dazed. She was lying flat on her back, her jeans wet and her head roaring. Her left ear rung the loudest. A trace of *pungent gun smoke*, an odor she recognized, bit at the insides of her nostrils.

Although disoriented, and feeling like she'd been kicked from her pony, she remembered being surprised by the intense *snap* of the gunshot.

"What happened?" she cried out. "I didn't pull the trigger!"

She glanced at the distant streetlight, only long enough to regain her bearings. She saw the stump, then the gray glob slumped at the base of the oak sapling, knowing that he had been shot dead. She almost cried, knowing that the dead man was an officer of the law, but she could not. Maria was dead, because of him. Plus, she, herself, was his intended target at the time of his demise. Her anger, over the whole ordeal, overshadowed any feelings of compassion. She glared at his undefined form, slumped like a dead skunk shot behind the pig barn.

"I can only cry for Maria," she blubbered, realizing nothing could change what had happened.

She instinctively became very alert. The acrid smell from the shooting was gone, rapidly carried away by the wintery wind. Tree tops swayed. The frigid air whistled through the dormant branches far above the crime scene.

Thinking clearly, it only took Margo a moment to realize that the gun-barrel had not been fully retracted when the shot rang out, and that her fingerprints were all over the officer's gun. She imagined how the cops would love to find easy fingerprint-evidence like that. And she was acutely aware that the deputy had been right about her reputation, one of a louche woman.

"My version of his confession would be worth squat, and my past sins would only drag me down in any legal proceedings," she decided, then heard a dog barking in the distance. "Probably a farm dog," she said with some concern, increasing her fear of getting caught. "I have to get out of here, and fast!"

First things first. "How to make it look like I was never here? Find the gun and wipe it clean. Otherwise, the evidence will point straight at me. But where is it?"

She was experienced enough to know that a powerful recoil would have flipped the gun, so it could be lying anywhere, probably far from the body. She took short steps in the darkness, methodically kicking her boots in the duff, hoping to easily locate the gun. She shuffled slowly, systematically, but quickly made it to the site of the shooting, only a couple paces away, without finding the weapon.

Having reached the slain monster, but not yet finding the gun, she almost panicked. She dropped to her knees and began to crawl, blindly searching the forest floor. A cold rain returned. She raked her bare fingers through layers of wet leaves, desperately trying to find the weapon.

In her frenzy to find the gun, she barely noticed the pain from brush that slapped her in the face and the blackberry thorns that tore at her skin. Finally, her desperate attempt to find the gun paid off; she found it lying much closer to the body than she had expected.

"Fingerprints," she bemoaned, keeping her chore focused. She groped for something to use, something that would work like an eraser. "My sweatshirt," she quickly decided, stripping it off. She began wiping her prints off the gun but couldn't see a thing.

"Like a suicide—yeah; make it look like he shot himself," she repeated in the darkness, blindly pressing the cold fingertips of the dead man against the metal surfaces, up and down the muzzle and on the grip. She carefully laid the pistol down on the ground, just about where she had found it, still holding it with her sweatshirt, not wanting to touch it again.

In a hurry to leave the scene, but still concentrating on details, she found the key and removed the cuffs. Freed from the tree, the body fell forward and into a heap, over the top of the gun. She held up the handcuffs to the distant light, still attracted to the alluring sheen.

"One too many clues to leave behind," she reasoned and tied them inside one of the sleeves of her soiled sweatshirt. "Besides, he said they're mine."

The dog barked again, much closer this time. She began a hurried escape. Snow was falling heavily when she stopped at the stump, wiggled the axe loose, and ran to her car. Under the bright light, she saw blood on her jeans. She scrambled, finding a paper grocery bag on the floor of her car, stuffing the blood-soiled sweatshirt into the bag and finding a place to lay the axe on the floor. Grabbing her baby's blanket from the back seat, she spread it across the driver's seat to avoid smearing any blood onto the upholstery.

She turned toward the farm, just as the heavy squall of snow was starting to accumulate.

Chapter 45
The Absconded Axe

Margo turned by her mailbox and quickly switched off the headlights, then slowly steered up her driveway. The yard light, midway between the barn and the house, lit up the entire yard, making her farm look as beautiful as a snowy Christmas card. And Flower, the expecting mare, stood fast in the shadow of the barn.

"God, I should have stayed home," she moaned in anguish, then saw that somebody's car was parked in her spot.

"Ernie—he's here! I can't let anyone see me, especially him!"

She veered off the driveway, crossing the grassy front yard and just missing the pile of discarded furniture that her parents had thrown out. She parked in the shadows by the Boxelder trees where her car was partially hidden. Snow flurries swirled, as she got out of her car. She feared that Ernie, or her father, would suddenly come around the corner of the house and confront her. No one came.

There was muted laughter coming from the trailer house. All the lights were on, lit-up like it was a holiday. She stealthily carried *the absconded axe* past the rear bumper of Ernie's new luxury-ragtop, then to the tool shed.

"Why bring home a souvenir?" she muttered. She knew why: he said it was hers; and for her, it was something to remember Maria by. "No one would understand, but maybe no one will ever notice it either. And I need an axe for splitting firewood." Comfortable with her rationalization, she leaned it against the inside-wall of the shed, then dashed to the house.

She avoided all switches on the wall. Reflected illumination, from the yard light, was enough to navigate the house in the dark, as she had the layout memorized since childhood.

She threw the bloody sweatshirt into a large garbage bag and carried it to the bathroom, a windowless room. There, she closed the door, turned on the light, and looked in the mirror for the first time since the shooting.

"Red dots!" she whimpered. "This is no good—blood—bloody spots everywhere!" She pulled at strands of her hair, finding dried blood that would not rub off.

"My clothes—my new cowgirl clothes—ruined with blood!" she cried. "And smears on my new cowboy boots! What should I do?"

It didn't take Margo long to decide that all of her clothes had to be thrown away. "I can't take any chances," she mumbled, methodically stuffing each item into the garbage bag.

After showering, Margo changed her mind about the boots and the belt, with its precious silver buckle. Determined to keep them, she frantically scrubbed the tooled designs on the leather and the fine stitching of each boot. She scraped and scrubbed until she was sure that the smears of blood were gone. "I'll use these in the barn and wear it off!"

While dressing into an old pair of faded jeans and a cotton shirt that she hadn't worn in years, Margo remembered the handcuffs. She dug into the garbage bag and retrieved them.

"Good; the key's still in the lock!" She smiled, pleased with her new acquisition. Under the bright light above the vanity, she admired the smooth nickel surfaces and the patent leather design. "They're elegant!" She spent several minutes, using her toothbrush to scour the copasetic shackles, meticulously brushing each tiny joint to be certain that all blood was washed away. "These are *keepers,*" she grinned, then placed them in a drawer by the sink.

She dashed back and forth through the dark house, in a hurry to leave. "It's Saturday night, and I'm going out," she said. "And I might need an alibi, so I'll have to make a decent showing in public."

While primping in front of the mirror, Margo was reminded of her greatest fear—crepey skin. "My neck!" she cried out, imagining the onset of premature aging. She found an old scarf in the closet and tied it like a neckerchief.

Deciding that her freshly scrubbed leather items were okay to wear that evening, she carried the garbage bag out, through the shadows. She put it into her trunk, then slowly drove down the driveway. She faintly heard the warning of the train whistle, in the distance, and turned the other way.

In the midst of the storm, Margo was finally on the road, headed for The Corner Bar, driving slowly through blustery waves of blinding snow that formed horizontal streaks across the low beams of her headlights. While approaching the Roadside Rest Area, panic struck. Her heart began to pound, and her legs were shaking, trembling fingers barely holding onto the steering wheel. In her peripheral vision, she saw the cop-car coated with snow, still parked beneath the light. Simultaneously, a frame-by-frame replay of the shooting began to flash before her eyes.

"I can't look!" she gasped. Without slowing her speed, she suddenly attempted a dangerous U-turn, desperate to avoid that horrendous scene. No traction. Her tires slipped on the fresh snow, her vehicle spinning donuts on the icy surface, taking up both sides of the two-lane road. She frantically steered to the right, then to the left, neither choice doing any good.

Spinning out, right in front of the dead officer's parked car, her engine died. The car rolled backwards, ending up stalled in the opposite lane. Had she crashed, then and there, she certainly would have ended up in the middle of the shooting investigation that was inevitable. The brief stillness, in the aftermath of the spinout, was of no consolation. She was still desperate to keep moving, and she had to get back on the right side of the highway, as oncoming traffic was getting closer.

Frantic to steer-clear of the crime scene, she re-started the engine and floored-it, swerving from side to side until she finally got her vehicle headed straightaway.

"I can't drive by there again." She was certain that she'd be arrested and do-time, probably for the rest of her life.

Chapter 46

To Bolster an Alibi

After driving in the opposite direction, the flashback faded away. Margo had a different nightspot in mind, not far up the road.

Bright neon lights illuminated the parking lot of the Lost Goose Rendezvous where she had once been touted *Queen of Nine Ball*. She turned in, then drove around to the back where she knew the garbage dumpster was kept. Parking next to it, she opened her trunk, grabbed the plastic bag, and tossed it into the dumpster—all done in one smooth motion as if she had practiced it. With the evidence gone, the events of the day were behind her.

The unpainted wooden door at the rear entrance hadn't changed, even after the many years that had gone by since her heyday. Across her mind flashed her goals for the evening, not only to avoid her old boyfriend but *to bolster an alibi*.

Inside the Lost Goose, the blended smells of pizza sauce and tobacco smoke, along with the distinctive sound of Bob Dylan on the jukebox, reminded her of the many times she had entered through that same door in the past. The laughter-filled room made her feel at home immediately.

Heads turned, along the row of bar stools, as Margo weaved through the crowd, grooving to the rocking beat of the music. She strutted to the center of the floor, feeling especially poised in her cowgirl boots and faded jeans. The heels of her new boots thumped in time with the pulsating beat. She added a cowgirl sway that brought an eruption of hoots from the sidelines.

The juke box suddenly broke into a Chuck Berry classic, the excitement spurring a provocative smirk that illuminated her now sassy-looking face. Fluffing her hair with quick fingers and thrusting her hips and flailing her arms, she looked like a professional go-go-dancer from the 1960s. Cheering voices urged her on, and a quiet middle-aged man tried to hand her a bottle of beer.

Somebody's quarter, in the slot, brought up another fast song, and Margo kept on dancing, putting on the sort of dated, sexy go-go show that many, in the younger crowd, had never seen before. Just as she was really into it, and many bar-patrons had gathered around clapping their hands, there were crude catcalls. "Take it all off!"

Suddenly fearing for her own safety, Margo stopped abruptly, turning a shoulder to those shouting hoots of "strip—strip"! To her, the chanting sounded like, "Smith—Smith", the name of her slain assailant, coming from an assumed group of tattletalers. She held her hands over her ears and escaped to the sideline.

Sitting alone, glancing around the room in a melancholy stare, she recognized no one. Teenagers—most of them, so it seemed. Even the old bartender that she once knew, and would have remembered, had been replaced by a young woman—barely 21 years old, if that—a kid.

A new genre of music suddenly blasted from the speakers, the clashing sounds not ringing any bells for Margo. Staying away from the *mosh pit* and all the flailing arms and legs, she reached for her throat, her nervous fingers stroking the knot on her bandana, then covering her ears as the tinnitus was intensifying.

The unharmonious sounds brought back the latent sound of the gunshot. And a vision of the deputy's limp body, slumped into a heap, flashed through her mind—not what she expected. She thought the flashbacks of the shooting would have stopped, by now.

"I'm going to leave," she mumbled, alarmed by the tormenting imagery in her mind.

Just as she turned to walk out the back door, a strong man's hand grabbed her arm.

"O-o-oh," Margo wailed flirtatiously, remembering that she needed someone who could vouch for her; an alibi that could be checked out, so she could be ruled out as a suspect.

She closed her eyes, feeling that her childhood dream about a beautiful princess meeting a handsome prince was about to come true. Who was this strong man who had spun her in to a twirl, like they could have been dancing? She was loving the feeling, being swept away by a tall stranger who knew how to swing a cowgirl.

Wanting to see the face of the bold gentleman, Margo whispered, "I'm feeling dizzy—"

"Margo, are you leaving?" the man asked. "You just got here."

She smiled, feeling his strong arm around her waist, allured by his gentle whisper, almost like a new romance was starting up. As her eyes opened, she was stunned; eyes frozen, as if she'd seen a ghost.

"Margo, are you okay?"

"Stanley! My God—Stanley—you scared me! What are you doing here?"

Stanley Nelson seemed as surprised as Margo was. "What do you mean, 'what am *I* doing here'? I've been waiting *on you*, in this *honky-tonk*, for two hours!" he complained. "Didn't you get my message?"

Margo faltered, like she'd been hit by a bullet. Stanley's voice seemed far away, muted by the recurring ringing in her ears; and she now saw Stanley as a cop, more so than as a boyfriend. Her heart pounded, pressured by feelings of guilt.

"Don't embarrass me in front of my friends; you sound like an Arkansas hick!" she barked, knowing she had no real friends left.

"Huh?"

"You said *honky-tonk* and *waiting on*. Nobody talks that way, Up North! What are you going to say next— *Y'all*? Sit down Stanley, before you make *a southern fool* of yourself! And don't ask a lot of questions. I don't feel good," she said, putting up a façade so her new secret—anything concerning the shooting—would not be discovered.

Stanley escorted her to the booth where he had been sitting. He pushed a paper plate, containing a few stale-looking potato chips and the remnants of a greasy hamburger to the side. He looked into Margo's eyes. "I was getting tired of waiting. Didn't your dad tell you that I'd meet you here?"

She looked away, trying to think of a way to side-step that question.

"You didn't return my calls. I stopped at the house. Your dad thought you'd be here, to show off your new shirt and cowboy boots. Looks like an old shirt, to me."

Margo gulped nervously, knowing that just minutes beforehand she had tossed her new, blood-soiled clothing into the garbage dumpster just outside of the back door, almost within sight of where she and Stanley were currently sitting.

"The belt . . . and boots are new," she said, wincing slightly. "I just bought them today." She kept her hands away from her humming ears, not wanting a naturally suspicious cop, like Stanley, to know why her ears were ringing.

"Oh; let me see those new boots," Stanley said, and tried to look under the table.

"Cut it out, Stanley!" she said sternly. "You can take a look, when I go to the little girl's room." Margo slid off her seat and walked toward the ladies' restroom, stopping at a safe distance—a distance far enough away that Stanley, hopefully, would not notice anything suspicious.

"What if they don't look new, with the scrubbing they got tonight?" Margo feared, fighting off a tear. She faked a grin, while pulling up on one leg of her jeans to show off the upper design of her boot.

Stanley smiled, not noticing that the leather was still wet from the scrubbing. He tipped the neck of his bottle toward her, in approval.

Margo went into the restroom and bawled.

Chapter 47
Beyond Suspicion

In the ladies' room, a young woman tried to strike up a conversation with Margo, offering her a cigarette, but Margo pushed her away, knowing how badly she craved it. "I'd be lying to my boyfriend, if I even touched it."

The sympathetic woman understood Margo's secret desire to sneak a nicotine-fix; she lit a cigarette and positioned it between Margo's lips, just as Eileen would have done for her.

By the time Margo returned, someone else was sitting at the table. She found Stanley standing on the other end of the barroom, watching two plowboys shoot pool.

"Nice boots," Stanley commented when he saw that Margo was back.

"You should get some, too, especially if you are going to ride."

"I saw the horse—well, all I could see with the yard light. It's kinda fat."

"She's ready to foal!" retorted Margo, barely able to fake a smile. She ordinarily would have laughed, but wasn't able to respond spontaneously.

"Your dad surprised me: you already own the farm . . . and bought that horse! I was just trying to make you smile. You finally did, just a second ago! I like it when you smile, Margo."

She looked away, rubbing both hands on her face to hide her profound sadness. She was wondering how Stanley could be so predictably gullible. "It's been a really, really long day."

Stanley offered a hug, and Margo reciprocated.

"When were you at the house?" she asked, trying to appear at ease.

He glanced at his wristwatch. "Who knows—your parents moved out of the house, since I was here last, and somebody else was parked in *your* spot. I talked to your dad, on the porch, and saw your mom, through the window; but I didn't want to bother her."

"I told you that I bought the farm, didn't I?" Margo asked, in a calculating way, knowing that she'd actually avoided the subject all week.

"No, you didn't; these major changes seem so secretive."

"Huh?" Margo was relieved that she and Stanley hadn't crossed paths earlier, at the farm, where he would have seen her face speckled with blood. "Let's play a game of eight-ball," she said, wanting to put an end to the questioning.

"Your dad told me that he sold it to you, but . . ."

"It was only yesterday—for Pete's sake—that we signed the papers!" she snapped, then remembered the shooting at the rest area, not wanting Stanley to know anything about it.

"Gee—you're awfully jumpy tonight, Margo."

"Don't get mad," she pleaded, realizing that she had erred in her impatience, and that she had to play the game differently now—now that the shooting had occurred. She wanted to remain *beyond suspicion*.

"A pool table just opened up. Do you really want to play a few games?" Stanley asked.

"Oh, Stanley!" she groaned, then stroked the skin on her neck with her painful fingers. "I really don't want to—not tonight."

"What's happened to your hands, Margo? Are those cuts?"

"Huh?" Margo held her hands in front of her face, noticing for the first time, the deep scratches on her fingers. She caressed the bloody scratches on two painful fingers, trying to think of a good excuse. "Ranching—occupational hazard," she said, having no problem coming up with a convincing lie. "Blackberry vines—scratches from all the fencing work."

"You look tired, Margo. You've been working too hard."

"Don't I know it! It's been a long week. I just want to go to the house. I'll show you . . . *our* new home."

Margo led Stanley out the front door, not wanting him anywhere near the dumpster by the back door. And thankful for a lull in the storm, she had Stanley follow her car back to the farm. Once there, she was relieved to see that her parking space was empty. She took the spot, which was covered with only two inches of new snow. Stanley pulled in, alongside.

"We need locks on the doors," she said, walking up the porch steps. "See?" She effortlessly pushed the door open. "Anyone could walk right in."

"Not having effective locks didn't seem to bother your parents."

"They never locked the doors—not even once—in the last forty years; but it's not the same world that Mom and Dad had. There are

222

crazy people—robbers and rapists, killers and drug addicts—driving back and forth on the highway. It scares me, that we could have an intruder. I want locks that work!"

Chapter 48
Keep On Snowing

The first time in Margo's house, since she had purchased it, was an awkward time for Stanley. Each time he tried to tell her something, or ask her a question, she dashed from room to room looking busy but actually trying to avoid contact with him. That seemed odd but he let it pass. He could tell her, later, about quitting his downstate job.

Trying to settle into their new home, Stanley began hanging his clothes up on his side of the closet.

"It feels like winter, all over again, blowing in on that strong wind!" he said, wishing Margo would stand still long enough to have a conversation.

Putting on her coat, she told Stanley that she had to go outside and check on her horse, to see if it was okay for the night.

The layer of wet snow made it sloppy to walk across the farmyard, and the steady, cold wind sent shivers throughout her body. Her visual check revealed the horse to be standing out of the wind and under the lean-to, just as her father had predicted. Since most of the hay had already been eaten or trampled, she tossed a few more flakes on top of the dwindling pile.

She hugged the mare's neck and shed a few tears, relieved that there'd be no detective-like questions from Flower. She hadn't had a chance to get acquainted with her horse since its arrival, several hours earlier, so she had plenty of conversation to unload on the unsuspecting mother-to-be. However, since Flower was content to strip another bunch of hay from the pile and keep on chewing, Margo decided that her horse was all right for the night. She changed her mind about talking, just then; she wasn't up to it.

Still traumatized by the shooting, the recurring memory of it persisted in her mind. In defiance of the cutting wind, she stared off into the darkness, to Highway 357 and beyond, enduring mental replays of the shooting that would not leave her alone.

"That stupid pig!" she said coldly of Officer Smith. "That rapist, drug pusher, and murderer got what he deserved! And . . . it's not enough—not enough to pay for killing Maria!"

She slyly looked behind, to see if anyone had followed her to the barn, or if anyone was listening to her solitary rant. Satisfied that Stanley was likely to stay in the house, she broke into her secret stash. She stood around the corner of the silo, out of the wind and out of view from the house, and lit up a cigarette.

Stanley was preparing for bedtime when Margo came back into the house. He laughed, "Hey, Margo, what are these handcuffs doing in the drawer of the vanity?"

Her heart almost stopped. Finding herself totally unprepared for that question, she drew from her old playbook—mystique—needing a prompt and convincing excuse. "I—I'm all moved in; just unpacked them today. Is there a better place for them?"

Confounded, Stanley didn't have a response to that, just as she'd hoped.

"I was going to surprise you with them, Honey, in the bedroom," she said, amazed how well she had lied and how easy it was to spit-it-out at the spur-of-the-moment. And she realized that she really liked those fancy handcuffs, apparently enough to be willing to take the incriminating risk.

"Where did you get them?" Stanley asked, less than amused, shocked that she possessed them, at all.

"Have you ever bought anything, off the cuff, at a yard sale? They're not just *any* handcuffs, they're . . ."

". . . kinky! I know where these are . . . usually sold. They're different than police-issue; that's for sure."

"Not good enough, or just the opposite? You like them, too?" Margo giggled naughtily.

Embarrassed, Stanley closed the drawer and complained about the long, tiring drive.

He finally got to tell Margo why he had been calling, that Sheriff Anders had called him.

"What—what did he want?" Margo asked with a panicky voice, thinking of the ghastly shooting and the inevitability of her facing a firing squad, or possibly just Life.

"There's a job opening, but he can't promise anything. I quit my job anyway—on the spot—just for you, Honey! And I moved out of the rental."

Margo stared straight ahead, in disbelief. "On. The. Spot?"

"Don't be depressed, Honey. I tried to tell you, but you never returned my calls. I packed what I could, into the car, and gave away the rest. The landlord said he'd return your fifty-buck deposit, in a couple weeks. So, I'm here . . . for good! Where's Toby, at Mom's place?"

Margo's eyes had frozen, in a wide-open position, at the prospect that Stanley was now home to stay. A city-slicker, now living on the farm he didn't want. And worse yet, a cop in her house; and a nosey one, at that. And she could be facing prison. For the rest of her life. How was she supposed to react?

"Where's Toby?" Stanley repeated.

The shooting had changed everything. Margo didn't know how to handle Stanley's untimely surprise-announcement, even though she'd begged him to quit and to move North with her. She was afraid that he'd find out; that somehow, she'd be accused of murder; and that would put an end to all of her plans—dreams she'd spent a lifetime in shaping, planning and conniving. How could it all end so suddenly? Right now, she couldn't rid her mind of the disastrous outcome at the Burntwood Prairie Roadside Rest Area.

And now, all this good news—Stanley here, permanently. It was too much.

"You ask about Toby? Mom has him, like he's her kid," Margo said, lying on her back and staring at the pattern of squares on the ceiling. Tears came to her eyes. "I'm sorry, Stanley, but I've been too busy to take care of him, lately. Every day that you were gone, I wished you were here—every day and every night. I can't do it all, by myself."

She rolled into the deep sway of Aunt Pearl's worn-out mattress, unable to show much surprise, holding both hands over her chest as if her heart would fall out if she'd let go. And, if her detractors actually saw her exposed heart, they'd see the lies. They'd think it's rotten to the core.

Her watery eyes dissolved the blurring ceiling tiles, as a vision of the dead deputy's snow-covered car, parked under the light pole at the rest area, froze in her mind. She clung to her feather-pillow, seeking enduring comfort.

Stanley fell asleep almost immediately.

Once Margo realized that all the questions had stopped, for the time being, she snuggled her pillow and stared into space. In the darkened room, the ceiling tiles came alive, partially illuminated by the reflected glow of the yard light. The perfect squares seemed to spin like ellipsoids, reminding her—over and over again—of the desperate events of that evening.

"I can never tell him. I can't tell anyone." She sobbed quietly, finally dozing off.

Nightmares tormented her mind. The shooting replayed dozens of times, like a recurring movie, finally awakening her.

She slipped away, down to the dining room where she could pace the floor without waking Stanley. At 2:00 AM, watching wind-driven snow streak past the vibrating windowpanes, she wondered what incriminating details she had forgotten to eliminate.

Looking beyond the steadily accumulating snowdrifts that had already obliterated her driveway, she held her gaze in the direction of the most notorious speed trap in Justus County. By morning, its notoriety would increase by logarithmic proportions.

"*Keep on snowing*," she whispered, like a trance, not wanting anyone to know that she saw him die. "Let the clues be frozen forever!"

Her stare was hollow, knowing that any reprieve she could gain, granted by the cold-hearted snowstorm, would not last any longer than the blanket of spring snow that would surely melt with the first persistent rays of sunshine.

The authorities would find everything, only a stone's throw from the parking lot where the abandoned squad car would stick out like a sore thumb, by daybreak.

She expected to be arrested before she could sleep another wink.

Desperately tired, she once again lied next to Stanley, hugging her pillow and visualizing deep snowdrifts forming over the despicable corpse—her stalker, attacker, and Maria's killer.

Stanley rolled over, hugged her, then sleepily whispered in her ear, "I love you."

Chapter 49
Sunday Morning Surprise
April 4, 1993

F oot stomping vibrations on the back porch shook the whole house. Then came Hank's loud voice from the kitchen, intended to wake up sleepy heads.

"Get up, Margo! You've got a *Sunday morning surprise!*"

"Oh—for-crying-out-loud!"

"What's happening?" Stanley asked, trying to rub cobwebs from his eyes, noticing that daylight filled the room.

"I don't know; must be trouble!" she said, quickly pulling a sweatsuit over her torso.

Stanley heard Margo's feet drumming down the steps.

Her father was standing in the kitchen doorway with a wide grin. Fresh snow caked his trouser legs, past the top of his boots, almost to his knees.

"Surprise!" he said excitedly. "You've got a horse to check on— remember?"

"Oh!" Margo held her hand to her mouth. "Did she—?"

"Yeah!" Hank couldn't wait to tell her. "You've got a colt layin' in the snow! I don't know why, but that mare busted out of the fence and gave birth to that little rascal, right out in the coldest, windiest part of the yard!"

Margo nearly panicked. She put on her winter coat, then snow boots, and called to Stanley, "Get your tail down here—now—and bring a blanket! We've got a foal, caught in the snow!"

Margo followed her father through the snowdrifts, taking long steps to stay within his stride, keeping inside his trail-breaking tracks.

The mare was hovering over the newborn that lied in the deep snow, licking the fur-like hairs on its face. Before Margo had a chance to get closer, she saw her brother's fast-moving, 4-wheel drive truck coming up the driveway. Clunks of crusted snow flew from the edges of the spinning tires, as he cut the first tracks across the wind-formed drifts of snow.

Brian stuck his head out the window, skidding to a stop. "Cop cars down by the speed trap, swarmin' all over the place! Yellow ribbons strung out everywhere!"

"Oh, Rowdy!" Margo reacted. She fully expected the news to unfold that day, but didn't want to appear knowledgeable of what had happened. "Can't you see that we've got our own problems? Flower had her baby in the snow! We've got work to do, or it might die!"

"Red Wilson called about an hour ago," Hank said, "looking for his ducks; guess they flew the coop. He said that both the sheriff and the state cops are down there."

"What else did he say?" Brian wanted to know.

"He wondered if his ducks might've landed here. I told him, 'Not on this place'."

"No, Dad—what about the cops?" Brian persisted.

"Well, somebody told Red that they found a dead body. We don't know . . ."

"A dead body?" Stanley asked, coming up from behind.

"Stanley, Margo asked for a blanket; go back and get the blanket!" Hank ordered. "We hafta take care of the colt first. We can talk about the shooting later."

Stanley returned and tossed a blanket to Margo. "*Shooting* usually means *murder*."

"Murder?" Hank repeated, echoing the chilly term. "That never happens, in these parts. Farmers, around here, are more likely to dance ya to death, not murder ya. It mighta been a heart attack, or somethin'. I wonder who it was that died."

"It must be somethin' *big,* since all the cops are down there— psychopath on the loose—a bloody massacre!" Brian supposed.

"Cut it out, Rowdy!" Margo said. Everyone laughed, except her. "A *psycho* in our neighborhood? You're nuts! Quit trying to scare me, like you always do!"

"Very funny, Rowdy; that's enough!" Hank said, chuckling at the sibling silliness.

Everyone turned to watch Charley Day navigating Brian's deep snow-ruts, his old doodlebug making it look easy.

"Who called Charley?" Margo asked.

"Your mother, of course," said Hank.

"What details did the neighbor give?" Stanley wanted to know.

"Red don't know shit; said he was afraid to stop and ask. Too many cops, and he didn't want anybody asking *him* questions." Hank said, then rubbed his whiskers while watching Charley Day wade a new path to the mare. "Pro'bly is a murder, alright. The cops are out, and the roads ain't even plowed yet."

Charley walked directly to the foal which still lied in the snow, Margo by its side. It only took him one second to size up the situation. "The momma's all right . . . and unconcerned," he told Margo. "I'm worried about the foal layin' in the snow, though."

"I hope he doesn't catch pneumonia," said Margo. "I thought you said *rain*, Charley!"

"Well—rain, then snow—kinda reminds me of old times, down in the Panhandle."

"I can't lift him. Is he okay?"

"He's fixin' to git up. Y'all git that blanket out of the way and let the handsome colt stand up, by himself, the way Mother Nature intended."

The colt lied still, so Charley began applying iodine to its navel, a minor medical procedure that had to be done. Margo flinched, seeing the blood-red color and shaking-in-her-boots, from re-living the shooting.

"I'm surprised that this scared y'all, Miss Margo," said Charley, showing her the label. "It's just a little disinfectant, so his belly button heals the way it's s'posta!"

Hey, Charley, since you just drove by the speed trap, what didja see?" Hank asked. "I'd like to know, since it's right in my back yard —so to speak."

"Hell—I don't know what's goin' on."

The colt tried to stand up, but his tiny hoofs slipped in the snow. Margo dropped to her knees and covered him with the blanket, trying to appear disinterested in the discussion.

Brian took a step closer, hoping that Charley would say more. He didn't want to miss a word. "What happened down there? I mean, *really*?"

"Well, there's a big commotion goin' on—for certain. *Poleece*, runnin' back and forth like-chickens-with-their-heads-cut-off; and directin' traffic—won't let y'all get a look; told me to *keep on truckin'*. Yellow ribbons . . . and snowbanks five feet high—hidin' somethin'—for sure."

"We're not gonna know anything about it, unless we go down there and find out, for ourselves," Brian said impatiently. "I'm goin' down there, Dad!"

"Now—now, Rowdy!" Hank said, holding him back, knowing that Stanley was listening and remembering that Stanley had heard Brian shooting his mouth off at the supper table, just a week beforehand. "It's no concern of ours. We'd better let the authorities do their work."

Bette came running from the trailer house, dressed in furry boots and a wolf-like hooded parka. "The radio says there's been a shooting at the Roadside Rest Area! The public should stay away so the crime lab can investigate."

"What did I tell ya, Dad?" Brian said. "They always bring in the hotshots, if it's a murder. Ain't that what the yellow ribbons are for?"

Stanley looked to Hank's eyes and nodded. "Whether it's a shoot-out or a homicide, you won't hear any more about it until the crime lab investigates," he said. "One thing I can tell you, this layer of snow is going to make it a lot harder to figure out what happened."

Chapter 50

Long-Legged Runner

Margo stayed close to Charley and the colt, but strained to hear what the others were saying. They were speculating, as to what sort of shooting-crime had occurred.

"You guys won't be happy, if one of our neighbors had the misfortune of a heart attack, or an accidental gun-discharge, or maybe a suicide, will ya?" Hank asked with a befuddled chuckle. "It hasta be *murder*, to suit both of ya; is that it?"

"I think somebody's dead at the speed trap; and I hope it's a cop," Brian lightheartedly joked, "one of those damn speed-trap jerks!"

Stanley stared suspiciously into Brian's eyes, with dead-serious precision. "If you get your wish, Brian Toralf, the sheriff will be busy; lots of speeding tickets to read through, looking for the single culprit, probably the one irate motorist who got mad enough to shoot an officer."

If looks could kill, Brian would be choking, by now, from the strangulating glare he was getting from Stanley.

"Oh—touchy; so-much for trying to kid-around with someone who has no sense of humor!" remarked Brian.

Again, the colt struggled to stand; this time, doing it on his own. His wobbly legs, all at oblique angles, seemed especially boney and weak but he was actually standing on-all-fours. Everyone gathered around, like a small cheering section at a game of dice.

"Oo-wee!" Charley hooted. "He's a *long-legged runner*! Y'all *is* in tall cotton, now!"

Margo looked proud. The others laughed at the shivering colt, watching him stand awkwardly, legs holding a sixty-degree angle and trembling, and his pointed hooves sinking into the loosely packed snow.

Stanley stood in the background, looking on from a distance, seeming to be evaluating each person's reaction to the shooting. And he probably felt out of place, not quite a betrothed man who hadn't yet won over the entire Toralf family.

The mare stepped closer, touched her foal nose-to-nose, and blew-out a loud snort that startled the onlookers. Everyone backed away.

"Leave them alone!" came Margo's panicky order. "Stay away and let the mother be alone with her baby."

"Y'all hep me get both of 'em to yonder barn," Charley said, "outta the snow!"

"Daddy, is the barn ready?"

"Aw—still workin' on it, Margo. There's a small space, in there, but it needs fixin'."

"I thought you did that yesterday, Daddy!"

"I coulda, if I woulda known the colt was comin' today!"

After the mare and colt got inside, Charley left; his rear wheels spinning until the snow-lugs got traction.

236

Margo sniffled, realizing the cops were probably digging in the snow, by now.

Working alone, inside the box stall, in spite of two animals in constant motion, Hank began to replace the broken boards, one at a time.

The mare stepped sideways in the box stall, instinctively moving her newborn foal from one side to the other, staying away from danger. The colt, now better than an hour old and with strengthening legs, pranced around his mother in the small space and sniffed at Hank's backside. Nursing had come naturally, already done swallowing his first meal.

Soon Hank became hungry, put his tools down, hooked the door, and began his trek to the trailer house. He knew he was late but didn't want to miss breakfast entirely.

He was following the snow-packed footpath when he noticed that a dead branch had fallen from the oak tree, onto the hood of Margo's car. He waded through the unspoiled snowdrift that surrounded her parking space, until he could reach the long piece of wood.

"Mighty heavy snow, to break this one off," he muttered, tugging at the jagged end of the branch, wondering if it had broken the window. With difficulty, he waded through the deep snowdrift, to the tool shed where he knew a broom was kept. The door was partway open, blocked by snow, frozen in place. Reaching inside, he moved a quite-new-looking axe closer to the wall, standing it next to two old axes so he could squeeze inside. After retrieving a broom, he began sweeping a foot of snow from the windshield.

"Hm-m, not even a tiny crack," he grinned, after closely examining the swept glass. But then, looking through the window, he spotted something odd: a yellow blanket, spread across the front seat, appearing to have a red stain.

"What's that—blood?" Hank quickly brushed snow from the door frame, with his bare hand, and opened the car door. "Well, I'll be darned; blotches of dried blood on Toby's blanket!" he said, barely aloud, after taking a closer look.

"Is Little Toby hurt?" he whispered to himself, aiming a questioning stare across the yard, all the way to the screen door of the farmhouse. However, remembering that his grandson was safe, inside the trailer house, his eyes tracked to the left, stopping at the door where everyone had gathered for breakfast.

"I smell a rat!" he said aloud, his eyebrows narrowing. "How can it be possible, that there's blood on Toby's blanket?" With an immediate suspicion, he stared at the trailer house door, as if he was trying to read the face of Toby's mother.

"Blood? It can't be Billy; he's not around. What about Brian?" Not believing in coincidences, a flurry of guarded thoughts raced through his mind. He frantically looked inside the car again and saw a smear of dried blood on the steering wheel.

"Oh, no—get it off!" He picked up a handful of loose snow, feeling it begin to melt in his warm hand. He smeared the partial liquid all around the steering wheel, to re-moisten the blood, then wiped it dry with the blanket.

Believing that no one was watching, Hank carried the blanket behind the trailer house, to the burn-barrel. Using his always-handy cigarette lighter, he destroyed the potential evidence along with other accumulated trash.

"We need a family meeting!"

Chapter 51
The Snowplow

When Hank entered the kitchen, he was relieved to see his grandson safely bouncing on his father's knee. He wedged past Brian, who was theorizing about the shooting, then slipped between the table and the wall, landing in his own chair. He noticed Bette's impatient eyes.

"Late, ain't I?"

No one noticed Hank's heavy eyes or his especially solemn expression. They were all done eating, but still crowded around Grandma's table, now listening to Margo's exciting re-telling of the new colt story.

Hank listened, too, and grimly sopped-up the last smear of egg yolk with a buttered piece of sourdough. Everyone was conveniently present for a family meeting, if he had called for one, but the timing didn't seem appropriate for a discussion of Toby's blood-stained blanket. And he hesitated to say anything to Margo, before talking privately to Bette; and Stanley Nelson was present, of course, so Hank wasn't about to violate the closely held family code of secrecy.

Later, back in the box-stall, Hank continued working around the mare and her foal. Stanley was leaning against the wall, and Bette was helping Margo rub the colt's coal-black hair, until it shimmered under the glare of the incandescent light bulb.

"The time's not right," Hank muttered, wanting a family meeting soon.

"He's beautiful, Mom," Margo marveled. "No Appaloosa spots, which could have made me rich, but I love the white star on his forehead." She suddenly looked around in every direction. "Where'd Stanley go?"

"He went to the house, to keep an eye on Toby, I suppose," Bette said. "With all the excitement, I forgot all about the baby."

"Me, too," Margo said, realizing it was literally true. Without explanation, she suddenly dropped the towel and grasped her head in both hands. She flinched, with the metallic sound of her father's hammer striking the heads of nails. Each pounding-blow reminded her of the sound of the fatal gunshot. She began to cry, not able to stop thinking about the shooting.

"What's the matter, Margo?" her mother asked.

Margo knew that she couldn't tell her mother anything about the shooting, but her mind was quick. "I forgot about Toby, Mom!" she cried and reached for a hug.

"That's okay, Margo," Bette said, patting her daughter on the back. "You can't be everywhere, at once. Stanley's in there . . . doing his part. You don't have to do it all yourself. Oh—by the way, Margo, I called Ernie to plow the snow," she added. "He'll be here soon. Don't have a fit about it; somebody has to do it! And he'll need Fifty Dollars for the job. The farm is yours now, so you get to pay."

Bored with pulling old nails, Margo slowly walked back to the house. She had never felt as sad as she did at that moment. She felt like crying but didn't have the energy. Besides, she was keeping a secret; and no one was listening, so what would be the point?

Brian was sitting at Grandma's table, holding Toby on his lap, when Margo looked through the doorway.

"How's Grandma?" Brian asked, when he saw her peeking around the corner.

"Oh—Grandma—the rest home! Don't bother me about that, Rowdy," Margo said, rubbing her forehead. "I'm hungry. Is there anything to snack on?"

She sat at one corner of the table and buttered a left-over piece of blackened toast. Her mother came in, from the barn.

"I just wanna know, have you talked to her lately?" Brian continued. "You must see Grandma every day, at work, don'tcha?"

"I've been too busy. Sometime next week—maybe. I'll make it a point."

"I saw her last week, Rowdy," Bette said. "She's doing okay, considering the confinement. She likes the cable television—you know—being in town; the luxury of it."

"I bet she misses the farm, even without all the modern conveniences," Brian said.

Margo glared at her brother, as if he were a dope. "She has Alzheimer's disease, Rowdy. She doesn't remember the farm; doesn't remember anybody—not a thing!"

"She remembered me," Bette said. "It took her a while, but after I explained who I was—her favorite daughter-in-law—she said she remembers me."

"Oh, God, Mom! That's not how Alzheimer's works!"

"I've got a gift for Grandma," Brian continued. "It's a carton of cigarettes. She pro'bly don't get a chance to go out and buy any, for herself, cooped up in that . . . old folks' home."

"Rowdy!" Margo scolded. "You can't give Grandma cigarettes—for God's sake!" She laughed condescendingly, "You're kidding me, right?"

"No. I wasn't kiddin', but I s'pose . . . they're not allowed."

"Bingo-o-o!" Margo was exasperated. "You want to break the rules at the rest home!"

"No smoking; betcha she don't like that rule. She'll let 'em know, not to mess with her!"

"She doesn't remember that she smoked."

"What—Grandma don't remember? She was a chain-smoker! What about withdrawal?"

"She . . . just doesn't remember."

"She must still crave it, don't she? Nobody can just give 'em up."

"She doesn't remember anything about smoking; it's all in the head!"

"Well, then, that must mean that all the researchers are wrong! It's s'posta be a habit—a craving that can't be stopped."

"It's an addiction. It's all mental; get it?"

Moments later, Margo was back in her own house, staring out the dining room window, her eyes trained on the movements of Ernie Niceski and *the snowplow*. She marveled at the efficiency of his V-plow, attached to his tall-looking, new four-wheel-drive truck. She told Stanley to go outside and give Ernie a new-looking, non-crumpled, One-Hundred-Dollar-bill to pay for the plowing.

242

"I want Ernie to know that I'll pay for any favors, from now on. I don't want him thinking, later, that I owe him anything."

Stanley couldn't have been more stunned-cold, if he had been hit over the head with an icicle. "Okay. I thought that maybe he'd just send a bill." He didn't have such a large bill in his thin wallet, but he counted out enough smaller ones to barely come up with the cash. He reluctantly went outside to pay the man.

"Ernie doesn't send bills; he just expects favors—always expects something," Margo said hatefully, to herself, while watching large snowbanks form along the driveway.

She suddenly had a vivid flashback, to the scene of the shooting. In the natural design of frost, crusted on the windowpane, Clarence Smith's pimply face seemed to emerge from the crystalline pattern. His psychotic eyes glared at Margo and his lips opened wide. She covered her ears, wanting to silence the death threats being hurled by the dead man's frosty image.

The *boom* of the back door, as Stanley returned, almost sounded like a gun blast.

He saw Margo's terrified look, from across the room.

"What's the matter?" Stanley said, not aware of Margo's frightening dilemma.

"Help me lie down, Stanley. I've felt sick . . . all morning."

"Is it the flu-bug?" Stanley asked. He took her hand and led her away from the window.

"All this talk about a killer is . . . scaring me. What if the murderer is running around our neighborhood? I expect locks on all the doors, Stanley—today, before the sun goes down! Do you hear me?"

"I know, but . . ."

"Don't argue about this, Stanley! It's for our safety! Go to town, right now! Buy some kind of locks. Get bolt-locks! As it is, anybody could kick the door in. What if that happens, and you hadn't done what I asked? It would be *your* fault, if someone finds us all dead, someday!"

"Install locks? I don't know how to do that."

"Then find someone who does! How are you going to be a ranch manager, if . . ."

"Maybe Hank knows how."

Chapter 52
Frost-Singed Ears

Home alone, since she had sent Stanley to town, it was too quiet in the old farmhouse, for Margo, allowing back flashes of the traumatic shooting to play upon her mind. Compounded with the spontaneous creaks and popping noises, all natural phenomena in the old house, it became a frightening place for her. Replays of the shooting would not go away.

She lied down on Aunt Pearl's old couch, curled into a fetal-like ball, and held her eyes shut. She cried herself to sleep.

Her power-dream was intense and frightening, where she fought off an onslaught of accusations from Sheriff Anders who attacked sharply, accusing her of murder. In his aggressive interrogation, the agile sheriff kicked her around the living room and slapped her face until her ears rang. The fast-moving lawman was out for blood, acting like both interrogator and prosecutor, combined into one aggressive madman-of-an-investigator.

Dreadfully asleep and repeatedly trying to scream, she finally cried out, "You've got the wrong girl!"

An oddly quiet stillness filled the room, being awakened suddenly but too late to hear the echo of her own screams.

Long shadows darkened the room, since the sun was going down. Being disoriented, from the frightful dream, she hadn't heard the sound of the actual sheriff's car door closing just outside her kitchen window. And she wasn't aware that Sheriff Homer Anders was waddling on the slippery surface of the driveway, like a duck-on-ice, heading directly for her back door.

Still winding down from her afternoon nightmare, she hadn't yet sorted out whether or not her frightful confrontation with Sheriff Anders was real or imagined. She suddenly heard something—a thud on the wooden steps and a knock on her door. She recoiled from her curled-up position and raced to look out the window.

"Oh—no! The sheriff is here!"

Too late to panic. Dream or no dream, she had to greet the actual sheriff who was knocking again. She kicked a pair of boots out of the way and opened the door.

"Good afternoon, Missus Nelson," Sheriff Anders said, speaking through the screen.

"Hi, Mister Anders!" Margo said cheerfully, running her fingers through her messy hair and trying to sound friendly, aware that she had an image to project. "What a surprise! Please come in, Sir. I'm not a Nelson, yet—you know." Margo knew the purpose of the sheriff's visit. She hoped the surprise in her voice sounded convincing. In her mind, it was hard to separate her fearful dream from the reality of the slow-moving sheriff who was actually speaking.

"I've met Stanley Nelson. He mentioned your paternal name, *Toralf*. Henry Toralf's daughter," Sheriff Anders said precisely. He took off his hat and gripped one ear, wanting his cold fingers to warm it up. "I'm sure you're a busy person, so may I get right to the point?"

"Ah—sure, whatever that might be—"

"You were at the discovery of that body, too—the boy—what's his name—can't think of it," the old sheriff started in, making a clumsy start in getting to the business of his visit. He was stuck, his failing memory not allowing his cold-numbed lips to enunciate the deceased man's name. He reached for his opposite ear, gently squeezing its numbness. "It's been a very trying day. I suppose you know why I'm here. You must've heard about the shooting at the Roadside Rest Area, by now."

"Yes—all the neighbors, too; a terrible *suicide* in our neighborhood," Margo said, being deliberate with her words. "That sort of thing just doesn't happen around here." She stared at the sheriff's bright-red, *frost-singed ears*. "I've got hot coffee—"

"Oh, thank you, Ma'am. Maybe—"

"If you're looking for Stanley, he drove into town just as soon as we got plowed out, to buy locks for our doors. He's the one who actually found . . . that boy that you mentioned. Now, this . . . bad news, today, has put a fear—a terrible fear—into all of us! We're *sitting ducks*, out here in the country, for any crazy person that might come around."

"Yes; I understand, Miss Toralf."

Margo offered the sheriff a chair at the kitchen table and promptly placed an empty cup in front of him. She poured steaming coffee, directly from the pot which had been percolating all day.

Sheriff Anders cupped both hands around the outside of the hot drink, absorbing all of the heat that he could from the steam. He lowered his partially numb lip to the cup-brim and held it there, against it for a moment, savoring its precious warmth more so than wanting to taste the bitter brew.

"It sure is too bad about my deputy—Clarence Smith—a good cop. I've still got to go visit his wife—uh-h—I mean, *widow.* I don't know what to tell her. Clarence was a dedicated family man—you know—two or three little kids, or maybe . . . grandchildren."

"It's a shame," Margo said, outwardly echoing the Sheriff's sentiments with the expected agreeable response but secretly thinking something very different of the despicable murderer.

The sheriff asked if she, or anyone else at the farm, had heard anything unusual the previous evening. Margo assured him that they hadn't, so the visit didn't last long.

She stood by the dining room window and watched the sheriff get into his car, jot down a short note into his pocket-sized notebook, and drive out the driveway.

"Whew!"

A few minutes later, Stanley Nelson carried two paper bags through the back door. "Honey, your dad said that he saw Sheriff Anders come into the house," he said, setting one heavy bag on the square table, with a clunk, and continuing to the refrigerator with the other.

"He was here . . . a while ago," Margo said, carefully weighing each word.

"Did he say anything about the temporary position at the sheriff's department?"

"No," she said, wishing Stanley hadn't applied.

"No problem. I went to his office this afternoon. He wasn't there, but I left a note with the dispatcher. Now, they know I'm here. If they need help, they can call.

"Hey—news from town—somebody really was shot. Killed. A Deputy Clarence Smith," he said. "I thought that everyone would be shook up about it, since that's all that anyone's talking about. But, no; it seems that this Officer Smith had rubbed the fur the wrong way, on lots of folks. Very few seem to have any sympathy for the guy."

"Well, of course—city people—all desensitized to such violence; but out here, in the peaceful countryside, the whole neighborhood is bound to be upset about it."

"So, what did Sheriff Anders have to say?"

"Not much; just notifying us of the *suicide*," she said, sticking to her own spin, hoping to influence Stanley's thinking, too. "I don't like having cops come to my door. They shouldn't be bothering me, not when there's a killer out there, on the loose!"

"Mister Anders is a harmless, old guy. He couldn't hurt a fly."

"Yeah? Some of these cops are just plain jerks! I wish they'd just leave me alone! I'm a law-abiding citizen!"

"I'm pretty sure that Sheriff Anders, besides looking for a witness to the crime, is working at improving public relations for his department."

"If cops want a better image, maybe they shouldn't hide in roadside parks with their radar traps!" she fumed. "I hate cops! Well, except for you, Honey."

"You sound almost like Rowdy! I tried to tell him that sneaky cops catch speeders. It may seem unfair, but it's not illegal for them to use devious techniques. Even so, we must show some respect for the deceased. Did you know him?"

"Who—a guy named *Smith*? Isn't that an alias that all crooks use?"

Chapter 53

The Legend of Justus County

April 9, 1993

Margo's second workweek was over. She paced near the employee exit, waiting for her shift to end. It seemed like a month, but it was less than a full week since the fatal shooting had occurred. She dashed that haunting memory from her mind. When the buzzer buzzed, she punched out.

Arriving at her farm, no time was wasted. Excited that the newness of her ownership had not worn off, she immediately went to her horses.

The spring air smelled fresh, and the dipping sun still shone brightly as Margo led the new colt, walking on the moist sand of the driveway. The surprise-snowstorm had melted, along with the rest of a forgotten winter.

She toyed with the loose end of the lead-rope and was almost giddy, testing her memory of Sheriff Ander's hapless visit, just five days earlier. She felt in-the-clear, the clumsy old sheriff not likely to make any headway in getting to the bottom of the shooting.

Brian was there, talking to Stanley. Stanley told of Hank's help in getting the new locks installed, plus removing all the old stanchions and junk from the barn that week.

"We filled the dumpster to the top," he said.

Brian wasn't impressed. "Any news about the *Speed Trap Murder*?" he asked.

"I haven't heard anything, but I'm not in-the-loop, either."

"Sounds like the investigation has dried up."

"You might not know about law enforcement professionals; there's a certain bond—a brotherhood. And in situations like this, they're working when you're sleeping. Wait until they converge on this tiny town. There's a killer out there; probably thinks he's a free man, smarter than the cops, but not for long. Just wait—"

Then, Margo, after walking the colt all the way around the house, stopped to compare the two clashing personalities, curious that the tetchy guys were having any conversation at all.

"Incompetent cops—makes me mad that nobody's been arrested yet!" Brian continued. "The biggest crime—ever—and what'll they do about it? Some paperwork, and that's about it!"

"I think it's a mystery, Rowdy," Margo cut in, barely holding back a confident smirk. "They can't solve it because . . . they can't figure out what happened."

Stanley had no reaction, his eyes open without blinking. Just listening.

"I didn't like him, but I respect the dead cop," said Brian. "He had a family—maybe. What the killer don't know, is that—us country folks—we take care of each other."

"Yes, we do. Farmers stick together . . . and help one another," Margo said piously.

"They'd better catch 'em fast, before we take care of it ourselves —how it was done, in the *old* days. Those short oak trees, down by the lake—the ones with the big side-branches—midnight hangings, in frontier days. Real justice, back then; ya find the guilty guy—*ZAP*— all taken care of!"

"Rowdy!" Margo was quick, in reproach. "Frontier justice, with a noose? That's just a story from the Eighteen Hundreds! You're going to give Stanley the wrong impression. We follow the law, out here, not some outlandish legend about a lynch-mob!"

"Well, *the Legend of Justus County* has a lotta truth to it; they didn't name it *'Justus County'* for nothin'!"

Frustrated with her brother's ignorance but impressed with the progress that Stanley was making on the barn, Margo was excited to schedule her new-owner celebration, a sort of barn dance affair. She had been thinking about it: as a veteran, it was logical to hold it on the Fourth of July. She planned it that way and wrote it on the kitchen calendar. And since Stanley was available every day, she saw no reason why the renovation work couldn't proceed at a fast clip, to get done in time.

If Stanley hadn't known much about carpentry, beforehand, he was learning it now—on the job. He stuck to it, making daily progress on Margo's to-do list while she was at work.

Late one afternoon, he received a long-anticipated phone call. He zigzagged across the yard, from one location to another, wiggling the extendable antenna, trying to find a spot that had clear reception.

The call was brief and vexed with static, but the message was certain. He hit the *off* button, just as Margo drove into the yard. He quickly walked to the oak tree, excited to tell her the news. She pulled into her parking spot.

"Margo, I've been waiting all week, and they finally called!"

"Hi, Honey! You shouldn't carry that phone-monstrosity around, outside. What if—what if it gets wet, or . . . something?"

"The Sheriff asked me to come to the office, tomorrow. I think he wants to hire me!"

Margo's shock showed on her face, the news troubling for her but exciting to Stanley. She woefully followed him into the barn. There she saw her father, quietly sitting on a sawhorse, holding down a board so Stanley could make a cut. The work had stopped, ten minutes previously, when Stanley's portable phone rang.

Stanley found a place to lay the phone down and picked up, where he had left off. He squared off a pencil-mark and picked up the cut-off saw.

"Tomorrow's Saturday," Margo complained, just as Stanley squeezed the trigger. The sound of the saw was overbearing, and the rotary blade threw sawdust in her direction.

"Time is of the essence," Stanley said, repeating words that Sheriff Anders told him. "Two weeks have gone by, since the shooting, and he's one man short."

"Really? Duh-h—one guy's dead. Of course, the sheriff is shorthanded!"

"That's not funny, Honey. They don't have the personnel to handle a murder case. That's what Homer Anders—the sheriff, himself—told me."

Speed Trap Murder

"Murder? I thought it was a suicide," she said, thinking wishfully. She nervously tried to gather the loose skin on her neck into the grip of her thumb and two fingers, but her supple flesh snapped back.

Chapter 54
Family Meeting
April 16, 1993

B rian came to the farm, just before mealtime, and got in on Stanley's job-news. Bette called "suppertime" and the Toralf family gathered around the table. Speculation, as to why the sheriff wanted Stanley to report to his office, on a Saturday, had the whole family in a stir.

"Does this have something to do with the shooting at the speed trap?" Brian asked.

"Rowdy—not during mealtime," Margo said, trading glances with Stanley.

Hank had been observing his daughter's attempt to turn the tide of the detailed investigation that was sure to come, especially if Stanley would be hired by the sheriff. And suspecting some sort of involvement, by his daughter, he had carefully waited for an appropriate point where he could enter the conversation.

"Ya know, Stanley—I really doubt if ol' Homer would have ya in the middle of somethin' this big; not a new guy," he began cautiously, matching stares with Stanley's professional eyes, testing his nerves for a favorable flinch. He hoped he had successfully interjected the only discouraging but discreet words he could think of.

Stanley sensed pressure from all sides but only listened. There were plenty of negative comments, concerning the capabilities of Sheriff Anders and how he ran *the department;* how it was a good place to stay away from and a bad place to work.

"Besides, if that government grant money is for public safety projects, like ya said, you'll get stuck with paperwork, not the responsibility of a high-profile crime investigation."

"Sheriff Anders didn't say what the public safety job might entail; and I'll not speculate," Stanley said. "I'll wait until tomorrow, to see what he wants me to do."

After eating, Stanley didn't want to be part of the sheriff-roasting, so he left the others to their derision. He took Toby to the farmhouse and put him to bed. And wanting to be well-rested, himself, before reporting to the Sheriff's Office the next morning, he went to bed early.

Later, after everyone else had left the trailer house, Margo's parents talked privately. This was an excruciating discussion, since Hank had postponed mentioning anything to his wife about the blood-stained blanket or the implications that pointed directly to their daughter.

"I didn't want the cops to have a field-day, pickin' Margo's car apart. That's why I kept it to myself, all this time," he said, reacting to Bette's criticism.

Bette hopelessly stared at Grandma Toralf's faded chicken picture and folded her hands, as if the old painting held some sort of hope for the future. "Margo has always been too independent for her own good! What are we going to do, Henry?" she asked with an expressionless face, mirroring the family's dilemma.

"Well, we're not gonna jump to conclusions. We don't actually know nothin'," Hank pointed out, his tightening fists showing his frustration. "Whether she did nothin', or if she did somethin', we can't squeal 'n send 'er to prison, either; it's a family matter. And we can't say or do a thing, until Stanley's gone. Too bad, the investigation has already started."

* * *

Saturday began before the sun came up. The possibility of Stanley being hired that day had him checking his watch every half-hour throughout the night. It had already been two weeks since he quit his old job; two weeks since Margo bought the farm; two weeks since the colt was born; and just two weeks since the baffling shooting at the Roadside Rest Area that left the Sheriff Department in disarray. In Stanley's mind, the old sheriff needed help badly.

After breakfast, Margo was at the door to see Stanley off. Trying not to show her anxiety, she stood quietly by his side, halfway out the screen door and clinging to his arm.

Bette and Hank stayed in the trailer house, waiting for Stanley to leave, peeking through Grandma's crocheted curtain that hung over the window next to the kitchen table. Whispering, Hank opined that it was his fault that he had allowed two weeks to slip away without dealing with the time-bomb of potential evidence that lurked inside of Margo's car.

Suddenly, Margo burst through the door. "He's gone! I've never seen him this way—so excited, just to get a . . . stupid job!"

"C'mere. *Family meeting*!" Hank announced.

Margo's surprised eyes spotted her father's tension. She backed toward the doorway.

Bette motioned for her to come back and sit down, not looking up from the flowery print on the tablecloth, already knowing what her husband would say.

"What is it, Dad?" Margo took a seat at the corner closest to the door, realizing she had been singled out. "We haven't had a meeting in years. And I'm the only kid here."

"We've got trouble!" Hank said firmly, getting right to it.

Margo scooted her chair halfway to the door, trying to seem detached from any sort of problem. "Stanley's barely out the driveway, and you're jumping all over me!"

"The cat's-outta-the-bag. Tell me about the shooting," Hank said impatiently, watching his daughter shift her eyes.

"Uh-h—what am I supposed to know about that? I've already talked to . . . Sheriff what's-his-name; and God knows I—I answered all his questions."

"I'm not talkin' about that ignorant, old sheriff. If he saw his own ass, he wouldn't recognize it! Besides, he's countin' his days to retirement. He'll never solve anything! I'm talkin' about yer fiancé. I think he knows you did it. Now that he's goin' to work today, we need to move fast; things to clear up right now—today—before he gets back. He'll be appointed Deputy—before suppertime—for God's sake!"

Margo's eyes fluttered, in her practiced *innocent princess* sort of way. "Besides Stanley being *nobody*, not even an officer, you know exactly what?" she asked and laughed uneasily, her heart beginning to sink. She glanced to the side, then gasped as if her breath had been cut off. She shifted in her chair, and out of habit, reached for her throat with caressing fingers.

"We've got a problem," Hank said, staring down his daughter's unsteady eyes.

"Why are you looking at me, that way, Daddy?"

"I found Toby's blanket; blood all over it. You know where I found it, don'tcha?"

"Ah-h—" Margo's mouth hung open, her eyes wide. That give-away, along with her adolescent-like denial, told Hank and Bette that their suspicions were correct.

"What other evidence didja leave, layin' around, besides Toby's blanket in the car?"

"Oh—the blanket!" She burst into tears.

"It's too risky, keeping something like that; blood never washes out," Bette said.

"You threw it away? Grandma made that blanket! It's the last thing she ever did, before she went away . . . and never came back."

"I betcha, if that car is searched by the crime lab, they'd find blood; it sinks into the upholstery and . . . everywhere."

"There wasn't *that much* blood, Daddy!" Margo blurted out without thinking, then sat silently, realizing that she had just admitted the obvious.

Chapter 55

Manic Moment

Hank sat in his inherited chair, wondering what his father would have done. On second thought, his father never had a kid, likely to be culpable to such an egregious crime. A previous family case came to mind, although it was not similar to Margo's predicament.

"Remember what happened to Billy—what did 'em in?" he asked. "Stupidity. He shoulda zipped his mouth but wagged his tongue in court. He sent himself to prison!"

"He didn't zip-it, because he did it!" Margo objected.

"Are ya sayin' ya didn't do it—you didn't shoot the cop?"

She knew, she should've walked away, but couldn't think straight, at the time. "A *manic moment*, so it's not my fault. It was a mistake, I'll admit, but I didn't pull the trigger."

"Good luck, with that excuse," her father said. "You'll get *Life*—worse'n Billy got!"

"Manic, alright!" Bette said. "If you repeat that word, they'll think you're crazy and throw-the-book at you!"

"It must've gone off by itself, when I pulled it out," Margo said, vacillating in confusion.

"*Out*—out of where?" Hank asked.

"Out of his mouth, except it was cocked; and when the hammer fell . . ."

"What—you say—*what*? It went *off* in his mouth?" He imagined a large, cranial exit-hole. "You blew his brains out?" Hank almost puked. "What were you thinking?"

"She never, never tells anyone what she's thinking!" Bette said, her cheek twitching. She held the nervous tick still, fingers shaking. Her eyes traveled up the wall, searching for some sort of peace, stopping at the old chicken-picture—the one with the mother hen teaching her chicks how to eat. It was so quiet in the room that she could almost hear the hen scratching corn.

"He was going to rape me, Daddy! That son of a bitch pulled me over and attacked!"

Upset with that news, Hank stood up from his chair, fire glowing in his eyes. He went to a window and stared at a puddle of water that remained from the melted snow.

"You should've told us—your own parents," Bette whispered. "Family can't squeal."

"I couldn't tell anyone. He said he'd kill me. I didn't want anyone to know."

"He threatened you?" Betty asked.

"He prob'ly got what he deserved," Hank said, "but it's too late now; no cop would believe ya. We hafta cover your tracks. No-tellin' how much the cops know, already. The biggest problem we've got now, though, is Stanley. He could see—maybe hear some small detail; anything that hasn't been released to the public. If any of it slips out, they'll nail ya!"

"He's not a problem; we're getting married, plus, I haven't told him anything about it."

"If ya wanna see things go haywire in a hurry, just wait 'til you've got a cop living under your roof!"

The silence in the kitchen had an eerie echo to it, and Grandpa's old clock that hung across the room from the chicken picture seemed to click louder than ever before.

"That constant tick-tock sound can get on a person's nerves," said Bette.

"We shoulda did somethin' a week ago," lamented Hank. "Hope it's not too late. We have two choices: either get rid of your car, evidence and all, or get rid of Stanley! He's too smart; too dangerous to have, right here—right under our noses! He could put ya behind bars! Kick 'em out, before he finds a spot of blood someplace."

"I can't," Margo objected. "I love him."

"Maybe you can get Stanley to commit suicide," Bette suggested, as a semi-compassionate gesture, "like Helga got Plunk to jump off the silo."

"What?" Hank seemed surprised. "The guy with the prostate trouble—whatcha-ma-call-it—Dambul? I thought 'ol Plunk Dambul fell—a farm accident."

"Helga called it *prostrate famine*. She got tired of—you know— waiting for a train that never arrived; she ran off with the milkman."

"Well, I knew that. So—what'd she do, push him?"

"Well," she half-nodded, "Helga hooked the door, so when he couldn't breathe—"

"What! There's no oxygen in a silo; he must have suffocated!"

"That's when Plunk fell . . ."

". . . and went, *'plunk'*!" Margo laughed, not able to stop herself.

"This ain't funny!" Hank said. "Are you tellin' me that Helga purposely caused it—a fall, impossible to survive? Murder? How'd she get away with it?"

"She answered all the sheriff's questions—"

"Yeah, with lies! That door can't lock itself. That's important information—missed!"

"Important? Oh, what can be more important than a woman's happiness?"

"I could never get Stanley to climb up that high," Margo said. "He's afraid of heights."

"That's what guns were invented for."

"Stop the useless, idle talk!" Hank said. "And forget about cutting your own throat, by doing any harm to that young man. The car's dispensable—the only choice that makes sense!"

"I'll vacuum it, Daddy. When it's clean, I'll sell it. It's worn out, anyway."

"If the cops go through it with a fine-tooth comb, they'd find somethin' incriminating."

"Junk it!" Bette blurted out. "There's more-than-one-way-to-skin-a-cat!"

"Now, there's the best idea! Once it's smashed down, into a pancake, nobody'll bother checkin' it for blood—not even Stanley!"

"I could go for that," Margo said, "but new cars cost a bunch, and I don't have it."

"Who said *new*? Get another *used* car," Bette suggested. "Pick out something you want and talk to Ernie. I bet he'd *give* you the money!"

"I will *not* ask Ernie Niceski for a loan!" Margo retorted angrily.

"I didn't say, *loan*! I said *give*," Bette clarified.

Hank nodded. "If he thinks there's any chance of gettin' back together with ya, Margo, he'd make it happen; he can afford it!"

"That's all you see in Ernie—his money!" Margo said. "I don't care about Ernie's money. Stanley's my man!"

"Oh, this game again—defiance, instead of common sense! There's a lot of good that can be said, for having money!" her mother asserted.

"Fiddlesticks!" Hank hollered, tired of the arguing. Dishes rattled on the tabletop, when his fist bounced off its surface. "Enough of this nonsense!"

A fearful silence ensued. Margo's nervous fingers toyed with the skin on her neck, and Bette simply smoothed the wrinkles of the tablecloth with the palm of her hand.

"There's no point in wasting any more time. We get rid of that car —today—before Stanley gets back, before he sits down at the family table as a sworn deputy! The car goes, your *only* choice. We don't want any more shootings, around here!"

Chapter 56
The Car Crunching

Hank was firm, staring at Margo until her thinking came into alignment with his. "I knew that'd be your choice," he said. "I called Joe already, down at the junkyard, so he knows we're bringin' it in."

"What—already?" Margo exploded. "You planned this without asking me? And you put me through all these questions—this charade?" Her watery glare showed that she felt betrayed. "Do I get paid for it?"

"You should; the scrap iron value, I'm sure."

"Ask him, Daddy. If I can't get what it's worth, I'll take it someplace else!"

"You should just be glad to get rid of it, under the circumstances!" Bette snapped.

"Ol' Joe already knows it hardly runs. It's rusted, beyond hope, from the road salt; not worth fixin' up. We haul it in, now, before anyone notices—especially Stanley!" Hank glanced at the old clock. "Joe's expectin' us, so we've gotta get goin'. Listen close, Margo; when we get there, we don't wanna say anything that'll arouse suspicion."

"Do we have to do this today?" she whined like a teenager.

"Don't argue with your father!" Bette scolded. "Anything with blood on it has to go, just like . . . the blanket. Your butt's sticking out-in-the-wind, and Dad's trying to save-your-hide!"

"Be sure to bring the vehicle-title with ya, Margo. "Joe can't take in a junked car, without turning in the title to the state."

When Margo came from the house, an envelope in her hand, she saw her father approaching, steering the old farm tractor directly at her car. He motioned for her to get out of the way. She jumped sideways and cringed at the impending collision.

Hank rammed the tractor into the rear of the car, bending the bumper and smashing a large kink in the trunk. Backing up and turning, he sideswiped it—both sides—rippling all the doors and fenders with the projecting tread-lugs of the tall, rear tires.

"What'cha do that for?" Margo yelled out.

Hank didn't answer. He bumped it a couple more times. When he decided that he had mutilated her car enough, he drove the tractor back to its parking-spot by the barn. When he got back to the scene of the car-crunching, Margo was waiting with hands on her hips and a teary look of disgust on her face.

"How's that? Looks like scrap iron, now!" Hank said with a chuckle.

"Hunky-dory. Thanks a lot, Dad!"

Hank grinned. "Now, Joe won't bother trying to tune-it-up and sell it. We don't want that thing drivin' up and down the road, not even with a new owner."

"By the time it's compressed into a small cube, it won't be worth anything," she griped.

"Steel weighs the same, smooth or smashed up. What's more important, a couple-hundred bucks for a worn-out car, or life in prison? Now hurry up, before Stanley gets back!"

Margo got into her smashed up set-of-wheels and miraculously drove it away. Actually, Hank had been careful not to damage any vital working parts. He followed in his antique pickup, a 1950 keepsake that hardly got used anymore. To avoid the main highway, and the specter of impropriety, they followed a series of back roads all the way to Joe's Salvage Yard.

Margo gritted her teeth, after Joe gave her only fifty dollars for the car.

She *rode shotgun*, while her father drove the old pickup back to the farm. Her heart flip-flopped, knowing that she'd successfully gotten away. The car and any associated evidence were gone. She hadn't felt this relieved in a long time.

Partway home, an instantaneous flashback of the shooting hit her, like a gunshot. She re-heard the powerful percussion, the sound ricocheting inside the echo-chamber of her own skull, and her left ear popped and rang loudly. She grasped both hands around her head, groaned, and squirmed on the seat.

"What's wrong?" her father asked. He pulled the truck over to the edge of the road and stopped. "Are you okay, Margo—My Little Princess?"

"The torment keeps coming back, Daddy."

Hank cradled his daughter's head in his arms, just as he had done in the early days, so far into the past that he didn't remember; but she did. She cried until the evil visions went away.

"I'll talk to Ernie . . . about a used car. Is that okay?" Hank asked softly, knowing what would soothe her pain.

"Ah—just so it's white."

Before Hank got all the way home, he wanted Margo to rehearse her response to Stanley's inevitable questions.

"I'll say, 'I junked it', and that's the truth!"

"It has to be a convincing story. Tell 'em that it was runnin' so bad that you got tired of the trouble—every day—so ya junked it."

"I'll tell him that it was an old, crappy car; and I hated it! He'll understand that. Then, I'll tell him that my dad got drunk and drove the tractor into it—accidently!"

"Now, don't get too carried away; he'll get suspicious!"

"Daddy! I'm not going to say anything stupid! I know he'll ask about it; it'll obviously be missing from the yard."

"You could just tell him that you got tired of the trouble with it . . . and sold it. He don't hafta know that ya junked it."

"Hm-m; you think too much, Daddy. I'll wait until he asks, then I'll tell him whatever I feel like saying!"

"Just be sure to . . . phrase it right; make it sound like the truth."

"Why? Lying comes so easily, Daddy. Is that something else I inherited?"

Chapter 57
Gung-Ho Investigation

It was late Saturday afternoon, by the time Margo and her father got home, surely time for Stanley to arrive; but he wasn't there yet.

Margo dreaded what news Stanley might reveal that night, as she tried to put the evening meal together. While washing lettuce, she looked out the kitchen window, noticing how empty her vacant parking space seemed. She hoped that Stanley wouldn't notice.

Pork chops burned in the fry pan while she paced the floor in the dining room, keeping her eye on the driveway. She didn't detect the scorched odor until she saw Stanley's car bounce through the pothole. Running to the smoky kitchen, she flipped the pan, tossing the overly-charred chops into the garbage can.

Outside, also watching for Stanley to arrive, Hank held a shear in his hand, pretending to be pruning the apple tree. He watched Stanley pull into his space, next to Margo's empty space. He was intent on being the first to speak with him.

"How was your first day on the job?" Hank asked, before Stanley got out of his car.

Margo tried to listen from the Kitchen window, but couldn't hear a thing.

"Fascinating!" Stanley said, stepping out of his car.

"Well—sounds like everything musta went good—"

"He signed me up, the minute I came in the door, then took me for a ride."

Hank was surprised but somewhat suspicious. He wanted to know if Stanley would be involved with the shooting investigation, but didn't want to seem too eager by asking a lot of questions.

"Traffic duty! I knew it!" Hank said, his laughter loud but premature.

"No; we drove out to the Burntwood Prairie Roadside Rest Area."

Hank could hardly believe that Stanley was already in on *the gung-ho investigation.*

"It was murder," Stanley said.

"How—how do they know that? It was s'posta be a suicide," Hank said, discretely pumping Stanley for more information.

"That was the first publicity, leaked purposely—you know—to throw-off the killer," Stanley said. "Narcissistic killers don't want to get caught; however, their pride likes to hear what the cops know—details of what they did. If a killer feels safe by hearing that it's a suicide, instead of what he knows actually happened, he'll think the cops are stupid . . . and not likely to solve the case. That's when a criminal is likely to get careless—make some mistakes. That makes him easier to catch."

"Ah-ha," Hank acknowledged, "the wheels and gears, turning—meshing inside the brain of that ol' experienced cop, Homer Anders. Pretty clever—"

Margo heard the thump of Stanley's feet on the wooden porch steps. She darted from the kitchen, so he wouldn't think that she'd been trying to listen.

"Hi Honey!" Stanley said, bursting into the kitchen with more enthusiasm than she had expected. He tossed his new deputy-hat onto the hook, by the door, and gave Margo a hug as she walked in from the living room.

"Your first day—betcha they put you out on the highway—Speed Trap Jerk Patrol!"

"No; nothing like that, Margo," Stanley said and laughed lightly. "That's almost the same thing your dad said!"

"What do you do at that . . . boring public safety job?"

Stanley chuckled and hugged Margo again. "That's funny, Honey! It's not what you think. Poor ol' Homer—swimming in paperwork, ever since the shooting at the roadside park. We're not too organized yet, but he sat me down and went over the evidence—crime lab stuff and witness statements. And he showed me a few things at the scene of the crime."

"Witnesses? Oh!" Margo was surprised. "Someone saw it?"

"There's not much that I'm at liberty to say—top secret evidence —you know."

"Stanley! Surely you can tell me . . . enough to put me at ease."

"Well, they know it was—"

"You stopped. What's the matter?" she asked, anxious that Stanley was holding back.

"Oh—nothing—just realized that I may have said too much, already."

"You haven't told me anything, yet."

"If I *do* tell you . . . *something*, you can't repeat it to anyone. It's a closely held secret."

Expecting Stanley to get down-to-brass-tacks, Margo was fretful that he continued with generalities, explaining that the Crime Lab did some amazing work, but it was his job to find a valuable clue, or two, in order to catch the killer.

"You're confusing me. Do you have an eyewitness, or not?"

"Don't I wish—"

"Oh-h-h—nobody? If nobody saw it happen, and they don't know what happened, how can they be sure of what didn't happen?" Margo said, fearing that Stanley was zeroing-in on solving the crime; and it was only his first day.

With that, Stanley was perplexed, wishing he hadn't said anything. "Critical evidence cannot be released to the public, so I cannot divulge certain things. Only the investigators—and the killer, of course—know the most crucial details."

"Like what? You stopped again!"

"This is all under investigation, so I shouldn't have—"

"Yeah, like I'm a risk! I'll tell the killer, so he can escape to Canada. Give me tidbits, Honey. Your police secrets are safe with me." She awkwardly faked a fainting spell, miraculously falling into a nearby chair.

Stanley quickly got her a glass of water.

She sipped a little, then said, "You're making me feel sick with all this terrible news!"

"That's it—no more talk about the crime!" said Stanley, just as Hank walked in.

After seeming dizzy and let-down, for less than sixty seconds, she suddenly stood up, in a tizzy, and marched to the door. "I'm going to talk to Mom!"

Chapter 58
Genetics

"Did Margo throw-ya-for-a-loop, Stanley?" Hank asked, a grin forming. "Nothin' like this has ever happened before—not around here! She's bound to be upset. Everyone is."

"Well, the sheriff wants to get on top of this case, right away. That should make everyone feel better," Stanley said, determined to waste no time in solving it.

After Hank left, Margo returned and quickly threw a supper together—a box-dinner of instant macaroni and cheese. Worried, she didn't utter a word all through the evening meal.

After Stanley got Toby to bed, he returned to the kitchen to help Margo at the sink.

She didn't want assistance, just details. "You said there were fingerprints?"

"No. I'm pretty sure, I didn't even mention it. If I had, I shouldn't have—"

"Oh—you and your rules! But I want to know, Stanley," she begged. "I promise to be strong, if you keep me filled in."

"Well, I hope I won't regret this, but . . . okay. Fingerprints: there are some—strange ones, at that," he said, shaking his head and knowing he should keep quiet; but he was also charged with making sense of the facts, and he was stumped. *If Margo has any free ideas, I could use the contribution.*

"*Strange* fingerprints—what do you mean, Honey?"

"Well, whoever did it—the perpetrator—planted the dead man's fingerprints all over the gun, except on the trigger; either not experienced with guns, or was in a hurry."

"Or, maybe *he* was afraid; what if the gun goes off?" Margo suggested, hoping to muddy up the investigation.

"He wiped his prints off and placed the dead man's prints on the weapon, obviously to make it look like a suicide. Three problems—woops—orders from headquarters, two areas of concern: no prints on the trigger, of course—puzzling; but the other problem is, the victim's prints on the barrel and on the grip were contaminated with blood—his own blood."

Margo's pulse raced, realizing that she had blundered in her attempt to reassign blame, but she tried not to appear distressed. Staying loose and trying to show indifference, the burnt pan suddenly fell from her hands and hit the floor with a zing, sounding almost like a ricocheting bullet. Her nervous fingers reached to soothe her throat.

The innocuous sound didn't interfere with Stanley's concentration. "It's an odd situation," he continued, actually hoping Margo could help. "With all the wetness—rain and snow—a dead man could, inadvertently, get some blood on his fingers; but it's highly unlikely—impossible—that he would have handled the gun *after* his own death."

Margo heard, nodded her head slightly, and stared out the window. The sun was low, casting long shadows from the barn and silo; not colorful and bright, but gray shadows—gloomy-looking ones. She now knew the apparent status of the investigation, expecting that, in the next moment, Stanley would make some sort of accusation.

"Someone else must have done it," Stanley continued, explaining the dead end he was facing, "then planted the dead guy's prints all over the gun, botching it up with the dead guy's blood. Implausible. Unbelievably stupid, or maybe what an amateur would do. The crime lab came up with that theory, before I started."

Margo calmly wiped off the table with a damp cloth. "If they had it figured out already, why did they hire you, Honey?"

"No suspect. I'm supposed to investigate and tie all the pieces of the puzzle together. Sheriff Anders thinks I can handle it. I'll probably catch the culprit, right away. Sounds like a simpleton who probably carries a bloody rag in his glove compartment."

"Hm-m—a blood-botching dummy?" Margo felt relieved that her father had forced her to dispose of her blood-stained automobile; however, she kicked herself over the botched-up evidence she had left behind—such an obvious mistake.

Stanley opened his briefcase, retrieving a glossy page that looked like it had been torn from a magazine.

"Mister Anders gave me this," he said, unfolding the colorful-looking article on DNA and Genealogy. "I've never learned this kind of—what-do-you-call-it—DNA science."

Margo raised an eyebrow, seeing the page and recognizing the topic. She touched her fingers against the rapid pulsating of her carotid artery. "*Genetics*," she said, knowing something about it from her college days but never expecting it to affect her personally.

"Yeah—that's the word; Greek-to-me but what Mister Anders says is *the future*."

Margo wandered away from the conversation, hoping that Stanley would give up on the difficult but technically precise study of genetics. She was sensing that any investigation, centered around molecular science, would quickly go beyond anything she knew about fingerprints; beyond any comprehension that she had gleaned in nursing school.

"How did we end up with bloody fingerprints?" Stanley asked, frustrated.

"Obviously, it must've been dark. Who could've seen it?"

"I never thought of that—darkness—impossible to see blood. The lab couldn't pinpoint the exact time of death—messed up estimates, with the snowstorm and rapid change in temperature. I was stuck on that point, trying to figure it out. Thanks, Margo; you're a genius!" He gave her a hug as she passively faced the other way, still staring out the window. "The perpetrator, who probably thinks he got away with murder, is in trouble now—now that I can figure out the timeline!"

Margo's heart leaped wildly, beating like it might implode. She felt dizzy. Holding her hand on her forehead, she wished that she hadn't made any contribution to the discussion.

"I am *not* your collaborator, Officer Nelson."

"That was good, Margo, like a pro! I was wondering how a killer could be so careless."

She stared out the window at the growing darkness, making a hopeless-sounding sigh. "Ah—don't tell the sheriff that I solved it for you, Honey; you deserve all the credit yourself."

"Oh, it's not over yet. I still have to find a suspect. If only, it hadn't snowed! And I still have to come up with *another* theory—how a trace of the dead man's blood got smeared on the *inside* of his pants-pocket. Now, isn't that a strange one? Still working on that—"

Margo knew the answer to that minor detail but would say no more. She knew it was her own fingers—her bloody fingers—that had searched the dead man's pocket for the key. She said she was tired, then went upstairs to bed, leaving Stanley with his papers at the kitchen table.

Once alone in the dark and staring at the ceiling tiles, Margo pined for a return to her simpler childhood days when her horse-ranch dreams made, even her significant problems, seem small. She felt like crying but couldn't.

Chapter 59
Talking To Oneself
April 18, 1993

It was a cool Sunday morning when Margo went outside to feed the horses, but the hidden warmth of the sunshine accumulated in the fibers of her drab-colored work shirt, making the spring sun rays feel almost like those of summertime. Sprigs of green growth seemed to have popped up, overnight, reviving the dormant grasses. The spring freshness was a far-cry from the conditions, barely two weeks earlier, when the freak snowstorm had blanketed everything.

She stroked the short hairs on Flower's face and combed her long mane. "Life's not complicated for you, Flower; you're lucky. If a horse does something wrong, no one cares. But for humans, if you break a rule, *the law* shows up and wants to put you behind bars," she said, starting up spontaneous communication with her horse.

"You're safe, if I lock you in the barn overnight, but if the boogeyman comes and locks me in a cage, it'll mean incarceration for a long, long time—justice—punishment for trying to defend myself. You'd be dead and gone, Flower, by the time they set me free. I might even be dead, myself, by then."

280

The new colt, also wanting attention, nuzzled against Margo's shoulder.

"You're so innocent, Little Colt. You've never done anything wrong in your whole life—your life of only two weeks!" she laughed and itched his ears, then brushed his coat with a currycomb, realizing that she had forgotten to give him a name. She tried to think of a suitable one, but her mind had been preoccupied for the past two weeks, searching only for a way to avoid incarceration.

Stanley was still asleep, which Margo didn't mind, since it gave her a chance to let her thoughts wander without having to answer any questions. She liked working alone, because it gave her repeated opportunities to verbalize new and outrageous ideas, just to see how each one sounded, to her. "That's what *talking to oneself* is all about; not a form of craziness that some mind-experts think it is."

Soon, she was deepening a hole with the post-hole-digger, almost ready for the next post.

As she sweated, placing the corral posts in a straight line, exactly where she wanted them, Margo tried to think of a way to manage Stanley's activities to somehow keep him in line.

"Control—manipulation—the only way," she spoke as she toiled. "It should be easy, though. No normal man would actually suspect a woman. If I keep all the wires straight and tight, like a proper fence, it'll look perfect; the finger of the law will never be pointed at me."

Later in the day, Stanley found Margo behind the barn stretching a long section of barbless wire. It was perfectly straight and tight.

"I'm tired," she said, when she saw him approaching.

"I'll help."

"No; come inside with me," she said with a sigh. "You get to peel the potatoes."

Stanley silently worked the paring knife, his mind preoccupied while the peelings accumulated. Soon, freshly peeled potatoes filled the pot.

"I know you don't want to hear it, but there's something that may interest you, Margo."

"You're not going to tease me with more crime lab details, are you?"

"There's not much more to tell you, except—well—after only one day of working on the case, I found out that the killer must have been a female," he said. "Guess what they found—"

Margo was intrigued but wary of saying something incriminating. She wondered if she should keep her mouth shut. A brutal crime is usually presumed to have been committed by a male, not a female. So, she had to ask, "A woman—why?"

"Prostate leakage."

"Huh—something they found with—what—a microscope? Why would that possibly interest me? What would it prove, except that Officer Smith was a male?"

Stanley laughed. "That's funny, Margo; but you must know, don't you—a nurse—someone who's familiar with normal bodily functions?"

"No. I can't imagine what you're talking about. If it's a disease, I may have studied it in college. If it's advanced cancer, I'd say, 'six months to live'."

"It's simpler than that."

"Don't even tell me. I don't want to know!"

"Good thing you stayed out of law enforcement, Honey; you're not cut out for it."

A vision of demised Deputy Smith's face suddenly popped into Margo's mind. She imagined Smith, aiming the sharpened blade of his axe and estimating the arc of his projectile while watching her run, then releasing the handle with the follow-through of a marksman; and herself watching it flipping toward her, approaching fast and doomed to fail, because she saw it coming and ducked out of the way. At that same instant, the empty pan that she was holding rattled to the floor, sounding like a thrown hatchet that missed its mark and bounced off a rock.

"What's wrong?" asked Stanley, remembering that Margo had also dropped a pan, just the previous evening. He stooped and picked it up.

"Ah-h—butterfingers," she said, relieved that the frightening vision faded away quickly.

She walked to the stove with Stanley's pot of potatoes. "You might be wasting your time on your new job, Honey; but it's good for us, as long as they give you a paycheck every week."

"Yeah—short-term, anyway. Good, for as long as the federal money holds out."

"As long as they pay in real money, that's what's important", she joked, feeling confident that she was playing Stanley successfully. "Can you set the table, Honey? Mom and Dad are coming over for Sunday supper."

Chapter 60
Strategic News Leaks

When Bette and Hank arrived, the dining chair for Toby had a stack of thick books piled on it; two mail-order catalogs topped with the Burntwood Prairie Telephone Book and Grandma's thick Bible. Stanley helped Toby with his plate while answering an array of questions from his prospective in-laws.

"So . . . how do you like your new job, Stanley—detective, is it?" Bette asked.

"Right, the job I've been trying to get for a long time. Too bad it's only temporary."

"Federal money's as good as gold. You need to stretch it out; milk it, for as long as you can!" Hank said with a delightful chuckle.

"Ha-ha! That's funny, Hank. Are you suggesting that I should avoid solving the crime, so I can draw my pay indefinitely?"

"Yeah! Why not? Play by *their* rules. And if ya get away with that, you should be a DFL candidate—run for the State House!" Hank joked and chuckled heartily. "If you join up with that pack-o-wolves, you could ride-on-the-coattails of President Clinton."

"That's a good idea, actually. Politics. I could run for Sheriff, like you say. Solving this crime could guarantee me the election!"

Hank's jaw stopped chewing, remembering that he had, indeed, made that suggestion. "I never thought of *that*—not when I first said it, that is." He swallowed slowly. "You should know, a crime with this complexity might not ever get solved. On the other hand, even the *appearance* of some success could propel you right into office." He saw amusement in Stanley's receptive eyes.

"First, of course, you'd hafta make a name fer yourself. Get your name into the newspaper—every week. Make sure ya get quoted, even if there's no progress on the case. Write your own press releases—for sure. Pat yourself on the back, like the others do, and give 'em tidbits of useless information—every week."

"*Strategic news leaks—*"

"Oh—you've heard of this?"

"You're a genius, Hank!" Stanley said with a chuckle of his own.

Margo's face was arrested with apprehension, miffed that Stanley seemed serious about actually running for office. Although she had tried to appear amused at its absurdness, she was irked by the possibility. She glared, when Stanley looked her way, and shoved the chicken platter in front of his plate. "Take some and pass it on!"

"Hey, Margo, it was your dad's idea!"

"Just what our country needs—another Arkansas hick, running for office!" she said.

"I didn't say *president*! I'm talking about pretty small potatoes, here—the sheriff-job."

"About yesterday—your new job," Hank said, having a leading point, "I thought they had other work fer ya—you know—*public safety work*, using that special federal appropriation. I've heard that it's illegal for the county government to spend it on somethin' else."

"Earmarked funds; they have an intended purpose, but—"

"In other words, they'll waste it on—let's say—unrelated investigations."

"We don't put it that way . . . at the office," Stanley said. "And I'm not the accountant."

"Stanley, don't go around telling people that you want to be Sheriff!" Margo piled on.

"Oh, I'm not going to mention it yet—especially at work! I have to slowly get people on my side, first—politicking, like your dad said. In fact, it might be a good idea to become affiliated with a political party. I don't know which one, though. I'm not a Democrat or a Republican, but I might have political aspirations."

* * *

Stanley carried Toby up to bed, and Hank stepped outside for a cigarette.

When she knew that Stanley wasn't watching, Margo slipped outside, too. She saw the red glow of smoldering tobacco, over by the oak tree.

"Daddy!" she began to cry, running to him. She stood in her empty parking space and told her father about the woman-killer theory.

"Hm-m!" Hank paused to think, then exhaled a humid cloud of gray smoke that elongated into spiraled ribbons. "That puts a new twist on things! I wish that Homer Anders was as stupid as everyone thinks. Remember, it was Homer that sent Billy away."

"What can we do, Daddy?"

"Now, don't you worry, Princess. I know a few good-ol'-boys, down at the County Building—damn bureaucrats but ambitious people who know how to throw their weight around."

"You have power and influence?"

Hank chuckled and drew in another puff. "Not too much—"

"We're just . . . nobody-farmers, Daddy. We can't even get the county to fix our gigantic pothole!"

Hank pondered the situation and took a long drag, making the tip glow fiery-hot. "Ol' Red Wilson is a long-time farmer, and he sits on the County Board. He owes me a favor."

Chapter 61
Guitar Practice
April 19-21, 1993

The next workday, Stanley scribbled something on the calendar and circled *Monday*.

After he went out the door, Margo looked to see what was going on. "Sixteen days," she read, then primped at her last-second mirror. "Fanatic cop—he's actually counting the days!"

Across the way, Hank sat at his mother's old table slowly stirring cocoa, in his cup, and watching Toby do the same with his bowl of oatmeal, using his fingers.

"Did you hear Margo this morning?" Bette asked. "What a mood she's in! Maybe we should buy her a car, or . . ."

"Not so fast, Mother. Ernie Niceski's working on a deal—remember? Problem is, Margo told me that Stanley thinks the killer is a woman. That's what set her off. You know how she gets; all wound up and says a bunch of crazy things. She don't mean half of it."

"She's fit-to-be-tied! I'm just afraid that, one of these days, she'll lose her head and say something like, 'get off my property'!"

"She's stressed out, to be sure, but not mad at us. Just think of the secrets she hasta keep from Stanley, right now! Once this investigation blows over, like a fart in a windstorm, everything should go back to normal. But in the meantime, she'll need us more than ever before. She's proven it, time and time again, Mother." Hank massaged his soft whiskers with his rough hand. "She'll be hearin' more stories, chances are, and lettin' her mind run wild—worse with each one. Those cops come up with all sorts of outrageous theories—ya know. Who knows what they'll say next? A lot of it is trickery, intended to mess with her mind!"

"That Stanley—playing games with Margo's head! What's he trying to do, throw her off-balance, get her to confess? I'm afraid he's going to find out. She might even tell him, in some hissy fit!"

"They seemed okay, together, last night."

"He's like a bulldog, always pulling on the chain. What can we do with him?"

"Nothing. We've already decided that; and especially, not now—now that he's into it; and now that they say a woman did it! We've gotta be smart, Mother. The whole family hasta be smart, like never before. We've gotta keep our future son-in-law on our side."

Hank lifted the handle on a small pail of potato peelings, mixed with other kitchen carvings, pork rinds, and eggshells, then carried the slop-bucket outside to feed the piglets.

* * *

That day passed quickly, as Margo was soon home. She loosely gripped the lead-rope as she walked the bouncing colt around the yard, something she looked forward to every afternoon. The rambunctious, young horse was growing steadily, gaining strength and confidence.

The colt suddenly kicked and bucked, pulling loose from Margo's grip, then ran in circles, the knotted end of the rope dragging behind, not allowing anyone to get close enough to catch him. Hank couldn't move fast enough, and Margo had no patience. She became furious but also fearful that the colt might run away, down the driveway, and get killed by a passing semi-truck.

When Stanley got home, he immediately saw the problem. He put a halter on the mare and led her into the yard, then circled the house with the colt's mother, the young one joining-the-parade and soon falling-in-line.

"Easy-as-pie," he said, after leading both horses back inside the fenced area, then closing the gate behind them. He was not expecting a disdainful glare.

Margo was upset that her efforts had been futile, but Stanley's technique was a piece-of-cake. She previously thought Stanley knew nothing about horses. It infuriated her that he had so easily solved the problem.

"Beginner's luck!" she said indignantly.

Returning to the house, she almost made it to her back porch when her mother came running outside. "They're burning Waco!" she cried out. "Margo, come and see the fire on TV; live pictures on the news. The FBI firebombed the protesters in Texas!"

"No! I don't want to see *real* violence on TV," Margo said, already over-traumatized by recent events. "Fire—the penalty for protesting; and without a trial? Everyone will die!"

"It's not Bill Clinton's fault—the zealots!"

Speed Trap Murder

* * *

That evening, Stanley showed Margo an order he had received in the office-mail. He was required to attend a week of special meetings, all to start the very next morning in Bemidji—no advance notice. He knew he'd never make it before 08:00, unless he drove during the night. So, he took off, soon after a late supper. And Margo knew why —training—crime lab coordination to catch crooks.

"Ironic," she told herself, pouted briefly, then tried not to think about it; instead seeming happy that Stanley would be gone, giving her something called *space*.

Excited to get started on her party-planning, she wrote *barn party night* on the calendar, then jotted down a few words on the back of an envelope and recited them to everyone she called: "Come to my Barn Party, July 4th."

By midnight, Margo discovered that she was truly lonesome without Stanley. "He drives me nuts, when he's here; but I can't stand to be without him," she admitted to herself.

By the next evening, since Stanley was still gone and spare time seemed plentiful, she dreamed of playing her guitar to a barnful of adoring friends. She was determined to learn how to play a song on her guitar; and she wanted to be proficient at it, before the night of her fast-approaching party.

It was dark in the barn. She didn't turn on the lights, since she was mournfully depressed from missing Stanley so badly. The sound box of her guitar boomed each time it accidentally bumped into objects in the dark as she climbed into the hayloft.

P. G. Knudson

She stood on the edge of the threshold and looked out, across the illuminated farmyard, squinting from the glare of the yard light. She shielded her eyes, then ducked into a dark shadow, off to one side of the doorway. There, the subdued light-intensity reflected her mood.

She sat on a bale of hay and hugged her instrument, holding it gently as she loved it very much. She caressed its curves and slid her fingers up the smooth neck, softly plucking one string at a time, wishing that she knew how to finger the high positions on the fretboard. The twang of the open E-string reverberated across the exposed rafters of the roof. A melody that she hummed to the harmony of a minor chord, and the blackness of the night, closely matched her dark thoughts.

Then, like a miracle had happened, she formed a sequence of correct fingerings, and the music flowed. At last, sitting on that bale of hay in the dimly reflected light, Margo was practicing playing her guitar. The chord progression, and the mournful song on her lips, temporarily took away the scourge of the once-constant images that haunted her. The peace it brought was good, and her smile, radiant.

The next day, the music still played in her mind, soothing her soul. Her time at work seemed fulfilling; happy to be needed. That evening, she was more determined, than ever before, to master her guitar. Little by little, *guitar practice* was showing positive results. She was happy, playing her fine instrument, but the steel strings pained her uncalloused fingertips. However, she didn't let that diminish her determination to learn. "I must know how to play before the deadline —the Fourth!"

After fumbling through a few tunes, Margo glanced out the open door, expecting to see an enchanting, full moon; but only a narrow,

292

yellow portion was lit up on the far-edge of the blackened sphere—disappointing—the *new moon*.

"I wish it was bigger and brighter!" she said to her instrument, as if the guitar wanted to see a golden glow as much as she did.

She tried playing another song, but her sore fingers refused to cooperate. The difficulty was depressing and her confusion, overwhelming. Her mind tried to switch to another song, as it had all week, but her declining mood was crashing lower.

Angered by her inability to produce harmoniously correct sounds, she leaped to her feet and ran to the always-open hayloft door. She tossed the guitar toward space, at the blackened sphere, as far as she could throw it.

TW-W-A-N-G!

Chapter 62

Never Awaken a Sleepwalker

It was finally Friday. Margo arrived at work on time but left early. She felt miserable, obsessed with Stanley's absence; not understanding how she could be glad that he's gone, but contrarily, didn't know how to handle her life without him always by her side. "At least, he'll be home soon—tonight!"

Margo was home, walking both horses when she saw Stanley's car coming up the driveway. She stood at her vacant parking space, holding both lead-ropes in one hand, watching warily as if Stanley was a stranger.

His car was getting closer. Her heart thumped with excitement, glad that he had returned, but she looked away; no intimate greeting, not even a *hi Honey* was forthcoming.

Stanley stopped short of the horses, excited to be home. "Any calls during the week?"

"Mom didn't say," replied Margo, projecting an attitude of ambivalence in spite of her pining for him during his absence.

Stanley gave Margo a hug, but she held back.

"It's getting interesting, Margo! We're getting close!"

"Close—close to what, the Waco outcome?"

"No!" Stanley laughed, seeing humor in the fact that Margo had an undefinable knack for keeping him sharp. "Surely you know, we're close to solving the murder case!"

"Is that what gives a cop a climax, the prospect of throwing somebody in jail? Can't you wait until Monday to talk-shop? Why can't you work a normal nine-to-five, like everyone else?"

"I talked to the profiler. She's got a Jane Doe scenario all figured out, but I didn't get to see it. It's in the mail. Homer should have it by Monday . . . or Tuesday."

"You say . . . *she*—a woman-profiler? What did she figure out?"

"Well, I already told you; it's a female killer. She just put the facts together and came up with a profile—you know—motives and the like, a list of possible traits and attitudes of the killer. Now, all we have to do is find that person!"

"So, it's that easy; is it? What about this idea: *gay psychopath murders boy, then commits suicide?* Is there still time to investigate how all these killings are probably connected, and the culprit might be a drug dealer?"

"The case is not *that* complicated, Margo. Let's talk about something else. I'd rather hear about what's going on with you."

Stanley got a dose of *silent treatment* for the rest of the evening.

Later, she rolled to him, hugged him, and began to tell him how much she needed him. "You are so strong, Stanley—steady. I love you, more than you can know. I don't know what I'd do, without you. When you were gone this week, I thought I'd go absolutely berserk. Don't ever go away again!"

Stanley didn't know what to say; and he was tired. They both fell asleep.

P. G. Knudson

Deep in the night, Stanley was awakened by squeaking bedsprings and a bouncing sensation. Margo was on her knees next to him, punching her pillow and tossing it to the floor. In the reflected glow from the yard light, Stanley watched her leap from the bed and pounce on the pillow, as quick as a cat, wrestling and punching it again. "We have to tell someone!" she said, her voice barely audible.

Sleepwalking? Stanley didn't interrupt her, since he had previously learned to *never awaken a sleepwalker.* He watched her pick up the pillow, go to the window, then pause momentarily to gaze across the yard. He admired the artistry of her naked body, silhouetted against the illumination from outside.

Margo suddenly slammed the pillow against the headboard, then disappeared, traipsing down the stairs in the dark. Almost immediately, she returned with a butcher knife gyrating in one hand. She jumped into bed, still holding the knife as a weapon.

Stanley's heart almost jumped out, when he saw the protruding outline of the large knife next to him. He kept quiet, remembering the past admonition concerning sleepwalkers. Lying just inches from her erratic movements, he nervously held his eyes partially closed, realizing that he had never asked anyone why a sleepwalker should not be awakened.

Margo suddenly stabbed the pillow. Feathers flew when she ripped out the knife and flung it across the room, paying no attention to where it stuck in the wall. She gently smoothed a place to lay her head, among the loose feathers that surrounded the knife-slit in the pillowcase. She continued sleeping, her eyeballs thrashing back and forth beneath her closed eyelids. She snored softly and peaceably.

Chapter 63
Family Stuff
April 24, 1993

Stanley Nelson was lazily conscious, falling in and out of sleep, when his skinny-dipping dream was interrupted by Hank's voice coming from downstairs.

"Margo!" Hank called out, for the fourth or fifth time but got no answer.

"What is it, Hank?" Stanley shouted back, squinting from the sun that glared through the curtain. He noticed that Margo's side of the bed was empty, except for dozens of scattered feathers.

"Is Margo up there?"

"No!" Stanley bounded from the bed, remembering Margo's bizarre sleepwalking performance. "What's wrong?"

He saw where the tossed knife had stuck. He pulled it out of the papered wall and carried it downstairs. There was a confusing frenzy of activity in the kitchen, both Hank and Bette dashing in-and-out of the house. No one saw him wipe gypsum dust from the blade and return the knife to its place.

Bette was stuffing some of Margo's personal items into a duffel bag. Stanley followed her out the door and stood on the porch, expecting some sort of explanation.

"Stanley, did Margo call you?" Bette shouted with frenzied voice.

"No. I just woke up . . . and she's not here! What happened? Did you look in the barn?" he asked, remembering the bizarre rope incident.

"I looked; she's nowhere!" Hank said frantically, opening the door of the station wagon that sputtered while it idled by the porch. "The old pickup's gone; she must've taken it," Hank said to Bette, breathing heavily as if he'd run a mile.

"What makes you think she took the truck?" Stanley asked. "Look, her car's gone."

"Oh, Stanley! Where have you been?" Bette asked sharply. "She got rid of her car!"

"Got rid of it? She never mentioned that. So, now she doesn't have a car?"

Betty looked the other way. "She drove the pickup to work, all week."

"We've gotta go," Hank urgently said. "We'll check *Four Corners*, first."

"Oh-h-h!" Bette cried, holding one hand over her mouth. "You stay here, Stanley, in case she comes back! She might call, so listen for the phone! Dad and I'll try to find her!"

"I think there's a low tire on the truck—almost flat," Hank mumbled, rushing to help Bette put the bags into the tailgate. He also threw in a hand-operated tire pump.

"I can go—"

"No; just family!" Bette said flatly. "Besides, you need to stay here with Toby!"

"We'll find 'er; she can't be very far away with that low tire," Hank said, getting into the driver's seat and slamming the door repeatedly, until it finally latched. The engine revved.

Stanley watched the faulty rear lights flicker on the old station wagon, as Hank peeled sand and pebbles all the way out the driveway. He turned toward the lakes, the opposite direction from town.

They seem to know where Margo went. And it's a family secret, apparently, since they won't tell me anything. Stanley was worried. *What is Four Corners . . . and where is it?*

Toby was still in his crib, just awakening for the day, when Stanley went into the trailer house to find him. He didn't like finding the crib, as a fixture at Hank and Bette's trailer home, which seemed to be a permanent arrangement and an impediment to a normal life with Margo. *This is wrong; something has to change.*

Stanley found a jug of milk and a box of dry cereal, then sat his son down for breakfast. He noticed a gray substance on Toby's cheek. He tried to wipe it off, but it was stuck on.

Gooey—almost like some kind of glue. Is this duct tape, again? What's going on here?

He found a washcloth and was able to remove the glue after a soapy scrubbing. He gave the baby a bath and changed his clothes, playing with him all morning while listening for the telephone to ring.

The phone did not ring; no calls, at all.

About noon, Stanley saw Hank coming up the driveway, not in the station wagon but driving the antique pickup truck. He carried Toby outside, expecting to greet Margo, holding his young son in his arms.

Before the truck stopped, he saw that Margo wasn't inside; only Bette sat on the passenger side.

"Did you find her?" Stanley asked.

"Yeah; she's fine," Bette said, a tremor in her voice.

"What's the matter, Mom?" Stanley asked, helping her to the ground. "Why didn't Margo come back with you?"

Ah-h, she's not ready yet," Bette said timorously.

"Tell me what's wrong, Mom!" he said, realizing that the problem was larger than anyone was willing to admit. "This doesn't sound like normal behavior, to me."

"Normal? Oh—who's to say?" Bette said flippantly. "Everybody's different."

"I'm worried. I want to see her. Is she at the hospital?"

"Oh, no; that wasn't necessary. We just talked to her," Bette said, now seeming to balk at the barrage of questions. "She felt much better, after we got her a hot hamburger."

"A *gut bomb*—that's all the help?"

Hank stepped in. "She was famished and just needs to spend time alone. She'll take a little drive in the countryside, in the station wagon, then come home for supper. That's what she told us. You're supposed to take care of Toby . . . and she'll see us all later."

"You let her drive, just killing time? She sounds incoherent; that could be dangerous!"

"She's got Dad's car, and she's familiar with it. She learned to drive in that wagon."

"Where did you find her?" Stanley asked.

"She was at the cemetery, behind the Four Corners Church," Bette said. "That's where her little brother Jeremy is buried."

"Yup; fourteen years," Hank said grimly. "I had a feeling, she'd be there."

"She's never told me about a little brother who'd passed away. Does she go there often?"

"We all go on the anniversary of Jeremy's death. Margo goes, by herself, if she's really depressed; except this time, it was bad!" Bette cried. "She didn't even know who we were. She screamed, 'Get away from me'!"

"This sounds serious."

"She scared me," admitted Bette. "It was *not really her*, at first; more like a zombie!"

"Now—Mother," Hank reacted protectively.

"Well, she didn't know who I was! Must've taken half-an-hour to convince her that we were Mom and Dad."

"How often does this happen?"

"Oh—all this stuff—this . . . *family stuff*!" Bette said in anguish. Hank suddenly grabbed her arm and tugged her toward the trailer house.

"I'm *family*—now," Stanley said, hoping for a better explanation.

"She'll be mad if we tell ya," Hank said. "You'll hafta wait and talk to her, yourself!"

"Does she take any medicine for this . . . problem?"

Hank exchanged glances with Bette, then turned away, not acknowledging the question.

"She'll be back tonight—good as new!" Bette reaffirmed, chokingly trying to muster a laugh. "She's doing . . . great; you'll see!"

Hank led Bette into the trailer house, leaving Stanley and Toby standing by the truck.

Stanley glanced at the truck's license plate, noticing something odd: *this plate expired in 1972, over twenty years ago!*

The afternoon passed slowly. The evening mealtime came and went, but Margo hadn't shown up. Stanley put Toby to bed, then poured a bowlful of dry cereal for himself. Later, he stood on the porch steps, watching for the station wagon to come into view.

Still later, he heard the muted sound of a telephone ringing, coming from inside the trailer house. From where he stood, pacing Margo's empty parking spot, he could only imagine that it was Hank who took the call.

Darkness had fallen when Hank suddenly started the pickup and drove out the driveway—alone. He hadn't mentioned why, and Stanley never got to ask.

I wonder who called. Stanley watched the old truck turn toward the lakes. He instinctively knew that Hank was on his way to rescue his daughter—somewhere.

Chapter 64
The Episode

Well-past any normal person's bedtime, Stanley saw headlights slow down, rock through the pothole, and come up the driveway. He paced, waiting for the pickup to stop. With the glare of the headlights, he could barely see Margo through the streaked glass.

Bette came running to the driver's window. "Where's the station wagon?"

"Can't find it, but I found our daughter," Hank whispered, so Stanley couldn't hear.

Stanley reached for the door handle, but Bette squeezed in, pushing him aside. She helped Margo step down to the ground. Hank rushed over and slammed the door, then stood like a sentry, between Stanley and the truck.

Stanley tried but failed to catch Margo's attention, her parents slowly leading her up the porch steps. She timidly walked into the kitchen as if she had never been there before.

"Hi, Margo," Stanley said cautiously, still trying to connect with her, recognizing that she was not bubbly as he would have normally expected. Her hair was wet and had been combed straight down, and she was wearing a flowery-white robe that was too big for her.

Her parents ushered her into the living room, the borrowed gown dragging across the carpet. She slowly sat down on her hand-me-down stuffed chair.

Stanley watched Margo's vacant stare, in disbelief, barely recognizing her drawn face, realizing he had never seen her in such a withdrawn state—beyond indolence. *Something is really wrong. She hates Aunt Pearl's old chair.*

Margo took a glance, like she'd never seen him before, then looked back to her mother, acting like a lost child.

"I think it'll be best, if you take a motel, tonight," Bette whispered to him. "She needs to get used to the place and start remembering . . . again."

Wanting to please everyone, Stanley agreed to leave. Hank waited in the kitchen, ready to escort him away.

"Where has she been?" Stanley asked when they got outside.

"There's nothin' wrong with her, if that's what you're thinkin'," Hank insisted.

"This isn't normal, is it? I think she needs a doctor."

Hank didn't respond to that, not treading on one of the family secrets. "It's only stress, possibly. After some rest, she'll be fine."

That's it? Stanley walked to his car. Just before turning the ignition key, and to his surprise, the opposite door opened.

Bette quickly got in and quietly closed the door. "Don't tell Margo or Henry that I talked to you!"

Stanley listened while Bette spoke.

"She's never had one this bad, before—*the episode.*"

"Is she mentally ill?" Stanley asked, expecting an answer.

Bette's eyes looked back to the porch, to be certain that no one had followed her. "She's been so-o good, lately. I never expected this to happen again, now that she's back on the farm."

"Where has she been all day, in a mental hospital?"

"*Oh, no!*" Bette half-whispered, not wanting to admit to anything. "She had a tough day; but she's responding quite well, don't you think?"

"What! This—episode? Has she gone untreated, all day?"

"Oh, she refuses treatment; it's an insult, to her!"

"Mom, I've held her when she's shaking, fighting some sort of internal battle. It's real; and I want to help her. Tell me, what can I do? Can't we take her to a doctor?"

"Unless she passes out, or something, there's not much anyone can do against her will. She quotes State Law at me, if I interfere. We just help her, as a family. That's our God-assigned purpose on earth—to help each other," Bette said hopelessly, trying to smile through her tears, determined not to tell Stanley that she and Hank would be on suicide watch that night.

"Did she tell you what happened?"

"Ha—never! Getting information out of her is like-pulling-hen's-teeth. She makes the same mistakes, over and over again, then complains. Rest is best—lots of sleep—the best fix."

"It's hereditary, isn't it?"

Bette looked away and quietly opened the door. "Go now! She won't let you stay here." She gently clicked the door shut.

* * *

After spending a sleepless half-night in a cheap motel, Stanley went to work. Miserable, not able to concentrate, he didn't stay long. He had to see Margo.

It was mid-morning when he drove into the farmyard. Hank was by the chicken coop, holding Toby so he could see over the fence. Stanley walked over to look, too. They all watched a hen sheltering a dozen baby chicks under its half-elevated wings, an amazing sight for a small child to see. After a short conversation with Hank, and with his permission, Stanley went into the house.

Margo only whispered, acknowledging his presence. Her mother sat next to her, guarding her like a mother hen would do, even hovering her arm over Margo's shoulder and spreading her fingers, almost like protective feathers. A normal conversation was not possible yet Stanley pulled up a chair and sat next to Margo, holding her hand and whispering in her ear.

Stanley commented that Toby, seeing the mother hen protecting her chicks that morning, probably has some sort of hidden meaning. "Maybe . . . a mother protecting her children?"

Betty's eyes looked down and she moved her arm away. "If you're referring to the chicken picture, I'm just taking care of it until Grandma gets better and comes back home again. She loves that painting!"

Unreal. Stanley almost wished he hadn't said anything about it. He lightly squeezed Margo's hand more firmly, and she reciprocated. She smiled, something he was hoping for.

There were a few more smiles, then Margo slept; and Stanley played with Toby. Each night, he slept in Toby's room, glad that he brought the baby's crib back to where it belonged—in his own room.

He helped the family, in the only way he was allowed to, just spending time with Margo and talking with her. Although it seemed to make a difference, the downside was that she became alert enough to initiate squabbles over nothing. When that happened, Stanley absorbed the blame for each instance.

He tried to avoid the argument trap by treading lightly, as if walking on eggshells to avoid upsetting Margo. But no amount of effort seemed to please her. He didn't understand why her sudden fits of depression were his fault, and why he could never seem to correct himself well enough, or soon enough, to suit her.

Slow recuperation was expected, but, during that week, Margo's overall outlook improved a lot. In fact, she told everyone that she felt great. Over the phone, she even promised her boss that she'd return to work on the very next Monday.

Chapter 65

The Eviction Document

May 7, 1993

A dizzy headache? Stanley was disappointed, hearing Margo's excuse for not going to work that day. "She promised."

Later, at the office, he stared at words scrawled with a felt-pen-marker across a manila folder, containing all the collected information on the death of Officer Clarence Smith. He held his eye on it but couldn't make his mind stick to it, worried about his seriously troubled girl. *She'd only had her job for a month when the episode happened. It won't go over well, if she misses too many days.*

He drove to the farm, keeping up the same routine—some work and some time with his family—with special emphasis on Margo's recovery. After another day of recuperation, Margo was able to laugh.

I knew her fiery spirit would return.

Surprising everyone, Margo returned to work the very next day—Wednesday—just two days late. Stanley was relieved but still concerned, as she had expressed anger over Maria's murder.

Late that afternoon, when Stanley got home from work, he saw that Margo had parked the seldom-used antique truck in her spot, but the house was too quiet.

"I'm home, Honey," he called out, his voice echoing through the eerie silence. *Something's wrong. Maybe she's outside.*

He walked across the farmyard, the abstract sky seeming like it had been swept with a wet but colorful paintbrush; and the sinking sun, parked on a pincushion of distant treetops; all majestically beautiful, but the golden horizon was marred with streaks of disturbing gray. Becoming very concerned, it was almost dark when he searched the pasture area behind the barn.

The Appaloosa nickered, then walked over to get a nose-rub. The colt, however, stayed where he was and seemed to be sniffing the short grasses. Stanley walked past a clump of dry thistles that hadn't been flattened by the previous blanket of snow, and found Margo lying on her stomach, sprawled on the freshly grazed bluegrass.

She squeaked a hopeless cry, as he stepped closer. Her face was flush, eyes tightly closed, and bits of dried grass stuck to her tear-streaked cheeks.

Stanley knelt next to her. Both horses sniffed at Margo's outstretched body. She squirmed, curling into a fetal-like ball.

"Margo, are you okay?" He gently touched her forehead, wanting to soothe her pain.

"Get away from me!" she snapped, her reddened eyes opening and oozing with hostility. She spun to her feet, bolted across the pasture, crawled under the fence, and ran to the house.

Stanley followed, wanting to help her cope with her mysterious affliction, whatever it was. When he walked into the living room, she was sitting quietly on a brand-new couch which had just been delivered that afternoon. The red-velvet cushions were still wrapped in clear plastic coverings.

"Go away. Leave! You scare me," she said in a strangely muted voice. She tried to whisper again but barely emitted a sound.

"What's the matter, Margo?" Stanley sounded both hurt and confused. "I can't *go away*; this is our home."

"This is *my* farm!" she said angrily.

"Everything was great yesterday; what's different today?"

"I don't want you," she sobbed. "Why would you stay where you're not wanted?"

Stanley stared out the window. *Not again! She needs a doctor.*

"Can't you see I'm having a nervous breakdown?" she said weakly. Her face was expressionless, and she appeared to be exhausted.

Bette suddenly appeared, then pointed—stage left—as if she was orchestrating an act.

Stanley acknowledged Bette's presence and also noticed that Hank was innoxiously sitting in the next room, staring down the driveway like he was expecting someone. Realizing that both of Margo's parents had been there all the while, for the act and probably for all the rehearsals, Stanley didn't leave. Confused, he walked toward the stairway.

"No! You can't stay here; not in your mental state!" Bette said accusingly. "Margo is in danger; no telling what you might do to her!"

My mental state? They're trying to turn this around, on me.

Bette's eyes followed a set of bright lights, quickly passing by the window. A squad car suddenly stopped at the back porch, colored lights flashing. Hank rose to his feet, keeping his eye on Stanley.

The emergency lights flashed into all corners of the room. Hank answered the knock at the door. Stanley was surprised to hear Aino

310

Pekka's voice. He waved *hi,* when Pekka asked for *Stanley Nelson,* and stepped over to greet him.

Then came Deputy Sheriff Pekka's official-sounding, high voice, "Are you Stanley Nelson, Sir?"

Stanley almost burst out laughing, as Aino's voice inflections seemed comical, to him, almost as funny as they had been in his jokes, told at the office.

"Why, of course I am!" Stanley said with a light chuckle, then looked into Aino's eyes for some hint that his visit was probably some sort of practical joke, especially since Aino sees him every day at the office and would definitely recognize him. "Aino, you know . . . me!"

"I hereby serve you this paper—" Aino continued in his falsetto.

"What are you doing?" Stanley asked, snatching *the eviction document* from his hand.

"Hey—look-it, Stan, the court has ordered you to leave the premises," said Officer Pekka, almost whining. "I had to do it—ya know. Judge Barnes signed it!"

Frustrated, Stanley panned his eyes across the page. "Margo, you signed this complaint today!" He turned to see Margo's face, but she had disappeared. *Stage left.*

"Get a room; spend money you won't let Margo have!" Bette jeered, then slipped away.

This is an act; she said one line and exited. "What's going on? Who's pulling the puppet strings?" Stanley asked.

Aino Pekka was unaware of anything irregular.

Hank stepped up defensively. "You'll hafta go, Stanley. Margo says, *out!*"

"I've never hurt her, Hank. I love her, and all I want to do is help her."

"Go tonight; come back tomorrow. She'll likely feel better in the morning."

"Why can't I just sleep here, on the couch? I won't bother her."

"She said she don't wantcha here."

"That's crazy!"

"That's one word that's not allowed, in this house. It's her house; what she says, goes! Go—now! You tell 'em, Aino!"

Aino moved in close and whispered, "Well, uh—hey—look-it, Stan; as an officer, you know not to git yourself into any domestic trouble. You'd better just leave the premises, Buddy, like the order says."

That is procedure. "Let me get a couple of things, first."

"Yup; git yer toothbrush, or anything else ya need for the night," Officer Pekka peeped out his practiced line. He waited in the kitchen until Stanley returned with a small overnight bag.

"Nothin' personal," Hank said, when Stanley walked past him and out the door. "I hafta protect my daughter—ya know."

Stanley showed that he was fully cooperating, by getting into his car and driving away, but wondering, *Is everybody off-the-wall in this family?*

The patrol car followed, escorting Stanley off the property.

Chapter 66
Submerged Car
May 8, 1993

Raindrops spattered the motel window and trickled down the outside of the glass. Stanley stared at the grillwork of his sporty-looking 2-door hardtop, rivulets of water cascading across it in the steady rain. He closed the curtains and plunged, face-down into the pillow, the only solution that made sense.

A restless night of soul-searching had left him tired and confused. He recalled that a colleague in Arkansas had asked him, just before he quit and followed Margo northward, "What do you see in that unstable woman from Minnesota?"

And he remembered the last time that he spent a weekend with his father at their peaceful cabin, something from his past that now seemed like a distant dream since his father had passed away. He wondered what life would be like if he had just stayed there in his inherited cabin.

Maybe I should go back.

He felt dejected from being rejected. Lethargy, a rare state of being for Stanley, made him want to stay in bed all day; but he got up anyway.

P. G. Knudson

The complimentary motel-donut tasted like cardboard. He tossed it into a garbage can and walked, between raindrops, to a truck-stop cafe across the street.

* * *

It was almost noon, by the time he drove out to the farm, hoping it was okay to see Margo and Toby. The rain had stopped, but the overcast sky gave no promise for a better day. The pothole by the mailbox, full to the top, splashed when he drove through it.

Entering the yard, he immediately recognized Ernie Niceski's powerful truck parked near the barn. Hank was on his knees, unhooking a tow-chain from his wrecked station wagon that had been missing for almost two weeks. Long, water-soaked weeds hung from the rear bumper.

Ernie popped the clutch and sped down the driveway, when he saw Stanley approaching.

Hank hopelessly watched Stanley walking toward him, the image of intimidating authority in a freshly pressed uniform.

"Where did you find your car?" Stanley asked, noticing that the entire body of the vehicle was streaked with mud.

Hank rubbed his chin, unintentionally leaving a streak of moist clay imbedded in his whiskers. "I wish I woulda got this done before you came out here," he said woefully. "Maybe you County Boys can overlook this little incident. It wasn't reported—ya know." He looked into Stanley's eyes, in a pleading sort of way.

"Where did you find your old station wagon, Hank?" Stanley asked again.

314

"It might be best if I don't tell ya. Then ya can't accuse me of lyin'. Promise me that you won't make me fill out a buncha bureaucratic forms; just tryin' to help my daughter." Hank's lower lip trembled. His eyes appeared to be floating in pools of water.

Stanley rubbed his fingers along the slippery, muddy residue on a door panel.

"That's red clay—ya know," Hank volunteered. "Deerfoot River —the only red clay in Justus County, as ya pro'bly don't hafta be told."

From his years of experience in law enforcement, Stanley knew exactly what sort of vehicular accident-aftermath he was looking at. Through a smashed window, he saw the layers of clay and sand that had invaded the interior, realizing that the vehicle had been under water and guessing that Margo had been the driver.

"She don't remember missin' the bridge or drivin' into the river," Hank said, causing a tear to spill and run down his leathery-looking cheek. "She prob'ly thought she was flying, sailing through the air that way. Her life was saved, by the skin-of-her-teeth. Our good friend, Ernie—you know 'em, the guy with the snowplow—just happened to see her go in. No one else was there. We can all thank that man for a heroic rescue, emergency CPR, and for illegally pullin' the *submerged car* out durin' the night when nobody'd see. If you've got an ounce of gratitude in ya, you won't—." Hank stopped, seeming determined to neither cry openly nor beg for mercy.

Staring at the wreck, destroyed by the slurry of clay and muck that half-filled the interior, Stanley comprehended the life-threatening accident—the plunging into Deerfoot River—that could have snuffed out life's breath from his beloved Margo. Yes, he was grateful for the life-saving efforts of the elusive Ernie Niceski—forever grateful.

The decision may not have been his to make, but Stanley said, "We can pull it with your tractor, out of sight behind those trees."

Hank, surprised with the leniency he was being offered, looked to the Maple grove east of the barn, to where Stanley's eyes were pointing. "That's just what I was thinkin'," he said, a thankful quaver in his voice.

After the flooded wreck was concealed under the canopy of the Maples, Stanley accepted Hank's offer to wash the clay from his hands at the trailer house.

Stanley was feeding Toby at Grandma Toralf's table, when Margo suddenly burst in, raging, "Where were you, for breakfast?"

Surprised, Stanley thought of the disappointing cardboard donut. "I was kicked out."

"Where were you last night?" she demanded to know. "I had supper waiting for you!"

"You sic-the-law on me, a deputy escorts me away, and now you ask where I was?"

"You're supposed to call me; then you get invited—"

"Supposed to—what? Do I look like a mind-reader? I can't guess what you're thinking."

"It's simple logic. When you get kicked out, you go; but you're supposed to come back for meals. That's the way it works."

"The way *what* works? Certainly not court orders."

"Then, just go!"

"I'm not used to getting kicked out, then expected to come home to eat. It doesn't make sense! Who invented those rules?"

"Go now, or I'll call the police!"

I am the police! Stanley felt like saying, but he didn't.

Margo rushed out the door, just as Bette was entering the trailer.

"I've asked you before, Mom, but you wouldn't give me a straight answer," Stanley said. "Is it hereditary? Wouldn't it be better, if we address the actual problem and get her some medical treatment?"

The fear on Bette's face made her eyes seem sunken. Her cheeks twitched and seemed to form new wrinkles, as Stanley watched.

"You and I have never had any such conversation!" she insisted. "And don't make me answer that question! I'd be in worse trouble than I am now, trying to help Margo; she's so ungrateful!" Bette sobbed.

"Margo just wants to be happy—normal, like everyone else," Stanley said.

"Normal?" Bette tearfully scoffed. "In this life, nobody gets to be normal!"

Chapter 67
The 1970s-Style Psychiatrist
May 10, 1993

S tanley awoke Monday morning in the same dismal motel, agonizing over his strained relationship. He knew he had an important job to do, and he was expected to get at it. No more pity party. He had a criminal case to solve.

Pulling on his uniform trousers, he wondered if he was on the right track. He also wondered if Margo would ever truly welcome him back. And he thought of little Toby and what life would be like, for him, if his parents couldn't get along.

Even though his stomach was rumbling, he skipped breakfast and drove through thick fog, just to report to the office an hour early. He poured over the Smith case, but didn't learn anything new, even after reviewing stacks of crime-scene photographs that showed snow crusted on top of everything. He wondered what key piece of evidence he must be overlooking, something that could tie it all together.

Trying to concentrate on his job but troubled by Margo's teetering health, he hadn't accomplished anything. With hunger pangs prodding him, he decided to go out for breakfast.

Before he reached *Gwen's Family Kitchen*, he saw somebody through the fog—someone he would recognize anywhere—Margo— his Margo. She was leaving a small office building. He eased over to the curb, then watched her get into her father's pickup truck and fade into the mist.

Reacting to a hunch, he got out of his car and walked into the building. Inside the hallway, there were two doorways. One smelled like a dentist's office and the other had the words *Dr. James R. Sworden, Psychiatrist* painted on the textured glass door.

Opening it, he saw a man leaning over the receptionist's desk, jotting down a note in a file folder. From a distance, viewed upside-down, Stanley recognized Margo's name at the upper right corner. He was polite but insistent that he must have a few words with Doctor Sworden, concerning the health of Margo Toralf.

"I am Doctor Sworden, Deputy . . . Nelson," the man said, reading from Stanley's name tag and seeming somewhat intrigued with his unannounced visitor. "It would be highly unusual, if I were to allow you to access confidential information concerning one of my clients," he began.

"She's . . . my wife—" Stanley tried to say bluntly but left it hanging.

"Oh—not a fugitive?" the doctor reacted, considering the official uniform.

"Well—uh-h—we have a little boy . . . and we're getting married soon," Stanley clarified, realizing he was in full-uniform and not wanting to misrepresent himself.

"Step into my office," the doctor said, hoping to quickly send this man on his way. He swept his fingers through the fullness of his

Seventies-style, long-feathered hairdo. Not a strand of the fully moussed, graying hair was out of place.

Behind the closed door, Stanley tried to explain his perplexing situation and that Margo recently had a brush with death. "She could have drowned in that car."

Dr. Sworden sensed the emotion revealed in Stanley's voice and apparently recognized the submerged-car story, from what Margo had obviously told him. He removed his overly-small-sized spectacles, polished the lenses with a white handkerchief, and reaffixed them to the bony ridge of his nose.

"Young man, I cannot talk to you—professional ethics, you know. I could lose my license to practice. But, if Mizz Toralf brings you with her, next time, then I'll talk to both of you, together."

Stanley's body language indicated that Margo would not agree to such a dual consultation. The doctor silently seemed to agree. He glanced into the file folder, carefully shielding it from Stanley's view.

"Just one thing—that's all I'll tell you. She just told me, this morning, that she's never coming back, so there is *no* next appointment."

"How will she get help?" Stanley asked, surprised that he had learned precisely nothing and that his talk with the esteemed doctor seemed to be over. "I don't know what to do."

Easily frustrated, the therapist plunged his backside into his swivel-chair, its wheels rolling him backwards across the small floorspace behind his desk.

"Sit down, Officer Nelson!" he said tersely, after his chair crunched into a potted Rhododendron. He pointed to a stuffed chair which faced his seated position.

Stanley sat down, hoping to obtain some useful information.

"She's a very troubled woman, and I haven't put my finger on it yet—the chronic condition, that is. As you can probably imagine, there are umpteen manifestations of this beastly affliction—whatever it is—and every individual seems to be affected in a different way."

What—he's her doctor and doesn't know?

"I'm sure that you know, as everyone else should, also, that no one can accurately presume that another person is—one could say —*'crazy'*. I run into this all the time, as a professional practitioner; but I can only look at facts. And, since I cannot read her mind, it's up to that young woman to let me see into her brain. You know—there's a matter of trust that has to be established. She must trust me; and she's not that far yet. You might say, at this point, that her demons are just part of a great-big experiment."

Stanley seemed unfazed by the therapist's unusual ramblings. "Where does this leave Margo? Is she paranoid?"

"Tsk, tsk—a word reserved for professionals! This is where our conversation must end, Young Man. If you want my advice, just be kind to her and—you know—just let her work her way through her own problems."

"What—her own way? This self-directed plan she's on is *not* working! That's all?"

"I didn't say *'that's all'*! It's psychotherapy; there may be more. It's also very complex, especially when the patient refuses to believe that anything is wrong with her! There's no simple solution. Our great scientists—you must know that they work very hard—have only come up with one new medication: lithium salts. That was back in Nineteen-Seventy-Eight, quite a long time ago; and that was after fifteen arduous years of research and development. Now, with the passage of time, I'm sure you feel as I do, that a *new* miracle-cure is just around the corner—serendipitously speaking, of course."

Stanley caught himself, almost glazing over. "Nineteen-Seventy-Eight?"

"Ah-h; could have been longer ago than that, plus or minus," the doctor remarked, seeming to have misplaced the date in a slurry of other mind-related facts. "Anyway, did you know that the experts are predicting incredible scientific advances, with the coming of the millennium?"

"Huh?"

"Oh, yes! Here we sit, waiting for that exciting date—the year Two Thousand—The Great Millennium—when astounding things will surely come to pass! What do you think I'm referring to?"

"I have *no idea*. Seven years? Doggone it—that's a long time to wait! Are you saying that there'll be a cure for Margo, by then?"

"Exactly—Uh-h, we hope so." He pointed his finger directly at Stanley's nose, almost touching it. "High school graduate—right?" He saw Stanley's slow nod. "Tell me, Young Man, what makes a brain function normally—presumably an educated brain, such as your own?"

"Ah-h—"

"You know the answer—chemicals!" the doctor spoke excitedly. "Everyone has them, functioning inside any brain. We all expect a brain to function perfectly; but for those who have trouble, for instance, they need a positive chemical adjustment. Do you follow me?"

"Ah-h—Yes, sir—so far—"

"Obviously, I'm over-simplifying this example—giving you the condensed version for the benefit of your twelfth-grade understanding. The scientific breakthrough that we're all anticipating will be a new chemical treatment. Then everyone can be—let's say —'normal'."

"So, we . . . wait?"

"Well, actually—right now—sitting in the wings, is a chemical drug that's actually been around for a long time. I shouldn't mention the name; don't want to jinx it."

"This sounds important. What's it called?"

"Ah—okay; just don't hold me to it. We're awaiting FDA approval of valproic acid, but it still could be a long way off," he said with a hopeful tone but followed by a scowl, suggesting past defeats due to severe side effects. "As far as the immediate future is concerned, get yourself invited to her next session."

"I thought you said, she's not coming again."

"Oh-h!" he chuckled and gave a quick wink. "They always come back."

Chapter 68
Textbook Drivel

Stanley was trying to memorize the name of the new substance, cycling it through his mind to sear it in his memory, so he tuned out the therapist's additional ramblings. As Dr. Sworden elaborated, seemingly talking in circles, Stanley kept the memorized term on the tip of his tongue, hoping that the doctor was on to something.

Trying to be courteous but checking his watch, Stanley started backing himself to the door, only half-listening to what sounded like a post-grad lecture.

The doctor realized that his guest was almost out the door but was determined to insert one last thought: "We all hope for the best, but of course, anything tragic can happen. A reckless accident, suicide or other self-inflicted injuries; even crimes."

All things that Stanley didn't want to deal with. He fumbled for the doorknob, behind his back.

"You're the new Justus County Investigator?" the doctor squeezed in the question. "I recognize your name from the Otter Tattler—a newsy little bulwark of journalism."

Stanley looked back at the serious-minded shrink who was still seated.

"Ah; yes, I am . . . investigator. Did I forget to mention it?"

"I can see, you're in a hurry, Young Man, but allow me to indulge. I don't think that I'm obligated to warn an officer of your distinguished caliber, but there's no harm in alerting you—some precautionary advice. I've heard that the death of former Deputy Clarence Smith is a bit of a mystery, still under investigation."

Stanley's ears perked up. He felt the sharp stare of the doctor's trained eyes. Standing by the door, the twitches in his fingers almost caused him to turn the knob.

"Eventually, as you go from suspect to suspect, you'll likely question the actual killer," the doctor said ominously, rubbing his hands together. "But you must be very careful when you cross-examine the killer of Officer Smith; no telling what might happen. Based on what I've been able to glean, the killer is a psychotic—possibly a calm-mannered individual yet a person with a dangerous, unpredictable temper that very few people are aware of. Not even friends or family."

"A psychotic—just what the profiler said! And how did you know that information?" Stanley asked sternly.

The doctor seemed surprised with Officer Nelson's sudden fervor. "Officer, I'm a certified professional, and this is . . . *textbook drivel*! And even if I had a confidential source, I cannot reveal it; you know that! But it fits a pattern, you might say, a pattern that you just might recognize when you come face-to-face with it. A psychotic person can be very unpredictable in *his* or *her* behavior, just so you're aware," the doctor emphasized. "Potentially, a dangerous person to be around, if he or she snaps. It's best not to get too close. A psychotic, you understand, can look you straight in the eye and tell you a lie, all the while knowing it's a lie. Still, he'll likely trick you, convince you he's telling you the truth. And it doesn't bother him that he's deceiving you. In the psychotic's mind, it's exciting to fool an officer of the law; probably more satisfying than committing any crime! I'm sure you've heard this before."

"They call that a *bald face lie*, down in Arkansas. I'm used to liars; you talk to at least one every day, when you're a cop."

The doctor sternly narrowed his thick, combed eyebrows. "Officer Nelson, this is no ordinary liar. Far-beyond—let's say—a politician-type who rarely tells his constituents the truth. Anyone who blows the brains out, from under a cop's hat, has serious psychiatric problems. You have to be careful, so this doesn't happen to a young feller, like you!"

Stanley's heart pounded and his senses went foggy, seeming to remember only the stern tone of Doctor Sworden's voice.

He has talked to the shooter! A chilly jolt shot up his backbone. His knees felt wobbly, realizing that the therapist had just revealed detailed information which had never been released to the public; but he acted like he hadn't heard his warning. Wanting to conceal his trembling, Stanley rotated the knob and walked out the door.

Chapter 69
The Aggravating Pothole

Gwen's Diner was almost empty when Stanley took a corner booth at the rear, pondering Doctor Sworden's words.

"Darn!" He forgot the name of the special cure.

Gwen's eggs and toast went down with difficulty, as the effect of the mere happenstance meeting with Doctor Sworden had left him shaken.

He stared at a fly that aimlessly ran in circles among the crumbs on his table, wondering if he looked that silly, himself; his dominant thought being the health of his precious Margo yet they seemed to be drifting apart. He was aware that he was spinning in circles with no solution in sight, but the question of *what would become of the two of them* was the farthest thing from his mind.

* * *

Back at his desk, he was still reeling from the chance-encounter that he had just experienced with the doctor.

He stared out the window, the fog not lifting. Frustrated that he was charged to investigate the Smith case, but the limited evidence did not support the facts already acknowledged, he hoped for a miracle—definitive evidence—but couldn't say it out loud. Secrecy was a lonely responsibility.

While watching a red Cardinal pecking the windowpane, Stanley was called to Homer's office for an impromptu meeting.

Sheriff Anders was brief and to the point: "We've been caught, or I should say, 'The Department has come under scrutiny', and I'll *not* be a party to misappropriation of federal funds. The county can't afford to lose this grant-money, so I hafta close the investigation."

Stanley was disheartened with the layoff, but relieved that he had not actually been fired. He turned in his badge and uniform but left his personal items in his desk, expecting to be back someday. He headed for the farm, wondering how he could tell Margo that he lost his job.

Barely able to see, as the fog had thickened, he almost missed the turn. Then, expecting the large pothole to be his guide so he could find the end of her driveway, he failed to splash his tires into it. The roadway seemed smooth, instead of rough like it had been—a deep pothole punished by years of tire-hammerings. After a cursory inspection, he saw the repaired spot where the perpetual pothole no longer existed.

"Someone fixed it!"

Safely home, he was apprehensive, wanting to present the news of his termination in a positive light; hopefully, to say it in such a way that Margo could see the silver lining on what he expected would seem like a dark cloud over their future.

The farmstead seemed deserted when he got out of his car. He faced the old gray barn that seemed to stand in ambivalent isolation, in its slow state of both deterioration and renovation. Its outline emerged, in its graceful simplicity, from the fog that was dissipating.

He saw a subtle irony in the weathered structure, in which he had labored intensively: much invested but possibly nothing gained.

Thoughts of his secluded cabin drew his mind away from his present crises. That peaceful, stress-free Ozark hideaway, tucked away in a mountain valley that his father called *Nelson Holler* spurred his memory; a place where he could fall asleep to the babbling sound of the creek spilling over pebbles on a simple ford-crossing; where he could spin a lure into the spring-pond and catch a trout for breakfast.

It occurred to him, that his cabin represented the only certainty he owned; that he could glean only a measly profit by selling it now and lose its intrinsic value; that he should keep his small piece of a mountain paradise, a logical place to return to, if necessary.

Hank suddenly appeared, coming from out of the mist. "Why are ya home so early, Stanley?"

Lost in his thoughts, Stanley almost jumped. "Hank! For a minute, there, I thought everyone was gone!"

"Investigatin' somethin' here, in my yard?" Hank asked with a timorous chuckle.

Stanley felt that Margo's whole family was against him, and it showed on his face.

"Come on, Stanley, lighten up a little. I was jokin'! You've been takin' that investigation job much too seriously! You really otta find a better job, one more suited to ya."

"Is Margo better today?" Stanley asked, knowing where she had been that morning.

"Seems okay; and she canceled that court-order malarkey."

Stanley was relieved to hear that bit of news. Commenting about almost missing the driveway, due to the heavy fog and the apparently repaired pothole, he said, "I wasn't expecting that the smooth road would throw me off."

"Hey—the fog was as-thick-as-pea-soup, when I turned in two hours ago. It faked me out, too! Ya expect the usual ol' bump, but it's as smooth as glass. *The aggravating pothole* was there so long, I thought they'd never fix it!"

"The investigation job is over," Stanley said, getting the bad news off his chest. "Someone pulled the funding; so, being the expendable one, I'm . . . gone!"

"Nah—you're kiddin' me! They ended your job . . . without solving the crime?" Hank said, already knowing that 'ol Red had come through for him. "Too bad—"

"I hope our friends and neighbors will understand. I didn't mean to let them down. I got close, but there are still a few loose ends."

"What kinda loose ends?"

"You know I can't tell you that, Hank. Someday, the sheriff might reopen the investigation. Cops don't give up until they get their guy—you know."

"Well, in the meantime, there are other jobs—" Hank scratched his chin and glanced toward the kitchen window, from where he seemed to know that someone was watching. "As much as you like that kinda work, it's time to just . . . let it go. Speakin' of jobs, Stanley—and I wouldn't want to bother you with it, except you're . . . part of my family—there could be a job opportunity that you might wanna look into—"

Stanley's eyes showed interest.

"I've got a friend who could use another truck driver . . ."

"Let me guess, his name is . . . Ernie—Ernie-something," Stanley said with mistrust, looking Hank directly in the eye.

Chapter 70

Bad News is Good News

Margo seemed happy when Stanley entered the kitchen. She met him with a long, soft hug.

"Dad told me your job is over. That's it?"

How does she already know this? Stanley wondered.

"Gee, Golly—fired—what a surprise!" she almost laughed, not being contrite but bubbly, just as Hank had indicated. "You should be glad that it's over. *Bad news is good news!*"

"I was expecting the hammer to fall, just not this soon. I had barely gotten the investigation started, when they sent me packing," he said, wondering how she could sound elated when he was feeling quite blue; but he was happy that Margo's brightening persona filled the room.

"What happens to your suicide case?" she asked, even knowing what her father had arranged.

"They *may* reopen it someday; there's no statute of limitations on murder—you know."

"Oh—I've . . . heard that," she said slowly, seeming especially disappointed. "So, what do you do now, pack your things and go back downstate—maybe to Arkansas?"

Stanley's knees felt weak, with the mere suggestion that he would abandon Margo and Toby. He had special obligations to fulfill, yet memories of the ebb and flow of the two years that he had spent with his lovely Margo—from sheer bliss to abject agony—played like a sped-up movie in the forefront of his mind. He saw past the bad and wanted to hold onto the good—the best of the enchanting memories.

"My life is here," he replied, looking into her eyes for something special but not seeing it. "I want to stay here with you and Toby—my family. We still have a wedding coming someday, don't we?"

"Ah-h—gee; sure, Stanley, but . . . not right away, of course. There's so-o much to sort out—you know—for our future. We don't even have the ranch in shape yet. And—"

"I thought our future would be something we'd enjoy together, like married partners rebuilding the ranch together—sweating together, dots of paint splashing on both of our faces at the same time; but I won't pressure you, Margo. I'll find a different job around here, somewhere, so we can be together."

"What kind of job?"

"Anything I can find. I'll start looking tomorrow—promise!"

* * *

After a week of job-hunting, Stanley was still jobless and Margo, impatient. There was one dead end after another; no appealing job prospects in Burntwood Prairie. And he was holding off on Hank's suggestion, as a last resort. Correction: no-way; he had no intention of driving truck for Ernie Niceski, the one man who still seemed to carry-the-torch for his girl.

Margo was dashing in-and-out of the kitchen, getting ready to go to work, as Stanley scanned across the *help wanted* columns that he had spread across the kitchen table, crossing out each dud as he panned over it.

"Mom says you're not trying, very hard, to find a job," she said provokingly.

"I'm trying! It's going to take a while to find someone who'd be willing to hire me, an outsider in this clannish community."

"Mom said you didn't leave the house until nine, yesterday!" she quibbled, applying hair spray at her last-second mirror, seeming determined to start an argument.

"Does she understand what *revising my résumé* means? Is she spying on me?"

"You're sounding like the paranoid one, now!"

"Why would your mother tell you something like that— monitoring how I make use of my time—to deliberately cause trouble between us?"

"You've got no business talking about me, behind my back, about my so-called *mental condition*. I am *not* mentally ill!" she screamed.

"Woah! How did this topic surface out of a discussion about me trying to find a job?" Stanley realized that Bette had told Margo everything from their private whisperings. Now, he knew it was a bad idea to discuss anything with Margo's mother.

"You need to get a *real* job—real soon! Look at all the work still not done on this place; it takes money! And speaking of money, when is that house in Arkansas going to sell? It's taking way too long. Lower your price on that thing!"

Quite some time after Margo had gone to work, and when Stanley was taking a break from fencing, his realtor called from Little Rock. An offer had been made on his far-away Ozark get-away. Stanley was relieved but battling reservations in his mind, wanting to keep his ace-in-the-hole but also wanting to please the love-of-his-life.

That evening, when Margo heard that Stanley finally had a buyer, she was ecstatic. Dollar signs danced in her mind. She took Stanley's hand and twirled across the kitchen floor.

Wanting her to be satisfied, Stanley decided to make a quick trip to the Ozarks to expedite the sale transaction.

"If I hurry, I'll be back by next Friday . . . in time for the full moon; it's a special one!"

"I absolutely *adore* the full moon. I'm tingling!" she said gleefully. "I can't wait!"

That night, the evening before Stanley's departure to Arkansas, they stood in the dark by the corral, both searching the cloudy sky for any bright spot. They embraced, watching the first quarter suddenly appear from behind a bank of clouds, far above the horizon. Margo was disappointed that the moon was only a wedge, glowing a small portion of its roundness, its soft light barely a dim glow. Stanley reassured her that the first quarter was waxing toward fullness and would surely appear, round and full—just how she likes it—by the time he returned.

Margo reaffirmed her love to Stanley, that night, but stopped short of setting a wedding date, a subject that seemed to irritate her no matter how many times he brought it up.

In the early morning, long-before dawn and just as the waxing gibbous moon phase was tailing in the western sky, Stanley drove out of the driveway, southbound on his cabin-selling trip.

Margo drove to work in a new-to-her minivan that was strategically delivered to the farmhouse, sometime after Stanley left and just minutes-before she had to leave for work—a temporary secret, until Stanley would notice it days later.

Knowing that Ernie came through on a great used car deal—not the sporty look, but rather, a soccer-mom's utility choice—didn't fulfill her desire for feeling rich. She avoided the nightlife that she normally relished, her cycling depression gnawing at the edges of her enthusiasm. And her job was demanding; behind at work, after missing many days, and over-tired each evening.

"Make that kid shut up, Mom!" she complained, when Toby fussed at the dinner table.

"He's just tired," Bette said. " I'll put him to bed."

"Yeah; you do it, Mom. I just can't deal with it."

As the week dragged on, Margo loathed that Stanley was gone. Too stressed to deal with her baby, she had her mother keep the crib at the trailer house. Each night, she went to bed early, but that didn't equate to getting more sleep, and it didn't reduce her dreaded nightmares. She thought about practicing music but remembered that her guitar was broken, suspended from a nail in the shed where her father had hung it.

On Thursday night, the last night that Stanley would be gone, she was almost asleep but obsessing over old bones that mattered to no one. Terrified of her recurring worries, she cried aloud, "Stanley cannot know!"

She lunged from bed, charged down the steps in the dark, and floundered for the drawer-pull, just below where the phone-cord hung against the wall. Turning on the light and quickly paging through the telephone book, she almost tore out one of the yellow-colored pages. Reconsidering destroying that page, since it was something that Stanley might notice and thus become suspicious, she instead found a felt-tipped marker and blacked-out the entire display-ad of Dr. James R. Sworden.

"Now, he'll never know."

Chapter 71
Strawberry Moon
June 4, 1993

When Margo got home Friday afternoon, she listened to Stanley's recorded message. He was right on schedule. With dreamy thoughts of blissful love, yet dragging her feet from fatigue, she went to bed early. She was too excited to sleep, though, knowing that Stanley would soon be there.

She crouched by the window, anticipating the rising of a romantic full moon, the one Stanley had promised. She watched a wispy trace of fog overtake the unlit part of the farmyard, hoping Stanley would arrive that very minute. "I love him and miss him so-o much."

Imagining herself as a bird on a perch, she admired the shiny roof of her almost-new minivan that was parked under the oak tree, below, a gift from an old friend. "Okay—it's from Ernie. So—what?" she burst out argumentatively, with no one to hear.

A head-splitting pain suddenly hit, like a bolt of lightning. She decided to lie down, after all. Afraid of the dark, she added Toby's teddy-bear-nightlight to calm her fears.

Almost immediately, weird-shaped shadows cast from the nightlight spooked her thoughts. The horrific replay of the roadside park shooting came to her mind. To stop thinking about it, she tried to replace that scourge with a recurring, desirable dream, perpetuated by lingering longings from her childhood. To be taken care of by a handsome prince and to live the life of a wealthy princess who didn't have to go to work—the unrealistic life of a true princess—was the dream she craved. However, a replay of her desired dream wouldn't come. Angered, she decided to recreate her perfect dream, the one with horses running across the south forty.

Still irritated, she began ruminating about her job, upset that her schedule had changed, requiring her to work an occasional Saturday. On-top-of-it-all, her supervisor had reminded her that she was being watched for missing too many days and for making too many mistakes.

She dreaded having to go to work, the very next morning. The only soothing thought was that of Stanley returning soon, that night; that he would hold her securely and gently kiss all her worries away, her best chance to escape the reality of her complex life.

"At least he's off-the-case. Maybe I'm safe, and we can—"

In mid-thought, Margo had fallen into a light slumber but knew that she heard the slow creak of a floorboard. One eye opened up. She listened again. There was a startling squeak of a nearby hinge. Realizing that the door to her room was slowly opening, she jerked to alertness. In the weak light, she spotted her 12-gauge shotgun that leaned against the wall, then lunged for it.

"Margo—No, Margo," Stanley cried out. "I'm home!"

Margo's eyes popped and her heart pounded, the gun already in her hands when she realized that it was Stanley's familiar voice.

"Stanley-y!" she screamed, seeing his hand already holding the muzzle of her gun, low.

He turned on the instantly glaring ceiling light. "Sorry—"

"What are you doing? I could've shot you!" she scolded. "Stanley, you scared me! Why are you sneaking up on me?"

"I just walked into the room—"

"You were tiptoeing around the house. Make some noise, like everyone else does. It's not normal to be so quiet!"

"I thought you were asleep, and I didn't want to disturb you. It's still early. Let's go down to the lake and watch the moon come up," he said, wanting to turn the frantic moment into a romantic one.

Margo was infuriated. "No, I don't want to! What is it that you're planning to do in the dark, by the lake, something you thought about mile-after-mile, ever since you left Arkansas?"

"Margo, you always say how much you love the full moon. The June moon is supposed to be spectacular! Tonight's the night, and it's happening right now!"

Margo's eyes locked onto the east window. Unable to break her stare, she parted the curtains. "Here it comes. Look how red it is; how big it is!" she said, her breathy voice pulsating. "Can you feel the magic, Stanley?"

Stanley stepped up, behind her, and put his arms around her waist. "Magic—"

Margo pushed him away, with a guttural pout.

"We're missing the *Strawberry Moon*!"

"You don't like my relatives! Why don't you talk to my cousin?"

"What? The greatest moon of the year is rising, and— Which cousin are you talking about?" he asked, bewildered with the sudden emergence of a totally new, unrelated topic.

"Gerald; he was insulted!" she said angrily.

"Who? When was this? I don't remember meeting Gerald. Where did this happen?"

"That time at the grocery store—remember *Butch*—the guy with jeans, down below his butt, the nerdy glasses, and the wacko hair?"

"Oh—the purple-hair guy. I remember him, complaining about the Whitewater Scandal; just didn't know what his real name was. He was pretty worked up about the corruption and cover-up going on in Washington D.C.; kind of an oddball, trying to convince me that the president's wife is an ambitious broad who wants to be president."

"So what? He's actually pretty knowledgeable about politics. He predicted that Bill Clinton would win the election—ya know!"

"I didn't know he was your cousin, but I talked to him."

"The complaint I heard, was that you totally ignored him."

"He saw me, in uniform, and asked what kind of work I do. He's kind-of-an-idiot."

"Of course, he sounds stupid; but he's my cousin. What choice do I have?"

Margo insisted that she was too tired to look at the moon, and it was *his* fault. She crawled into bed and buried her head under the covers, then tightly stretched the sheet around her head, like she was closing off the entire world.

Stanley crawled into the deep sway of the mattress, alongside Margo, not wanting to argue about anything. "Go to sleep, Honey," he whispered.

"How can I sleep, wondering where you are? I miss you too much when you're gone. Don't ever leave me alone again—promise?"

"I sold it and signed the papers, Margo. I don't have to go back."

"Mom told me, you called. Where's the money?"

"It's safe. I already had an account, down there, so I just put it in the bank."

"You banked it . . . in Arkansas—a zillion miles from here? You made your own account, without telling me? Stanley, we're going to be married. You can't keep secrets from me. I have to be able to trust you!"

"It's not a secret. I've always had that account, ever since . . . long before we met."

"It's too late! You kept it from me . . . all this time. I can never forgive you!"

"What did you expect me to do, drive all this way with thousands stuffed into my pockets? I had to put it somewhere, where it's safe."

"You're afraid I'll get my hands on your damn money and go on a spending spree!"

"Margo, I didn't say that!"

"Doesn't it make sense, put it in our joint account so we can use it . . . on the farm?"

"I've already done that, rebuilding this place, buying fences, stalls, and probably the horse."

"And you did a great job, Honey. Everyone has complimented you on what a good job you've done, making the stalls."

"When can we put my name on the papers?" Stanley suddenly asked, surprising her.

"Well, not yet!" The worn-out bed springs went silent. Both fell asleep and they missed the much-anticipated, spectacular rising of the very special full moon.

After a while, Margo awakened, still agitated. Instead of going back to sleep, she became more and more irritable, then impulsively decided to go to work, early. She quickly showered and stomped about, definitely wanting Stanley to know that she was leaving the house.

He was befuddled. "We finally get to share a full moon together, and then, look what happens; you're in a bad mood, all of a sudden. Do you know that we've *never* been able to share a full moon together?" he asked, not understanding that Margo typically acts up, with the onset of a full moon. "It'll be the middle of the night, when you get to work. You don't have to be there for another . . . five hours!"

Stanley looked out the window and watched Margo drive out the driveway in the bright moonlight. *What's this—a car I didn't know about—another favor from Mister Nice Guy?*

Chapter 72
Crazy Night-Owls

Since Margo had gone to work very early, and Stanley was still full of travel-caffeine, he went to the barn and turned on a light. His tools lied just where he had left them. Seeming to be full of energy, quite an oxymoronic condition since he had just driven over a thousand miles without sleep, he decided that it was time to put the jack to work and straighten the sagging ceiling.

It was quiet in the barn, except for the ratcheting sound of the timber-jack. The central beam was slowly raising the sagging framework, one notch at a time, vibrations building up in every board that felt the upward force of the tool. With each stroke of the handle, popping sounds resonated throughout the skeleton of the old building. Then came a sudden boom, thundering and shaking the entire structure. Dust fell from the cracks above.

Aware that the whole barn could crash, in catastrophic failure, Stanley ran for the exit. Decades-worth of old hay-dust formed a choking cloud that followed him out the door.

"Oh, Margo, if you could only see this!" he lamented. "Straightening this old barn is hardly worth the effort."

It was hard to see the single incandescent light bulb that hung from the ceiling, as more dust fell through the cracks of the hayloft floor, clouding the air, drifting past the light bulb and past the jack, falling to the floor where he had been standing.

Now outside and looking back at the straightened structure, squinting through the earliest rays of morning sunlight, he saw the last cloud of musty dust slowly drifting away from the barn.

"It's still standing!" Eyeballing his work, he surmised that the old barn must have been jacked up far enough.

"Stanley! Come for breakfast!" came Bette Toralf's shrill voice, shouted from a distance.

Stanley looked across the yard and saw his future mother-in-law, waving from the deck of the trailer house. He waved back and headed in that direction.

He walked past Margo's parked minivan, his first opportunity to actually get a close look at it. *She went to work; is she back already?*

"I know you're just trying to please Margo," Bette said, when Stanley walked into her kitchen. "I saw your lantern, out there in the dark; heard you pounding, trying to make Margo's dream come true. We'd all be better off, if one of her other dreams came true—the one filled with fire. She'll probably burn it down someday, then collect the insurance money."

Stanley seemed surprised at Bette's incendiary comments, but chose not to say anything, knowing that she would repeat anything that slipped from his lips. The aroma of bacon and eggs made him hungry.

"Did you talk to Margo this morning? I thought she was at work," said Stanley.

"Oh—she was there but faked a sick spell, so she could come home. She doesn't want breakfast. With the mood she's in, I doubt if we'll see her for the rest of the day."

"Where's Toby—up yet?"

"Don't bother that kid!" Bette snapped. "I finally got him to sleep. He's been awake all night, like the rest of you *crazy night-owls*!"

"Where is he?" Stanley asked, starting to walk down the dark hallway. He began opening a door when Bette suddenly stepped in front of him, blocking the entrance.

"Don't go in there and wake him up," she insisted, bracing her hand against the door jam.

Stanley detected an odd smell coming from that room. "What's that funny smell?"

"Nothing!"

"There's a definite odor; you smell that?"

"Oh—I remember, now. Aw—I spilled some . . . nail polish remover—that messy stuff! It's harmless, so Toby's okay; don't worry about him!"

Since Stanley didn't know what polish remover smelled like, he held off but remained suspicious, remembering his previous concern over the questionable use of duct tape.

Chapter 73
Grandma's Magic Medicine

The next morning, Stanley was fitting a new post to the beam when Hank showed up. He excitedly announced that he and Betty were taking a camping hiatus, beginning that morning. "The Walleyes are biting, and Uncle Pugg rented a pontoon boat!"

"We'll be fishing on Lake Winnibigoshish with Aunt Pearl and Uncle Pugg for a couple weeks," Bette told Margo before she and Hank drove out the driveway, pulling their pop-up camping unit with the old pickup truck.

Stanley worked steadily, skipping lunch. By mid-afternoon, he was tired and thirsty, needing a break. He put his tools down and walked to the house.

"Stanley! What are you doing in here? It's not quitting time yet, is it?" Margo nagged.

"I just came in for a drink of something—something sugary; maybe a little snack, too."

"Well, there's no food here! Check at Mom's place. She might've left some pop in her fridge, and maybe some candy bars. And remember, since Mom and Dad aren't home, we've got Toby over

347

here. You'll need to take over, for Mom, when I go to work—if I go at all."

"Honey, are you feeling any better? You look . . . sad," he said, trying to tread lightly, not wanting to step on any sensitive, proverbial eggshells.

"I'm doing good; it just takes a while to get over the sick headache. It's nothing, really."

"Maybe you should see a doctor. It's scary to see you so depressed."

"I wish everyone would stop saying that I'm depressed! I'm perfectly normal; and I'm not old enough for menopause, in case you're ignorant! It's just my new schedule at work. I'm okay, and as smart as any doctor. I passed all the exams and I know what I'm doing. How many times do I have to tell you—a thousand?"

"I'm going to check on Toby. Is he upstairs?"

"Don't go up there! I've had to listen to that miserable crying all day long. He's finally asleep; leave him alone!"

"I'll see for myself," he said, moving quickly up the stairs, remembering that Margo's mother had told him basically the same thing, just the previous morning.

The hinges squeaked when he opened the door to the nursery, and the floorboards popped and creaked, but no amount of noise seemed to disturb the baby.

Margo scampered up the stairs and caught up to him. "No!" she pulled at his elbow.

Stanley immediately saw his son lying motionless in his crib, with a silvery-gray piece of tape stretched across his mouth. "Margo! What did you do?" he cried out, horrified that his son was gagged with duct tape.

"Stop—don't look, Stanley; don't bother him!" she pleaded, then dug her fingers into his shoulder and cried, "Don't be mad!" She pulled at his arm, trying to drag him away.

"What's the tape for? Is this how you and your mother get him to stop making noise?"

She faked a fall to the floor. "I told you not to come in here! It's not what it looks like."

Stanley gently pulled at a corner of the sticky tape, peeling it off Toby's delicate lips.

"Mothers have the right—"

"There's no motion; he's limp. I can't tell if he's breathing, Margo."

"Of course, he's breathing!" She reached over and shook the boy. "He's okay; see?"

Stanley tried to lift his son, but the baby's head flopped backwards.

"No, I can't see; he's knocked out! What did you do to him, Margo?" He lifted his son from the crib and held the unresponsive child in his arms, catching a whiff of a strange but familiar chemical in the air. "What's that odd smell—the same, funny smell at your mother's place—polish remover?"

"I don't smell polish remover," Margo said, slyly reaching her hand to the top of the dresser. She moved a small glass bottle to where it couldn't be seen, behind a framed photograph of their baby.

"What was that?" Stanley asked, suspicious of her maneuvering. "What are you hiding?"

"Nothing. I just straightened the picture. You almost knocked it on the floor, Stanley! You should be more careful! What if the picture fell . . . and the glass broke . . . and Toby got cut? It would be *your* fault!"

Stanley stepped over and reached behind the picture, finding the hidden bottle. He held it in one hand, expecting to read a list of ingredients.

"The label has been torn off! What's in this bottle, Margo? This could be a life and death situation! What is it?" he demanded to know.

Margo showed an expression, not unlike that of a dog getting caught sucking eggs. "You're raising your voice at little ol' me?"

"What is it?"

"Well, it's *not* polish remover," she said, almost with a laugh. "It's —it's—I don't know what it is; just something that Mom uses— *Grandma's magic medicine.*"

"The smell—something poison? You're both using this stuff— both you and your mother!" he said, his voice shaking.

Margo cringed, stepping backwards and holding both hands over her mouth. "Is he breathing?" she asked, seeming fearful for the first time.

"He's still knocked out. You're a nurse—for God's sake! Wake up the baby!"

Margo pointed to the baby's changing table, as the place to lay him down, and she opened the window, letting in fresh air.

"I can't believe you used this—something dangerous," he said, handing her the bottle.

"It's safe; it's like . . . nothing. Mom uses it all the time," she said dismissively, then tossed the bottle out the window when Stanley was looking the other way. She moved to Toby's side, getting ready to administer mouth-to-mouth resuscitation.

Toby opened his eyes, before his mother's lips got close. He squirmed; first moving his legs, then his arms. Just about the time that Stanley thought he was coming out of the sedation, the toddler began thrashing about, violently kicking and screaming.

"Toby—are you all right?" he asked. He could hardly hold his terrified son still. "What's going on, Margo—convulsions—hallucinations?"

Margo's face went blank, clearly having no idea, as to what she should do.

"Help—do something!" yelled Stanley. "Hold his legs, so he won't hurt himself!" After a few seconds, Toby's violent reaction began to subside. By the time he stabilized, Stanley was nearly exhausted. "Whatever's in that bottle is bad stuff. You could've killed him, Margo!"

"He's okay now, isn't he?" she said piously, then stared out the open window, feeling the breeze on her face. "You tried to scare me, Stanley, and tried to make me a dunce. Don't ever do that again—not to me!"

"I can't believe your callous attitude toward your own son. You knocked him out with some sort of dangerous chemical, for your own convenience!"

"I wanted *quiet*! He gives me an awful headache; drives me crazy! Oh, God—why did I want a baby anyway?" she screamed. "All this—this stuff—important stuff I'm trying to get done; all the fences, the planning for the party, the horses, my happiness!" Margo cried and hopelessly pulled at her hair. "I have the right to be happy, don't I? What's more important, my happiness, or—?"

Stanley finally saw the *real Margo*—the narcissistic woman that he loved but who hated motherhood.

"Should we call a doctor?" he asked, wondering if the worst was over.

"No, I'm an educated professional! Don't you think I know what I'm doing?"

"No, I don't! You've been endangering the life of our son! How many times, now?"

"Oh—cut it out! I'm not going to be interrogated this way; not in my own house!"

"That's *it*; it is *your* house, isn't it? And you're in charge . . ."

"Oh, Stanley, shut up and get out to the pasture; get that fencing done! And you haven't even started painting yet! The Fourth of July is practically here! How will we ever be done, in time, if you don't get your ass moving? You're slower-than-molasses-in-January! I'd like to get this ranch whipped-into-shape before I'm ninety years old! Now, I suppose you expect me to make supper! Can't you see, I'm coming down with a nervous breakdown?" she screeched.

"No, I can't tell—not at all. By the way, what *is* a nervous breakdown, anyway?"

Margo abruptly calmed down and seemed to actually ponder the question. "I don't know; that's just what they call it," she said in a suddenly fading voice.

"It seems to me that it's just an excuse, given to overlook a bigger problem."

"Go away; leave me alone, Stanley. I'm going to lie down," she said weakly, in a strained whisper. "And when I wake up, I don't want to see your face! Take your shit with you and get your ass off *my* property!" She walked slowly out of the room, not looking back, suddenly transformed into a virtual invalid, struggling to walk down the stairwell, clutching the railing each step of the way.

Chapter 74

The Rescue of Baby Toby

Stanley's hands were shaking, the confrontation with Margo very upsetting. He hadn't wanted their lives, or their love for each other, to deteriorate in this way. His attention remained with his mistreated son. He looked into his dilated eyes, alive but overly sedated.

The status quo was unacceptable. He had a decision to make: should he remain, trapped in a downward spiral and allowing the abuse of his son to continue? Or what—leave? What would that solve? Who would help Margo? But if he didn't leave, who would save Toby from the abuse? Whom could he trust? Certainly not Margo's mother.

He only saw a quagmire coming, recognizing a dead-end predicament—an impossible situation. *How do you help someone who refuses help?*

The decision should be easy, he thought, recalling the lies of both Margo and her mother; how they both endangered Toby's well-being and possibly his life.

"Are you okay, My Little Guy?" he asked, seeing an improved response from his year-old baby. He saw mental fog; clearly, Toby was still under the influence of the unknown chemical substance that had been forced upon him.

He had to act quickly, to rescue his son from this abusive environment. Toby's short bath, the unexpected packing of clothes, and the hurried preparations for an unplanned trip proceeded methodically. *Her order is clear; she wants both of us . . . gone!*

It grieved him to suddenly have to decide, yet it had seemed like he was living in an insane asylum. Deep down, he wanted to stay. Even though she had ordered him to leave, how could he ever get his lovely Margo off his mind? He wished there was a way to turn it all around, to get her some *real* help and make everything okay; but understanding that *the rescue of Baby Toby* was more important than anything, he zipped the stuffed bags closed.

The final decision was made: *leave now. Save Toby from the chaos and the abuse before his mother wakes up.*

After ascertaining that Margo was napping on her new couch, Stanley began to scrawl a short note; but there were more thoughts to convey than there were appropriate words to spell it out. He left both the pencil and the paper, with its unfinished goodbye, lying on the kitchen table.

The emptiness that filled his core reminded him that he had lost everything, except his son. And he knew there was no use in pining or lamenting his losses, as it was too late to do anything about any one of them.

* * *

P. G. Knudson

Approaching the only traffic light in Burntwood Prairie, Stanley still hadn't decided where he would go; not even which way he should turn—North or South. It crossed his mind that his now-lost Ozark get-away, which he had just given up for the love of Margo, was gone forever; so, there was no ace-in-the-hole.

* * *

Margo eventually awakened, now alone. She read the unfinished pencil-note, then blacked-it-out, angrily scribbling over Stanley's words until the lead broke.

Her life was over. She was sure of it. Without tears and showing no remorse, she found a bag of potato chips, turned on the TV, and lied down again.

Chapter 75
The Lost Years

The summer days of 1993 blurred into weeks, then into months. Before autumn, Margo had lost her job. No wonder, staying in bed, sometimes for weeks at a time. By wintertime, with the frigid air and inevitable snowdrifts, and with her having no income, Hank struggled to make the mortgage payments. He paid the taxes, too, so his heirloom farm—his daughter's would-be horse ranch—would not be taken away by fiscal sharks who prey upon the misfortune of others.

Months turned into the first year, then into subsequent years. Stanley never called, and Margo rarely repeated his name. If she ever thought of Toby, nobody ever heard her mention that she had a son.

In *the lost years*, which had passed by with no contact between Stanley Nelson and Margo Toralf, their separation seemed permanent. Her memory of her fledging family had only haunted her mind during her darkest moments, barely remembering the day that Stanley rescued Toby from her unspeakable abuse.

Eventually, the calendar advanced to a critical point in the election cycle, well into the fourth year of President Clinton's first term in office and the beginning of yet another political season.

P. G. Knudson

With the passing of time, and a lingering love for Margo which could not be explained, there came the surprising return of Stanley Nelson to Burntwood Prairie.

Was there to be a reuniting? Not likely. Or, was there a ghost of a chance?

Chapter 76
A Sight for Sore Eyes

March 27, 1996

It was an early spring morning, much like the one when Stanley first visited the farm, when he dialed her number. Margo was trudging to get to her fourth new job when her phone rang.

Counting the number of rings but not lifting the receiver, she grabbed her car keys and glanced at her last-second mirror, deciding that her eyeliner was flawless. On the ninth ring, she lifted the receiver from the wall, her speech already prepared. "Sorry, I'll be a little late," she said, expecting that the call was from her new boss.

At that same instant, Stanley stood in a local phone booth, feeding quarters into the slot, hearing the payphone chime, coin-by-coin, until Margo's voice finally came to his ear.

"Hi Margo," he said cheerfully, like nothing had happened.

"You—you!" she said, instantly recognizing his voice. She promptly lit into him, a surge of hatred spewing from her lips. "You're making me late for work and . . . it's Rowdy's birthday; and I've got to bail my boyfriend out of jail."

What's this? "Toby will be ready for kindergarten, by next year."

359

He listened for her more-pleasant voice but only heard a click, then the dial tone.

* * *

The next day, unannounced, Stanley paid a visit to the farm. He first drove past the place, realizing that his pining for Margo's love had driven him to this point.

"It looks the same," he whispered to himself. *Except for the new house on the corner of the south forty. Is that Brian's name on the mailbox?* He slowly turned into the familiar, narrow driveway where pussy willows bloomed in the watery ditches.

With a wrench in one hand, Hank Toralf was on his knees and leaning over his lawnmower when a half-dozen of his hens scampered past him, getting out of the way of an approaching vehicle. The sporty 4X4, which he didn't recognize, was inching its way closer, the slow-rolling tires barely making a sound on the soft sand.

"*Big Sky,*" Hank mumbled, reading words off the license plate. Rising slowly to his feet, he seemed shocked that it was Stanley Nelson who smiled through the mud-speckled glass.

"Hi there, Hank," said Stanley.

"Hey, Stan—*a sight for sore eyes*!"

"I've got a four-year-old boy, here, who wants to see his grandpa."

"Oh, Toby!" Hank said joyfully, straining for a full breath of air and rushing to the other side of the vehicle. He opened the door where Toby sat. "For goodness' sake—you big boy! You came to see Grandpa?"

Stanley helped Hank undo the seat harness. Hank lifted Toby up, with great pride, enveloping his arms around his grandson. "Do you remember me?"

Only inches from Hank's hoary face, Toby stared at the wrinkled old man.

"What's the matter, Toby? Do you think I'm Santa Clause?" Hank's familiar, jovial chuckle rang out, making him sound almost like the fabled carrier of good will.

"How've you been doing, Hank?"

"Well, I'm behind-the-eight-ball; grass growin' wild, and I can't get this ol' mower goin'!" he said, in disgust. "Are ya lookin' for Margo?"

Bette rushed from the trailer house, to where she saw the men standing on the driveway.

"Look who's here, Mother," Hank said to her, as she approached.

"Land sakes—what are you doing here?" she said, sounding friendly but giving him the cold shoulder. She turned her attention to Toby. "Oh, my—what a big boy you are!"

Hank handed the youngster to Bette. Toby was wide-eyed, not recognizing his grandmother. Perhaps it was the stylish change she had made, to narrow-framed glasses.

"Can you talk?" Bette asked, trying to lure a reaction from her bashful grandson, using tricks—flashing eyes and an exaggerated smile—but he just stared at her. "Well, you're handsome; sure to drive the little girls wild!"

Bette addressed Stanley but didn't face him. She brushed at Toby's hair. "Margo's not here, if that's who you came to see."

"Aw-w—she went to work," Hank said.

"I don't see Flower in the corral," Stanley said, "just a bunch of chickens."

"Aw—the horse—"

"She died," Bette cut in abruptly. "It happened, all of a sudden."

"Lyme Disease," Hank said. "The ol' gal was too-far-gone, by the time the vet got here."

"Sorry," Stanley said. "I didn't know; no communication—"

"Aw—nothin' we could do about it—six-a-one 'n half-a-dozen of the other—ya know. We buried 'er, back behind the barn. And, of course, Margo sold the colt."

"I'll tell Margo you came by to say *hi*," Bette said dismissively, ignoring Stanley's attempt at restoring relations. She handed Toby to Stanley and turned away, as if she was in a hurry to check on a boiling pan of water.

Acknowledging the time-to-go cue, Stanley opened Toby's door. "Tell her I'm back. I'll stop by, again, someday after work."

"What—not just passing through? You work around here?" Hank asked.

"Yes, I do," Stanley said proudly. "I got the detective position at the Justus County Sheriff's Office—a permanent job."

"They needed a detective? Homer usually handles everything. I wonder why—"

"Unsolved crimes, and Mister Anders has decided not to run for office this fall."

"It's about time—that old fart! He shoulda retired years ago!" Hank said.

Bette cautiously strolled back, after overhearing the extended conversation. "You can't stay!" she said in an irritated voice, accentuated by an involuntary twitching of her upper lip. "Get out of here! You'll just cause trouble. Margo can't take the stress—you know!"

Stanley bristled from the open hostility, only wanting to engage in meaningful conversation. "I thought that—maybe—you folks would still be in the South, for the winter."

"South!" Bette erupted, nearly unglued. "We couldn't go anywhere, with Margo; you know how she gets. We had to . . ."

"Now, Mother—we stayed home because it never got cold, this winter," Hank cut in protectively, for Margo's sake. "Well, with all the *global warming* and the *hole in the ozone layer*, all destroying this planet—one day after another—we're damn-lucky to be alive!"

"Huh?" Stanley grinned, spotting Hank's clever sarcasm that slammed the partisan scams.

A wintery breeze caused Bette to shiver. She pulled at the arms of her sweater.

Not equating his cold reception to the chilly spring day, Stanley was hopeful that he'd be able to see Margo again.

"Aw—you didn't say—what unsolved crimes are you talkin' about?" Hank discretely asked, still wanting to protect Margo from the law.

"All of them! Homer called me at the ranch by Lewistown. He wants everything wrapped up before his last day."

"Lewistown—Missouri Breaks country, huh?"

Surprised that Hank was geographically knowledgeable, beyond the State Line, Stanley said, "Yeah, I worked for a private detective agency and did some cattle-wrangling."

"Hm-m; you say . . . Homer's last day; you must mean election day?"

"That's right. And thanks for that tip, Hank. I already got myself on the ballot."

"Hm-m. You've got yer work cut out fer ya. Aw—at least that shootin' at the speed trap was solved; too bad how that clumsy deputy shot himself," he added slyly, fishing for a reaction.

"That's still an active case. And it falls on me—the homicide detective—to solve it, now that Homer Anders hired me—again. This time, I'm on the regular payroll!" Stanley's smile could hardly be contained within the stringy muscles of his thin face.

"I'll be damned!" Hank's surprise was due to the shocking news of Stanley's reinstatement and the fact that he was now running for office. And, of course, this news dashed any hopes that the shooting investigation would die and be forgotten.

"I'll be around, talking to all the neighbors, too, in case anyone remembers anything," he said, before re-seating Toby and strapping him in.

Bette and Hank watched the four-wheel-drive vehicle go out the driveway.

"Is that a tear in your eye, Henry?"

Hank was hoping that she hadn't noticed. "Mixed feelings, I guess; upset that Margo could be facing jail-time, but proud of the boy who's carryin' our family heritage. That's our grandson in that car. Ain't it nice that he came to see us?"

Chapter 77
Back In Town

Margo showed up—lunch break—about two hours after Stanley left. She knew that he'd called but hadn't listened long enough to realize that he was *back in town*. Dismayed, she stood by her car and stared at the weathered gray boards of her dilapidated barn.

"Stanley never finished anything," she said woefully. "I didn't get to have my new-owner party. I've been wanting to fix it up, myself, so it'll at least be clean enough for a barn party on the Fourth of July—eventually."

"Maybe this can be the year," her mother said. "I'm sure you'll somehow get the gumption . . . and have it in shape, by then."

Later in the afternoon, when Margo was back at work, Brian drove in and parked under the spread of the oak tree.

Hank looked up from the lawn mower. "Didja get it?"

"Nope; they don't carry parts for that carburetor anymore," Brian said. "The guy laughed; offered to sell me a new mower, instead."

"Wanna hear another funny story? Stanley's back."

Brian had no apparent reaction. "Should I just haul it to the dump fer ya?"

"I said that Margo's old . . ."

Brian Laughed. "That's wild, Dad; you're crackin' me up!"

"He was here this morning, Toby in the back seat. The boy seemed like a stranger, except he looks a lot like Margo—dark brown hair and brown eyes—a good-lookin' kid."

"What did Margo do? She keeps a twelve-gauge shotgun, leanin' on the wall, right by the back door—ya know. And she sleeps with it, too!"

"She wasn't here—good thing." Hank glanced at Brian's truck. "She'll be back soon, though. You'd better get your truck outta her parkin' space, unless ya wanna deliberately aggravate her, like ya usually do."

"Nelson—the loser; thought we'd never see that dope again! He did Margo a favor when he left . . . and took the kid with him. Margo's too crazy to raise a kid, and he's too stupid to be a cop—what a pair!"

"Well, he's back now—*back*, as the homicide detective. He's reopened that case."

"What—the suicide of that speed trap cop?"

"That's what we all thought, until now," Hank said, measuring his words, still not wanting Brian to know about the details.

"What a way to go! Shot in the face with his own Three-Fifty-Seven, one honkin'-big gun!" Brian marveled.

"Who told you that? Was it Stanley?"

"No—"

"Ya know somethin'? I watch the ten o'clock news every night. Not once, has that ever been mentioned—neither the shot to the face, nor that information about the gun! Whatever you do, Rowdy, don't repeat any of that stuff! I wanna know, who told you it was a Three-Fifty-Seven?"

"What difference does it make—who cares?"

"Well, when they're on a fishing expedition, this is the kinda information that cops troll for. Anyone spewing out that sorta detail is always assumed to be . . . close to the crime. If you end up bein' the sucker they're trollin' for, then you're the one who gets hooked—guilty, or not! And Stanley's the investigator. If you don't like cops askin' ya questions, you'd better be careful! Just tell me, who told you *that* detailed information?"

Brian's eyes showed a degree of acquiescence. "Well, besides the fact that everyone knows that Pimple-Face Smith carried a hog-leg, I heard it one night at The Corner Bar. It was Charley Day who knew all about the gun. I remember, Margo got too sick to drive herself home, hearin' all that scary talk. I took 'er home."

"Charley Day?" Hank wondered what must've been said, in front of Margo. "Did Stanley ask you anything?"

"Yeah, he did, but I told him I had a good alibi. I was at Old Man Martin's Dairy Parlor, washin' teats and wrestling those damned milking machines. And he knows that's the truth. Who'd ever make up an excuse like that?"

"Oh, I imagine . . . he hears some pretty outrageous ones, in his line of work."

"Well, my present line of work is *not* my intended line of work. I gotta find a better job, Dad. Do you know how long it takes to milk sixty-five cows—even with milking machines? It's ruinin' my social life. I hafta get my nights back, Dad!"

"Well, we all hafta be careful of what we say, now that Stanley's back."

"Gotta go. Don't worry, Dad. I'll move my truck. I don't wanna get crosswise between Margo's parking space and her scattergun!"

Chapter 78

The Lost Steer

It was a successful Saturday night at The Corner Bar, for Margo. She had made a spectacular trick-shot and won everything. Her opposition paid up immediately and stormed out of the bar, to a wave of humiliating laughter.

Margo hooted and danced a circle around the table, her pool-sharking sidekick, Eileen, joining in. Margo hadn't seen her brother, Brian, come in.

"Margo!" he called out, then walked over.

"Don't stand there, staring down my blouse, Rowdy," she said, drawing a practice-bead for another special shot on the eight-ball, her body stretched partway across the table.

"That view is for the marks!" Eileen said with a zesty laugh.

"That's not me," Brian said. "I'm not a sucker for your money-vacuuming scheme."

"You don't have any money!" Eileen said with a taunting jeer.

"Wadda ya want, Rowdy?" Margo asked gruffly. "You know, you're supposed to stay away when I'm doing this."

"Looks interesting; think I'll have a beer and just watch."

Irked, she angrily said, "You know I can't work, with my brother watching!"

"Have you seen Sergeant Stanley Nelson yet?" Brian asked provocatively.

"Get outta here, Rowdy!" she uttered, gritting her teeth, already knowing that Stanley was back and restarting the murder investigation.

"He'll pro'bly come in here with his note pad and pencil—ha!" Brian joked but saw the anger on his sister's face.

"Okay, I can lip-read. I'll go, this time, but the hot-shot detective, Tin-Horn Stanley—gun belt and all—will likely be here, chasin' all your friends away!" he said, laughing as he walked to the door.

Shortly after Brian left, an unexpected visitor showed up at the bar. Sheriff Homer Anders, dressed in shorts and a Hawaiian shirt, recognized Margo and sat next to her on a stool.

"Do you remember me, Mizz Toralf?" the out-of-uniform sheriff asked.

Margo glanced to her side but drew a blank, definitely not interested in striking up a conversation with a strange old man who looked like he'd escaped from a senior care facility.

"I dress casually, when socializing," Homer Anders said, triggering her memory.

Realizing whom she was sitting next to, she wanted to stay on his right side, especially if it was true that the investigation had reopened.

"Sure—I remember you, Homer!" She let out a spontaneous-sounding laugh and gently nudged Homer's arm, as if he were a mark ready to be taken.

"I wasn't expecting to see you today, but since I found you, may I ask you a question?"

"Is this official business?" Margo asked, trying to stay calm.

"No—nothing official; not since that lost-in-the-storm surprise."

"What . . . surprise?" Margo asked, her curiosity stimulated.

"Your neighbor, aw—whatcha-ma-call-it—looking for his beefer. You knew about that, didn'tcha—*the lost steer*?"

"Lost steer?" Margo's surprise-reaction was partially a quest for relevance.

"Well, it's one of those odd things you run into, during any investigation. Who'd ever expect that someone would walk right in, on a crime in progress? Seems that . . . whatcha-ma-call-it, looking for his black steer—black as a bear, I'll tell ya—had his dog with 'em, down in the woods behind the roadside rest area. Darn critter got loose, just before that spring snowstorm—ya know—ha! What a deal, huh? Can you imagine, looking for a black cow in the dark? Ya ever chase loose cows in a storm?"

"Cows? Ah—yeah; the cows got out, lots of times," Margo said, recalling the part of her childhood spent in the neighbors' woodlots, looking for stray cows. After a second, the thrust of what Homer had just told her, about a neighbor looking for a lost steer by the roadside park, piqued her memory—the sound of a barking dog, after the gun went off. That memory sent an eerie chill up her spine.

"Well, anyhow, this guy was following cleft hoof tracks, in the dark, with a flashlight! Have ya ever done that? Ha-ha!" Homer had to laugh. "Them cows—sure a pain, sometimes! What was I saying?"

"Ah—a black steer . . . and . . . someone with a flashlight—"

"The Black Angus? Have I already told you this one?" Homer asked, innocently senile.

"No, Mister Anders. What about the guy with the flashlight?"

"Oh yeah; now I remember. He saw something at the roadside park, that night. The dog tried to run toward the gunshot, but he held it back—choker chain—ya know. He said there was *a second car* under the streetlamp."

"My car!" she mouthed the words silently, knowing that this fact could do-her-in if it was ever confirmed. She stared past Homer Anders, the unlikely barroom storyteller, seeing the row of distillates displayed on the wall behind the bartender, as a blur.

Barely listening to the rest of his story, she sharpened her focus on a bottle of tequila, a tempting choice, but she knew that it would do her no good; and she wanted to stay on top of her game. Her mind must stay clear to get past this setback.

"We never saw a second car," Homer continued but was cut off when someone touched him on the shoulder, from behind.

"What are you doing in a place like this, Homer? Ain't this against your religion?"

Homer turned around, to the laughter of the young man who had just affectionately slapped him on the back.

"Well—what a coincidence—Yancy Jensen! We were just talkin' aboutcha! You know your neighbor—ah—Mizz Margo—don'tcha?"

Margo's mouth hung open and her eyes looked like they were about to pop out of their sockets. A rush of blood seemed to fill her head, like a spilled beaker of water, nearly drowning out the sound of the men's voices. She looked into the face of her neighbor, Yancy Jensen, someone she should have known but didn't recognize.

The next thing she knew, she was shaking hands with the rather tall and handsome Yancy Jensen, who she hadn't seen since he was a short and skinny underclassman in high school.

Yancy took off his baseball cap and raked his rough fingers through his red hair. "Margo Toralf! Who could forget the girl who used to trot, bareback, past my house—bareback and bare-chested! And you joined the Army . . . to spite your parents!" He laughed and gave Margo the once-over glance. "Man! I can't believe it. You don't look like anyone from the Army!"

Margo cooed with the compliment but gave a somewhat abashed smile, never expecting that anyone in the community would remember any of those things.

"Ah, I quit. That was a long time ago, Yancy," she said, hoping he didn't have any more memories to mention. She stroked the skin on her throat with jittery fingers. "I hear you've taken over your parent's farm."

"That's right—a new generation. Who woulda thunk it, huh? Stop by and meet my wife Becky. She'll show you the new house, still under construction; doin' it myself, a little at a time, one paycheck at a time. I hear you bought your dad's place."

"Yeah, just recently. Why don't you and . . . Becky plan to come to my new-owner barn party on the Fourth of July? You too, Sheriff Anders. I'd love to see you both!"

Both men agreed to attend Margo's party on the Fourth of July. She listened to the two men talk, hoping to hear more about the lost-steer incident, but neither man mentioned it. She wondered how much Yancy Jensen knew about the shooting, and if he had actually seen her car parked alongside the dead deputy's vehicle.

"What was that question you were going to ask me, Mister Anders —the unofficial question?" Margo asked, her heart palpitating.

"Oh—what was it? I can't remember," he said with carefree chuckle.

"That dumb old sheriff," Margo muttered to herself, after she had excused herself from the conversation. "Maybe there's nothing to worry about. But that nosey neighbor, Yancy Jensen, has me concerned; he saw my car; he knows! And what else did he see? And why can't he have a failing memory, like everyone else?"

Chapter 79
Rusty Widow-Maker

Sergeant Nelson was at his desk when a plump paper bag suddenly fell, dead in front of him and on top of all his papers. It reeked of fried onions. He looked up and saw Aino Pekka's feckless grin.

"Gotcha a double-burger with the works, just like ya wanted," grunted Officer Pekka. "Try not to scarf it down in one bite. Ha-ha!"

"Is it any good?"

"Who knows? I don't eat that crap anymore—high cholesterol; it'll kill ya."

"This case is weighing me down," Stanley said, taking a big bite.

"Which one?" asked Aino, glancing at the file label. "Oh, that dead kid—Martl—the homo and dope-pusher. The crystal meth and marijuana problems were cut in half, after he disappeared.

"And don't waste your time on that confusing fingerprint report— the Clarence Smith monstrosity. I studied it a thousand times when you were gone; ain't no prints, except for Clarence's own clumsy smudges. That whole case is a can-a-worms—plenty of truly confusing shit. Look-it, it's an open-and-shut case. The whole deal boils down to common depression. It got the best of that imbecile— that neurotic sonofabitch.

"I can picture it—Clarence, on a cold miserable night; nothing to do but sit out there, at his wretched speed trap. No traffic to stop and harass, because of the snowstorm. He prob'ly just sat there, watching the blizzard swirling all around him—pretty depressing, even for that pathetic jerk!

"Don't say nothin' to the boss, but I think that stupid, poor-excuse-for-a-cop shot himself. He was insane enough to do it—ya know! He staged the crime scene pretty-well; almost made it look like foul play," he said, emitting a high-pitched laugh, a cross between his normal hacking-chuckle and the sound of a hyaena.

Stanley felt the hairs on the back of his neck rising into the thin fabric of his undershirt, giving his skin a creepy crawl. His stomach turned and he felt nauseous.

After Aino grabbed his empty lunch pail and left for home, Stanley just stared at the wall. Now, he was more confused than before; and thanks to Aino's contribution, it all seemed a little spooky. He knew it was more complicated than Aino had opined; there had to be more to it. He was determined to dig deeper.

First, he popped an antiacid tablet into his mouth.

* * *

At that same time, out at the farm, Hank decided to mow the lawn with an old push-mower his father had retired to the tool shed, years beforehand. He remembered using it when he was a kid. After a little oiling, the reels moved smoothly. It was ready to go. After only one pass, though, Hank let go of the handle and staggered away, then leaned against the apple tree, panting heavily. He wiped his sweaty brow on his sleeve, remembering that it worked a lot easier in the past.

"What are you doing, Daddy," Margo suddenly shouted, running to him. "Stop pushing that *rusty widow-maker*. You'll give yourself a heart attack! How am I supposed to get you to the emergency room before you kick the bucket?"

"Someone's gotta cut this grass!"

"Why not use the gas-mower? I thought you fixed it!"

"Can't get parts anymore."

"You mean, it's obsolete? We'll buy a new mower—today. I'll go with you, Daddy!"

Margo rode *shotgun* in the family pickup, while Hank drove.

He liked how Margo could sometimes make a split-second decision, like deciding to buy a new lawnmower at the spur-of-the-moment; but he also knew that she had another decision to make. The most-pressing issue had to do with Stanley Nelson's return, the need to come to grips with Toby's need for a mother. He had noticed Margo's ambivalence concerning Stanley's return but wondered why she showed no interest in her young boy, his grandson. There were things he wanted to know, and she was being tight-lipped about it.

"Ya seen Stanley yet?" he asked.

"Nope."

"He has Toby with him. They live in town, I think."

"Ah, Dad, do you really think I'm interested in this conversation?"

"You might hate Stanley, but don't forget Little Toby! And then, there's the revival of the murder investigation. I'm sure your mother filled ya in."

"Everyone knows; by popular opinion, it was a suicide."

"That's not what we're hearin', now. Stanley told me, himself, that the murder case is still open; he's workin' on it. Old Man Anders wants it solved before Election Day. That means, before he quits in November!"

Margo stared out the side window, absorbing but not wanting to admit the legitimacy of her father's concerns. "Nice Black Angus herd at the Jensen farm—"

"What happened with Stanley's phone call, this morning? Is Toby . . .?"

"Didn't Mom tell you? They're coming for supper, sometime this week."

Chapter 80
The Red Stain

Stanley sat on a large Basswood stump at the Burntwood Prairie Roadside Rest Area, reading from the Crime Lab Report that lied across his lap, searching for understanding. His attention was drawn to the two-inch-diameter oak sapling where the bullet trajectory had stopped, dead center, splitting the wood and lodging in the stem. He found the small tree, a short distance from the stump, damaged but remarkably still alive. He could see the stiff fibers in the center of the shattered area, from where the crime lab had extracted the fatal bullet.

What a stroke of luck that this tiny tree somehow caught the speeding bullet! Otherwise, it could have disappeared in the woods, never to be found. What were the chances? We've had the mangled bullet, all this time, but why the problem with the evidence?

* * *

Being nearby, he decided to stop at the farm. Margo was sure to be at work, so a quick visit was certain to be hassle-free.

Hank Toralf was struggling with a large, woods-run fence post, when he stopped in.

"Hey Stan, grab me an ax outta that tool shed. There's a big ol' knot stickin' out too far on this darned post; it'll never make it to the bottom of the hole."

Stanley ducked into the cramped shed and saw three axes leaning against the wall. He chose the best-looking one, the short one with the shiny head and polished handle.

"Where did you find that new ax?" Hank asked. "All of mine are old and dull."

"It's the only one that looks sharp, Hank."

"Hm-m; must be Margo's . . . or Brian's."

Stanley was positioning his feet to take a swing at the knot but paused when he noticed a discoloration on the handle of the tool.

There's a reddish stain, deep into the fibers of the wood, right next to the axe-head. Could it be blood? He resumed his windup and chopped the knot off. His mind raced, silent questions about *the red stain.*

"Good tool! Do you mind if I borrow this?"

Hank nudged the air, a slight nodding of his head, indicating that Stanley could take it.

Stanley set the axe aside and pitched in, helping Hank set the post. He hung around and visited, for a few minutes, but had the stained axe-handle on his mind. He waved to Hank when he drove away, the axe in his trunk.

He returned to the nearly forgotten crime scene and took the axe from his trunk. Under the trees, the mid-day sun was only partially blocked by the thin, spring-forest-canopy. He approached the perimeter where a yellow ribbon had once encircled the place where the slain deputy had fallen, then walked to the stump where he had noticed an axe-mark, earlier that morning. He compared the shape of the axe-head with the single axe-mark, on the top surface of the grayed stump. He took a swing, sinking the axe-head into the soft, decaying wood. The new axe-mark was aligned, right next to the old mark.

"Looks like a match, to me; but could it be, that all axe-marks look the same?" He looked over the lab notes, once again. *No mention of an axe in the report, but the axe-mark on the stump is definite. If there was an axe, it had to have been removed before the snowstorm, because there were no tracks in the snow. Do I dare ask Margo about it? Was she here, or was this just a lucky-find at a yard sale?*

Using a magnifying glass, he zeroed-in on the discoloration that seemed to be confined to the porous, vascular tissues of the wood fibers.

If it's blood, it soaked inside the pores where it couldn't be wiped off.

* * *

Back at the office, Stanley was determined to apply what he had learned about using DNA sampling techniques to resolve his suspicions. After following some detailed technical instructions for isolating a DNA sample, he managed to obtain a suitable laboratory sample of the substance that comprised the stain, extracted from deep in the wood fibers. He mailed the specimen to the State Crime Laboratory; sent with some apprehension, since the DNA analysis technique was so new, in 1996, that he didn't know any officer who had actually tried it.

Remembering that he and Toby had a special dinner-date, that evening, Stanley rushed to the babysitting service. He picked up his son and drove directly to Margo's farm.

Chapter 81
Special Dinner Guests

Margo anxiously stared out the dining room window, keeping her eye on the driveway while setting the formal table for *special dinner guests*, something rarely done at the farmhouse. How the arrangement for this dinner-meeting had actually come together was a mystery to her, but she was sort of glad for it. At least she and Stanley had successfully talked, over the phone, agreeing to give it another shot for Toby's sake.

For Stanley, a lot was riding on the success of this particular evening. And for Margo, it was her first chance, in almost three years, to actually see Stanley; and especially to see her baby boy.

Setting and resetting the dishes in varying placements, she happened to be facing the wrong way, not seeing Stanley's car come up the driveway.

Stanley parked near the oak tree, with some apprehension. After all, he hadn't seen Margo in a long time and his departure had been under arduous circumstances.

Toby clutched onto two of his father's fingers, as they walked to the back porch. Bette opened the door.

Margo almost dropped a bowl of applesauce, when she was surprised by Stanley's voice at the door. She dashed in the opposite direction, into the living room, as if she preferred to stay out of sight. When her mother announced that Stanley and Toby had arrived, she timidly made her entrance.

It was a tense moment in the quiet room, Stanley seeing his lovely Margo step around the corner and stand stiffly near the archway. Beautiful, looking like a movie star, she smiled but remained aloof. The extended but estranged family gathered around the table without any particular greetings, probably because everyone knew each other.

It seemed apparent that Bette had done all of the cooking, but the Toralf family was trying to present Margo in her best light. And it seemed, to everyone present, that the family dinner was probably the only opportunity for Margo and Stanley to reconnect, if that was possible, at all.

The reuniting, after a long time of being apart, was more strained than antagonistic, but in a pleasant sort of way, considering there was no shouting. They seemed like courteous strangers.

Toby's presence had a neutralizing effect on Margo's past antagonistic attitude. She put on her best face yet held a rigid smile, realizing that she had been feeling better but was fearful of her plight, should Stanley put the pieces of the shooting-puzzle together. Not revealing her private thoughts, she acknowledged their strained relationship and admitted that all of her problems were her own fault.

Hank didn't seem to remember that he had loaned Stanley the axe, and Stanley avoided mentioning that he still had it. He certainly didn't mention anything about waiting to hear the lab results from the DNA testing. While the dysfunctional family sat around the table, he wasn't thinking about solving the shooting, but rather, the hope for reconciliation with Margo.

During the course of the meal, light-hearted discussion about the unpredictable, nice spring weather somehow led to various scenarios for Toby's potential success in life. Although both were discussed, it was not decided whether 4-year-old Toby should become a farmer or a doctor.

* * *

After Stanley and Toby went back to town, Hank and Bette whispered, rehashing the bizarre homecoming.

"Seems, to me, that he's back—back, for good," Hank said.

"I hope he leaves us alone," Bette said. "It's been so long, and . . . he shouldn't suspect his own family."

"We're *not* his family, remember? And you saw the coldness around the supper table tonight. He's back, alright, but I don't think there'll be a wedding."

"How are we going to get rid of him?" Bette asked. "If he finds out . . ."

"How's he gonna find out, Mother? We talked about this before; we hafta tighten our lips, around here—that's all. The only way that he'd suspect anything, is if someone says something . . . that they shouldn't. We hafta keep Margo out of it, and especially Rowdy."

"Well, Stanley shouldn't suspect Margo, and she won't tell him anything."

Chapter 82
DNA Analysis

The morning meeting was all business. Sheriff Anders' said, "It's up to you, Stanley, the new generation in law enforcement. Go with the new policy. Learn it and do it."

Stanley returned to his desk, feeling the weight of his responsibility and pondering the Sheriff's directive, that *DNA analysis* would now be the central emphasis in investigating all future homicides.

With the new goal in mind, and to clear his mind, he gazed out the window at nothing. Focusing on the new science, he was just beginning to understand its significance. Even so, he doubted his ability to learn it, surmising that Sheriff Anders was optimistic but also knowing that neither of them actually knew very much about the potential for DNA analysis or the science of it.

He switched his attention to his campaign posters and finalized his order, adding 250 bumper stickers, one advertising banner, and a dozen balloons. *Balloons? Odd for a practical man, but why not make it fun? It's not childish. I'm running for sheriff!*

Inspired by the Sheriff's confidence in him, Stanley set his political campaign aside and immediately dug into the old files, looking for unsolved cases that could benefit from DNA analysis.

He was mulling over the sheriff's instructions when the mail arrived. He quickly opened an envelope from the State Crime Lab. His hunch, about the discoloration on the axe-handle, had paid off.

"Human blood," he mumbled, skipping through the confusing parts of the report. *And two subjects, huh?*

He stood from his chair, then dashed to the evidence room and brought the new-looking axe back to his desk. He stared at the ominous but simple tool as it lied on the desktop in front of him, cushioned only by the latest printing of the Otter Tattler.

Knowing what the report stated, he tried to comprehend that the clean-looking, small axe had probably been used for killing someone, or more than one. And he thought about how the combined blood, from two subjects, had been concentrated into one stain, drawn into the vascular fibers by capillarity. He stared at the rather drab discoloration, which seemed barely noticeable after apparently surviving a considerable effort to scrub it off.

He called the crime lab, trying to ascertain just what evidence he had stumbled upon. He was reminded that the lab found no connection between the shooting at the Roadside Rest Area and an axe of any kind. And this blood-discovery, lifted from the porous wood fibers of an axe handle, was not a match for any samples taken at the Smith crime scene. However, it had the potential to be connected to one or more unrelated axe crimes.

Expanding on his hunch, Stanley followed the lab's instructions in locating possible corroborating samples. He immediately thought of

Maria Richardson, Margo's friend who had reportedly been killed by a hatchet. He reopened her folder, then stared at the photograph. Seeing the picture of the axe cut in her back caused him to think of another possible case.

He had wondered about the little-publicized death of Martin Martl, but now, for the first time, pulled his file, too. He read the brief description and saw several nearly identical, blurry pictures of an axe cut, also located in the center of his back.

"What?" *Martin Martl, too? I didn't know this, and I was the one who found his body!*

Stanley quickly ran it past the Sheriff, to bring him up to speed and to seek advice.

"Darn!" muttered Sheriff Anders. "I never thought I'd ever see such a conundrum."

"What do you mean?"

"That's two—two axe murders; two in a row, with the same weapon. If it's a *serial killer,* which it looks like *now,* there'll be a third, then probably a fourth. God, help us—"

Stanley, with shaky legs barely holding up his heavy responsibility, rushed back to his desk. *Is Homer right? What do I have, here, evidence of a serial killer?*

He knew what that meant. His hands moved quickly, packaging up the old blood samples, one from each of the axe murder victims. He was in a hurry to get the package in the mail, that day, before the post office closed. *The crime lab needs these samples, as soon as possible. Let the DNA chips fall where they may!*

He knew the process would take a while, since he had learned that old blood samples must *grow* in the laboratory for an unspecified length of time.

Chapter 83

Handprints

Margo paced near the service door of the Burntwood Prairie Children's Clinic, anxious to punch-out as soon as the big hand hit the 12. She and Stanley had talked on the phone and agreed to a new first date; nothing elaborate, just meet at Gwen's Family Diner and see what happens. She tried not to show her excitement, but alone in the car, she cried out, "I've got a date!"

The diner was not a dimly lit nightspot, but rather, an innoxious place to retry nervous smiles, share a simple meal, and warm up to meaningful conversation. They took a table, not in the far corner but close to the front entrance.

After the early dinner date, when the bungling couple actually shared a few comical moments from days-gone-by, they drove out to the farm, then took a walk. They ended up strolling across the south forty as the sun was sinking low. Stanley didn't ask about the new ranch-style house that Brian had obviously built on the corner of the field, and Margo acted like it wasn't there.

The warmth shared by holding hands, along with more familiar laughter, led to a gradual reigniting of the flame that they had previously known. During the next few days, with the growth of a productive summer, Margo and Stanley began to feel closer again. It was almost like walking a stony path, but both seemed determined to trek it one step at a time.

Another afternoon, just before the second invitation-meal at the farm, Stanley walked with Toby across the leased-out cornfield. Toby had fun, running through the ankle-high corn plants, almost knee-high for a small boy. Stanley loved breathing the fresh country air and virtually watching the corn stalks grow. It made him feel attached to the land.

Margo's mother had prepared the evening meal, although Margo told her that she was capable of doing it herself. With the help, Margo found time to enjoy playing hide-and-go-seek with Toby, which was encouraging to Stanley. She was so pleased with the reuniting of her family that she told Stanley to check out of his rental, in town, and bring Toby back to the farm.

With her *men* back on the farm again, Margo revived her plan for a special celebration on the 4th of July.

"I've already invited all my neighbors and my relatives, plus Sheriff Anders and Yancy Jensen," she whispered to herself. There wasn't much time to actually prepare, since it was already past the middle of June.

Stanley picked up where he had left off, on the renovation project, three years earlier. He was surprised that the timber-jack still stood in the same position, holding up the main beam of the barn. He finished cutting and installing the new posts, then began painting and fixing other things in the barn. And he found Margo's cracked guitar, hanging in the corner of the tool shed. He took it to a luthier for expert repairs.

One day, when Margo got home, she curiously followed a set of dual tire-tracks in the sand, to the barn door. Inside, she saw Stanley on his knees, silently troweling freshly poured concrete.

"Stanley! You filled the gutters . . . for horses!"

Stanley loved the return of the magic twinkle that brightened her eyes.

Overjoyed with the progress, Margo helped Toby press his handprint into the soft concrete. Toby took his father's hand and pushed it into the mud, too. His mother found a short stick and scratched names and dates into the cement, before it hardened. "Handprints—what fun!"

Chapter 84
Jug Band
July 4, 1996

The boom of a canon in the distance, the traditional kickoff for the community fireworks, rocked the darkness along the western skyline. Stanley looked toward town and saw the bright flashes of light that ensued, colorful embers bursting and scattering in the air over the familiar enclave, Burntwood Prairie. He and Margo had skipped the traditional July 4th festivities—apprehension over last-minute preparations for their barn party which was to follow immediately.

The July humidity got sticky that warm evening, and fireflies zig-zagged in flight, randomly blinking across the blackness of the pasture.

"Guests will be arriving soon, Margo," Stanley said, knocking on the closed bedroom door, knowing that she had been overwhelmed with angst, earlier. He knocked a second time, then a third. "Margo!"

Brian's truck rumbled up the driveway. Stanley saw the headlights turn to the barn. He ran to see if Brian had delivered the items that Margo wanted.

"I borrowed a stock-tank from Yancy Jensen; got it half-fulla ice," Brian said excitedly. "Where's the beer?"

"Everything's in the hayloft."

Using the hydraulic bucket on the tractor, Hank hoisted the tank of ice, high enough to clear the hayloft door. Brian and Stanley managed to drag it, from there.

Margo suddenly marched from the house, clearly in an edgy mood. She handed Brian the American Flag and two hastily-made *no smoking* signs.

"What are these for?" Brian asked.

Margo's expression of exasperation was aimed directly at her brother. "Duh-h—hazard reduction—you moron! I don't want to have the fire department out here, tonight!" she growled. "And it's the Fourth of July—for Pete's Sake! If you don't know what the flag is for—"

Brian balked, since he disliked his sister's sarcasm and her impatient huffing.

"I'll hang the flag myself," she said angrily, then proceeded to display *the colors* on a bracket located on the side of the light-pole.

Brian reluctantly took the signs into the barn to install them, shaking his head. *"Barn-party-mania,"* he muttered, not caring whether she heard or not.

"Put one upstairs . . . and one down," Margo yelled out. "And get your piece-of-crap truck away from the barn. I need that space for my guests to park!"

"We put the drinks . . ." Stanley cautiously started to say, pointing upward.

"Don't wear that shirt, Stanley, it makes you look like a cop!"

"I am a cop. At least, I'm not wearing my service weapon."

"Please, Stanley; it'll spoil the party. Living here, you have to *know* your neighbors, not as a cop but as another neighbor. This is the friendly, American countryside, not the impersonal big city; get it?"

A long and low barge-like sedan, badly in need of identifying chrome and a paint job, pulled into the yard. The boat-sized body almost scraped the sod, as it left the driveway and parked under the bright mercury-vapor yard light. The car backfired when it shut off, black smoke puffing from the tailpipe and white steam hissing from under the hood.

"Who's that?" Stanley asked. "Looks like he lives in his car."

"Is that you, Bummer?" Margo called out, her voice suddenly sounding cheerful.

A ragged, aged hippie stepped out, onto the meticulously mown grass.

"It's me, Margo. Hope I'm not late!" Bummer's tenor voice rang loud, sounding almost like a song-lyric. He grabbed his guitar, from under a layer of miscellaneous clothing and empty cereal boxes, then walked to where Margo and Stanley were standing. Without much fanfare, Margo showed him where the gathering was to occur.

"It's a van," Stanley said, as another set of headlights slowly came up the driveway.

"That'll be the rest of the band. Show them where to go," Margo said. "Don't forget what I said about that shirt!"

Stanley gave a friendly wave to the driver, as the van slowly pulled up to the barn. He turned to ask Margo another question, but she was already halfway to the house.

Just then, a third vehicle arrived, a pink foreign sports car—brand-spanking-new. A thin, haggard, mystery woman with teased frizzes on top of her head got out of the two-seater. Two young boys piled out and followed close to her heels, hiding their faces. The woman, who seemed too old to have small children, not to mention her thick makeup, carried a tidy-looking picnic basket.

"Hi, I'm Dawn. Where should I put this casserole?" she asked Stanley.

"Oh, food—Dawn, just . . . follow the band," he said, pointing to the hayloft. "I have to go, change out of my uniform-shirt."

Moments later, Margo and Stanley came rushing from the farmhouse. Stanley carried the recently repaired guitar and was still clicking snaps on his shirt sleeves when a sleek black car drove up the driveway.

Awestruck, Margo watched in silent apprehension. The luxury vehicle stopped next to Bummer's relic-of-a-car, situated so Old Glory, gently waving in the background, made it seem like some dignitary from Washington D.C. had just arrived for her very special Fourth of July celebration.

A tall cowboy, wearing a wide-brimmed straw hat, stepped out of the impressive-looking car. When Margo saw the mop of red hair, sticking out from under the hat-brim, she knew who it was.

"Nosey Yancy Jensen," she murmured, under her breath.

A stylish young woman stepped out, too, and the attractive couple held hands as they walked over to where Margo and Stanley were standing. Yancy extended his hand, and Stanley was honored to shake it.

"Yancy! I'm so glad you came!" Margo said, also latching onto his hand. "I went to high school with Yancy," she excitedly explained to Stanley while rubbing Yancy's hand. She giggled shamelessly, admiring the fluffy hair that seemed too bulky to fit under the spread of his hat. She winked, "I always loved that red hair!"

Stanley was surprised that Margo's sudden exuberance far-exceeded the definition of a positive mood-change. And her coming alive, in this way, must have been embarrassing for the Jensens, and was contrary to her average mood over the past month.

"Meet my wife Becky," Yancy said, a little taken back by her brashness.

Becky Jensen was aghast with the swooning but polite enough to shake Margo's hand.

"Becky's not from around here," Yancy said. "She's a bit more-refined than the locals. I found her in Milwaukee five years ago. We've been married ever since!"

"Who's the band?" Becky asked, of the assembly of old, hippy-looking minstrels, all gathered at the open door of the hayloft. The plonky sound of out-of-tune strings fell flat in the humid air.

"Just some Bluegrass friends of mine," Margo said, "fellow amateurs."

"Amateurs?" Becky remarked, almost reeling from the clashing noises. "And what is it that they're playing?"

Knowing that the guys were just tuning up, Margo surmised that Becky was not *into* traditional music-making.

"It's *hillbilly*—sort of—simple songs about living and dying. Songs about loving and being loved. Songs about emotions that everyone can relate to. Overall, a pretty-good thing."

Becky had a defenseless look, and Margo seemed to be playing offense.

"It's not as uptown, as you're used to—I'm sure—but you might like it, Becky. A little Bluegrass never hurt anybody."

"It's a *jug band*," Yancy quietly advised his wife.

"What's that?" she asked.

"That's when the band plays a song, and the rest of us hillbillies pass the jug!" Margo interjected with a hilarious laugh.

Chapter 85

Ghost of Plunk Dambul

Most of the guests seemed to arrive at the same time. Margo outdid herself, in greeting everyone. The eldest gentleman stopped to talk, while the others went inside and climbed through the hay-chute.

"I came, like I said I would, Mizz Margo," the humble old man said.

Margo had to look twice but recognized Sheriff Homer Anders, dressed in the same flowery Hawaiian garb she had seen him wearing, once before. "Mister Anders, you're a handsome devil tonight!"

Homer blushed.

"Go ahead; lay it on, Girl," she murmured, her whisperings masked by her infectious laugh. "Make this dunce into a loyal friend —the key word being l-o-y-a-l!"

"It's so late to start a party," he said. "I usually go straight home, after the fireworks."

"Oh, I understand, Homer," she said. "You know Stanley, though —the Arkansas Honky-Tonker! We'll be up, past midnight, I suppose!" she said with an especially boisterous laugh, teasing an old man who, she presumed, always went to bed before 9:00 PM.

With no one else around, Margo took Homer by the arm and stepped away from the open barn door. "I've been so-o afraid, ever since your deputy shot himself," she said quietly and persuasively. "Now, I hear it might be murder. Is there anything you can tell me, so I can feel safe?"

"Well, I can't say much, Mizz Margo. The leads all dried up, a while back. Stanley's the guy to talk to now—you know. It's in his hands. You've heard that I'm not running for office again, haven't you? There'll be a new man in charge, by election day."

"What about the . . . *lost steer*? Whatever became of that?"

"You should ask Yancy Jensen; he found that ornery critter, the next morning." Homer laughed, recalling the coincidence. "That cussed-out steer was first on the scene, layin' in the snow all night long, right next to Clarence Smith's dead body, like a lost puppy would do. In fact, Yancy's the one who called Nine-One-One!"

Shocked, her mouth dropped open and her wide eyes looked away, not expecting that sort of surprise. She darted to the shadows, just as Stanley saw Homer standing outside, alone.

"Hey, Homer! Come on in," Stanley said. He hadn't seen where Margo went. He led Homer to the stairs, who eagerly followed, the sound of guitars warming up, beckoning.

Somewhere in the tall grass, hiding on the dark side of the silo, Margo wheezed, the humid air seeming stagnant. "I can't believe it— the stupid cow! And Jensen—he knows everything! Stanley's never mentioned any of this, and he's probably going to talk to Yancy tonight."

Inside, Homer took one look at the primitive board-ladder, a slippery and strenuous-looking climb, and changed his mind.

Margo watched Homer get back into his car. Craving a nicotine-fix, she reached behind a loose board on the barn wall, knowing exactly where to touch in the dark. She retrieved a package of cigarettes, from her secret stash, and lit one. She was unseen, except for the bright circular glow where tobacco was on fire, powered by her nicotine-starved inhalation. Her body trembled, watching the departing glow of Homer's taillights.

She saw it in her mind, Yancy's steer shielding the dead body, keeping it warm. No wonder, the time-of-death calculations were off. Then imagining, she seemed to see herself lying between the dead deputy and the black bovine that wore a crusty coat of accumulated, wet snow.

She suddenly jumped with fright, certain that she felt a cold wet nose touching her arm. What had seemed like a moist bovine nose, was just the cold iron ladder that traversed the silo-wall, wet with the July dew, condensed from the humid evening air.

"Oh—you—*ghost of Plunk Dambul*!" she panted, remembering her mother's account of Dambul's death. "Why are you hanging around *my* silo?"

Shaking, Margo bravely placed her hand on the cold iron rail, just to affirm that it was only an inanimate object that had startled her. She ran her eyes up the narrowness of the iron ladder, all the way to the top, barely seeing its outline against the night sky.

"I'm not afraid of ghosts!" she said, her voice shaking. "And don't let that old Homer Anders scare you either," she said to herself, realizing that the hapless old sheriff, who she had thought was on her side, could actually become her demise.

Chapter 86

Secret Enemy of Horses

Margo burst into the glow of the yard light, running as if she was escaping a stampede of Black Angus, her boots wet from the dew-laden grass. She would have kept running, but saw the lights of a familiar truck coming up her driveway.

"Charley Day, my only friend. Save me!"

Charley's old truck pulled up alongside her. His raspy voice sang out his open window; a lyric from a Bob Wills song, sounding like he was into Bluegrass and was ready to dance. He rolled to a stop.

"Hi Charley," she tried to smile, in somewhat of a gloom. "Come, the party's just starting."

"What's the matter? You seem down-in-the-dumps—you poor cowgirl! Where are the horses? I don't see the mare and . . ."

"I lost her, Charley. Flower's dead."

"Aw-shucks!" Charley pounded his fist into his opposite hand. "She was kinda long-in-the-tooth—" He took off his hat, held it against his chest, and looked to the starlit sky, a show of reverence for a good horse, lost.

"It's not your fault, Charley. It was Lyme Disease." Margo's eyes welled up. "You don't know how I cried, when I lost Flower.

Afterwards, Dad said her colt was too hard to handle, so I had to sell him. I'm sorry, Charley. A better cowgirl would have done a better job. And, if my boyfriend had been here, it might have been different, too. Nobody wanted to buy a wild-ass stallion, full of piss and vinegar, so I had to practically give that beautiful colt away," she whimpered, a tear disappearing into the grass.

"That damn Lime Disease—*secret enemy of horses*!" Charley lamented, too angry to shed a tear. "I was fixin' to give y'all a warnin', like I did for Maria. Thought I done-told-ya, but musta forgot."

He reached into his truck and retrieved a half-consumed bottle of beer. He tipped it, as a greeting to Stanley Nelson who had just appeared close by, seeming to be listening. A halo of glare outlined Stanley's slim frame, as Charley squinted to see who it was that stood there.

"Did you know Maria Richardson?" Stanley asked.

"Huh?" Charley strained to see, the bright bulb beaming squarely behind Stanley's head. He didn't recognize the soft-spoken man who had overheard him mention the dead woman's name.

"Know her? You betcha!" Charley said, then took a long gulp, emptying his warm bottle. "Sold 'er a horse, maybe a month before I heard about the *hatchet murder*, a tag some Fargo newspaper-guy made up. Other folks say it was a tomahawk; want y'all to believe it was a Chippewa buck, who did it—ya know—the *blame it on the Indians* excuse! Well, I know all the Chippewa and Sioux guys, around here; sell horses to 'em all—ya know. None of 'em woulda did it. Had to be one of those doggone lumberjacks, throwin' a wood choppin' axe. The cut was too big, for a tomahawk!"

Margo listened dispassionately while Charley ranted, coldly envisioning the pimply face of the demised deputy who had brandished the glossy-handled axe; the same axe that she thought now stood in the corner of her own tool shed, not 30 yards from where they were standing.

"He got what he deserved," she almost said aloud, nearly evoking Charley's knowledgeable words that confirmed, in her own mind, that it truly was Clarence Smith who had killed her best friend.

"She was a *real* cowgirl—that Maria!" Charley continued. He angrily tossed the empty bottle against the silo-wall. Glass shards ricocheted into the tall weeds. "Damn coward, whoever did it! Somebody's gonna catch up to that bastard, someday! Hope it's me. Yup, I'll show that sonofabitch howda throw an axe!"

Margo's body shook from the resonance of Charley's angry curses. Her mind flashed back to her purported opportunity to run, from the *deputy-monster* at the rest-area-crime-scene.

"Maria was my friend—my last *real* friend, on earth. I hope it's you, Charley, that confronts the killer . . . and not me!" she said coldly, consciously distancing herself from any involvement yet revealing her latent anger.

Chapter 87
The Widow

Stanley was shocked by the intensity of Margo's angry rhetoric, more so than by Charley's threatening words.

"Stanley, meet Charley Day, the horse trader who sold Flower to me," Margo said, forgetting that the two had met before.

"I was here, that snowy morning when the colt was born," Stanley said, proffering his hand to the elderly Indian cowboy.

"Hmm!" Charley shook Stanley's hand, with a weak grip, having no idea who Stanley Nelson was. "That's the same mornin' that Clarence was found dead at the speed trap, shot point-blank with his own gun, so they say."

"You might not remember me, but I remember you," Stanley said, noticing that Margo had left him standing alone with a guest. *Almost showtime, for her.*

Charley was confused and possibly drunk. "Who—what do y'all do, Son?"

"I'm Sergeant Stanley Nelson, Sir—homicide detective."

"Oh-h, the new guy—Clarence's replacement—the murder investigation, over three years now. Y'all haven't made a lotta progress! Don'tcha think it's about time to solve that case?" he said acrimoniously, having an axe to grind. "My baby sister's been waitin' long enough!"

"Who do you mean—your *sister?*"

"Why—my sister, Dawn, *the widow* of Clarence Smith!"

Surprised, Stanley remembered where he had sent a mystery woman—Dawn.

The sound of a wailing fiddle suddenly broke into the murmurs of conversation that filled the bare skeleton of the hayloft. Immediately, the sounds of guitars strumming, the bass plucking, and a bright-sounding mandolin joined in, to the cheers of everyone in the barn. The grayed timbers resonated throughout the wooden structure and the toe-tapping sounds, plucked in rhythm and harmony, were spilling out across the farmyard. Stanley dashed to the hay-chute ladder, and Charley followed.

Stanley was in a hurry, since the musicians were already into the introduction to Margo's opening song, and he didn't want to miss any of her act. He scampered up the cedar rails and leaped to the landing, seeing his lovely Margo standing next to Bummer with a microphone in her hand. And her parents, sitting on a bale of hay, were anxiously waiting to finally hear the song that their daughter had promised.

The band began like a whirlwind, aggressively picking out the notes of a western tune, keeping the crowd guessing until Margo moved the microphone to her lips and belted out the opening line, making everyone believe that she was a cowboy's sweetheart, hushing all the small talk.

Excited, Stanley moved closer, wanting an unobstructed view. He leaned against a pole-truss, listening to her yodel the soul out of that song. He grinned with pride, not only that Margo sang well but that she seemed to be back to her real self. She was beautiful. Radiant, like a star.

The next song was a mournful ballad, but the melody struck a chord with Stanley. "That's one of her favorites, even though its theme is sorta cold," he said.

Charley heard the comment, leaned his back against the other side of the same truss, and shared a comment of his own. "Cold—the right word for her," he said, "and hot. That young woman—she's a firecracker, ain't she?"

"She's great," Stanley said, watching her sway as she sang.

"Y'all pro'bly get called out here often, one kind of trouble or another." Charley could not seem to stop talking, except when he broke pace to open a new bottle, fresh from the ice-tub, and gulped a cool swallow. "Almost like *firewater*," he said with a warm smirk and a wink.

Stanley looked away, hoping that someone else would step up to talk. He noticed that Aino Pekka had shown up and found a bale of hay to sit on, next to the beer-tank. He barely recognized him, as Aino —the goofball—looked almost like a rodeo clown, wearing an exploded straw hat, facial makeup, a red-rubber nosepiece, and oversize bib-overalls.

Stanley's glance continued around the hay room. He homed in on the overdone makeup of the mystery woman, her lips caked with bright red lipstick, and, what looked like, pink paint covering the circles under her eyes—Dawn—sitting with the two boys on the opposite side of the dance floor. He had missed out on the subtle gossip, that deceased Officer Smith's surviving wife was present.

Is she Charley's sister? I didn't know that Clarence Smith's widow is one of our neighbors!

Chapter 88
The Barn Party

Margo had everyone's attention at *the barn party,* a feast-for-the-eyes. It was truly *her* night of the year, if not the decade.

Charley chummed up to Stanley, gently elbowing him, "Those high-strung dames—they're hot, when they're in the mood. Just try to find a time, though, when they're in the mood! Ha!" He slapped his knee, stricken with laughter, numbed by the alcohol that was doing the talking.

"Do you have something against Margo?" Stanley asked seriously yet keeping his cool.

"Nah; sold 'er a horse a few years ago and sold 'er dad a horse—ages ago—when that girl was a kid. She used to be a helluva cowgirl, in her younger days. Now, if y'all get too close, she'll pro'bly take all your money, then turn y'all out to pasture like a gelding! She can find another stud, anytime she wants one—ya know! I've seen her work the crowd, down at the pool hall. A bag-o-tricks, I'll tell ya that! Hey—starin' at that double-barrel harness-package, from across the pool table, a man can forget what he's doin' and lose the game . . . and all his money!" He chugged the rest of his bottle.

"Hey—that's my future wife you're talking about!" Stanley protested, finally sounding offended.

"What? Y'all gettin' married—really?"

"Yeah, didn't she tell you?"

"This is confusing shit, Cowboy. Why buy a cow, when the milk is free? Ha!" Charley laughed, scraping the bottom of the barrel for probably the oldest joke in all of Minnesota.

"We already have a little boy. I'm *in* . . . for the duration."

"Well, I'll be damned!" Charley apologized for the disparaging words, like a sincerely nice drunk. He tipped his empty bottle, a toast, then stepped away. After taking about one-half of a stride, though, he hesitated in his tipsy mode. Looking back, he had something to add.

"Before you marry that young woman, y'all need to watch out." He pointed squarely at Bette Toralf, across the dance floor. "Her mother, that treacherous old bitty, took a butcher knife to their family dog," he said, watery eyes forming. "That little puppy didn't do nothin' too bad; may have sucked an egg or killed a chicken or two, but what farm-dog hasn't? Anyway, if that insane old woman ever comes at y'all, with a butcher knife, you'd better run like Hell!"

Stanley gulped, realizing that he hadn't pressed Margo for any details about the demise of her dog. *A butcher knife, huh?* He wondered if Margo was like her mother, remembering the strange incident when Margo also wielded a large knife, then stuck it in the wall. And he remembered her bizarre antics with the hayloft-rope, while she was wide-awake. He felt uncomfortable, standing directly under the double-knot of that same barn-rope, a potential hanging-rope. He grabbed the dangling end, tied it to a truss, then stepped away.

Charley Day laughed, making a high-pitched neigh as he staggered to the beer tank, found a fresh bottle, then seemed to head toward the band. Partway across the floor, though, he changed direction. He hooked his fingers around the hemp twines of a bale of hay and began to slide it across the plank floor. The crowd turned and watched, the weight of the bale slowing his momentum.

I've heard it before, Stanley thought as he let Charley's brazen comments go, watching him barely holding onto the bottle and swaggering, the heft of the hay-bale dragging next to the heels of his boots that clunked across the floor.

Stanley saw the Jensens, happily experimenting with the choreographed boot steps of a line dance, to the beat of the doghouse bass. He waved across the room to Toby, who was allowed to stay up late. Toby sat next to Bette, but on his grandfather's knee, watching his mother sing. Bette and Hank proudly watched Margo, who was shining in her new life that she had wanted so badly.

Suddenly, the whole barn shook. Charley had thumped the bale of hay onto the floor, next to where Dawn Smith sat with her grandsons. He sat down next to his sister. A side-by-side semblance of their family-line was plain for everyone to see.

Stanley quietly nodded, as his guessing was over. And he realized that the loss of Deputy Clarence Smith's life was affecting many different people.

Chapter 89
Palsy-Walsy

A flashy cowgirl who wore white stars on a red and blue striped blouse, and with red feathers tucked under her hatband, suddenly stopped at Stanley's side.

"Hi-ya Cowboy!" the sexy-sounding gal said, flirtatiously hooking one arm around his waist and giggling in a mildly intoxicated manner. "You don't know me yet, but I'm Eileen—*palsy-walsy* with Margo, like . . . since forever!"

Stanley knew who she was and politely listened to her line, but mostly tried to keep his eye on his wonderful Margo. Training his ear toward the band, he didn't want to be interrupted while listening to Margo perform the classic song, *"On the Banks of the Ohio"*, and he wanted to hear all of it. It was a 19ᵗʰ Century murder-poem, encapsulated within a beloved, almost-primal tune—author unknown.

Before Margo finished singing the cryptic line, where the girl in the song dies, imagery of Smith's axe striking Maria in the back played on her mind. And she visualized a replay of Clarence Smith's brains spraying into the darkness. She forgot the rest of the lyrics, her unwitting eyes locking onto those of her nemesis, Dawn Smith, a neighbor she'd never met but one who stared back lustrously, as if she knew something that no one else did.

BOOM was the amplified sound that the microphone made, after it slipped through Margo's fingers and bounced off the plank floor. Guests hushed, as Margo rushed down the hay-chute and ran outside.

Seeing the fright on Margo's face, Stanley quickly followed.

Gerald Toralf, Margo's easily offended cousin *Butch,* cornered Stanley when he got outside. Using the tip of his brown bottle, he repeatedly poked Stanley in the chest, pointing out what was wrong with all the politicians in Washington, D.C.

"You know—the *Whitewater Scandal*? At first, it was just about the money and the cover-up," Butch said, clearly wound up. "Then, the White House counsel-guy, Vince Foster, suddenly turned up dead! The whole country is pretending there's nothing wrong, like we're all numb to it! Is anyone paying attention? They're getting away with murder, and no one seems to care!"

Stanley pretended to seem interested in Gerald's jabberwocky, but his immediate concern was for Margo. He had his protective eye on her, as she ran across the yard to the house.

Butch persisted; but he was easy to ignore, while listening to the fiddle wail the melody of a foot-stomping classic Bluegrass tune.

Stanley headed for the house. *She needs me.*

Chapter 90
Moving-Target Practice

Most of the month of July was hot and dry. Margo's farmed-out cornfield shriveled up prematurely, but the renewed loving relationship of the reconciling couple flourished.

The heat of summer eventually disappeared, with the onslaught of an August cold front that brought daily rains to the parched prairies of Minnesota. With the cooling trend, the Toralf family was gearing up for the annual deer-hunting season.

One afternoon, after work and before he turned into the driveway, Stanley thought he heard a gunshot. He stopped by the mailbox and stuck his head out the window.

BANG! Another gun blast, and it sounded like it came from the house.

Stanley sped up the driveway and stopped near the oak tree. A torrent of gunfire made his adrenaline spike and his gut drop, ready to seek cover. He cautiously got out of his car and sought the protection of the large oak tree, then saw Brian's head bend around the corner, from behind the trailer house.

"Don't look now, but Tin-Horn Stanley's here!" Brian announced to the others.

Margo pulled the trigger one more time.

BOOM!

The percussion of her 12-gauge shotgun echoed through the woodlot and across the fields.

"How's it goin', Sergeant?" Hank yelled out good-naturedly, acknowledging Stanley's arrival.

Relieved that the family was at peace, Stanley poked his head around the end of the trailer house, where he saw Margo's grinning family clustered, each holding a long gun. A row of empty, plastic milk jugs hung from bushes along a trail that extended far into the woodlot.

"*Moving-target practice*," Margo said. "Just keeping sharp, for the deer hunt. Are you going to buy a hunting license, Honey?"

"I . . . haven't thought about it," Stanley said, the excessive pitter-patter in his chest already fading away. "How many deer can one family eat? If you each shoot one . . ."

"There's never enough venison!" Brian cut in with a hilarious laugh. "That's if *you* can hit one!"

Stanley ignored the group-laughter, understanding there was usually a victim in Brian's brand of humor and that his snide remarks were always intended to sound disrespectful. Everyone knew that he and Brian had clashed, ever since their first meeting. He nodded his head, acknowledging Brian's remark as a challenge.

"You don't have to decide today, Stanley," Margo pleaded quietly, not interested in exacerbating the tension between the two of them.

"Stanley's gonna be too busy for huntin', in the fall," Hank said. "He'll be shakin' hands and kissin' babies, with the election comin'."

"The deer are safe—safe with me; is that it, Brian?" Stanley asked, seeming to press the issue, taking up Brian on his skill-challenge.

"Bucks only—between you and me!" Brian retorted with fists tightening.

"Biggest buck wins!" Stanley rebutted, sounding like he was committing to the annual family-deer-hunt.

"Gotta be more than six points—farm rule!" Brian was quick to add. He grinned, as if Stanley was suddenly his buddy.

"Farm rule—" Stanley pondered, looking Brian in the eye. He grinned, too. "A good rule. I like it!"

Brian smiled widely, showing his perfect set of white teeth, except for the open space where one tooth had been knocked out, in a bar fight, years before. He stepped up to Stanley and offered his 16-gauge. "Wanna try a practice-shot?"

Stanley was tempted to say, "I don't need practice," but knew that he didn't want to perpetuate past friction between the two of them. He nodded, accepting the offer.

Margo, Hank, and Brian stepped out of the way. Bette came from the trailer house and tied yet another empty milk jug onto a Hazel-nut bush, along the footpath.

"It's loaded," Brian warned, when Stanley looked over the simple mechanism.

"Slugs?" Stanley asked, without opening the single-shot magazine.

Brian nodded and suddenly dashed to the closest target. He gave the jug's rope a vigorous swing, dove for cover, and braced himself for the loud percussion to come.

Watching the swinging jug, Stanley quickly went into action. Dropping to one knee, his single shot rang out immediately, hitting a line of three milk jugs in a row.

"Nice shot!" Margo cried out, with a wild-hearted laugh, not expecting Stanley to hit more than one target, if any at all.

Brian stood awestruck, as the gun smoke cleared, drifting past his face. He said nothing, not wanting to openly recognize that Margo's beau was an excellent marksman.

Stanley calmly ejected the spent shell and handed the empty gun back to him.

"Not bad, for a cop!" Brian finally said.

"Hey—be nice, Rowdy," Brian's mother warned.

Chapter 91
Lame Duck Sheriff
August 20, 1996

A somber *lame duck sheriff* opened his door and beckoned officers Pekka and Nelson to enter, subtly indicating that he was going to miss this place. Sheriff Anders brought the reality of the political atmosphere into focus, then wished them both the best of luck—*may the better man win*—and sent them out to kick butt.

"Wait! In the meantime, there's serious work to get done; and I mean, right away. Time is of the essence. The election is getting closer every day, and the voters have some serious concerns that land right in our laps; none bigger than the crime spree that has tarnished the image of Justice County."

Aino snickered, like a schoolboy, but Stanley homed in on the serious tone of the boss's voice. He knew that the homicide cases were his primary responsibility and saw no humor in the tragedy of any one of them. And he was aware that perfection was important to Anders. He didn't want to disappoint him, especially knowing that Homer was ready to accept any outcome on election day.

"It's time to draw conclusions on all the pending cases," the sheriff continued. "I made some promises, and, by God, I'm gonna

417

keep 'em! I don't want a single loose end, when I hang-it-up in November."

Stanley wondered how he could possibly accomplish everything in such a short length of time, lacking corroborating evidence and, especially, having no new clues.

"I know you'd like to solve every detail, on every case, Boys," the sheriff said, "but our knowledge of what really happened is very limited, in almost every case. We've *got* what we've got, and we *know* what we know. That's all. The rest is up in the air. But it always is. Get the evidence together and make a recommendation that I can take to the DA. Then it's in *his* lap."

After the meeting, Officer Pekka cracked a side-joke, then wished Stanley well in the impossible job of solving all the homicides in the next six weeks, or so. He smugly walked straight to his patrol car and went on traffic duty.

While standing next to Homer's bookcase, Stanley spotted an old newspaper clipping pinned to the wall in plain sight. He scrutinized the faded print-article that featured a lineup of axe-throwing competitors.

Curious, he asked the sheriff about the picture. Homer explained that Clarence Smith was an axe-throwing enthusiast, a rather benign activity, then pointed him out—second man on the left.

Back at his desk, Stanley felt the pressure to *wrap it up*. He wanted to but knew he couldn't prove anything. He dug into the pile of unsolved cases; three file folders, including the case that he had promised Margo he'd solve—the Maria Richardson file. Its contents had been spread across the top of his desk for at least a month. Reviewing Maria's file, again, he found nothing new. There was one short but useless note to the file, signed by Officer Clarence Smith, indicating that he was continuously searching for evidence. *Oo-oo-o —the agony of dead ends!*

In the idle records concerning the unsolved death of Martin Martl, he found that Martl's criminal record was short and amateurish but never arrested locally. Although the coroner's report indicated that Martl had been killed with an axe, there was no additional evidence collected, beyond that specified in the crime lab report, just a similarly written note to the file signed by Officer Smith. The dozen blurry-looking photos, all of a single axe-wound, were of no help. And he was surprised that there had been no arrests for drug-dealing, even though it was widely rumored that Martl frequently sold contraband through the window of his car.

Next, the third file, the mystery of what happened to Clarence Smith—the most intriguing case yet the most confusing one. The ballistics report created more questions than it answered. And what role did his personal revolver play in the tragedy? It had been wiped but still had some blood on it, including the botched fingerprints. He wished he had conclusive evidence. As it existed, the District Attorney would laugh him out of his office.

He remembered how Officer Aino Pekka had summed up the case. He was almost tempted to accept that Pekka's assessment was probably the most convincing argument—well, except that Pekka's opinion didn't agree with the lab findings.

He pondered inconsistencies in the known facts and enumerated other problems with the case—no suspect, no witnesses, no anonymous tips, no enlightening revelations, and the limited evidence was contaminated. The finding of the body was credited to a stray steer, found lying next to the corpse; but its owner was clueless. He closed the file folder and stared at the wall.

One thing especially bothered him—Margo's possible involvement, although her name didn't appear anywhere in the record. He hadn't told anyone that some circumstantial evidence seemed to point to her, but he didn't want to believe any suggestion that she could be involved.

What should I tell Homer? Time is running out; and I've got . . . nothing.

Chapter 92
The Karyotype

Time was slipping away. The elusive evidence Stanley needed was still in hiding, and the calendar pages were flipping by, in a blur; and the election, too-close-for-comfort. He could be seen campaigning at the Justice County Fair, but his mind was always divided between Margo's health and the delays inherent in processing the DNA samples. If Homer was right, Stanley really needed the results of the DNA analysis to solve these cases.

Near the middle of the week, a large manila envelope from the crime lab was delivered.

Stanley opened it and poured over the lab results, wondering how the DNA comparisons would match up, if at all. He found *the karyotype* to be both complex and intimidating. He wondered what a ninety-five per cent probability-of-a-match meant and whether or not a percentage was a reliable number.

A phone call to the forensic scientist helped him understand that the combined blood stain was from both Maria Richardson and Martin Martl, each a very close match. It was almost a certainty that both victims had been killed with the same weapon.

These people were killed in different places, and on different days, but their blood was combined into one stain. The killer must be the same person, using the same axe for each murder—Homer's fears, of a serial killer, confirmed.

Alone in his office, he stared out the window, not satisfied that he knew everything he wanted to know. Since the axe found in Margo's shed contained the most damaging evidence, that could make her a prime suspect. *That can't be! She wouldn't have killed her best friend. I need something that will pass Homer's logic test.*

"Who is Maria's murderer?" *The axe is the key; if I find the true owner, I'll have the killer. How does the karyotype, a fancy-looking graph, help me find and arrest that one person who fits the numbers?*

"And what's the connection between Maria Richardson and Martin Martl? Or is there a connection? Martl was found by the swimming hole, and Maria was found miles away on the county line. And Margo was the last person to see Maria alive," he said, asking himself the tough questions, going through an agonizing thought process, "and I found the murder weapon in her tool shed!"

It doesn't look good, for Margo.

Stanley walked down the hall to show Sheriff Anders the lab results. And he summarized the lab's interpretation of the karyotype.

"Hm-m, blood from both Martl and the Richardson girl; all in the same sample," Homer said thoughtfully. "Just as I thought, we've got a diabolical killer running loose; and we don't know who it is!"

"Sir, I found a sporting catalog in your bookcase, a while ago. There's an axe, just like this one, on page twenty-two. I sent an inquiry letter, last month, hoping to get lucky. If we can determine who purchased this specialty axe, then we might have the killer."

Sheriff Anders agreed.

Speed Trap Murder

* * *

The next day, Stanley received a response from The Avid Competitor, the sporting goods catalog he found in the bookcase. The company's executive officer confirmed that the subject axe had been purchased from their mail-order catalog. And he offered the name and address of the purchaser.

Shocked, not expecting his detective work to pay off this easily, Stanley immediately took the letter to Homer's office.

Sheriff Anders stood silent, then slowly eased into his chair, seeming weak; perhaps dumbfounded by the truth contained in the two-sentence letter, trying to fathom all the ramifications. He read the letter again, almost as if he was wishing it would read differently the second or third time.

"It was Clarence," Homer finally said. "He bought the axe; it was his; and the combined blood stain—he must've done it, to both of them."

Stanley read the pain and disappointment in Homer's eyes, the shock of knowing that his trusted deputy, Clarence Smith—the wanna-be axe-throwing champion—was probably the killer.

"I'm so sorry," Stanley said, patting Homer on the shoulder.

The axe is the only incriminating evidence I have, but it only applies to the axe victims; no resolution to the question, "who killed Officer Smith". He must be the axe murderer, but it will never be proven, now that he's dead. He either killed himself, or someone killed him. It seems to me that he had the axe with him at the rest area, but by the time the crime lab showed up, someone had taken it. The axe, in itself, could have convicted him of the two axe-murders. But his own death? That's an unrelated circumstance. It's well-known that he had enemies. Any one of them could have shot him.

Back in his own chair, Stanley was puzzled, his thoughts still buzzing 'round and 'round. *Is the answer this easy—Smith, the killer?*

Aware that the lab found no amount of evidence connecting the axe to the shooting—only to the axe-murders—he was back to square-one. *Unless Smith killed himself, my job is not over!*

How did Margo end up with the axe? And what's her connection with Clarence Smith's axe, or with Martin Martl?

He pondered the mystery of how Margo and Maria had almost discovered Martl's body on the day of the trail ride. And he wondered if the Martl connection was purely coincidental, or if Clarence Smith was the one who had disposed of the body in the woods.

Perhaps Clarence Smith had just killed the boy and hid the body when he saw the two women on their horses. "I betcha," he said aloud, glancing at his watch and realizing that he was almost late for supper at the farm.

But first, it was time to finish his talk with Sheriff Anders. It was time to lay everything on the table. Everything.

Chapter 93
Storybook Doll House
October 4, 1996

It was one month before Election Day when Stanley Nelson drove out to the Smith residence. It seemed strange, to him, to be driving the official vehicle so close to home. He followed the lakeside turns, shady from the umbrella-like treetops that nearly formed a tunnel over Shoreline Way. Driving through newly fallen leaves, he came to a dead-end, stopping in the spacious yard of a quaint house situated on the shoreline of Lake Splendor.

He recognized the pink convertible parked by a white picket fence. *Wow—like a storybook doll house! How did Officer Smith afford this place?*

He walked the path through a well-kept rose garden and knocked on the front door. A plain-looking woman, dressed in flannel pajamas and old tennis shoes, opened the intricately carved door. Her dark brown eyes widened with interest, brightening her otherwise sullen face when she saw Stanley's finely pressed uniform and brass badge.

"Missus Dawn Smith?" Stanley asked, expecting a younger person. He remembered once meeting her, but she looked a lot different today, although he remembered her frizzed hair.

"Officer Nelson," she said, timidly holding her boney-looking fingers in front of the furrowed lines on her face, feeling awkward being seen without makeup. "I remember you—the barn party on The Fourth. Too bad it ended so abruptly. We never had a chance to talk."

"I'm sorry, Madam, about the death of your husband Clarence. You must be tired of all the questions."

"I'm used to it, and . . . a lot of time has gone by. Police work was part of our lives."

"Ah-h, yes, of course; sorry for the long delay, but . . . there wasn't much evidence."

"Do you like coffee, Officer Nelson?"

"No thank you, Missus Smith. I just have a couple questions."

"Fire away," she said. A small smile appeared, her shyness fading.

"Had you written to The Department, requesting that your husband's axe be returned?"

"Yes, I did. He sometimes took it to work. That's why—"

"Help me understand, Missus Smith, why . . .?"

"Please call me *Dawn*; and I'll call you *Stanley*, like friends would do. Is that all right?" she asked, smiling gently.

"Ah, yes—friends; that's okay with me, Dawn," he said, reciprocating the gesture. "Tell me—what about the axe?"

"It's for throwing, but it's good for splitting kindling, too."

"A pretty-fancy axe, for chopping firewood. Why did Clarence have a *throwing axe*?"

"Oh, he was in the lumberjack competitions. It's a sport. He never won, but he tried."

"Interesting," Stanley said, remembering the newspaper clipping pinned to Homer's wall.

426

Dawn gazed across her splendid yard, past her professional-looking tennis court, pointing to an all-wood target which stood to the side of a large pile of dirt. The boards were weathered gray from the deleterious effects of alternating snow, rain, and sunshine. Most of the black-painted rings were badly faded.

"Clarence could hit it—dead-center," she bragged of his skill.

Without saying another word, she began walking directly to the target, leading the way, walking past the tennis court, then stopping by the large pile of dirt, an earthen backstop for Clarence's home-shooting-range. A wood post by the dirt backstop was riddled with bullet holes, the top of it shattered, long splinters hanging from its backside. And at head-height, there were torn remnants of paper-plate targets, one stapled upon another. And more bullet holes.

Pivoting to the axe-throwing target, Dawn proudly expounded on the sport of axe throwing, sounding like a professional.

Stanley stared at the axe-marks that scarred the periphery of the center of the target and its few concentric rings, then contemplated the distance and how Clarence Smith must have thrown the axe at his victims, just for fun—sick amusement.

"Do you throw?" he asked, noting her knowledge of the sport.

Her reaction was a dismissive laugh. "He was in the red, most of the time, and his *kill shot* was . . . almost-always perfect," she said, her words explicitly direct. "Why he never won, I'll never know."

Kill shot? Stanley's mouth almost dropped open, surprised that the widow was so forthright. The photo of the axe-cut in the middle of Maria Richardson's back popped into his mind. "Did you say . . .?"

Dawn laughed, seeming to enjoy the shock factor of the term she used. "If I had my way, I'd re-name it *the ultimate shot!*" She reached

427

to the upper right of the target, touching a small blue dot past the outer ring—a secondary target which was much smaller than the red bullseye. "This is the most exciting part of the contest!"

Stanley understood that hitting the small, blue dot would be a greater challenge, for an axe-thrower, than hitting the much larger bullseye. He ran his fingers across the dozens of narrow axe-slits that riddled the spot of blue paint, impressed with the consistent accuracy.

"He was good—deadly good!" she said, not hiding her pride. "But I'm just as good!" she giggled. "Half of those marks are mine!"

Glancing near his feet, Stanley spotted something barely visible under the mown grass, a glimpse of brass sheen. He nonchalantly kicked at it, loosening it from the sand, revealing that it was a discarded shell casing. It had obviously been there for a while, possibly a few years. When Dawn turned to go back to the house, he picked it up. With one glance, he knew the make and the caliber. He slipped it into his pocket.

Stanley stopped at the patrol car and popped the trunk-lid, exposing a new-looking axe. "Does this belong to you, Dawn?"

"No Sir." She spun the handle in her fingers. "Too long, too thick, and poor balance. Clarence's axe was perfectly balanced for throwing," she said. "This one will wobble and fall short. It has to make a flip—once in twelve feet—before it hits the target."

She handed back the axe, which Stanley had just purchased that morning. Next, he unrolled a towel exposing a second axe which was somewhat shorter. The polished hickory handle outshined that of the first axe, and it had an *evidence tag* tied around the handle, from where the DNA samples had been taken. Stanley said nothing, to avoid bias, awaiting her reaction.

428

"Oh my-y—that's it—his prized axe!"

"I'm sorry, Dawn. It's evidence in the axe-murders of Maria Richardson and Martin Martl. Do you recognize either of those two names?"

Dawn Smith very briefly went silent, just staring at the evidence tag. "I only know what I read in the paper," she said remorsefully.

She looked up, despair showing on her face. "Are you implying that Clarence did it, just because he owned a throwing-axe?"

"We found blood, from each victim, on the handle, Madam. I'm sorry—"

"How?"

"New technology, something that was never available in the past. The method is so new, this is the first time that our department has used it. It allows us to positively tie blood samples, directly to a specific individual. It's called, *DNA profiling*. Have you heard of it?"

Not seeming surprised, at all, Dawn Smith stared straight ahead and thought for a moment. "Yes; new science, since my days in college. I've done some reading, the *double helix* and the *mapping of the human genome*. Fascinating topics, actually, having to do with genetics—right down to the microscopic genes," she said, sounding very knowledgeable.

"Yes; that's it," Stanley said, impressed that Dawn Smith probably knew more about genetic profiling than he did. "Now we can compare blood from a victim to blood found somewhere else, like on this axe; probably the biggest advance, for law enforcement, in the last hundred years."

With the weight of human tragedy on his shoulders, Officer Nelson quietly closed the trunk and got his briefcase from the car. He held a legal paper for Mrs. Smith to sign.

Dawn Smith hung her head. Her drawn face had been previously drained, indicating that there were no more tears possible. Showing no emotion, she signed the pre-printed statement, claiming ownership of the axe and requesting that it be returned to her when the Richardson and Martl murder cases were closed.

Chapter 94
Red-Velvet Ribbon

It's a 30-06 shell casing, Stanley thought, feeling it jiggling in his shirt pocket, hurrying through the tight curves along the lake, then speeding all the way to Burntwood Prairie.

Stanley handed Sheriff Anders the clue that could blow the Smith case wide open.

Anders rotated the 30-06 shell casing in his fingers, knowing that the fatal slug had passed through Smith's brain, then lodged in the center of a two-inch oak sapling. He listened intently, paging through the ballistics report and occasionally nodding his head. "Finally—evidence that aligns with the official findings!"

Stanley nodded, knowing that all the hooey concerning Smith's .357 sidearm was mostly popular speculation.

"Of course, there are procedures to follow," the sheriff continued. "If we fire this down to the lab, we should hear-back in a week or two."

"Homer, are you sure we should wait that long? What about your favorite line, *time is of the essence?*"

Weighing the potential flight risk, Sheriff Anders seemed to agree with Stanley's hunch. "What are we waiting for?"

* * *

Soon, both officers stood at the front door of the quaint house on Lake Splendor, hoping they'd found the break they were waiting for. When the door opened, there stood Dawn Smith, dressed in an all-white tennis uniform and assuming the stance of a tennis pro, ready for a fast ball—anything. She looked 25 years younger. This time, her hair was long and in a ponytail, her facial makeup fully deployed, and she held a decorated shoe box in her hands. It was tied shut with a red-velvet ribbon.

"I've been expecting you, Sheriff Anders," she said, offering him the box. "Is this what you're looking for?"

Something was askew, but Homer saw that the ball was in-his-court. Rather surprised, he accepted the apparent gift-wrapped box.

"You don't have to open it; you should know what it is," she said. "It's Clarence's service weapon, the thirty-eight-caliber furnished by the department."

"Ah-h; thank you for returning it," Sheriff Anders said, but was not buying the ruse. He sniffed the package. "This hasn't been fired in a long time, has it?"

"I don't believe so. Clarence carried his own—you know—like the *Lone Ranger.*"

"Ah-yes." Homer almost smirked but cleared his throat. "I'd like to see the thirty-aught-six, if you don't mind, Missus Smith." he said, cleverly referring to information only known to those who have read the ballistics report, or to a person with personal knowledge of the shooting.

A brief stare down ensued—Homer and Dawn. Her stern face held but her eye twitched.

"Is it in the house?" Homer asked, sounding like a sympathetic friend.

There was a long pause, then she looked down. "I—I keep it in the bedroom," she said, sensing that the gig was up.

Stanley guardedly accompanied the Sheriff into the house, wary of trouble as Mrs. Smith led them through the living room and down the hall.

"No one else is here. My daughter took her boys to the ranch—my brother's place."

The antique long gun stood in the corner, an arm's length from her pillow. The 30-06 bolt action rifle looked clean, not recently oiled but modified for a generation-3, 1990 night-vision scope—a state-of-the-art upgrade.

Except for the scope, Homer recognized it as a 1920s era carbine, similar to the model he borrowed from his grandfather at age ten for his first deer-hunt by Wilderness Swamp.

Stanley nodded, knowing that the brass shell casing in his pocket would surely fit. He held it up, so Dawn would see it. She did, and she recognized it. She had noticed that Stanley found it in the grass, earlier, lying where ejected, where she had practiced at close range.

Homer Anders picked up the rifle, switched the safety to vertical position, held the muzzle low, and operated the bolt action to open the breech, to be sure the weapon was not loaded. To his surprise, an empty shell casing, just like the one Stanley was holding, extracted and flew onto the bedspread.

Stanley's head almost snapped back, realizing that the murder weapon had been found.

Dawn's face revealed an expression of surrender, that after three years since the shooting, she had failed to pull the bolt to eject the empty shell—the same piece of brass that once encapsuled the fatal bullet.

Stanley flipped the spent casing into an evidence bag.

There was no doubt. Dawn knew they'd found a match. She began to explain, how she drew two eyeballs on a paper plate, then stapled it to the top of the post. Then, practicing—

"Did you shoot your husband?" Stanley asked.

She continued, wanting to get this over with, "I saw his squad car parked under the streetlight, right next to . . . that other car. It made me mad; he was doing it again!"

"Doing what?" Stanley asked.

"You know—his latest obsession—the *bloody* kill shot!"

Stanley shuttered, listening to her rationalization; how she drove past the speed trap, hid her sporty car on a woods-road, then scurried all the way to the place where she would squeeze the trigger on her husband's deer rifle.

"I'm not sorry," she affirmed. "He threatened, many times, to shoot me between the eyes. I won't tell you the things he said to our grandbabies."

"How did you get a shot off, with somebody standing in front of him?" Homer asked, cleverly ascertaining if someone else was there.

"You're talking about Margo Toralf," she said.

Homer didn't let on, that this was the first confirmation that Margo had been at the scene of the crime. No one else knew either, not for sure.

"She didn't know that I snuck up, from behind. It was already dark, but I saw 'em in the night-scope. I'd never hurt her; she was his next victim—you know. Margo, somehow, got the drop on him and had his three-fifty-seven crammed in his mouth. I heard her spewing out the riot act, but I knew she couldn't do it."

"Couldn't do what? How could you know what was on her mind?" Homer asked.

"Not what was *on her mind*," Dawn said, "what was *in her hand*. She didn't know about the half-empty gun. Clarence always kept three open chambers in the cylinder."

Stanley knew this was true, from the crime lab report. *The hammer had fallen into an empty chamber. That revolver did not fire, whatsoever.*

"Margo was in my way, and I didn't want to accidently shoot her. And I didn't want her to shoot him, either. He was *my* problem, not hers. It breaks my heart that she's driving herself crazy, now, thinking she's the one who shot that devil." She looked to Stanley, then to Homer's understanding eyes.

"I'm glad I did it! The world is better-off. Surely the investigators know the difference between the bullets—a three-fifty-seven or a thirty-aught-six. They're not alike—ya know."

"How'd you get a clear shot?" Stanley asked, concerned that Margo's life had been in danger, from both the front and the rear."

"I'm too short, but I stood on top of a stump," she continued, "my toes tucked under the axe handle; barely enough room to sight over

435

her shoulder, just missing her left ear." She almost began to laugh, apparently pleased with her prowess.

"Clarence installed a night-vision scope—his folly," she snickered. "It was an easy shot, right between the eyes, just what that dirty bastard deserved!"

Chapter 95
Strategic News Leak

Hank dashed down the two-track to the mailbox, after tossing a handful of chicken feed onto the sandy driveway, a diversion meant to keep the chickens from following him all the way to the county road. It worked; a dozen chickens scrambled after the bouncing kernels of grain. He found only the Otter Tattler in the mailbox.

"Good—no bills to pay," he mumbled, then walked back to the trailer house.

It was Bette who first noticed Stanley Nelson's picture in the newspaper. "Henry, you have to see this!" she said, moving his signature cup to the side. "Page one—Stanley—all dressed up in his uniform. And he's smiling. Is he all done with the case?"

"Hm-m; we haven't heard about this," he said, reading the headline: *DNA Evidence Connects the Dots*. He recognized the inserted picture of Maria Richardson, but not the other victim. While digesting that bit of news, he turned the pages and glanced at Aino Pekka's display-ad for the upcoming sheriff election, aligned next to President Bill Clinton's re-election campaign advertisement, just for the purpose of comparison. Then, back to the featured article. He read the surprising news again. "It looks like Stanley has made a *strategic news leak*."

"Is the investigation over? The whole thing points at the dead deputy—Smith," Bette said, expecting different results from the long-drawn-out shooting investigation.

"Hm-m." Hank took his time. "The death of the deputy—Smith—is not mentioned; just that he's responsible for the serial axe killings!" He stroked his soft, silvery-looking mustache. "It just says that blood from both hatchet-murder victims was found on an axe owned by the late, Deputy Clarence Smith."

"Well, that says . . . nothing!"

"Sounds like Stanley wrapped up the axe investigations with some sort of new, scientific method. Smart!" he quipped proudly.

"Stanley gets the credit for connecting the dots," Bette mused, still showing confusion on her face. "I just want to know, is Margo getting away with murder?"

Hank found another article on page 3, grinned, and his eyes twinkled. "Son-of-a-gun!"

"What now?" Bette asked.

He pointed to a small-print headline, "Widow Arrested for Shooting Death of Her Husband."

Bette read the two-sentence article, amazed.

"To answer your own question, Mother, you hafta learn to read between the lines; the speed trap murder case is as good as dead!"

Bette looked to the chicken picture on the wall.

"Ya know—I was gonna vote for that useless Aino Pekka," Hank said, "just so Stanley would lose the election. Now, I just might change my mind!" He chuckled and grinned, then leaned back in his chair.

Chapter 96
The Crayon Drawing

Word of the widow's confession rocked Justice County. All three murders were solved, almost overnight, as it seemed.

When Margo heard the news, she could hardly believe it, especially since she was there and thought she remembered it differently; but she knew she didn't pull the trigger, a detail she had stuck to from the beginning. Still, she was mystified that Dawn Smith had confessed.

Who could have known that Dawn Smith gunned her husband down in a hateful fit, precisely at the same moment that the hammer fell on the pistol in Margo's hand?

It seemed so long ago, and it was; but now, knowing that she was in in the clear, Margo wondered why she had blamed herself for the crime. It was Clarence Smith that terrorized the county, not her. She should be ecstatic that it was all over and that she was free. Relieved but confused, the false guilt she had carried for over three years crept back into her thoughts.

Her mind obsessively racing, and standing at the kitchen sink with a bottle of pills in her hand, she contemplated throwing the whole works into the garbage can. Why not? After years of misery, she had been periodically skipping her doses anyway.

"Who needs these?" she said, almost tossing them; but then, she heard the unmistakable rumble of a finely tuned engine.

Looking out the window, she saw a shiny-new red pickup truck, pulling an empty horse trailer. It stopped outside the window. A political advertisement dominated the side door: "Vote Stanley Nelson for Sheriff".

"Stanley!" she cried out. Overcome with excitement, and the unsettling symptoms of medication-withdrawal pulsating through her veins, she allowed her bottle of medication to slip through her fingers. It rolled across the kitchen counter, stopping at the back-splash. Pulling on her cowgirl boots, she dashed out the door, skipping all the steps, floating, dazzled by spears of glaring sunlight that flashed in her eyes. She hit the ground running.

A brisk breeze blew the truck door shut, as Stanley retrieved a custom-made cloth banner—a *Vote Stanley Nelson for Sheriff* advertisement. He held the large, rolled-up banner under one arm, excited to show-it-off to the woman he loved. He had just brought the new axe to the tool shed, hoping that Margo would never notice the difference, and was lifting Toby to the ground when he saw Margo coming around the corner of the house, her hair in flight like the mane on a horse.

Toby ran toward his mother, a huge smile on his face, carrying a hand-drawn picture.

"What's this?" Margo asked excitedly, of the rolled-up banner, running to Stanley but not noticing that she had run past her son.

Toby tugged at her leg and tried to give *the crayon drawing* to her, but Margo ignored him. She seemed perturbed that her young son wanted to interrupt. She turned to shout at him but stopped when she got a glance at the drawing: a sketch of a barn, a horse, and a small boy with his mom and dad. Something clicked in her head, and it seemed important.

"I know what you want, Mommy!" Toby said excitedly.

Margo knelt for a closer look. She carefully lifted the limp paper from her son's hand, protecting it from a strong gust of wind. She stared at the colorful lines of scribbled crayon.

"It's a picture of our farm—red barn . . . and . . . horses! Stanley, did you see this?" she asked excitedly. "He sees it! He sees my dream!"

Stanley grinned, since he had helped Toby make the drawing. "It's a perceptive picture, Sweetheart, drawn just like you've described it a thousand times."

Margo's eyes met with Toby's. Her misty eye glanced at the picture again, then back to Toby's innocent smile.

"I love you, Mommy," said Toby.

Margo gasped, a primal thrust suddenly overriding her negative impulses. She felt like a caring mother, once again, and hugged her son. Knowing that she had mistreated him, in the past, it was hard to understand how a child can be forgiving. Stinging tears flooded her eyes.

"I have something to show you, Margo," Stanley said, of the advertising banner, and began to unroll it. He wanted to see the expression on Margo's face when she saw the picture-perfect design, the advertisement that would surely win the sheriff-race.

"Stanley, this is a great campaign ad! And I love the color! I know just where to hang it, so everyone'll see!"

"Honey, there's more. There's a horse auction tomorrow at the sales barn, not so far away," he said cautiously, not wanting to interrupt the touching moment of Margo connecting with her son. "I thought we'd need a truck and a trailer—"

"We're getting horses?" she asked, then smiled. "That's all I've ever wanted." Within seconds, her expression flattened. Fright crept, like a paralysis, across her face. Her lips trembled, "Stanley, what about—you know—?"

Stanley wondered why she had seemed happy, then suddenly, unhappy. He knew that she had already heard the good news, that all of the murders had been solved.

She had something to say, but her mind was fuzzy, her cursed affliction creeping in and a bit of withdrawal cycling through her consciousness. "What about—you know—reality—what *really* happened at the speed trap? I just can't take it! There's the depression-reality, too."

"You are so-o close to conquering this . . . scourge. You almost said it. Name it, Margo; just identify it; say it out loud, so you can put it behind you," Stanley pleaded.

"That's what Doctor Sworden says."

Stanley's eyes grew large. *She almost expressed it.*

Margo quickly covered her mouth, realizing that she had unintentionally revealed her secret therapist. "I just want a *normal* life, Stanley, but the reality—I can't cope."

Chapter 97

The Miracle of Closure

"I know what happened at the speed trap, Honey, and so does Sheriff Anders. It's all out there—everything—and you're innocent. You can let it go, free as a bird."

"That's easy for you to say."

"That murderer, Officer Smith, killed the kid, then Maria; but you slipped away. You remember, don't you? He was planning to eliminate you, too, just like he did with the others. No one would blame you for defending yourself. Unfortunately, there are no witnesses. On the other hand, Smith's wife confessed to the shooting. That's all we needed; plus, the murder weapon, of course, which she turned over to us—all, a perfect match."

Margo hadn't snapped out of her gloom—no surprise, no relief in her eyes.

"I've never mentioned that some of the evidence once seemed to point at you, but I always knew you didn't shoot anybody. You've never been a suspect, My Dear; not in my book. You had Smith's revolver in your hand, but it didn't fire a shot—proven by the lab."

"What?"

Stanley detailed, how Smith's angry wife had stood behind her, with her husband's deer rifle, and fired the fatal shot. "We've always known about the rifle, ever since the bullet was recovered at the crime scene, but we didn't know whose it was or who did it. Who could've guessed?"

"But the guilt I've felt, always waiting for the accusations to come; my fight for justifiable homicide; begging for mercy, only to be locked up—forever!"

"None of that was necessary, Honey. You should've said something. I'm sorry you went through all that mental torture, but it was top secret—ya know—until we had the shooter. It wasn't until this week that Dawn Smith confessed and turned in the murder weapon."

"Well, isn't that just fine and dandy! You solved the crimes, but Maria is never coming back. What do her parents get out of this? What do I get—my only true friend, gone forever?"

Stanley moistened his grim lips, hoping he could find the right words to say. "Consider the Martl family; they finally know what happened to their son, the evidence pointing to his murderer. And Maria's family can finally allow their hearts to rest, knowing who killed their daughter and that justice for them has been served. As you know, just as with Maria, he intended to kill you, too, at the speed trap. For all of us, it's not much but it's over; it's closure."

"Closure", Margo repeated, echoing but not liking the term.

"It's an amazing concept, actually—*the miracle of closure*. It's what everyone in Justus County has wanted, and now they have it! And do you know the best part? The voters are satisfied that the crime wave is done with, and I get the credit for it!"

444

"What about Mister Anders? What does he think of it?"

"Homer? He's happy. He assured me, the election will go our way, and there's no evidence against you! Believe me, he knows you didn't do it. And he's okay with all of it, and gallantly riding off into the sunset, himself, with his cowboy hat on and with an untarnished record. And he's proud of you, just like I am. He loves you, Honey, almost like *family*."

Chapter 98
Descent of the Red Banner

Margo hugged the rolled-up banner, her eyes easing across her view of the farm, wanting the better future that Stanley's victory at the polls would provide. It was hard to fathom the truth about the shooting, but she wanted to. She wanted to show her happiness, but sadness held its stubborn grip, not letting go.

"There's something I've never told you, Stanley. It's my brain; not too serious but a little neurotic—you know—some sort of imbalance, according to . . . my doctor. It sometimes messes up my thinking. Actually, I'm perfectly fine, most of the time. He prescribed something, just a simple medication," she rambled, vague in her elaboration, hoping Stanley didn't know that she had been skipping her doses. "I know it's been bad, but I'm cured now."

A bit confused with the half-truths, Stanley looked for sincerity in Margo's deceptive eyes, realizing that she was holding back, preventing her own progress. He figured that it would be hard for her to lay it all on the line, on her first try, but was impressed with her apparent intentions.

"Good progress, Margo; keep taking your medicine," he said, keeping up the encouragement. "I'll be there to help, every step of the way! These are exciting times; everything's going right for us."

"What will happen to me, Stanley?" Margo cried. She buried her face in both hands.

"Honey, you've confronted your reality, a great first step. It's yours to conquer, and you can do it! Just keep on trying. Margo, there's so much for us to look forward to!"

Realizing that Stanley was her strongest advocate, Margo wiped her eyes and turned her face into a strong gust of wind, re-imagining the thrill of a galloping, bareback ride.

"Horses? Really? Do I get my ranch?" Feeling that her vacillating state of depression had vanished, for the last time, Margo gripped Stanley's hand and shouted to the sky with unbridled excitement, "My dream—I get to have it, Mom!" Topping that outburst, with a hoot, she started to laugh. "I will shout it from the tallest place on this farm!"

"Back to the topic of horses," Stanley said, delighted to hear Margo's laughter again, "one for you, one for me, and . . ."

". . . and, maybe, a pony for Toby—a small one," she added, with a long-awaited and exciting giggle, tightening her grip on the rolled-up banner, "a really small one. After all, he's only four! What kind of a horse ranch will this be, without horses?"

Hank and Bette came, almost running, wondering what all the excitement was about.

Stanley turned to Toby. "What do you think of that, Son?"

"What, Daddy?"

447

"Why—the thought of you having a horsey of your own—a real pony! Won't that be fun? Are you excited, too?"

Toby didn't respond but had a distant stare; one like Stanley had never seen from his son before. Repeating his last question, Stanley saw Toby pointing to the sky. He was unaware that Margo had impulsively sprinted away, to display the banner from the highest point on the farm.

"Look, Daddy! Look, Grandpa and Nana—Mommy's flag!"

In horror, Stanley saw the flash of red—his red advertising banner —high in the air, halfway up the side of the silo, unfurled and flapping in the wind. His heart almost stopped, seeing Margo holding it, stepping higher on the ladder, already near the top of the structure.

"No—no, Margo; not up there!" he yelled, imagining her feet slipping off the iron rungs and falling. His voice got lost in the strong wind, running as fast as he could, to rescue his beloved Margo.

Hank shouted, "No—Margo-o!" He tried to run but fell flat on his face, blood splashing on his reading glasses that fell to the dirt. Before he could stand up again, he saw the flutter of the banner, held up momentarily by the buoyant breeze. Then it fell, plunging straight down.

"No—no, Margo-o-o!" Stanley hollered, too, seeing only *the descent of the red banner*, drifting away from the silo and landing on the paddock.

Chapter 99

A New Friend

Hank rushed at Stanley, fear and anger mixed with streaks of blood across his face, thrusting both fists into the chest of his would-be son-in-law. He began a wind-up but held back, not willing to take a swing. "Where's Margo?" he shouted in Stanley's face, out of breath from his short run, certain he had seen his daughter fall to her death.

Flustered, Stanley was nearly in a panic. There was yelling, all around him, making it hard to think.

Betty was hysterical. "What have you done to my little girl—you crazy idiot! Where is she? Is she dead?"

Hank saw the red banner lying in a crumpled heap, then rushed to it. He lifted it, looking dumbfounded. There was nothing under it, except a short bush which had held it up slightly. "Where is she? I saw her fall, didn't I?"

"Look, Daddy!" Toby said, pointing high.

Stanley looked near the top of the silo, then heard a faint cry in the wind.

"Margo!" he shouted, barely seeing her inverted body hanging against the curved wall.

Suddenly, from out of nowhere, Brian was on the scene, pushing past his parents and scrambling up the D-rungs, just as he had done in disobedience, as a kid. Now, his past experience in climbing that same set of slippery, iron rungs would help save a life. Reaching Margo, he took hold of her hand and called for a rope.

"Her foot's stuck, prob'ly broken. She might fall!" he yelled down to the others. He saw that her boot was precariously wedged behind the D-rung from which it had slipped, her leg jammed against the concrete silo-wall, and she was hanging upside-down.

"Hold on, Margo . . . and Brian," Stanley called out, realizing that Brian might not be the hellion he thought he was. "A rope is coming!" He knew where he could find a long rope.

Yancy Jensen suddenly showed up with an extension ladder, something he was using on the construction of his house. Driving by, he had seen the chaos and didn't hesitate. He quickly untied the ladder from his truck, and Becky helped him carry it to the silo.

"It's too short," Hank said, frustrated, then wondered what was keeping Stanley.

Margo was tough, staying calm in spite of the pain, sharing old memories with her brother while he stood below her on a lower rung, holding her from crashing to her death.

Hearing Margo groaning in pain, Stanley came running, the rope dragging behind him.

The three young men worked together, combining the height of the ladder with the length of Margo's favorite rope. Brian slipped one end of the rope through the top D-rung, tied a loop under Margo's arms, and somehow managed to free her foot, slowly hoisting her down to Yancy's ladder, then safely to the ground.

Margo whispered a secret to Stanley, then added, "On the counter. Just bring one pill."

For Margo, her experience seemed like a rough ride gone bad; and her rescue, like angels had descended from the sky. Her appreciative eyes melted onto those of Becky Jensen. Her grateful smile gleamed through a happy tear.

"Neighbors help neighbors," Becky said, soothing Margo's brow with a moist towel, sounding like *a new friend*.

THE END